# Praise for *The Aral*

"Frank Wilem's powerhouse thriller *The Aral* starts fast and never slows down as he weaves an intriguing tale full of twists."
-*New York Times* bestseller Dianna Love

"If you like Clive Cussler's Dirk Pitt, you'll enjoy Frank Wilem's Quint and his loyal team. He takes us on a journey that starts and ends in Key West. But strap on your seat belts and get ready for a dangerous journey deep into Russia full of surprises.
-Ricky Mathews, president and publisher of New Orleans' *The Times Picayune*

"Watch out Lee Child . . .Frank Wilem is coming on strong!"
- *USA Today* bestselling Author Mary Buckham

It's just outstanding . . . I couldn't put it down. I thoroughly enjoyed it and highly recommend it.
-Mary Perkins, librarian

## The Keys

Ever considered just getting into the car and heading to parts unknown? Most people have—few actually do. Quint not only considers ditching his cheating wife and dead-end job for a tropical escape, he does it—and heads for the Keys. And then the fun begins. Quint is thrust into a race to find a shipwreck with clues to the world's most valuable treasure while battling rogue naval forces, and a vile cadre of pirates and thieves, who are also committed to snatching the treasure from the grasp of ancient history or from anyone who gets in their way.

## The Pass

**Fact: A live nuclear bomb lies in shallow water off the U.S. coast – one of dozens lost around the world!**
Based on this true event, Quint and Dawson are tasked to locate and recover it–a mission that quickly becomes a wild race against a group of terrorists bent on detonating the bomb in their twisted jihad against the U.S. With one of the worst hurricanes in history bearing down on them, Quint's team is pushed to the limit as they struggle against overwhelming odds and a well-armed enemy.

# THE
# ARAL

## Frank Wilem

# ACKNOWLEDGEMENTS

I would like to acknowledge the encouragement and support of my wife, DeeDee. Karen Slade Bryant worked tirelessly editing the final manuscript and formatting it for publishing.

Also thanks to my father, Mary Page, Mary Perkins, Nel Ducomb, Darlene Holtgreve, Pam Williams, Ben Young, Bill Webb, Marshall Lynch, Greg Robins, Mike Joyner, Andy Chapman, Ricky Mathews, and Julie Jones for their contributions during the novel development and the Killion Group for the cover design.

A special thanks is due Mary Buckham who provided guidance and suggestions that dramatically improved the final product and to Dianna Love, who has been most generous in sharing her experience.

# DEDICATION

This book is dedicated to my loving wife, DeeDee, and our daughter, Brittany, who gave me encouragement and support throughout the writing process. Thanks to my son, Chris; my father; and the rest of my family for putting up with me.

I'd also like to dedicate it to the many who have died as a result of one of the worst man-made ecological disasters in the history of the world.

# PROLOGUE

Dean remained motionless, peering through the ship's porthole across the surrounding Uzbekistan desert. The thud of the hulking figure slinging a sledgehammer on the bow of the next ship over had awakened him from his shallow sleep.

*Probably a scrapper looking for some piece of overlooked junk to trade for a loaf of bread.* But it was the antique rifle, some sort of blunderbuss-looking weapon, slung over the man's shoulder that worried Dean.

The last thing he wanted was to catch a bullet from a chance encounter with an innocent. Then have the nearby villagers, drawn by the boom of the man's old cannon, come marching out after him, armed with knives and pitchforks.

The next-to-last thing Dean wanted was to kill one of the remaining locals, guilty only of having the misfortune to live in this godforsaken hell hole. Of course, before long most of those living nearby would be dead from cancer or one of the many other diseases running rampant.

Dean cursed himself for remaining on the bridge of the rusted fishing trawler. It had been a mistake to opt for the chance of a slight breeze through the broken-out windows rather than the safety of the stifling hull below decks. Now he was trapped.

A bead of sweat fell from his nose as he eased away from the porthole and slid down onto the hard steel floor. He twisted the cap off his canteen and drained a quarter of it to replace the fluids the arid desert sucked from his body. The smell of rotted fish, old diesel fuel, and the Aral sea filled his nostrils. Flecks of paint stained brown-red clung to the backs of his arms and the legs of his desert-camouflaged fatigues where they had rested on the deck.

He longed for the cool night air that had washed over his face twelve hours earlier during his parachute jump from the back of a stealth plane, so new that its very existence was a secret. While the heat was oppressive, at least the earache from breathing pure oxygen during the high altitude jump had finally eased. *Now, if only my ankle would quit throbbing. Or better, if I hadn't ended an otherwise perfect landing with my left foot in a hole.*

The corner of his balled-up parachute peeked out from the battered ship's console where he had stashed it the night before. He kicked it back out of view, wincing as another bolt of pain shot through his ankle.

With the scrapper's location fixed by the continued clanging sound, Dean risked removing his left boot. Gasping from the pain he probed the joint, praying that it was only twisted and not sprained or worse yet, fractured. After wrapping it tightly with tape from his pack, he grunted as he eased the boot back on and laced it tight.

The throbbing from his ankle was distracting. No matter, he'd carry on; it wasn't his first time dealing with such injuries in the field. Opting against taking the stronger meds in his kit, he chased two more ibuprofen down with another mouthful of water.

Half an hour later, silence drew Dean's attention, and with his hand firmly grasping the barrel of his M4A1 carbine, he struggled to his feet, favoring his aching left ankle. After flipping off the weapon's safety, he once again peeked at the adjacent ship and breathed a sigh of relief.

Stooped over from the weight of a heavy piece of steel on his shoulder, the intruder was trudging away past the row of decaying ships toward the village. The loose sand upon which he walked gave no evidence that a sea had ever been there.

The scrappers had performed their work well. The boat in which Dean hid appeared as if it had never been completed. Rather, it seemed sentenced to remain like a partially completed hull, forgotten in the corner of some defunct boat yard in the middle of a sweltering desert.

Dean moved to the far side of the bridge and scanned the area to the west. Seeing no other threats, he eased down beside the open doorway, hoping it might offer more relief from the waves of heat that washed over him. Wearily, he lay down, cushioning his head on his equipment pack, relegating his body to the metal deck of the decrepit wheelhouse. The eight-hour wait for his contact to arrive at dusk would seem more like thirty.

He checked to make sure that the paper trash from his last meal was secured back in his pack. Should he be forced to flee his hiding place, he wanted to leave no trace behind. Then he closed his eyes to get a few more hours' rest, confident that if the need arose he would awaken as he had earlier with the scrapper.

His mouth formed a slight smile as Mia entered his thoughts. Though her full lips and even fuller figure had caught his attention less than a year before, he knew she was the one. Even her name, Latin for "star of the sea," was perfect. Simply perfect.

They were at a party. Her slinky cobalt blue dress hugged her body, and flowing auburn hair graced her alabaster shoulders. As he drifted off to sleep, she clutched his arm tightly whispering a better offer in his ear—an offer he readily accepted.

The shadows were long when the sound of an engine in the distance woke him. He glanced out the door to find a plume of dust, beneath which a dot grew rapidly larger.

"What the...?" He watched the Tomcar, a dune buggy-type vehicle developed by the Israelis for combat use, come to a stop, ten yards from the starboard side of the ship where he was hiding. As the dust plume slowly faded in the still air, a lone man emerged, his goggles raised above a grime-encrusted face, leaving a raccoon-like clean spot. His loose-fitting clothes were stained the same color as the desert.

Dean cautiously poked his head out the door of the ship's bridge, the M4A1 carbine clutched tightly at his side. "Your ride has arrived," the man shouted in a heavy eastern European accent. "Now, how was I to verify my identity? Oh yes, 'I have your fish.'"

Dean emerged from the rusted wheelhouse to give the challenge response with a grin, "And they smell rotten."

"Like your grandmother." Sherzod laughed at Dean's double take. "Ah, so you are the mighty American who has come to save us all, praise Allah. I am Sherzod, honored to be your humble servant." The man gave an exaggerated bow, his air suggesting he was unlikely to be servant to any man.

"Okay, Sherzod," Dean replied, stumbling over the name, "you can drop the sarcasm, or I might just have to demonstrate our true superiority."

"Oh, great warrior, please spare me for I must care for my family," Sherzod's voice filled with mock fear.

Dean found himself warming to the guide with his wry sense of humor. "You a comedian in your spare time?"

"Sort of. Living here demands a strong sense of humor. Ready to take a ride?"

"I hate leaving my deluxe accommodations." Dean jerked his thumb toward the decrepit hull behind him. "But I suppose duty calls." With his bag on his shoulder, he dropped down from the ship's deck, landing mostly on his right leg, and then walked to the Tomcar, unable to mask his limp.

"They sent me a spec-ops gimp?"

"No, just a clumsy one." Sherzod laughed, and Dean stowed his pack in the rear of the Tomcar before climbing in, grunting at the pain from his ankle.

"If you wish to still be able to see when we get there, I suggest you put these on." Sherzod handed Dean a set of goggles before roaring off toward the distant Aral Sea. Unable to hear over the deafening sound of the engine and the wind, they rode without speaking over the rough desert terrain. Dean fought to keep his kidneys from being liquefied by the constant pounding against the vehicle's metal sides and roll cage. Sherzod seemed to view each dip and rock as a challenge, refusing to slow and never braking.

Under his "trust-but-verify" philosophy, Dean glanced repeatedly at the GPS in the comms unit on his wrist to confirm they remained headed toward their target. As they rode, his mind, numbed by the drone of the racing engine, drifted. Once again he thought of Mia and his sudden urge to quit pushing his luck before it ran out.

Dean knew they were reaching the point in their relationship where it would either move forward or die. He had been there many times with many other women, always accepting the end. Problem was he had never before felt this way about anyone.

*Maybe switching to a regular job and spending the rest of my life with the woman of my dreams isn't such a bad idea. Have the family I've always wanted.* By the time they reached the shore, he'd vowed to make this his last mission.

"We're here," Sherzod yelled as he slowed the Tomcar for the first time since leaving the derelict ships. "The beautiful Aral Sea, or what once was." It was nearing sunset, and reflections off the polluted water's surface flattered it.

"Enjoy your ride?" Sherzod asked straight-faced.

"Splendid, much smoother than I would have expected. A testament to your driving skill, no doubt," Dean's tone dripped with sarcasm.

"Excellent." Sherzod accepted the compliment as if were sincere. "Now you will experience my seamanship. Actually, we could walk; the water is only chest deep. But few sane people would enter these waters polluted by nasty chemicals. Besides, it would take time we don't have if we are to keep to your schedule."

"The boat will be fine." Dean helped Sherzod unload an inflatable from the back of the Tomcar and lug it along with a small outboard engine to the shore. Daggers of pain shot up his left leg from the injured ankle, and he paused to wash a couple more ibuprofen down with a slug of water from his canteen. Half an hour later, the boat was inflated with the outboard fired up.

Heading into the chop from the evening breeze, only the small size of the motor prevented Sherzod from making this leg of the trip as unpleasant as the last. With his bag held between his knees, Dean sat on the middle seat clutching a hand-strap on either of the inflatable's tubes. The spray that blew over him quickly evaporated in the dry air, leaving a thick deposit of salt on his skin and clothing.

"How long you been doing this?" Sherzod grunted as the inflatable bounced off a wave.

"Nearly ten years, give or take. How about you, what do you actually do?"

"I'm from Russia, spent a few years in the Spetznav. But now, just a concerned citizen." Sherzod smiled.

"Citizen or mercenary?"

"We all have to eat."

"You from here?"

"Close enough to hate what the dumbass Soviets did to this place." Sherzod saw Dean's puzzled look. "By diverting most of the water from the Aral Sea's tributaries to boost Russia's cotton production, they shrank it to a fraction of its former size, leaving a desert in its wake teeming with pollutants. The U.N. Secretary-General calls it the world's greatest man-made environmental disaster."

"Really?"

Sherzod gave Dean a surprised look. "How much they tell you?"

"Just what I needed to know in order to bring back samples from some sort of chemical lab on Renaissance Island where you're supposed to be taking me."

"Chemical lab?" Sherzod laughed. "The island is home to 'Aralsk-7,' the largest biological weapons lab and manufacturing facility ever constructed. They forget to mention that little detail?"

"Need to know, I believe they call it. The military and their secrets."

"Only this is not so secret," Sherzod continued. "Dust storms mix shit off this island with more shit left behind in the sand, and the people in the nearby villages breathe it. Tuberculosis and eye diseases run rampant. Throat cancer here is nine times the world average. Several people were recently infected with anthrax, and a 9-year-old boy died of the plague a year ago. No damn place to raise a family, I can tell you that."

Dean shook his head. Suddenly the relative safety of the derelict ship seemed appealing. A feeling of foreboding crept over him as he stared ahead at the low island and the boxy shadows of buildings silhouetted against the setting sun.

They approached the north end of the island, and Sherzod slowed the inflatable. Dean could now make out the outline of the housing units, the windows vacant, mostly broken. He felt the hair on the back of his neck stand up as he first caught sight of the sterile-looking, gray concrete lab buildings. They loomed in the distance with stores of bioweapons reputedly still remaining and fully capable of wreaking untold havoc.

Sherzod drove the boat up onto the beach before killing the engine. Unsure what filth might be carried in the air, Dean found himself breathing shallower. He was relieved when Sherzod withdrew two gas masks from his shoulder bag and tossed one to Dean. "Though they did find live anthrax bacteria in the soil back in the mid 1990s, you probably won't actually need this until we enter the lab building, at which time I definitely suggest you wear it."

Though dreading the discomfort of the full mask, which would soon fog, adding to his misery, Dean immediately pulled the strap over his head and donned it. The two men dragged the inflatable farther up onto the coarse sand and headed across the white strip to an area where a dock stood some distance from the water.

"At one time we could have tied up there. But as you can see, due to the retreating waters caused by our incompetent leadership, we must walk."

Dean slung his pack onto his shoulder, and the two men trudged in silence through the loose soil toward the dock. The ibuprofen had kicked in, and the pain in Dean's ankle had eased.

An aluminum skiff, nearly buried in the sand, sat beside the dock. Ahead, abandoned trucks stood on flattened tires, and faded yellow bulldozers waited futilely to be pressed into service once again. A red playground set, its empty swings swaying in the slight breeze, stood outside an abandoned elementary school. The building's raw concrete exterior appeared ghostly in the waning light.

Broken bottles and debris lay scattered everywhere. A decaying, olive-drab gas mask lay by the roadside. Dean heard the crunch of a glass petri dish shattering beneath his foot.

"Creepy, isn't it?" Dean nodded in reply. "During the heyday of the Soviet bioweapons program, over 1,000 scientists lived here with their families. But the entire facility was abandoned after their immediate evacuation was ordered. Check this out."

Dean followed Sherzod through the unlocked door into an apartment on the bottom floor of a two story building. The beam of Sherzod's flashlight pierced the musty air, illuminating a modest but neat and lovingly-decorated living area. A crocheted pillow bearing some Russian phrase sat propped at the end of a pale green couch. Pictures of a man and a woman holding a baby lay on a table beside an overstuffed chair, presumably forgotten in their hasty departure.

The dining table stood in a nook at the far end of the flat, still set as if the residents might return for dinner at any moment. But the blackened remains of a moldy loaf of bread on the counter gave evidence that it had been a long time since the occupants had taken a meal here.

Dean followed Sherzod to the master bedroom where the bed was still made, and pressed uniforms hung in the closet. It was as if the residents had just stepped into the bathroom to shower.

A shiver ran down Dean's spine. He felt like an unwilling participant in some science fiction horror movie. Neither man spoke as they stepped off the front porch to continue toward the lab building.

Dean checked for security cameras but found only bare wires where they had once hung. The two men climbed the stairs of the lab building, and Sherzod donned his mask before they entered through an unlocked door.

"It's completely unsecured!" Dean shook his head in amazement. "Incredible!"

Sherzod handed him his light, withdrawing a second one from his pack, along with a folded drawing of the building layout. As with the living quarters, the lab appeared as if everyone had simply left for the night. Only the occasional mound of packing material and glass from a few shattered windows indicated otherwise.

Upon entering the lab building, Sherzod seemed to gain a sense of urgency. Dean imagined he was eager to finish so that they could escape the hellish place. A hint of an antiseptic smell reminiscent of a hospital still permeated the building.

They turned left down the first linoleum-tiled corridor continuing at a brisk pace to the end of the dreary, gray hallway where they entered a stairwell. Their heavy boots echoed loudly on the metal steps as they descended the two flights of stairs to the basement.

Consulting his map as they emerged from the stairwell, Sherzod proceeded straight and then took the first right, walking until they reached a pair of heavy metal doors. While Dean couldn't read the wording, he took the skull prominently printed on the large sign affixed to each door as a warning and cinched the straps on his mask tighter.

Without breaking stride, Sherzod burst through the doors into a cavernous room. Their steps shattered the silence as they strode quickly across the expanse. Sealed 55-gallon metal drums, many corroded and leaking their contents onto the floor, were stacked four high in endless rows. Dean followed Sherzod's example carefully avoiding the puddles as they continued onward.

Just as Dean began to make out the far end of the building in front of them, Sherzod glanced at his map and abruptly swung his light to the right down a smaller corridor, at the end of which stood a stack of diesel fuel-filled barrels. The two men tilted the heavy barrels, rolling them on their bottom edges off to one side, exposing a small door with another ominous sign affixed to it.

"Russian safe," Sherzod said, as he removed his 9mm pistol and blew the padlock off the door. "Russian key," he added, with a broad grin.

Dean laughed. "Well, let's be careful. I'd rather not have a Russian funeral." He shined his light about, amazed at the wall of cardboard boxes stacked some ten-feet high filling the gymnasium-sized room. Holes in the boxes revealed them to be filled with glass vials. He paid scant attention to the bits of cardboard, the thick deposit of rat droppings, or the rat skeleton which lay on the far side.

Sherzod walked rapidly down the cardboard-box corridor, seeming even more eager to complete this part of their mission. Dean could hear him muttering to himself as he read the labels on the boxes. Still walking at a brisk pace, he pivoted to turn left when his foot slipped, causing him to stumble and fall into the stack of boxes before him.

Too late, it dawned on Dean that the bits of cardboard were from rats chewing on the boxes for nesting material or perhaps food, thereby weakening them. He looked on in horror as the adjacent stacks collapsed like dominos showering Sherzod with glass vials. A burst of popping sounds echoed in the room as a handful of vials shattered on the floor, splashing a rainbow of liquids all over Sherzod and onto Dean's pant legs.

Sherzod lay on the floor, stunned amidst the broken glass and the mixture of various liquids, his gas mask knocked askew. Instinctively, he leaped back to his feet. He brushed away the broken glass and liquid that streaked his chest, turning the dust on his uniform to mud. As the grim realization sunk in, he stopped brushing and looked up at Dean. His face was a mask of horror, his body beginning to tremble. "I think we're dead."

Dean staggered backward. Sherzod fell to his knees, knocking his gas mask to the floor and clawing at his throat. His mouth and nose gushed blood. It didn't take a PhD to figure out what was happening.

Dean watched helplessly as the man toppled over and, after convulsing for only a moment, lay motionless. Dean stooped to snatch the few intact samples of each color vial he could reach without getting too near the wet stained concrete floor. Then he ran, his injured ankle forgotten in his adrenalin-fueled flight.

Once outside the room, he paused. He withdrew a small protective metal case into which he carefully placed the vials. He then began winding his way back through the cavern of steel drums. Twice he made a wrong turn and his heart raced, fearing that he was lost.

When he found the stairs, he took them three at a time. Once back at ground level, he burst from the stairway. He ran down the hallway and through the front entrance into the still heat of the night. Brushing his gas mask aside, he vomited on the steps outside.

He wiped the bile from his mouth on his sleeve and rinsed his mouth with water from the canteen. He spat on the steps before taking a long pull of the tepid water. The image of Sherzod dying so suddenly, so painfully, was burned into his mind.

*Maybe I should have tried to help him rather than cutting and running,* he berated himself. But in his heart he knew there was nothing he could have done to save the man. Certainly, he too would have died had he tried.

For several minutes, Dean sat on the front steps collecting his thoughts while he caught his breath. The plan had been to conduct a full reconnaissance and retrieve samples of any suspected biological warfare agents in an organized manner. He was then to return to the derelict ship for extraction the following night. But now, he was no longer confident he would still be alive by then.

With his pulse returning to normal, he retrieved a camera from his pack and photographed each vial. He then opened a mini-laptop computer and typed a quick summary of events. Linking the digital photos to his summary, he initiated an encrypted burst transmission to his command center via satellite before replacing the computer in his pack.

He checked the area about him for threats with his night vision goggles. Then, still spooked by the events, he slid his gas mask back in place and headed toward the inflatable. The injured ankle, forgotten in his panicked rush, was now complaining and he paused to down another dose of ibuprofen.

*I didn't actually touch Sherzod or have skin contact with any of the broken vials. Since he died nearly immediately, maybe I'm okay. I don't even know what that stuff was, so maybe you have to actually have skin contact to be infected. Yeah, that's it,* Dean said to make himself feel better, while ignoring the rainbow stains on his pant legs.

After finally reaching the boat, he tossed the gas mask aside before wading into the putrid water to wash the liquids from his pants. The wind had died and the air was still as he pulled the boat off the beach. He shoved off with one foot before stepping in. When the boat had drifted a short ways from shore, he fired up the small outboard, slipped on his night vision goggles, and cranked up the throttle.

With only one passenger, the boat skimmed over the placid dark waters toward the waiting Tomcar. He kept the throttle wide open as he neared the shore, driving the boat well onto the beach with the outboard protesting loudly once free of the water. After killing the engine, he limped from the boat to the vehicle, pausing only to wash down another pill for his aching ankle. He headed into the desert without a backward glance at the abandoned watercraft.

As he drove through the quiet dark, the shock gradually wore off. With plenty of time before sunrise, Dean chose to drive slower, easing over the various obstacles Sherzod had taken earlier at full throttle. Though he felt giddy to have survived, Sherzod's tragic death took the edge off his relief.

*It's time to get out of the service. I mean, how many more close calls before my luck finally runs out? I've done my duty and then some. Time to settle down, have a couple of rug rats. Yeah, I'd like that.*

Without thinking he wiped his runny nose before it dawned on him, *Why is my nose running in the desert?* Even in the greenish light of the night vision goggles he could tell the dark stain on his hand was trouble.

He stood on the brakes and grabbed the light from the seat beside him. After wiping his hand on the leg of his fatigues, he rubbed his nose again. Eyes closed, he muttered a silent prayer, knowing what he would see when he opened them. He glanced down a second time to see his fingers, illuminated now by the flashlight, covered in a thick layer of blood. It felt like a fist slammed into his stomach.

"Nooooo! Damn it all! Damn it all to hell," he yelled into the night and then sat sobbing. Sherzod had been right—they were dead.

Collecting himself, he drove on. *Maybe, if I make it to the ship, I can last until they extract me and get medical attention.* But he knew it was wishful thinking. Soon he'd join Sherzod; nothing could save him.

He sped back to the rusting ships, parking the Tomcar behind the rotten hulk farthest from the village in hopes it wouldn't draw immediate attention. He grabbed his pack and, for no particular reason, returned to the same ship in which he had sought refuge earlier.

He climbed atop the bridge where he sat cross-legged, typing his last message. After hitting transmit, he removed his comms unit, switched it to beacon mode, and strapped it to a rotting antenna bracket, camouflaging the unit with a dirty rag. He then staggered inside the ship's bridge and collapsed onto the wheelhouse floor.

An hour later, Dean was dead.

# CHAPTER 1

Beady onyx eyes, each protected by a sharp horn, swiveled on stalks as the alien-looking creature scanned the area before it. It assumed a defensive posture, legs splayed out from its armored body, small antennas probing the space in front searching for sustenance. There the invader sat poised, unflinching, ever vigilant.

That is, until an unpleasant nudging sensation at the back of its body forced it forward in its lair. It never saw the loop of heavy plastic that snaked up its tail and then tightened—it was captured.

Quint pulled the snare from the coral cave and deposited the lobster into his bag. This was his sixth and final one, making his season opening day's limit. *Not bad; half a tank of air left and already finished.*

His buddy Dawson was hard at work on the opposite side of the coral head when a sizeable lobster shot out, erratically propelling itself backward with thrusts from its powerful tail. Casting aside his own bag of lobsters and snare, Dawson kicked frantically with his fins while pulling himself along the bottom in hot pursuit, showing little regard for the reef.

The harried lobster darted first one way and then the other in its desperate attempt to shake the madman. Quint's belly laugh sent clouds of bubbles rising to the surface as he watched Dawson's comic escapades.

Minus two legs and an antenna, the lobster shot into a shallow crevice dead-ending into a coral head with no protective cave. Dawson slammed his hand down, pinning the hapless creature to the bottom, and then quickly folded the creature's tail against its body to thwart its further escape attempts.

Mustering his remaining dignity, Dawson calmly swam back to retrieve his equipment and place the "bug" in his bag as if nothing had happened. While rubbing a red splotch on his leg, he signaled Quint that he too had just scored his limit.

Dawson claimed to have the uncanny ability to contact any piece of fire coral within 100 yards. A careless moment while pursuing this last lobster and, bingo, his skin was ablaze.

When Dawson flashed his pressure gauge showing he had plenty of air, Quint reciprocated before heading left, to continue the dive with their remaining air and bottom time. Quint closely guarded the location of this favorite dive spot off of Big Pine in the Florida Keys, offering the dual advantage of being little known and holding numbers of plump lobsters.

Quint freed a strand of sandy blonde hair caught in his mask strap as he swam. Fighting an unending battle against a growing paunch, he had managed to keep his fortyish-year-old body in good shape. Most days he would run five miles as he once did as a SEAL, but today this dive would count toward his daily dose of exercise.

His wetsuit top offered protection against fire coral while concealing a collection of old wounds. With the index finger of his left hand, he rubbed an itch near the long scar on his left cheek just below his dive mask.

Quint smiled at a parrotfish struggling to dislodge a remora glued to its side intent on catching a free ride on its unwilling host. No matter how erratically the parrotfish swam, or how hard it bobbed and weaved, the parasite refused to be dislodged. As Quint swam past, he saw the parrotfish duck through a thatch of soft coral and disappear below a coral ledge, nearly colliding with a bewildered triggerfish.

Approaching the end of their dive, the two men worked their way up the sloping coral bottom into shallower water, gliding past purple sea fans waving in the gentle surge. Just above a school of horse-eyed jacks cruising past, Quint spotted the mooring ball line. A cloud of yellowtail hovered nervously beside it in hopes of an easy meal.

He was absorbed watching the ballet performance of a pair of queen angels when a mass of auburn hair waving from behind a coral head and a pair of fins frantically stirring the sand caught his eye. He signaled Dawson before bolting off with several hard kicks. Rounding the coral head, he found a female snorkeler, struggling to free her right arm from inside a coral cave.

Quint saw the panic in her eyes as she desperately waved her free arm. In a single motion, he jerked his spare octopus regulator free of its retainer and thrust it toward her. She snatched it from his hand and greedily sucked in air, slowly relaxing as her lungs filled.

Ignoring the bare breast which had escaped from her bright red swimsuit top, Quint's quick glance at his pressure gauge confirmed that his tank was nearing empty. He eased beside her to peer into the coral cave.

A long yellow spear shaft was connected by a lanyard to a length of surgical tubing wrapped tightly around the woman's hand. Deep within the coral cave, the eye of a large grouper, impaled at the far end of the shaft, stared back.

Quint handed his bag of lobsters and gear to Dawson. He pulled a razor-sharp knife from its sheath on the shoulder strap of his buoyancy compensator.

He then reached inside the cave and, unable to see with both of their arms filling the opening, groped until he felt the lanyard and began sawing through it. A moment later, her arm was freed. Quint took his gear back from Dawson and swam toward the surface with the woman adjusting her swimsuit top.

"Thank you! I thought I was a goner!" she yelled breathlessly once her head broke the surface. After releasing Quint's spare regulator and pushing her mask onto her forehead, she turned to him. "I popped that grouper. Thought I got a good shot until he ducked into that cave. Guess I had the sling wrapped too tightly on my wrist when he ran," she explained in staccato fashion, the adrenalin apparently still coursing through her.

Quint motioned for her to follow him to his boat, where he politely ducked to one side. She tossed her fins onto the deck above before climbing aboard. Immediately, she turned to take his lobster bag, tickle stick, and snare.

She set them aside as he handed her the rest of his gear and pulled himself onto the boat. A minute later, Dawson joined them after passing up the woman's yellow pole spear along with the still-struggling grouper.

"Hi, I'm Marcia," she introduced herself, and the two men did the same, standing together in the back of Quint's center console boat.

Quint handed her his own towel and then used his t-shirt to dry his shaggy hair before giving her a stern look. "You might be a little more careful about what you spear."

"More like, where I aim. I'm really not an airhead novice. I've speared fish before, just missed the kill shot this time. But I do appreciate the advice and the rescue even more," she laughed with a low, throaty sound. "I know you're not supposed to dive alone and rarely do. But since I'm vacationing by myself, it was either that or not dive. Plus I figured it was no big deal since I wasn't using scuba. It would appear I was wrong." As she bent over to work the water from her hair, Quint punched Dawson for openly staring.

The woman stood a few inches shorter than Quint's six feet. Her lack of body fat and slender, muscular limbs gave her an athletic look, maybe a runner. The accent placed her from Boston, or perhaps New York.

Strips of pearl-white skin peeked out from the edges of her swimsuit, contrasting with those areas burned red by the sun's savage rays. She wore the air of someone who could handle herself, though Quint suspected she was more shaken by her near death experience than she let on.

"Where you from?" he broke the awkward silence while Dawson remained mute, continuing to study the woman.

"New York. But I did a lot of diving with my father when I was a kid. We took daddy-daughter dive trips each year, but that's been a while back. Maybe I'm a little rusty."

She wrapped the towel around her shoulders to ward off the chill of the evaporating water and perhaps Dawson's probing stare as well. "Should have put on the sun block a little earlier," she grimaced as the cotton touched a burned area between her shoulder blades.

"Classic tourist mistake, though I didn't take you for a typical one." Not a traditionally handsome man, his face was weathered by the sun and the sea. He turned his bright green eyes toward her and caught her staring. She blushed and quickly cut her eyes toward Dawson.

Also fortyish, his piercing blue eyes gave him a slightly menacing air, though not intimidating, despite a nose that looked to have been broken more than once. His dark brown hair was cut a couple of inches long and left to fend for itself. A touch of grey peeked out in front of each ear.

He stood slightly over six feet tall, and Marcia had to squint as she looked up into his face shadowed by the low sun. "Looks like somebody got overly friendly with the fire coral."

"Yeah, I get too focused when hunting bugs, and that's the price I pay," Dawson grunted, as he unzipped his shorty wet suit and eased it down past the angry red welt.

"I always offer to pee on it to help relieve the pain, but he never accepts my kindness," Quint laughed.

Ignoring the comment, Dawson turned to Marcia. "What do you do?"

"Security," she replied.

"You any good?"

"The best." Her cocky tone suggested she was only half kidding.

"Guess I need to—"

"Want to join us—" Dawson said at the same time. They both stopped, and she motioned for Dawson to continue, "You're welcome to come help us scarf up these lobsters."

"I appreciate it, but I need to get my rental boat back before they close. Rain check?"

"Sure," Dawson sounded uncomfortable, seeming unsure whether she was sincere or just being polite. He untied them from the mooring ball while Quint fired up the engine and idled toward her boat tied-off to a neighboring buoy.

"Thanks again, guys. See you around." Marcia climbed from their boat and took her spear with the grouper as Dawson handed it over. A minute later, she was under way.

"There's just something about her I like," Dawson said combing his fingers through his hair. "But I think she liked you."

"What?" Quint asked.

"Come on, we both saw her eyeing you."

"Don't be stupid; you're the macho ladies' man." Quint laughed and steered toward shore. "Plus I've got my hands full with Evie."

# CHAPTER 2

By the time they had cleaned the boat and stowed their gear, the sun was resting against the horizon. Quint drove down to Ramrod Key where he parked his truck alongside a green compact sedan at the Looe Key Tiki Bar. While he ordered two Kalik beers, Dawson headed for the kitchen around back bearing a bag with a half dozen lobsters. The heavy smell of grilled seafood filled the air.

"Brought you some nice ones. How about you grill up a couple for us and keep the rest?"

The cook looked up from the grill, wiping his hands on a stained dish towel as Dawson entered. "Hell, yeah! I'll even throw in some of my world-famous black beans with yellow rice to go with them. Have 'em done in a jiffy."

Dawson nodded and headed toward the bar.

Quint took a pull on his beer and wiped away a few drops of moisture that had fallen onto his t-shirt from the clear glass bottle. Hard-working ceiling fans barely moved the thick air, and calypso music blared from speakers hung just beneath the palm-frond ceiling. He liked the tune, though it played louder than he preferred.

On the wall behind the scarred wooden counter hung a mirror, partially obscured by dusty shelves filled with half-empty liquor bottles. Quint set his beer back on the counter and studied the reflection of a man sitting alone at the far corner table. His lime silk shirt and starched gray pants were much too formal for the casual bar.

Quint shifted his gaze back as Dawson returned to the bar, and handed him one of the frosty bottles of Bahamian beer. As Dawson reached for it, he froze, arm still raised, eyes fixed on the man Quint had just noticed.

"What are you doing here?" Dawson snarled.

"That's not much of a greeting." The man rose, carefully smoothing his pants. "Especially for the brother you haven't seen in, what, eight years? Just before... the, uh... accident." Dawson jerked, as if slapped by the memory of the wife and daughter he had lost in a fiery automobile accident.

After a short pause the man continued. "Just in the area and thought I'd drop by," he laughed heartily while approaching Quint. "You must be a friend of Dawson's, and a friend of his is a friend of mine. Preston is pleased to meet you," he said, with his hand outstretched.

Quint shot a puzzled glance toward Dawson, who answered with a shrug. Baffled by both the man's peculiar habit of referring to himself in the third person and the revelation that Dawson had a brother, Quint shook Preston's hand, doing little to disguise his confusion.

"It would appear that Dawson hasn't told you about his brother, has he?" Quint shook his head. "Figured. Hey bartender, a Manhattan for Preston and another round for them. I imagine we'll be chatting for quite some time."

"Not with me," Dawson muttered beneath his breath, and then asked again, "Why are you here?"

"Can't Preston come to see his brother without his motives being questioned?"

"No," Dawson replied bluntly. "*Preston* never does anything that doesn't benefit *Preston,* and brotherly love isn't a likely reason." Dawson wheeled about and headed back toward the kitchen where he caught the cook's eye. "Make those dinners to go."

"Man, I cook you up a masterpiece and you want it to go?" the cook snorted indignantly.

"Let's just say an ugly problem reared its head." Dawson returned to the bar a few minutes later with an armload of carry-out boxes. "Let's go before our dinner gets cold." Quint looked up in surprise but elected not to comment.

"Hate that you boys have to leave. Maybe we can finish our conversation later." Quint reached for his wallet to pay his bar tab when Preston grabbed his hand. "Preston's treat. Enjoyed meeting you."

Quint thanked him for settling the bill and followed Dawson out to the truck. "So what's the deal with you and your brother?" he asked, as he pulled out of the parking lot. "Except for the whole third-person thing, Preston this and Preston that," Quint laughed, "he seems like a nice enough guy."

"Think so? Well, you don't know shit about him." Quint chose not to press the issue as he drove to Dawson's place. He parked out front and followed his buddy inside the modest frame house, which backed up to Florida Bay.

The screen door squeaked and then banged closed behind them as their footsteps echoed across a wooden floor desperately in need of waxing. A sour, moldy smell hung in the air only partially disguised by the cinnamon air-freshener. Quint skirted the overstuffed easy chair and grabbed an armload of beer cans off the side table, leftovers from the previous night. For the millionth time, he straightened the landscape print that hung in a cheap frame beside the television. Quint worked hard at being a good roommate but felt the time was ripe to find his own place.

After Dawson fetched forks and a couple of beers, the two men each sat down in one of the mismatched chairs beside the garage-sale-refugee dining table to work on their dinners.

Quint peeled a chunk of meat from the split lobster tail branded with grill marks and dunked it in the melted butter before popping it in his mouth. A fork full of yellow rice stained black from the beans followed close behind.

Halfway through their dinner, Dawson finished chewing a mouthful of pressed Cuban bread and broke the heavy silence. "Sorry for snapping at you. I haven't seen my brother in years. He caught me off guard."

"What's the deal?"

"I don't want to talk about it."

"Okaaay," Quint replied, deciding it was best to drop the subject. Besides, he had little interest in getting in the middle of a family dispute. "The lobsters are great." Dawson nodded his reply without speaking.

They finished their beers, and Dawson rose to fetch another round before turning in. "By the way, can I borrow your truck to run errands in Key West tomorrow morning?" Dawson asked, handing Quint a bottle.

"Try not to wreck it," Quint laughed, tossing him the keys.

Quint was in the midst of a particularly erotic dream about his girlfriend, Evie, when Dawson headed out early the next morning. A short while later, a persistent knocking roused him awake. He opened the door in his boxers to find a green compact sedan pulled up out front and Preston holding a bag of doughnuts.

"I woke you, didn't I? Sorry. Dawson here?"

Quint glanced down the driveway and noticed his truck was gone. "No, it appears he's already left to run errands." He hoped that the bag of doughnuts had something to do with the trace of white powder on Preston's upper lip.

"Crap. It's a shame to waste fresh doughnuts; mind if I come in? We can have breakfast together and maybe finish our conversation from yesterday." Finding it awkward to refuse, Quint opened the screened door and motioned him in.

"Uh... nice place," Preston said, stepping over a pair of Dawson's dirty shorts. "You guys been roomies long?"

"A few weeks. Hurricane destroyed the boat I was living on so he's letting me crash here until I find my own place." Quint put on a pot of coffee, noting that he was nearly out of vanilla creamer.

"Dawson's a great guy; I'm lucky to have him as my brother." They continued to munch on the doughnuts while Preston chattered away.

"So what's with you and Dawson?" Quint finally interrupted as he grabbed another pastry from the bag.

"I came here in hopes of fixing things, which as you witnessed, hasn't gone well so far. But I'm determined to keep trying until I either succeed or concede that there's no chance."

"What caused your falling out?"

"It was my fault." Preston studied his coffee for a moment. "I was sort of a wild child growing up, always getting into trouble. Dawson was always the stable, practical one. He put up with a lot. But I guess the thing that really tore it was a woman." Preston paused to wipe doughnut grease from his hands while seeming to collect his thoughts.

"Dawson had feelings for a woman who was cheating on him. When I tried to clue him in, he became angry, refusing to listen. So, in an effort to protect my little brother, I did something which I deeply regret—I stole her away from him. Not because I cared for her, but to break up the two of them. He never believed me. It ended our relationship, and the brother I loved was gone," Preston finished softly.

Quint drummed his fingers on the table. To Preston's credit, he did seem to be taking the blame. "So why try to make amends now after all this time?"

"Things have changed."

"What things?"

"I'm, I'm... dying," Preston said and then stopped for a moment. "I'd been having problems. They bounced me from doctor to doctor while they ran this test and that prescribing a never ending array of meds. I probably took a suitcase full before they finally stumbled on the real problem—cancer."

"Can't they treat it?"

"Sure, they offered the usual radiation and chemo. But by the time I was finally diagnosed, the cancer had spread through the lymph nodes and into my bones. Truth is, I'm going to die, and I'd prefer not to be whittled away to nothing while spending my final days hairless and puking." Preston looked down at his feet in silence.

"How long you got?" Quint asked, pushing away the napkin with the remains of his breakfast.

"Days, maybe weeks, but not months, I'm told." Preston's voice broke, and his eyes suddenly filled with tears. "Quint, I admit that I've done things... a lot of things, of which I'm not proud. But I've changed. It hasn't been easy, but I've seriously changed. I just want to make things right with Dawson. I want my brother back before I die.

"Maybe I don't deserve the chance, but since he's the better man, I was hoping he'd cut me some slack. You care for him; help me patch things up. Please help me," he begged, openly sobbing now. "You're my only hope to reconnect. If not for me, do it for your best friend. Please!"

Even without Preston's abrupt onslaught of emotion, Quint found himself warming toward the man and feeling compassion. Unsure what else to do, he sat uncomfortably until Preston excused himself to use the bathroom. A minute later, he returned having regained his composure.

"Forgive me for losing it like that."

"Look, Preston, I'm not sure I can help you. But Dawson's like a brother to me, and I'd hate to see him miss the chance to square things before you... uh... are you going to tell him?" Quint asked, as he refilled his cup. Preston refused more coffee with a shake of his head.

"No! And I beg you not to tell him either. I don't want him doing anything out of pity."

"Okay, then how can I help you?" Quint rinsed out the coffee maker as he awaited Preston's reply. *So much for staying out of family squabbles.*

"Besides talking to Dawson, tell me what you can to bring me up to date on his life. Perhaps that will help me better connect with him."

Eager to change the subject, Quint began to speak. "After spending a few years together as SEALs, Dawson and I sort of lost touch. Then I ran into him down in the Keys still trying to cope with Cathy's death. I talked him into helping me run my charter boat to Venezuela. It's a long story, but we put together a team and went looking for a sunken Spanish galleon. We got lucky and made some serious money. Then a few months ago, Dawson and I got our team back together and formed a company to take on new projects."

"To look for more wrecks?"

"Perhaps, but the company has a much larger scope."

"Sounds exciting. Tell me more about your team... I mean whatever you feel you can share without breaking any confidences."

Quint hesitated for a moment before deciding there was little harm in telling him about the various members and their quirks. Preston seemed enthralled with learning more and pressed Quint further than he had intended to go.

"A few months back, we met this guy Rogers. His company, Vector, does work for the feds and our first project was for him. It uh... involved helping the government find some... missing equipment." Quint avoided going into further detail about the more sensitive areas of their work and anything else he considered confidential.

"So what exciting projects are you into now?"

"For the past couple of weeks, we've been licking our wounds. But we've scheduled a meeting to consider our next project. Where you staying?" Quint changed the subject hoping to gain closure.

Preston looked down, appearing ashamed. "Uh... nowhere in particular."

"What's that mean?"

"Uh... in my car. I sold my house before coming down here. Figured I wouldn't be needing it much longer," he laughed while fidgeting with his napkin. "The funds were supposed to have been wired to me by now, but there's a glitch with the title. An earlier mortgage was paid off, but evidently the bank never released the lien. My agent assured me they'll work it out, but it could take another couple of weeks. And then on top of that, a pick-pocket stole my wallet when I was up in Miami."

"But you paid our bar tab yesterday."

"I know. It was stupid. But I wanted so badly to get off to a good start with Dawson. The few bucks I have left won't last long anyhow. I may have to give up and go back if it takes much longer to get my house funds."

Quint hesitated for a moment, alarm bells going off in his head. *If he does have cancer, he really doesn't have much time. And I can afford to loan him what he needs. If he's lying, then I risk losing a few bucks to help my buddy. Would he do it for me? Without a doubt.*

Quint heard himself say, "How much you need to get you through?"

"Gosh, things are expensive down here. For a place to stay, food, and fuel, more than I care to imagine."

Quint left the room. A minute later he returned and handed Preston a check. "This loan should see you through. Pay me back when you close on the house."

"That's really generous, but Quint, I can't take your money. I'll manage. If I have to leave, maybe I can still make it back before..."

"Don't be stupid."

"Dawson would be pissed."

"He doesn't have to know." Quint was surprised at how easily he offered to deceive his best friend.

"I really shouldn't accept it, but I guess I don't have much choice. God bless you." Preston clutched Quint's hand with both of his. "Well, now that I can afford it, I'll go find a place to stay and take a much-needed shower. Give me your cell number so I can get back in touch with you to settle up. And Quint, please, I beg you, help me square things with Dawson while I still have time. Please."

Quint nodded. As he watched Preston walk out to his car he wondered if he'd just helped or screwed his best friend.

# CHAPTER 3

"What's with the cloak and dagger stuff? I mean I like the Hogfish Grill and all, but..." Quint asked as he took a huge bite of his fish taco. He had been puzzled when Rogers suggested meeting at this out-of-the-way place on Stock Island just north of Key West. While it was Quint's type of place, Rogers usually preferred to meet in Miami at his headquarters or on occasion in the team's modest Key West office.

Quint figured Rogers to be pushing 60 though he kept himself in great shape. Had it not been for his thick gray hair, combed straight back from a high forehead, he might have been mistaken for ten years younger. He had a strong jaw and clear eyes, one slightly lower than the other. He had the knack of always appearing well-groomed without seeming obsessive about his dress.

After requesting the meeting a couple of hours earlier, Rogers had arrived in his company's private jet, impeccably dressed, as always. To avoid appearing too out of place, he left the coat to his Italian-cut pinstripe suit in the modest airport rental car. With his own ragged shorts and faded Marty Wilson-designed t-shirt standing in stark contrast, Quint was afraid to hazard a guess as to the cost of Rogers' cologne, the scent of which wafted across the table.

"I guess between discovering a mole working for me and finding a bug planted outside of my office window,

I'm somewhat more paranoid these days." Rogers dove into the restaurant's signature BLT sandwich, which substituted lobster for lettuce.

Quint had chosen a rickety table near the raised stage area where the house band played in the evenings. While lacking an overhead fan, it was set away from the other tables, offering more privacy somewhat at the expense of comfort. Not that any area in the restaurant was what one might call cool.

Rogers waited for the waitress to replenish their drinks before proceeding. "Interested in an all-expense paid trip to Vozrozhdeniye, or Renaissance Island as it's known in English?" When the two men stared back without blinking, he continued. "I'll take that as a no. You may recall that after your little adventure hunting nuclear bombs off the coast of the Pass—"

"You mean the little adventure in which you left us to fight off terrorists in the middle of a hurricane? That little adventure?" Quint interrupted.

"Uh... yes, that would be the one." Rogers' company, Vector, had hired Quint's team under a highly classified sub-contract to find a lost nuclear weapon for the government.

"Yeah, wasn't that the same one where you promised us a treasure ship full of gold and silver?" Dawson asked while wiping a spot of sauce from the middle of his t-shirt emblazoned with a tail-walking blue marlin.

"Wait a minute. I never guaranteed you'd find it. I simply said there was a Spanish treasure galleon believed to be in that area."

"It was bait for us to take the job," Dawson replied flatly.

"Look, you were well paid, and besides, we've already had this argument. You shouldn't dwell on life's little challenges," Rogers protested.

"Little challenges, huh?" Dawson replied.

Quint studied a crude original painting of a large hogfish mounted on the wall across the restaurant while he savored the ensuing silence. Rogers squirmed, seeming unsure if they were really mad or just screwing with him. Finally, he took a different tack. "You two know much about bioweapons?"

"Should we?"

"Depends. We have a problem."

"We do, or you do?" Dawson asked through a mouthful of fried hogfish.

"I guess, I'm here to answer that question." Rogers looked him back straight in the eye.

"In answer to your earlier question." Quint broke the staring contest. "Anyone not living in a cave these past few years has heard about the scary anthrax attacks."

Rogers nodded. "Yes, but aside from those few cases in which it was sent through the mail, the reality is that anthrax really doesn't pose much of a threat.

"Weaponizing the anthrax bacteria to infect people on a large scale is quite difficult. It takes some 10,000 spores to successfully infect a human. Furthermore, it can't be passed from one person to another and is treatable with antibiotics. So, while it may cause alarm, in reality it's not the threat most people think. But there are plenty of other things to worry about."

"Such as?" Dawson asked, casting an uneasy glace at Quint.

"VX nerve gas for one. See this penny?" Rogers picked up a coin in his palm. "A drop of VX that would barely fill the middle of the 'O' in the 'One Cent' is enough to easily kill three men. Ever see what happens when a man is exposed to VX? His body starts to—"

"Hey, I'm trying to finish my lunch here," Dawson protested.

"Point taken," Rogers chuckled and changed topics. "Another thing that keeps our folks up at night is worrying about the highly contagious smallpox virus," Rogers continued. "In 1977 the disease had been eradicated, but the World Health Organization permitted one lab in the U.S. and one in the Soviet Union to possess a sample for research purposes. You can probably guess where this is headed—this gave the Soviets the ability to develop smallpox as a biological weapon."

Quint stopped chewing as a chill ran down him. "But don't we have smallpox vaccines?"

"We do. Over 10 million doses, in fact. But even if they're still viable after all these years, we'd need 30 times that existing supply to inoculate all U.S. citizens. But it gets worse."

Quint noticed Dawson shifting on the hard wooden bench, nervously tapping his fork against his glass. He didn't seem to like where Rogers was headed, and in honesty, neither did Quint.

"U.S. Army-funded researchers have confirmed that Soviet scientists successfully engineered a genetically altered strain of smallpox into a super-virus for which there is no method of prevention and no cure. This bioweapon has the potential to wipe out most of... say New York City in a week."

Quint tossed his napkin on the remains of his uneaten fish sandwich. "Asking us to battle terrorists in the middle of a hurricane is one thing. Bioweapons are a completely different beast. I feel like I need a shower after just listening to you." Dawson nodded as he waved the waitress over to refill their drinks. "Rogers, this is all very interesting, but let's skip to the part where you tell us what you're asking us to do."

"I was getting to that, but since you're so impatient, I'll cut to the chase. We need you to go to Renaissance Island as I said to start with," Rogers said solemnly.

"Where the hell is Renaissance Island?" Dawson asked.

"Near Uzbekistan in the Aral Sea," Rogers replied.

After a long pause Quint broke the silence. "And you need us to go there because...?"

"That's where I was headed. In the late 1980s when the U.S. succeeded in securing the Soviet's pledge to shut down their entire bioweapons effort, some 60,000 biological warfare scientists and technicians were out of a job. A number of labs and manufacturing facilities were then left with hundreds of tons of nasty toxins and diseases. The Ruskies felt that the potential danger didn't warrant the considerable cost of providing ongoing security much less the expense of incinerating all the remaining bioweapons material. So in many cases, they simply locked the doors, boarded up the windows, and posted warning signs on the buildings where the weapons were stored."

"And Renaissance Island is one such place?" Dawson asked.

"Not just one, it's where the Soviets built their largest bioweapons testing and manufacturing facility."

"So, the answer to my question," Quint said, "is that a genetically altered strain of smallpox for which we have no vaccine exists. And it, along with a generous stash of VX and a bunch of other nasty stuff, is just waiting for some terrorist group to stumble upon it." Rogers nodded.

"You want us to put our asses on the line to go fetch tons of this nasty shit for you? I don't think so." Dawson punctuated his last statement with a sweeping motion of his arm, knocking over Rogers' tea.

"No, we want you to destroy it," Rogers replied calmly while mopping up his drink with a soggy napkin. He paused while the waitress brought over a well-used rag to finish cleaning up and then refilled his glass. Once she had walked away, he continued.

"We can provide a believable cover story for you as a research group engaged in an oceanographic survey of the Aral Sea. That area has its own set of problems."

"But if all this happened over twenty years ago, why is the U.S. Government just now getting involved?" Quint asked.

"Unfortunately, concerns over the remaining Soviet nuclear and rocket bases took precedence."

"Wow!" Quint responded. "And let me guess, the U.S. Government doesn't want our military traipsing in there to deal with it for fear that such trespassing might trigger an international incident."

"Bingo. Needless to say, if U.S. forces were caught during such a covert operation, it would cause an enormous political problem if not a military one. It would also shine a huge spotlight on an issue we don't want illuminated, increasing the possibility that terrorists might go after these nasty weapons."

"Hold on a minute. My bullshit detector is going off. Rogers, have your guys already taken a shot at it?" Dawson asked in a steely voice.

Rogers sat silent for a moment before responding. "Well... sort of."

"Sort of? What the hell does 'sort of' mean?"

"We sent in two men to locate the cache. They found it, but had... a little accident."

"The kind of accident where they're no longer breathing?"

"Yeah, that kind. The guide died immediately when they literally stumbled onto a cache containing VX nerve gas among some other goodies. Our guy must have gotten a smaller dose, or was exposed to something slightly less lethal and was able to make it back to his extraction point. But by the time we got to him, he was dead. We retrieved his body along with the samples he collected. The vials contained Bubonic-Q, VX, and the aforementioned genetically altered form of smallpox, confirming our worst fears.

"The Uzbekistan government spotted us in the process of extracting his body and found the vehicle he had used. While they're not exactly sure what we were up to, it put the kibosh on another military incursion."

"But you think they'll be okay with us simply going in and blowing their shit up," Dawson said, with blatant sarcasm.

"We see this as a low-risk operation," Rogers replied.

"Low risk? Maybe for you." Dawson slammed his glass down hard and then grabbed at it to keep it from spilling.

Rogers took a deep breath. "Other than the explosives you'll need to destroy the bioweapons you don't even need to go in armed. Your biggest concern will be running afoul of the authorities. But if it looks like you're about to get caught, you'll just ditch the explosives and claim you blundered into the area denying any knowledge of what it is."

"Now *that* makes me feel better. But if it's all the same to you, if we do go in, we'll go in armed," Dawson said firmly.

Rogers nodded in response. "With the publicity surrounding your recent search and salvage exploration, your cover would hold. Anyone checking would simply confirm that you are who you claim to be. Then they'd probably release you with nothing more than a slap on the hand and a stern warning."

"It's the 'probably' part that concerns me." Quint folded his arms against his chest.

"Yeah, and I'm not so sure their little slap and warning would be as innocuous as you might have us believe," Dawson added.

"Worst case, we'll buy you out of prison. But as always, we do have other alternatives. We can use a cruise missile, but incinerating these biological agents is tricky. It could destroy the building and disperse the bio agents without generating enough heat to neutralize them."

Rogers paused as the waitress delivered the check. He handed her his credit card without even glancing at the bill and then waited until she was out of earshot to continue. "However, by having your team place explosive charges directly on the cache of diesel fuel drums, which we know to be situated nearby, our people are convinced that the bio-agents will reach critical temperature before the building collapses. It's crucial that the mission be conducted at night from the standpoint of stealth, and also when the winds are calm to minimize the chance of affecting the nearby populace."

"And what's the going rate for travelling to the other side of the world and sneaking into the world's biggest cesspool to blow it up?" Quint asked straight-faced.

"Given the risk associated with this mission, the U.S. Government is prepared to pay your team $40 million plus expenses and to provide you with whatever weapons and material you require. And, as you've insisted in the past, you can keep the toys you don't break, provided you don't require anything too exotic."

Dawson shook his head. "I don't know, dealing with bioweapons is scary."

"Yeah but $40 million is a lot of money."

"True, but hard to spend if you're dead," Dawson shot back.

"How soon do you need an answer?" Quint asked warily.

"As you might imagine, if we're discussing the use of your team, we need it yesterday. Recent Internet chatter suggests that a wacko terrorist group is sniffing down this path. So we need an answer within ten days and for your team to be prepared to execute within the next 60 days if not sooner. Otherwise, we'll be forced to proceed with an alternative," Rogers replied as he added a tip to their bill and then signed the receipt.

Quint appeared deep in thought as they rose from the table and headed out to the gravel parking lot where they stopped beside Rogers' rental car. "If the team accepts the mission, I'm sure we can be ready to mobilize within your timeframe. I'll let you know as soon as we can schedule a meeting so that you can personally brief the team. And Rogers, I suggest you come well prepared. I'm guessing they'll be even less excited than Dawson was about the idea of blowing up a bioweapons dump."

# CHAPTER 4

Quint missed Evie. So when he heard his phone ring as he stepped out of the shower and saw her name appear on the caller I.D., he snatched the phone off the bathroom counter. "Hello," he answered, struggling to keep the phone from getting soaked.

"Busy?" she asked, the sound of classical music playing softly in the background.

"Nope," he lied, unwilling to miss a chance to speak with her. He continued to towel off while listening at the same time. Evie was left deeply scarred from being kidnapped, held prisoner, and repeatedly raped by terrorists bent on obtaining a lost nuclear weapon.

After she broke things off to give herself space, Quint spent many sleepless nights sitting in his parked car down the street, watching her house. It comforted him just knowing she was there sleeping safely. More than once, dawn was breaking as he started his car to return home. Her struggles to cope left him feeling helpless, especially when she refused his calls and most of his attempts to see her.

"I've been missing you and needed to hear your voice."

"Evie... I've wanted to talk to you too, but y–"

"Quint, it's okay. You shouldn't feel guilty."

They talked for a few more minutes before Quint decided to push things. "Evie, what do you think about having dinner tonight, maybe Louie's Backyard?"

"I'm not ready yet. I'm afraid I'm still not... I hope you understand."

"No problem," Quint replied, though it most certainly was.

"We'll talk more later. Bye." She abruptly ended the conversation before he could think of another approach.

Quint was ready to be back with her, even for just one night of normalcy. He wanted that. He needed that. But clearly it was not going to happen—at least not any time soon.

While he respected her needs, it did not make her absence in his life any easier to accept. With no interest in other women, he coped with the loneliness as best he could. As he found himself thinking more about being with her and less about the advantages of being single, he came to realize that he wanted to remarry and have a family. But her disinterest in having kids was troubling. *Maybe I should discuss it with her. But how do I do that?* he wondered, certain that she was nowhere near ready to deal with the subject.

Exhausted from a hard day, Dawson climbed on a bar stool at the Schooner Wharf Bar for a much-needed beer. He did a double take at the sight of a parrot on the bar drinking from a bottle of beer his owner held for him.

The onslaught of development in the Keys had done away with many of the locals' hangouts, but this one lived on with its rustic charm intact. Dawson liked the familiar feel of the ramshackle place, decorated with old boat propellers and an array of junk suspended overhead.

"Well lookie here, the great Dawson himself," yelled the huge Jamaican bartender.

"And the one-and-only Julius." Dawson carefully avoided one of his bone-crushing handshakes.

"What'll you have?" Julius stretched, the muscles in his massive arms and broad shoulders nearly bursting his muscle shirt.

"Beer."

"What kind?"

"Cold and wet, my friend. Cold and wet." Dawson was nearly finished with his beer when Quint ambled in.

"Ever notice how big boobs are a real plus on a woman unless her stomach sticks out farther, in which case she loses all the points?" Dawson nodded at a large woman leaving the corner table with her date.

"You keep sucking down those beers, and the women will be making fun of your big gut."

"Ouch, man, you're plain mean. Julius, switch me to Jack and soda and a mojito for my partner here."

"Quint, ain't seen your sorry butt much since your last birthday celebration. Boy, you sure tied one on that night. " Julius squeezed a lime into a glass and began crushing mint with a pestle.

"That I did. Took me two days to recover. It's why you haven't seen me since," Quint laughed, his smile quickly turning to a frown as Julius delivered the icy drink. "Man, I don't need this."

Julius thrust the drink into his hand, ignoring Quint's protest. "Got to drink it, wasting it'd be alcohol abuse."

"What's a man to do?" Quint tasted the drink, "Well done." Julius smiled and left to wait on another customer. Quint stared at the drink for a moment before taking a deep breath and looking up at Dawson. "Preston stopped by."

Dawson stiffened and whipped his head around. "When?"

"Right after you borrowed my truck this morning."

"What did he want?"

"He came looking for you but then plead his case with me."

"Did it work?"

Quint took another drink and noticed two men carrying a large set of speakers toward the stage. "A little, I suppose."

"Humph," Dawson muttered as he emptied his drink and motioned to Julius for another.

"You know me; I don't get in your business."

"You don't know what all he's done."

"He told me some of it, even took all the blame. Why not give the man a chance?"

"I've done just that. More times than I can count."

"It's different now," Quint said and took another slug of the mojito.

"How so?"

Quint paused, picking a piece of mint off the end of his tongue and then continued deciding to tell Dawson and break a confidence. "He's dying. Cancer."

Dawson watched one of the band members struggling with a microphone stand for a moment before turning back to Quint. "And you would know this how?"

"He told me."

"And you believe him?"

"I understand you've got history with him, but it's been a while. If he really is dying, what's the harm in trying to end things between the two of you on a good note?"

"And what if he's lying?"

"What if he is?" Quint looked him square in the eye. "But if it's true, you have a chance to have closure with your only brother while there's still time."

Dawson took a long pull off his fresh drink and then for a moment traced patterns in the moisture on the bar's wooden surface. "I appreciate you encouraging me to do the right thing. I guess I agree. But the first time he starts up with his shit, we're done."

"Agreed," Quint replied, toasting him with the remains of his drink. He looked over at the stage where the local band was nearly finished setting up. One of the musicians was tuning his guitar while another did rolls on the drums. Their specialty was playing Jimmy Buffett songs and in a display of wry humor, they were dressed in black and yellow calling themselves the "Buffett Wanna' Bees."

"Those boys don't seem too serious about much of anything. I haven't heard 'em yet, but already I like 'em," Dawson laughed, changing the subject. "Speaking of Buffett, my favorite philosophy of his is, 'Lotta truth in a full bottle of whiskey, lotta lies in an empty one.'"

"Looks like you're hard at work on emptying one," Quint replied dryly. "Isn't that Marcia?" He pointed at a brunette wearing white shorts and a hot pink sleeveless blouse seated on a bar stool nearly twenty feet away. She seemed to be enduring the bragging and annoying pickup lines of a boorish but determined man seated at a table beside the bar. He wore civilian clothes, but his haircut and demeanor suggested he might be police or maybe military.

"Yeah, I was about to ask her to join me when Mr. Redneck Romeo latched on."

"Is he drunk or just stupid?"

Dawson shrugged. "She's a new victim. His last one got fed up and left just before she came in."

Finally, it appeared that Marcia too had had enough and spoke up in a voice loud enough for everyone to hear. "Why don't you go find someone with bigger tits and fewer brains who'll buy your crap?"

The put-down caused Dawson to spit a mouthful of his drink and roar with laughter, slapping his open hand on the bar. The red-faced man glared at him while beating a hasty retreat, but was still in earshot when Dawson piped up. "Excellent! I score you a ten for your public service in ridding us of an asshole."

"Didn't see you," Marcia said with a smile as she approached. "Consider it partial payback for saving my life."

"I'm throwing in the towel." Quint rose to leave but then leaned closer to Dawson and quietly added, "I don't want to be a fifth wheel."

"You're not going to hang around to check out the band?" Marcia asked, a hint of disappointment in her voice.

"He can fill me in tomorrow."

"I'm not too far behind you," Dawson replied. "Julius, another round for me and the lady."

"You clean up good," she said, taking a seat beside Dawson.

"As do you. I see you've gotten better at keeping the stuff covered that's supposed to be under wraps." Marcia blushed at his joking reference to her recent bikini wardrobe malfunction and changed the subject.

"So, your hobby's hanging out at bars?"

"I could ask you the same question," he grinned. "However, I'm somewhat of an expert on drinking."

"By profession? You have a micro-brewery or used to own a bar?"

"No, by avocation. My expertise is all from direct experience. Not limited to the grape, the hops, or sour mash, I'm a drunk-of-all trades, so to speak." Beginning to feel the liquor, he looked her in the eye, "You know what I like about you?"

"What?" her face formed in an expectant grin.

"Everything," he replied with a leering smile. Marcia rolled her eyes, laughing despite herself at his corny humor. "So, how long you going to be down here?" he asked.

"Not long enough. I head back to New York on Sunday."

"Come down often?"

"I wish. How'd you end up in the Keys?" Marcia asked.

"Long story. What do you do?" Dawson was determined not to divulge much about himself.

"Well, I used to be a waitress," Marcia replied, "but one night I finally had enough of taking crap off petty customers and quit. I had no idea what I was going to do until I stumbled onto a chance to work for a security firm." She related an incident that led to her all-expense-paid trip to the Keys. "And then my job with the security firm led to... let's just say, other opportunities."

Dawson nodded, choosing not to press her on the subject.

"Okay, your turn. I'm not telling you anything else until you ante up about yourself."

"Fair enough," Dawson replied. Perhaps spurred on by the alcohol, he told her about Preston and the recent encounter, which was weighing heavily on his mind. Though he rarely discussed such personal matters, Dawson felt relaxed with her and found himself sharing more about his brother than he had intended. By the time he finished, the band had cranked up, making further conversation difficult.

Julius' shift had just ended when three men entered the bar and took seats on either side of the couple. Redneck Romeo was with them, and Dawson smelled trouble. No one spoke as the men worked on their drinks and dug into their food when it arrived. They were finished eating when the band took another break.

The man seated beside Marcia blew his nose and tossed the thin napkin on his half-eaten plate of food. "Want the rest—just help yourself."

Marcia ignored him as the one wearing a red shirt beside Dawson asked, "Who the hell are you?" making it clear they came looking for trouble.

"Dawson."

"Dawson what?"

"Just Dawson."

"Like Sting or something, just one name?"

"No, I got all three. Just particular who I tell 'em to," Dawson said with a smile.

"He thinks he's tough," Redneck Romeo spouted off.

"That the case?" Red Shirt asked.

"Tough enough," Dawson replied.

Red Shirt stood threateningly. "Maybe that's what got your nose broke in the past and might just get it busted again."

"Bring it on," Dawson said calmly.

"Come on, guys, don't be starting no trouble," the bartender said, his hand beneath the bar resting on a Louisville Slugger.

Dawson headed for the bathroom to give things a chance to cool down. When he returned to the bar, he ignored the full glass of beer that sat before him and ordered another Jack.

"Hey, you got a beer right there in front of you. I bought it as a friendly gesture," Red Shirt protested. Marcia cut her eyes toward the beer and gave a small shake of her head, confirming Dawson's suspicion that Red Shirt had doctored it.

"Thanks, but I've got enough friends, and I've switched to Jack," Dawson replied. "Here, help yourself." He slid it over to the man, spilling some on the bar.

"That's not nice," Red Shirt growled.

"Guess I don't do nice." Dawson had just raised his fresh drink when Red Shirt sloshed some of his beer onto Dawson's shirt before shoving him off his stool. Pretending to be focused on his sodden shirt, Dawson let loose with an uppercut, and the fight was on. He landed three solid hits on Red Shirt before the second man joined in with a kidney punch from behind that took Dawson's breath away.

"I don't see why my buddies should have all the fun with your boyfriend," Redneck Romeo said, as he rose to join the fracas.

"Hey, it's already two against one. Stay out of it!" Marcia stood up in protest. Romeo made the mistake of shoving her onto her barstool before turning back toward the fighting men.

She leapt from the stool and drove her foot into the back of his knee while jamming her elbow into his kidney. Grabbing the mug of beer, she brought it crashing down against the left side of his face. Romeo collapsed into the pool of liquid, a shiner already forming on his left eye.

Marcia proceeded across the room where Red Shirt was holding Dawson while the second man pummeled his stomach and face. She swung her elbow down into the small of Red Shirt's back, and as he released Dawson to face her, swung her other elbow into his ear. Before he could react, she kicked him hard between the legs, collapsing him onto the floor.

When Marcia looked up, the bartender caught her eye. "I called the police. You best be gone before they get here." With the sound of sirens in the distance and Dawson once again engaged in a fair fight, she took his advice and left.

The door to the prisoners' visiting area opened, and Dawson shuffled in. His torn shirt was matted with blood, and he sported an impressive black eye with a matching swollen lip.

"You look like shit." Quint laughed.

"I'll take that as a compliment."

"Sometimes I think you've got an 18-year-old brain in that 40-year-old body. Enjoy your evening?"

"Do you really have to ask? By the way, you'll like this. As soon as they locked me up, my cell mate says to me, 'You didn't dress right.'"

"You didn't dress right to go to jail?"

"Nope, he tells me how he always wears a jacket to use as a pillow. I told him he was far more experienced than I ever hoped to be."

"So, what the hell happened last night?" Dawson described the episode leading up to the fight with the three men. "I thought you always avoid fighting unless the other guy starts it?"

"It was just a matter of time and, since there were three of them, I decided to get on with it. Wasn't one of my better decisions, given the amount I'd had to drink. I'll say this, the boys were good." Dawson rubbed his eye. "And that Marcia can handle herself. Said she's worked for a security firm. We oughta sign her up.

"Anyhow, I was still trading licks with the last guy standing when a couple more dudes join in. I figure they're more of Redneck Romeo's buddies and get into it with them, too. Next thing I know, we're headed off to jail. How was I supposed to know that they were plainclothes cops?

"Now, how about you work on getting me out of here while I head back to my cell to finish the nap you interrupted?"

Quint chuckled. "Getting you out ain't gonna be child's play. I mean, being drunk, fighting, and the coup de grace—assaulting two officers, who I understand are both in the hospital. What were you doing, trying for the law-breaker's trifecta?'"

"I admit it wasn't one of the high points of my life."

"And it ain't over. I'll go see what strings I can pull to get you out. But it won't be cheap, and this is on you, dumbass."

"You're so sweet. Wake me when it happens."

"That may be a while, so make yourself comfy."

A few hours later, Quint returned to the jail having arranged for Dawson's bail. "That's some shirt. It gives new meaning to the phrase, 'Now we don our gay apparel,'" Quint said, pointing at Dawson's pink flowered shirt.

"Hardy, har, har. It's the best the police department had in their donated clothing locker. It's still better than the blood-and-vomit-covered one I was wearing."

"I saw your friend Marcia and thanked her for you. She told me where she works. Maybe we should check her out."

"Maybe. You know what really pisses me off? I didn't get to finish my drink."

Quint shook his head in disbelief. "I considered letting you sit in your cell and stew, but I need you to work up the background on Renaissance Island. I have a feeling we're going to need it for the team meeting I set up for this Monday."

# CHAPTER 5

Monday morning, an hour before the team meeting was scheduled to begin, Quint entered the conference room he had rented in a hotel off Roosevelt on the north side of Key West. Its most attractive feature was the low price. The disinfectant failed to mask the musty odor that smelled like someone had stuffed seaweed inside the building walls. Several dark blotches marked the avocado green strip of carpet between the scarred walnut table and the edges of the room.

Quint caught a whiff of freshly brewed coffee and saw Kira standing before a stained aluminum coffee urn unlike the gleaming chrome ones to be found at the nearby La Concha or Ocean Key House. Being a punctuality fanatic, he felt a flash of irritation at not being the first of the team to arrive.

Kira helped herself to a Styrofoam cup from the stack and then proceeded to build a coffee, cut with plenty of cream and double sugar. A head of long, thick, naturally blonde hair framed her model-like face, belying how tough she had proven to be since joining the team.

"It would appear that the morning sickness is behind you now." Kira looked up and nodded. "How's the little one coming along?"

"At least he's letting me eat in peace now," she laughed through a mouthful of cherry Danish, one hand held against her stomach.

"Where's Colin?"

"Dropped me off to go find a parking space. I sort of like being pampered," she smiled. "Pulled out all the stops on renting this place. Sure we can afford it?" She toed a torn spot in the carpet with her sandal.

"Look, I need your help," Quint said in a low voice, ignoring her comment. He took her by the elbow and guided her past the coffee service and the continental breakfast buffet to the far corner. "It's about Dawson." Quint thought he saw a slight flush pass across her face.

"What about him?"

"You know how private he is. Well, Preston, his estranged brother—"

"Dawson has a brother?"

"It would appear so. Popped up a few days ago."

"Why estranged?"

"Uh... it's probably best not to dwell on that; they're trying to put it behind them. Preston takes the blame and appears to have come here bent on mending fences. None of it is really any of our business except that he's probably only got a few weeks to live... cancer," Quint added in response to her puzzled look, as he realized he had betrayed Preston's confidence yet again. "He seems to think that getting to know more about the team and Dawson's current life might help him reconnect. I think we should do what we can to help them, so I took the liberty of inviting him to stop by for a few minutes this morning."

"You invited him to a team meeting?"

"No," Quint quickly replied. "Just to meet everyone before we get started."

Kira nodded. "And you want me to help pass this on to the others."

"Precisely. Speak of the devil." Quint spotted Preston entering, bearing a greasy sack of doughnuts, which he placed alongside the coffee service. Quint caught his eye and he headed over to join them. His orange silk shirt, dress slacks, and Italian loafers stood in stark contrast to Quint's cargo shorts, t-shirt, and deck shoes. As they shook hands, Quint was surprised to notice Preston's was freshly manicured. *That's what my loan bought?*

"You must be Kira. I must say that you're even more stunning than Quint led me to believe," Preston laid on the charm.

Kira smiled, clearly enjoying the flattery.

"I see you're with child. It amazes me how some expectant mothers blossom, becoming even more beautiful when carrying a baby. And you must be Colin, the daddy-to-be," Preston said, extending his hand to the mid-40s man who had just walked up and placed his arm around Kira's waist.

Colin, a Brit hired by Dawson, joined the team to handle operations. His muscular chest strained the buttons of the shirt on his six-foot-tall frame, and his square jaw looked like it could crush nails.

"And you would be...?" Colin replied, as they shook hands.

"Oh, sorry, I'm Preston, Dawson's brother." Quint noticed the comment drew the attention of several other team members who had just arrived, all unaware that Dawson had any siblings. "That's a beautiful engagement ring. Colin, you have good taste and will be lucky to have such a lovely wife."

"We're still not engaged," Kira quickly replied. "The b-baby was a surprise... I m-mean a blessing but a surprise, nonetheless. Actually, I found the ring some time ago and bought it, figuring that eventually I'd find a husband to go with it. If not, at least I'd have a nice ring." Quint saw Kira glance at Colin, who appeared to be lost in thought while studying a spot on the ceiling.

"You said you're Dawson's brother? He never mentioned having a brother," Colin finally said, changing the subject.

"That's not surprising. We haven't... been on the best of terms. It was my fault. He's a great brother and a terrific guy."

Kira glanced at Quint before turning back to Preston. "This Saturday we're having a shower, really more of a casual party—no gifts—to celebrate the baby. We've rented Margaritaville, Jimmy Buffett's place, on Duval Street and plan on doing it up right. I insist you join us. Maybe we can work on your brother then." Kira gave a conspiratorial wink.

"Preston would be honored to attend," he said and then caught Quint's eye. Excusing himself, Quint accompanied him to the far corner of the room.

"The advance I had requested on my home sale funds just came through," Preston said in a low voice as he handed Quint an envelope. "Here's part of what I owe you."

"You didn't have to do this." Quint had never heard of getting an advance on the equity from a home sale.

"I knew you'd say that, but Preston hates to be indebted. I hope to pay the rest back soon," he replied, before a booming voice erupted from the far side of the room.

"These doughnuts are incredible. Where'd you get them?" Leo bellowed through a mouthful of pastry.

"Preston brought them." Quint walked toward Leo with Preston following close behind.

"Back home they're called tato-nuts," Preston replied. "None of the bakeries here sell them, but I found a woman who makes them in her home and charmed her into making a batch for the team."

"Leo, this is Dawson's brother, Preston," Quint introduced the two. Leo brushed a handful of crumbs from his beard and a few more off his considerable belly before extending his hand, a look of surprise on his face.

"Leo, you must share some of your dining adventures with me. I too enjoy occasionally forsaking traditional fare to sample the exotic, though from what Quint tells me I'm not quite as bold as you. Any recent tales to tell?"

"Why yes," Leo replied, seeming pleased by Preston's use of exotic rather than weird, as most of the team members characterized his tastes. "Last week, I got a chance to visit this Syrian restaurant in Miami to try *kibbeh nayyeh.*"

"I've heard of that. Minced goat meat combined with bulghur wheat and olive oil. I believe it's served with pita bread, am I right?"

"Why... uh... yes," Leo replied. "You know about it?"

"Well, actually, I haven't tried it, but it's reputed to be a manly breakfast in Syria. Did you enjoy?"

"It was even better than I imagined. Then I tried the—"

"Preston!" Dawson, who had just entered the room, exclaimed. "What are you doing here?"

"Chatting about places to eat with my new friend, Leo." An awkward silence followed before Preston continued. "Quint invited me to stop by for a few minutes while you guys were having breakfast. Don't mean to overstay my welcome, so I best take my leave," he said before proceeding toward Dawson. The two men stepped out the door and chatted for a few minutes before Dawson returned and headed straight for Quint, who saw him approaching and pocketed the envelope he was still holding.

"I just invited him to join us for breakfast," Quint replied before Dawson could speak. "He wanted to get to know some of the team in hopes of being better able to reconnect with you." Dawson nodded without comment and continued on to get coffee.

"Okay, once everyone has their fill of grease-sponges, we'll proceed with our meeting," Quint announced as Mimi, who had entered late, slid into a chair beside Kira.

Though she was from a poor family in which higher education was a fanciful dream, Quint was impressed with how hard Mimi had worked to become a critical part of the technical team. Short and more than a few pounds overweight, she wore her black hair in a goth style that did little to complement her muddy eyes, thin lips, and chubby face.

"Who was that sharp-dressed, good-looking guy I saw talking to Dawson?" she whispered to Kira.

"Dawson's brother."

"He has a brother?"

"Evidently."

"Who's got a brother?" Dakota ambled up munching on a doughnut, taking a seat in the row behind them next to Leo. An American Indian, Dakota had the broad shoulders, general physique, and complexion to match. His head was shaved except for a round spot in the back, from the center of which sprang a long braided pigtail. After years spent captaining an endless array of oilfield supply boats, he claimed that if it had propellers, he could run it.

"We were just talking about Dawson's brother," Colin replied.

"Funny, he never mentioned him before." Dakota stopped speaking as Quint rose.

"Okay, let's get started," Quint brought the meeting to order. "Today, we have three candidate projects to consider. I believe Kira has a briefing prepared on the first, so if you care to start off—"

"Mr. Chairman?" Leo interrupted, his left hand stroking his bushy black beard.

"Yes, Leo," Quint replied, looking somewhat annoyed.

"As de facto parliamentarian, I would like to request a reading of our Limited Liability Corporation's mission statement, as specifically required in paragraph 11 of the bylaws to be performed at each formal board meeting, or at least once a year at the annual partner's meeting. If you don't have a copy, I brought mine along."

Quint bit back a groan. Leo was not only the group's epicurean of unusual food, but also its stickler for protocol. "Why thank you, Leo," Quint's voice held more than a hint of sarcasm as he accepted the dog-eared sheet of paper, stained with what appeared to be some sort of food, the specifics of which Quint preferred not to imagine. "Leo's right, so in accordance with our by-laws, I'll now review our mission statement."

*"The three purposes of the LLC are the pursuit and acquisition of objects with intrinsic, historical, or other value; the neutralization of special threats for which conventional remedies are inappropriate or otherwise impractical; and missions involving the rescue of key personnel assets or execution of other programs deemed worthy for humanitarian, scientific, or other such purposes.*

*"The Company will be operated as a for-profit business entity under the control of the board, comprised of all shareholders. Unless otherwise agreed, the LLC's board will select projects with an acceptable risk-reward ratio, preferably those offering significant economic upside. Projects may have multiple objectives, with some deemed to have a higher purpose than financial gain."*

He concluded and handed the sheet back to Leo, who accepted it with a barely disguised smirk. "Now, if there are no further such items requiring our attention," Quint looked directly at Leo, "we will proceed. Kira, would you care to take the floor?"

Kira took a moment to hook her laptop to the projector positioned at the near end of the table and focused it before launching into her briefing. When she finished, Dakota gave the next presentation. As he concluded, Quint sent a text from his cell phone.

"That concludes the briefings for the first two candidate projects. I've invited Rogers to brief you on the third project before we vote," he added as he saw him entering the room in response to the text. "Rogers is the CEO and principal stockholder of Vector, who you may recall hired us on behalf of the U.S. Government for our last project. A few of you have already met him, but for those of you who haven't, I present Mr. Rogers, who just happened to be in our neighborhood." Several members of the team struggled to suppress their laughter. Quint connected the projector to Rogers' laptop before taking a seat.

"It's a beautiful day in the neighborhood," Rogers began, playing into Quint's joke about the kids' television host. Mimi's distinctive snort punctuated the laughter as the team roared. "Now that everyone has enjoyed Quint's little barb, I'd like to express my appreciation for the opportunity to brief all of you on the project I am proposing for your consideration. I know Quint has already provided a summary of our recent discussion, but I'm here to elaborate and answer any questions.

"Renaissance Island is home to the world's largest biological weapons lab and testing facility. The esteemed Dr. Hawker describes it as 'the closest place to hell' you'll ever see in this lifetime. Situated in the Aral Sea 2,300 miles south of Moscow and east of the northern end of the better-known Caspian Sea, this location was chosen for open-air bioweapons testing because of its isolation and 140°F temperature range, which makes it less likely that microorganisms could survive and spread.

"The test site was located at the southern end of the island, here," he said, aiming a laser pointer at the satellite photo in his PowerPoint presentation, "due to the prevailing winds from the north. Detectors were mounted atop these telephone poles to help study bioweapon dispersal patterns. The buildings located at the northern end were military barracks and housing for the scientists and their families. They even had an elementary school and an airstrip," he added, with another swirl of the pointer.

"What's that big building at the top?" Mimi asked while making herself a plate of fruit from the buffet.

"The lab building," he replied, highlighting the rectangular shape, "where we believe a sizeable cache of nasty bioweapons is stored. The scientists there were charged with creating some of the world's most deadly germs for use as biological weapons. We have reason to believe that a plot is currently under way, perhaps imminent, to acquire some of these bioweapons."

"And you want us to destroy them?" Kira asked with a look of disgust.

"Yes," Rogers replied, launching off on a twenty minute monologue outlining the proposed plan before inviting questions.

"How do you propose we overcome our lack of local knowledge?" Leo's typical skepticism was evident in his voice.

"We've recruited a local contact. He'll act as your guide and provide whatever help you're likely to need... assuming you choose this project, of course," Rogers added.

Quint saw Dakota, sitting near the back of the room wearing one of his signature t-shirts—*I know right from wrong- Wrong is the fun one*—rise to speak.

"It's pretty hot there. Would we have to wear HAZMAT suits?"

"No, one of the good things that came out of our otherwise disastrous recon mission is that there is no serious threat on the island, provided you're not in a dust storm or the like. You won't even need to wear breathing gear until you enter the lab building, at which time you'll definitely want to have it on. Just to be safe, we can provide you with a portable sensor system to monitor the air quality while you're on the island."

"Where will we set up our base operations?" Leo asked from the buffet, as he placed the last of the pastries on his plate, making his fourth helping.

"In Moynaq at the Oyabek hotel, which—"

"I've been to Moynaq as a young boy!" Leo interrupted. "It's a fishing city with a big cannery on the fourth-largest lake in the world. We stayed in that very hotel for a couple of days when travelling with my father. I loved the place. This will be great; I can't wait to see it again." Rogers responded with an odd smile but no comment.

"While the payoff for this project in terms of dollars is substantial, the humanitarian aspect cannot be valued," Rogers added. "I know you have other worthwhile candidate projects, but I hope you'll give this one serious consideration."

"So in summary, there's an unguarded cesspool filled with the most deadly cocktail of lethal germs known to man, and you want us to do something about it," Dakota said from the back of the room.

"I suppose that's an accurate though somewhat blunt description."

Dakota nodded and paused for a moment before he continued. "What's the deal on the operations base Quint keeps telling us you're working on getting us in lieu of the bonus we earned on our last mission?"

Rogers laughed. "I knew you'd ask so this morning I checked on your request. My contacts agree that if they are to continue the use of your services, as they wish to do, a non-U.S.-based operations center offers numerous advantages.

"They liked your choice of the little-known island off the coast of Cuba, too remote to offer much commercial appeal or no particular strategic advantage, as witnessed by the fact the Cubans have abandoned it. It would appear that no one at the working level in their, or our current administration recalls that it was used in the '60s by the Ruskies until they abandoned it after the Cold War ended, nor that it was earlier developed by the Germans near the end of WW II. They also agree that with its high elevation, deep water, and airstrip, it's perfect for your needs.

"As you earlier suggested, U.S.-Cuban relations have been warming behind the scenes, and much to my surprise, the deal may actually be possible. As we speak, our guy is headed down for a face-to-face chat. I guess they want to avoid any unwanted ears. So, now it's up to the Cubans, though I believe everything is on track."

"It's been on track for too long. It's time to arrive at the station," Dawson replied.

Rogers smiled, "I hope that by the time you get back from your next mission, it will be done."

Quint walked back to the front of the conference room. "Thanks for the sobering overview. I feel obliged to note that the risk is much higher for this project than the two we reviewed earlier. Working with biological weapons is not to be taken lightly. Any other questions?" The team sat in stunned silence.

"I think I best take my leave at this point. Thank you for granting me an audience, and again, I hope you'll take on this project," Rogers shook Quint's hand before exiting.

"Okay, I believe we're ready to vote," Quint said. "As usual, it'll be by secret ballot. Simply write the number of the project you support on a folded piece of paper and pass it down to Mimi, who will act as our 'Price-

Waterhouse' to tally the votes." A few minutes later Mimi nodded at Quint, indicating she was finished. "And the winner is?"

Meekly she rose and in a quiet voice announced, "It seems Renaissance Island was the nearly unanimous choice."

"Nearly unanimous?" Quint asked.

"Yes, we had one dissenting vote."

"Very well. As you all know, it takes a majority of the LLC partners to proceed with a project, but anyone wishing to opt out is free to do so. In so doing, you agree to forego your share of the profits and, of course, any losses which might result. Everyone interested in being a part of this mission, please raise your hand."

The right hands of everyone in the room immediately rose. Quint smiled, "I was pretty sure of your response, but for the sake of completeness, anyone who wishes to opt out, raise your hand."

They all looked around, but no hands went up. Quint wondered why someone had voted against the project but chose to remain in. "I'm concerned that whoever voted nay is uncomfortable bowing out in front of the group. So, you have 24 hours to reconsider and contact me privately," Quint said.

"Thanks to those of you who briefed us on the other two candidate projects. Please save your presentations as they may be reconsidered at a later date. Dawson, I believe you're prepared to continue Rogers' briefing in more detail to help us formulate our plan."

Dawson walked to the front of the room and set his coffee on the table. "Rogers covered most of the key points, so I'll attempt to fill in some of the detail. The island has many features of interest for the local tourist. A must-see is the world's largest burial ground for anthrax," he paused for the laughter to fade.

"Seriously, after transporting hundreds of tons of the bacteria here, the moronic Russian general in charge decided it would be a shame to waste all the valuable stainless steel drums in which it was contained. So, dispensing with environmental niceties, he ordered a massive pit to be dug in the sand, into which he emptied the barrels. He then had his men throw in a little bleach in a half-hearted attempt to kill off the annoying biological bad stuff. Twenty-five years later, a team of U.S. military scientists tested the soil and found the lethal anthrax bacterial spores to be doing just fine.

"We don't have time today to go into the entire history of why, but suffice to say the Aral Sea is drying up, and the island will eventually be linked to the mainland, which is one reason for the increased sense of urgency in dealing with this problem."

"Why not just take the lab out with a cruise missile?" Colin asked.

"Two reasons," Dawson replied. "The U.S. administration doesn't want to risk pissing off the Soviets and having them reciprocate in some other theater where their interests lie, or worse, initiate World War III. Thus they prefer that it appear to be destroyed by some sort of 'natural' event perhaps related to residual chemicals. Secondly, they prefer the bioweapons be incinerated to neutralize them rather than risk dispersing them in an explosion."

An hour later he wrapped up and Quint took the floor to assign everyone tasks. "We've got a lot to do in a short time. We'll meet back here in a week. Oh, and our destination and everything about our mission is sensitive, so please tell no one." As the team was leaving, Quint saw Colin in a heated conversation with Kira. "Problems?" Quint asked.

"Yeah. I don't think a pregnant woman has any business going on this one."

"You made your point, and I appreciate your concern," Kira replied. "Believe it or not, I'm not interested in putting myself or the baby at risk. But this is what we do. And while I'm fully prepared to exercise caution, the baby is not very far along, and I refuse to be treated like a China doll. I'm part of the team; I'm going, and that's final."

"Look, how about this? In exchange for your passing on this project, I'll agree to do the motorcycle tour you've been talking about, or at least part of it."

"I thought you were dead set against it."

"I was, but I'd much rather have you riding across Central Asia on a motorcycle than on a boat in the middle of the most polluted lake in the world, and then messing around on an island loaded with bioweapons."

Kira thought for a moment before replying. "I'll go for the motorcycle trip but not in lieu of being a part of the team on this job. Afterward I promise I'll take a break until the baby is born," she said, and then looked at Quint, who had remained silent.

"Colin has a point."

"Not you too! One overprotective worrywart is enough," she replied adamantly.

"Dawson and I have already discussed this. You can go with the team, but you're not going to the island."

"But that's not fair. I should be—"

"Kira, it's final," Quint said firmly.

She started to say something, but instead stormed off while shouting over her shoulder, "We're still doing the bike trip when this is over." She started for the door, but realizing that Colin had the car keys, opted to refill her coffee.

"I appreciate your support. She's one bull-headed woman," Colin said.

Quint nodded. "Have you two decided on a name for the baby?"

"No. She's adamant about not knowing the baby's sex. I think she should pick the name, but I'm making a list of both girl and boy possibilities to at least have some input." Colin dangled the car keys as he walked past Kira and then without speaking left to get the car.

Quint approached Kira to make peace. "I'm sorry, but that's just the way it has to be."

"You made your point," she shot back.

Quint paused for a moment before deciding to drop the matter. "Were you the one dissenting vote?"

Kira blushed and looked away before answering. "It was a secret ballot, right?" Quint nodded. "You're not supposed to ask, but yes, it was me. I voted for the project that I presented, but once the team made its decision, I wanted it to have unanimous support. I'm not a sore loser," she said.

Quint nodded and then changed the subject. "How are things coming on your search for another team member?" Kira had been tasked to hire someone to fill in for her while on maternity leave and also to staff up the team to meet its growing needs.

"I've gone through a stack of applications and resumes but haven't found anyone who really jumps out at me. Why, you got someone in mind?"

"Actually, I do. Her name is Marcia. She works in security and seems to be able to handle herself. You might want to add her to the list." He gave her phone number to Kira and saw her dialing as he left.

# CHAPTER 6

*Two Years Earlier*
*New York City*

Beatrice had not been blessed with great beauty—a fact beyond her control and for which she could not be blamed. But it was as if she had decided that if ugly was her strong suit, she would play to it.

Beneath her Groucho Marx eyebrows, a pair of thick glasses rested on a broad nose, magnifying her otherwise beady, narrow-set eyes to a ridiculous extent. Makeup seldom graced her high forehead or narrow cheeks. Scrawny arms hung beside an emaciated body draped in a drab, ill-fitting dress apparently cut from a set of 1950s drapes. Her abdomen protruded past the shrunken breasts, seemingly at odds with her scarecrow frame. Her personality was equal to the task of total ugly.

Two years before meeting Quint and Dawson, Marcia worked as a waitress and had the misfortune to not only work at one of the Beatrice's favorite restaurants, but to have the very table the woman invariably chose. Nearly all of Marcia's customers found her service outstanding—but not Beatrice.

The sound of tires on the wet pavement from passing cars signaled the opening of the diner's door. Framed against the glass rectangle, made black by the moonless city night, the "witch" entered that dreary November evening. Having given up on trying to persuade, cajole, bribe, or intimidate other servers into taking the woman, Marcia took a deep breath, resigned to her fate.

The restaurant was maybe half full; the rain had kept the crowd from filling the place, Marcia supposed. She saw the woman scan the restaurant through rain-spattered glasses before heading to her usual table on the left side of the restaurant beneath a yellowed poster of James Dean sitting on the back of the driver's seat of his bathtub Porsche.

"Good evening. Nice to have you dining with us again." Marcia shook the rain from the woman's umbrella and placed it along with her damp coat on the opposite chair. Like most of the diner's furnishings, the chair's chrome frame was deeply pitted, and the torn vinyl seat showed the wear of nearly 50 years.

"Good evening? Don't know what's good about a miserable, rainy night like this." Beatrice smoothed the water off her frizzy hair, twisted into a ragged pony tail.

"It's not all that bad. They've dropped the forecast for snow, and it is supposed to be warmer tomorrow than expected."

"If you believe that then you're more stupid than I imagined," Beatrice spat, always seeming to seize the opportunity to berate someone she was confident would endure her tirade for fear of losing their job. Biting her tongue, Marcia placed the menu alongside the place setting on the worn Formica tabletop. After giving Beatrice time to make a selection, Marcia returned with the standard cup of hot tea to take the order.

"So what would we like tonight?"

"Well, *we* would like a decent meal, but fat chance that *we'll* get it here."

"Well, I am sorry you feel that way—we honestly try to please you." A slight grin crept over Marcia's face as she imagined smashing her fist into those thin lips, devoid of any lipstick, and breaking that jaw protruding from her face in simian fashion. "But tell me, if you feel that way, what brings you back?"

"Are you being smart with me?"

"Not at all. It's an honest question."

"Well, this is about as far as I choose to walk at night, and the other nearby restaurants are even worse."

"Hmm, I see. Well, what can I get for you?"

"Last time the broiled chicken breast was nearly edible so I suppose I'll try that—but do try to make sure it's cooked. I don't wish to contract salmonella."

"Okay, well-cooked chicken breast. What would you like with it?"

"Well-cooked? Make sure it's not overcooked and dry; I don't like it dry. Give me the mixed vegetables but hold the cauliflower. I'll take a salad and do try to hold the dressing. A little vinegar and lemon on the side will do nicely. Oh, and a cup of broth to start—hot broth, if it's not too big a challenge."

Not trusting herself to speak, Marcia simply nodded. She took it as a personal challenge to please the woman and often times doted on her at the expense of her other guests. But she was trying to find good in a person where there just simply wasn't much to be found.

She retrieved the menu, and halfway back to the kitchen heard the woman already calling her name. For a moment, she considered remaining in the kitchen with its cocoon of warmth and chicken soup smell. But pausing just long enough to turn in the order, she returned to the table.

"Did you not hear me call you?"

"Yes, but I was turning in your order."

"Oh, in a hurry to get rid of me?"

"No, just trying to give you fast service. Now, what can I do for you?"

"Look at this cup, it's not clean," she said, holding the cup as if it were a dead rodent.

Marcia examined the cup. "I'm afraid I don't see what you mean."

"Are you blind as well as stupid? There below the rim on the inside by the handle. It's clearly food, why I doubt that cup has even been washed. I'll be lucky if I'm not sick before I leave."

Finally, noticing a small imperfection in the ceramic cup, Marcia replied, "Ma'am, that's not food; it's simply a defect in the cup."

"What? You dare call me a liar?"

"I didn't say that, but I believe you are mistaken."

"I am not mistaken. *You* are the one who is mistaken; it is food. I demand a new cup, a clean one if you can manage it." Marcia controlled her temper and returned a minute later with a fresh cup—doubly inspected. Back in the kitchen, she carefully inspected a bowl and ladled soup from the steaming hot pot. Relieved that the woman had gone to the bathroom, freeing her from another exchange, Marcia set the bowl down with a soup spoon and two packs of crackers, before retreating into the kitchen.

For the fiftieth time, she looked at her watch eager for the evening to end so that she could return to her modest apartment and curl up in bed to watch a movie. A few minutes later, Marcia stopped at Beatrice's table, "How's the soup?" She asked with all the enthusiasm she could muster.

"Not bad, I suppose, that is if you like tepid soup and stale crackers."

"Well I'm sorry, but the soup was hot when I set it down."

"Indeed, I doubt that soup was ever near the stove. I choked down what I could. Take it away." Seldom did Beatrice complete a meal without sending at least one item back. Never did she have a meal without some complaint, the nature of which often paled in comparison to what the staff actually did to her food once it was back in the kitchen.

Without comment, Marcia snatched the bowl and strode back to the kitchen, trembling with concealed anger. Once inside the kitchen she threw the bowl at the garbage can on the far side of the kitchen. Colliding with the wall above the garbage can, the bowl shattered, most of the pieces falling into the can. Jimmy, the cook, jumped. "Damn! Nice shot," he remarked. "What's got your panties in a wad?"

"As usual, the customer from hell."

"What, she didn't like that big loogie I spit in her soup while you were getting her crackers?"

"Jimmy! You didn't!" Marcia replied, laughing despite herself.

"Sure did. You know it's the little things in life I enjoy."

"You're bad," Marcia said with a chuckle, his shenanigans taking the edge off her anger.

"Why don't you quit? I know for a fact you've had other offers."

"I know, but Bob needs me."

"That he does, but he damn sure doesn't do much to show it. All he can do is count his money. That, and ogle the new young thing that started last month. It wasn't right him taking her side in that little tiff you two had. Of course, with her spending most of her time batting her eyes and seizing any opportunity to flatter the old fart, he probably didn't even hear your side of it for staring at her tits."

Marcia nodded as she pulled a bottle of aspirin from her purse and downed two.

"You okay? You don't look so good."

"Think I'm coming down with the flu. Didn't sleep too well either after... uh... oh, never mind."

"Oh no, you're not doing that shit. You know how I hate it when you start to tell me something and stop like that. Problems with that piece of crap you call a boyfriend?"

She nodded without commenting.

"You need to dump that creep."

Marcia looked up, her eyes watery. "I did," she said in a weak voice.

"Caught him cheating didn't you?"

She nodded again. "That and learned he maxed out my credit card. After a WW III-class encounter, I sent him packing."

"Good for you, girl. He may be good looking but he'll never make it as an actor with his complete lack of talent and training."

She wiped her eyes, straightened her apron, and forced herself back out of the kitchen. The salad course went okay with the woman even commenting that it was better than usual, though her tone suggested it still didn't meet her expectations.

As Marcia entered the kitchen with the empty salad bowl, Jimmy handed her a plate, "One well-done chicken breast with mixed veggies, hold the cauliflower. You want to do the honors or shall I?"

"Jimmy, don't you spit on her food again."

"Okay, okay."

Marcia delivered the plate and then returned a few minutes later. Before she could ask how the meal was, the witch lit into her. "You call this food? I never had chicken this tough. The broccoli is mushy, and look right here."

Marcia looked where the woman was pointing with her knife. "What? I'm afraid I don't know what you're trying to show me."

"You *are* blind! Why it's cauliflower. Did I or did I not specifically request no cauliflower?" Marcia now saw the offending vegetable, a piece the size of a BB.

"Take it away now before it makes me any sicker," the woman yelled as she shoved the plate away. Had the plate not skidded off the table to shatter on the floor, spreading broken China and dinner remains across the room, Marcia might have continued to hold her temper.

Instead, she stomped behind the counter at the back of the restaurant, grabbed her coat and purse, and then snatched a bucket of table scraps from the bus boy's cart. Reaching the woman's table, she proceeded to dump the food scraps onto her head.

"There, maybe you'll find something that suits you in that, you miserable, petty bitch," Marcia exclaimed as she walked out for the last time, yelling to the bus boy, "Tell them to mail me my final check." The last sounds she heard before the door closed were Beatrice's shrieks over the applause of the regular customers and staff.

*What am I going to do now*? Marcia asked herself a couple of hours later after the euphoria of standing her ground had worn off. The savings that her frugal lifestyle had enabled her to put aside would last only a couple of months, enough to regroup—but what then? For the next several days after walking out of the diner, she sought refuge in her tiny apartment, trying to answer that question.

One thing she had decided for sure—there would be no more waitressing.

*In fact, no more working in a situation where I have to take shit off of anybody,* she promised herself. With no other job skills and only a high school education, she faced bleak prospects.

# CHAPTER 7

"Thanks for letting me stop by," Quint said and gave Evie a quick hug, careful not to risk upsetting her by overdoing the affection. As always he was taken with the highlights in her dark brown hair and her girl-next-door look. He followed her into the living room and after accepting her offer of a glass of water, opted for the smaller upholstered chair.

"You seen Lefty lately?" she asked about his one-armed Vietnam vet friend.

"Not since taking him to his dialysis treatment last week. Why?"

"Just wondered. I check on him every couple of days, so don't worry if you have to be away unexpectedly."

"Thanks. I do worry about him, though the last time we went to dialysis, he seemed more clear-headed than usual. Losing his arm and his mind while defending our country and then having the kidney problems on top of that is more than anyone should have to contend with," Quint said, and then paused for a moment before continuing. "How've you been?"

"You really need to ask?"

Quint studied the piping on the front of the chair's arm, tracing it with his finger. "I'm, uh, going to be gone for a while. Maybe two weeks."

"Could you maybe tell me where?"

"Eastern Europe." Unable to divulge the full truth of the sensitive job, he figured at least that answer was partly true. He would be passing through there before arriving in Central Asia.

Quint grew quiet again and looked at the floor as he fingered the deep scar transiting his left cheek. "Evie, I miss you, and I worry about your withdrawing like this. Uh... I'm... uh... headed to Kira's baby shower, really more of a casual party with the team. I... uh, hoped you might come with me, at least for a while. I mean, you wouldn't have to stay long; I just thought it'd be good for you to get—"

"That's sweet, Quint, but I don't think so," she said, looking directly into his bright green eyes, her voice faltering only slightly. "I'm still not ready."

Quint fought the urge to press his lips to hers. "I don't mind being patient, but please, you have to start letting go of the pain."

"That's easy for you to say. You're not the one constantly waking up in a cold sweat."

"Evie, I don't pretend to know what it was like when you... I mean when they—"

"I was raped, Quint. You can say it. I was raped and raped and raped, over and over again! You can say it. I was raped."

"Okay, I don't know what it was like to be... raped. What I do know is that it happened. As horrible as it was, it happened. But now it's over. It's been over for a very long time. You have to put it behind you."

"Dammit, Quint! You think I like this? Don't you think I'm trying? Don't you think I pray every single night for the nightmares to stop?" Quint was silent, smart enough to realize he had no good answers. But her pain-fueled anger took issue even with his silence. "What, no clever come back? I can't believe you're not being supportive."

"Are you shitting me? I've been walking on egg shells while I put my life on hold waiting for you to work through this. Waiting in hopes that we could be back together."

"And now what, you think it's time to reconsider?"

"I didn't say that." Sensing this was futile, Quint turned toward the door to leave as Evie continued.

"Well, I'm sorry not to be meeting your schedule. Maybe you need to move on. Sorry to have ruined your life waiting on damaged goods."

"Evie, I—"

"Just go!" she screamed. "And take back your stupid ring. Have a nice life," she yelled as she slammed the door behind him.

Quint stood there for a while in shock, uncertain what to do. For months he had waited patiently for her to start the healing process, all the while doing anything he could think of to help. Having her act like this was heartbreaking. He stooped down to pick up the old wedding ring from his first marriage—a gift given in jest during better times as a token of his feelings for her. He needed a drink.

Quint entered Kira's party and headed for the bar. "Give me a tall gin and tonic, heavy on the Bombay Sapphire and lots of lime." He knew he shouldn't have come but was confident his sour disposition would provide the solitude he needed to cope with his Evie situation. He downed the first half of his drink in one gulp and then stood alone watching the crowd.

The room was noisy, and most of the team had arrived. A table near the door was piled high with baby presents. Quint now wished he hadn't heeded Kira's specific instructions not to bring anything. Maybe later, he would pick up some sort of gift, though he had little idea what to get for a baby.

He had finished his first drink and was starting in on his second when Dawson walked up. "It appears your brother is having a grand ol' time."

"That's my brother—life of the party and quite the little chatterbox. He's been busy telling everyone that he's turning over a new leaf and only wants a second chance."

"You gonna give it to him?"

"Hell if I know. Problem is, it's not a second chance; it's more like a fiftieth," Dawson replied and left to get a fresh beer.

Curious, Quint eased close enough to hear Leo and Preston without being too obvious. "Have you tried to work things out with him?" he heard Leo ask Preston after Dawson had walked away.

"Boy, have I. I'd do anything to patch things up with him," Preston said, his voice breaking. "Maybe it's just too late, and despite everything I'm willing to do, there's just no fixing things." Quint recalled the suddenness with which Preston had moved to tears during their earlier conversation and for a moment, questioned the sincerity of his display of emotion. He had known men who could shed "crocodile tears" on demand and wondered if Preston might perhaps be one. But the thought was fleeting, and Quint continued to eavesdrop.

"Dawson and I have had our share of disagreements, but he's a decent guy. Reuniting with family would be good for him. Maybe the two of you ought to go somewhere to work things out,"

"I'd love to, but I can't afford it until I can sell my oil stocks."

*Oil stocks? Preston has oil stocks?* Quint wondered.

"How much would it cost?"

"I was thinking about doing something really nice like taking him to the Manava Suite Resort in Tahiti."

Leo withdrew his wallet as he turned to the end of the bar and found a pen. Hoping not to appear obvious, Quint turned away but a moment later, saw Leo return to hand Preston what appeared to be a check and then heard him say, "It's a lot of money, but if it helps the two of you, it's worth it."

"Leo, that's just too much. I can't—"

"Just make things right with Dawson. You can pay me back when you sell your stock."

Quint was surprised. *Preston is selling a house and now stock?*

"God bless you, Leo. You're a prince, but please don't mention it to Dawson, or anyone else for that matter. Let me get your phone number and address so I can repay you." Leo complied before heading for the bar.

*Another loan? I wonder if all is as it would seem,* Quint wondered as Preston headed over to speak with him. It took only a minute before Quint's one-word answers and sullen disposition had Preston excusing himself to the bar.

With two drinks under his belt, Quint was feeling slightly better. But still upset after his episode with Evie, he still wasn't in much of a party mood and left.

Mimi was off in a corner standing alone when she saw Preston heading over. "Preston finds you ravishing this evening," he said while tucking his expensive jet-black silk shirt into his matching slacks and smoothing their knife-like crease.

"Why, thank you. You look quite nice yourself." Mimi was flustered and could feel herself blushing at the rare compliment. Dressed in a plain, un-tucked white blouse with cream-colored slacks, she wished she had followed Kira's fashion advice rather than wear comfortable clothing that did little to hide her extra pounds.

"Would it be presumptuous to offer you a drink? Or would I be risking the wrath of your significant other?"

"No... I'm single. In fact, I just got back from England visiting the family of the man I cared for but who... uh... recently passed." She struggled to keep a sad smile off her face. "I would love a drink."

"Well then, shall we?" Preston offered his arm to guide her to the bar. "Champagne?" Mimi eagerly nodded her reply. "Bartender, your finest champagne for this fine lady. Cristal or Dom Perignon if you have it."

"We have Andre," the bartender said with a slight roll of his eyes.

"Excellent, that will do nicely, and Preston will have an Angel Dust." Mimi accepted the champagne flute while watching the bartender mix a half-ounce each of whiskey, gin, and dark rum in a tall glass.

"What's that?" Preston asked.

"A Liquid Angel Dust," the bartender replied, the irritation thick in his voice.

"Oh, goodness, no. I wanted an *Angel Dust*. Let's see, it has one part Anis, two parts crème de coconut, one part Martini Bianco, dry, of course, one part—"

"We ain't got no Anus," the bartender interrupted. His slight grin suggesting he might have intentionally mispronounced the name of the liquor. "Got a second choice?"

Preston stared back before quietly replying, "Make it a brandy crusta, and be sure to use an entire spun lemon peel." The bartender sloshed a glass half full of brandy, tossed in a couple of slices of lemon, and slammed it down, spilling some on the bar. Before the sputtering Preston could comment, the bartender was already serving another customer.

Mimi saw Preston continue to stand there, his face turning a dark red and his left hand balling into a fist. It looked like he was about to step around the bar when Mimi saw him look at her and stop. He picked up his drink and walked toward her. "Can't say much for the surly bar staff here," Preston said as he maneuvered Mimi to the far corner of the room. "So how long have you been with the team?"

"Since they started. It's been the job of my dreams."

"Well, from what Quint tells me, you're considered quite a valued team member."

"Really?"

"But of course. It seems you've a bright future with them, especially given your personal sacrifices."

Mimi blushed and felt embarrassed as she saw Preston glance at the missing index finger she had lost to pirates. She placed her hand at her side before changing the subject. "The worst part was nearly dying deep in the Venezuelan jungles from a gunshot wound."

They continued to chat for the next few minutes before he excused himself to head to the bathroom. He returned sniffing and talking much faster. Mimi noticed a few white smears on his dark shirt. As they circulated through the crowd, she stood by patiently while he animatedly regaled anyone who would listen with tales of his past.

The praise he showered on the men had them warming to him, and the flattery he heaped on the women had them swooning. Mimi noticed he seemed to have a knack for locking in on and fussing over the attribute of which each person seemed most proud.

Finally, the crowd began to thin, and gesturing at Mimi's empty glass Preston said, "Why don't we leave here and find a quieter place to chat over another drink?" She nodded and eagerly followed him from the room.

# CHAPTER 8

Quint watched Dawson as he examined the various artifacts cluttering Professor Hawker's office while they waited for the bioweapons professor to arrive. A number of fossils lay scattered on an ancient wooden side table. On one end of the same table, a plastic tub contained a number of irregularly shaped, rock-like objects. Dawson examined several and, as his interest waned, absently tossed one in his hand.

"Sorry, my class ran long," the mid-50's professor said when he finally appeared. Dressed in jeans and a well-worn t-shirt, he looked more like he was attending rather than teaching at the university. "I'm blessed with a bright group of students this year, eager to learn and full of questions." Dr. Hawker noticed Dawson tossing the rock-like object. "So, you share my interest in coprolites, eh?"

"In what?" Dawson replied a confused look on his face. "You mean this?" he said, gesturing at the object he held in his hand.

"Yes, that's a coprolite. As you may have guessed, I'm an amateur paleontologist. Since my wife passed on, it helps me fill the empty weekends."

"Oh, I figured this was just some sort of rock or mineral. What's a coprolite?"

"Fossilized dinosaur poop," he replied. Dawson quickly dropped the object back into the plastic tub and wiped his hands on his pants leg while the professor and Quint chuckled. "So, gentlemen, from what Rogers tells me your interest is not in my amateur paleontologist talents, but rather in my knowledge of bioweapons."

Quint nodded. "Yes, he claims you're one of this country's foremost experts on the subject."

"I don't know about that. Rogers is always stroking my ego."

"We appreciate your seeing us on such short notice. We don't have much time before our departure for Renaissance Island. Rogers suggested that since you visited there a few years ago, perhaps you could help us prepare for what we're likely to encounter."

"Of course. I apologize for not being able to travel to brief your entire team as he originally requested. In addition to my teaching duties, I'm involved in other high-priority bioweapons projects and couldn't afford the time." Hawker paused to pluck a dog-eared folder off of his desk and then motioned for the two men to follow him. He left his office and climbed the stairs to the next floor where he continued down the hallway to a small conference room.

"I think this type of conversation is better conducted where we're less likely to have unauthorized listeners." Hawker cleared his throat. "Effective biological weapons should produce consistent results, be highly contagious, and have a brief incubation period. They should be difficult to identify, easy to produce, and must be stable. Many Soviet bioweapons offered most if not all of these attributes. Ideally, the designated target will lack immunity and have limited access to treatment while the attacking force carries protection," Hawker said. "Now let's talk about the facility."

"This drawing shows the lab building where it is believed they were storing the remaining bioweapons." Hawker opened the manila folder and withdrew a yellowed blueprint. "Security was heaviest here, and when I approached this building one evening, they were all over me," he said pointing to the blueprint. "I assume they had video cameras monitoring the place—though I doubt that would still be the case."

After walking them through the building layout, he finished his briefing with an overview of the particularly lethal materials they might encounter, how to handle them, their corresponding exposure symptoms, and treatments. "You must be very careful; there'll be lots of nasty stuff there that can kill you in a most unpleasant manner. I wish I could help you more." The two men nodded grimly and left the room after thanking him for his help.

"Is it too late to back out?" Dawson asked in jest.

"Unfortunately," Quint replied without smiling.

"How'd your meeting with Hawker go yesterday?" Rogers asked as they took seats in his spacious office, heavy with walnut and leather.

"I think Dawson was most impressed with the coprolites." Quint laughed at Rogers' puzzled look but continued without explanation. "Hawker told us everything he knew about what the Soviets were developing and scared the crap out of us in the process. He gave us this blueprint," Quint unfolded it and spread it out on the table.

Rogers studied the print for a moment before pointing to a spot. "Based on what we learned from our man, the weapons were stored in the basement located about here. In any case, having this should be most helpful." Rogers reached for a box beside his desk. "Here's a medical kit you may need in case you experience a contamination event. Our folks briefed Kira on how to handle the antidotes for those agents for which we have a defense. You may also need this." Rogers handed Quint a second small box filled with half a dozen cans of bug spray. "This stuff works a lot better than what you get at the discount store.

"Your contact there is a man named Boris. We're sending a pile of food and other supplies along with you. I suggest you host a dinner for him and his family upon your arrival as a courtesy. According to Uzbek customs, he should do it, but we're certain that he doesn't have the food. By preempting that situation, you can save him embarrassment. He may not say much, but trust me, he'll appreciate it.

"We'll be sending some parts that he had requested. From what we understand, he has access to generators salvaged from the fishing boats but no spare parts to repair them. Maybe you can get one running to power the lights and fans. Have fun," Rogers finished.

"Oh, by all means," Quint replied sarcastically as he rose to leave.

The next day, Dakota wandered into the office where Quint was arguing with Dawson over having a GPS transponder surgically inserted beneath his arm. These devices would enable each team member to be tracked should they get lost or captured. Dawson, for reasons unclear to Quint, was adamantly opposed to it.

"Look, Dawson, it's slightly larger than a grain of rice but may save your worthless hide. Everyone else already has theirs implanted, and you need one too." Quint re-filled the shot glass in front of Dawson with tequila. Having tried logic, reason, pressure, begging, and threatening, Quint finally resorted to tequila. Dawson had just finished his fifth shot.

"Yeah. Man up," Dakota said, needling Dawson.

"If I do it will you all shut the hell up?" Dawson asked Quint in exasperation.

"Yep," Quint confirmed.

"Your word?"

"Yep."

"Then let's do it. I know you'll give me no peace until I do."

"Hang on a minute." Quint left the room and called the doctor friend of his he had arranged to have on stand-by.

"He's agreed to it. Get here fast." Less than ten minutes later, there was a knock at the door, and the doctor entered the room. He laid a pouch on the table beside Dawson's chair, dampened a cotton swab from a small dark glass bottle, and wiped the area under Dawson's left arm. As he waited for the local anesthetic to take effect, he removed a small scalpel and a plastic case.

Lifting Dawson's arm, he made a small cut and then used tweezers to remove the grain-sized GPS/transponder from the plastic case and place it in the incision. After closing the tiny slit, he wiped it with gauze and applied surgical glue before placing a small butterfly-shaped bandage over the area.

"How long is this going to take?" asked Dawson, his speech somewhat slurred.

"I'm done," said the doctor.

"That's it?"

"Yup."

"Now I feel like a wussie," Dawson said sheepishly.

"Told you," said Quint.

"Yeah, I still don't understand how the likes of you stole our country," Dakota chimed in, continuing his ongoing Indian-white man banter. Dawson's reply was interrupted as Dakota removed his ringing cellphone from his pocket. "Well, hey, Preston," he said, as he wandered into the next room before reappearing a minute later.

When he saw that Dakota was off the phone, Dawson slurred, "What did my brother want, to suck the Injun blood from you?"

"No, Mr. Smart Ass. As a matter of fact, he bought me a collector's edition of a book I had mentioned to him. Don't know how he found it, but he got me a 1931 first edition of *My Indian Boyhood,* written and signed by Chief Luther Standing Bear. I'm going to meet him for lunch and pick it up."

Before Dawson could fire another insult salvo, Quint interrupted. "Wow! That's pretty cool, Dakota," choosing to conceal his surprise at Preston's largesse given his recent loans. Dakota smiled and started to leave, but Quint caught him just outside the door.

"Glad you seem to be doing better," Quint said. Before coming to work for the team, Dakota had captained a boat for a woman named Lolo, leaving when her husband found him servicing more than her boating needs. After being abused, she had shown up while the team was involved in their last project, but her budding romance with Dakota ended abruptly when she was killed by a terrorist.

At first it seemed that Dakota was upset, but after a pause, he replied. "Even if my ancestors are right, and Lolo's spirit is in some animal or bird flying around as they believed, it doesn't make a shitting bit of difference to me. She's gone, not coming back, and that's that," he said firmly and louder than necessary.

Sensing it bothered Dakota more than he let on and was concerned that it might affect the man's performance during their next mission, Quint started to reply but saw Kira approaching and decided to let it go.

"I followed up with your suggestion about hiring Marcia."

"What did you think?" Quint said, walking back inside with her.

"I think we should hire her. After our telephone interview, I checked out her references and former employers. Seems her most recent job involved classified stuff so I didn't get a lot of details. She started out as a waitress, of all things," Kira said. Quint grabbed a couple soft drinks from the small office refrigerator and took a seat beside her at the table.

"But after she had enough of that, she caught a break with a security firm and sort of found her calling. They put her through a bunch of training, and she quickly became one of their best. Then she caught the attention of a guy whose company does private contracting in the Middle East and was looking to recruit women. With no family or close relatives being a plus, they ended up hiring her and putting her through even more training. Everyone I spoke to sang her praises."

"I did catch one break and got the name of her instructor at sort of a private industry boot camp. It turned out to be one of those friend-of-a-friend deals so he spoke with me off the record. When I asked him if I should I hire her, he said, 'By all means. If I were you, I'd sure want her on my team.' So, I asked him how she did in his training course."

"And?"

"She failed," Kira replied with a grin.

"Help me out here."

"It's why she failed. She was paired with another woman, who probably would never have passed under the best of circumstances. Marcia had the course nailed, but during their final two-day survival test, her buddy broke her ankle. Marcia refused to leave her and carried her out on her back. While she finally did finish, it was not within the allotted time, so he couldn't pass her. But the only reason she failed was her dogged loyalty to her partner."

"So make her an offer." Quint drained his can and crushed it in his hand before tossing it in the trash.

Kira took a long drink before replying. "I want you to talk to a couple of her contacts first. After that, I'm ready, provided we're still on the same page. But you'll have to do it fast if you want her to be joining us before we leave for Europe."

"Is that even possible given the short window?"

"All things are possible," Kira replied.

# CHAPTER 9

She entered the ship's large salon, its expanse bathed in light reflected from the azure waters of the Bahamas. Her motorized wheelchair controls lay atop the same green pillow that concealed her grizzled hands. A claret-colored wig framed a face concealed behind a white porcelain mask, its garishly painted features giving the appearance of a red-headed Geisha. This effect was further underscored by the emerald kimono, which matched the pair of eyes that peered out from behind the mask. A hint of sandalwood incense filled the room.

She stopped her chair at the head of the table and silently studied the nine men seated before her. Dumbstruck by her image, the men feigned interest in the papers on the table in front of them or the view beyond the yacht's windows.

Finally, she spoke in a mechanical voice reminiscent of a female Darth Vader-like character. "Welcome, gentlemen. I see that all of you have been served." Nodding at the coffee cups and glasses dotting the table, she continued. "Does anyone need anything else before we proceed?" She paused to slowly pan the table, and each man shook his head, none daring to utter a peep.

"Very well, let's begin. The reason you are here is to discuss a job for which you will be handsomely paid.

From this point on, everything you see or hear must remain in confidence.

"Through our well-placed mole, we've learned of a cache containing glass vials of some very... exotic material. You have been hired to help us retrieve them and perhaps help us capture a few of our... adversaries. Each of you has a set of skills which, I believe, uniquely qualifies you for this team. You have all been advised of the risk inherent in this job and have agreed to participate. In front of each of you is a sealed envelope containing a complete dossier on the mission.

"Inside the envelope you will also find a form on which you may indicate how you prefer to receive your funds. Be sure to include any necessary wire transfer instructions. Assuming things go as planned, it will be the easiest money you'll ever make.

"Arnold," she said, gesturing toward a tall, sandy blonde-haired man who spoke with a Russian accent, "will be your leader. Aside from the planning time, which I expect to take no more than a day, you should be able to complete this mission in only a few more. Each of you will now retire to your staterooms to review the documents. After our break, we'll reconvene here to begin formulating a plan for the execution of this mission.

"This concludes our meeting. Oh, one other thing: You are grown men so we have not confiscated your cell or satphones, but as one of the conditions of your employment, you have agreed not to use them while you are here. In fact, you should already have removed your SIM cards and battery to be certain that no one can locate you here. I wish to emphasize the importance of this from a security perspective. Until later, ta ta." No one commented on how incongruent her departing phrase was or on her bizarre appearance.

The masked woman entered the owner's suite, the automatic doors swinging closed behind her. Her aide, dressed in a navy blue skirt and white blouse embroidered with the number "34" above the ship's name, scurried over with a lighted cigarette. She pressed the unlit end into a yellowed tube mounted on the arm of the woman's motorized chair. It was part of a device resembling a water pipe with a small pump to provide the necessary suction to extract smoke from the cigarette.

The aide placed the opposite end of the tube through the slit in the woman's mask that formed her mouth. Incapable of showing expression through the ceramic mask, the woman nodded, adding, "That will be all," in her mechanical voice. She then glanced at the aide's neck and added, "34." Each crew member was required to have the ship's name and a unique number tattooed on his or her neck. While by no means foolproof, it was a rudimentary security measure and eliminated the nuisance of remembering everyone's name.

The aide set the suite's master remote control unit on the pillow in the woman's lap and vanished, seeming eager to be dismissed. After her aide had shut the door, the woman continued into the expansive living area and pressed a button on the remote control unit. A panel on the wall facing her slid smoothly to one side, revealing a floor-to-ceiling mirror, the only one in the suite save a small handheld one in the bathroom.

Rolling closer to the wall, she snatched off the wig, dropping it to one side before removing the uncomfortable mask and casually tossing the porcelain veil aside to shatter on the floor—no matter, she had cases more. The Persian cat that lay on her bed looked up sleepily, aroused by the noise before stretching and closing its eyes once again.

For several minutes she sat, head bowed, triggering the water pipe to deliver a steady stream of smoke, which she greedily inhaled to fill her lungs. After slowly exhaling, she gathered her will before raising her face to gaze into the smoke-obscured mirror.

For an instant, she saw the flawless white skin that once covered the perfect features of a face framed in silky-thick burnt sienna hair. She imagined the face that once turned men's and women's heads alike to admire her stunning image whenever she entered a room. She pictured the image of herself standing at a cocktail party, a martini in one hand, cigarette in the other, tendrils of smoke slowly oozing from her mouth and nose, reeking sexuality.

Seeking to hold the image in her mind a moment longer, she pressed the control for the plastic tube to deliver another burst of smoke. But as the curtain of smoke thinned, her reflection slowly re-emerged along with reality.

Charred and blackened skin clung to a skull where hair no longer grew. A glass eye lacking an eyelid stared unblinking while the lid on her one good eye fluttered rapidly from the smoke, its overworked tear duct struggling to keep it damp. Her gums and a few remaining teeth on one side of her ruined mouth lay exposed, no skin or flesh to conceal them. The other side of her face was fixed in a frozen sneer. Smoke drifted from two holes in the front of her face where a perfectly formed nose once sat.

The elbow of her right arm rested on the stump of her left wrist holding the cigarette tube between the bones of her first and second fingers in a claw-like hand. The remainder of her scarred body lay concealed behind the silk robe as she sat leaned to one side of the chair.

For a moment, she imagined her parents' contorted faces as the flames licked at them. She could no longer recall what had angered her enough to burn them alive, or her sister a few years later. But the trail of burned buildings and ruined lives she had left afterward was business, a requirement of her work as a hired assassin. It was work she was quite good at. It was work she enjoyed.

Her mind drifted and she found herself outside the house where Quint and Dawson stood in the window above. Once again, she felt the weight of the phosphorous grenade in her hand. As if viewing the incident from above, she saw her arm draw back and then the bright light of the horrible explosion. And then she felt the pain as the phosphorous burned her as she had burned so many others—taking her looks, both of her feet, one hand, and severely damaging the other. It was what fueled her hatred and psychosis as she stared at the image before her.

By the time she finally snapped out of the trance, the sun was low in the sky. Her cigarette had burned itself out, leaving only a blackened stub in the end of the plastic tube and a pile of ashes on her green robe. She clawed at the ashes, knocking most of them onto the carpet as she worked the joystick in her lap to swing the chair around. With the master remote, she commanded the panel to close back over the mirror.

Her name was Syndy, though she often went by her alias, The Torch. She now drew strength from studying her image in the mirror. While her reservoir of evil and hate had once seemed limitless, it now required periodic recharging. In the beginning, she would forget her horrible disfigurement only to have a chance glimpse of her reflection bring reality crashing back.

Then she had learned to channel the emotions each time she went through this exercise. First she was filled with self-pity at the sight of her ruined body. The pity soon turned to anger, then to fury, and lastly into a violent rage—the fuel she needed to continue her life as a horribly disfigured cripple.

She paused at an expanse of glass at the far end of the room and stared out over *Syntillate's* stern and the sparkling blue sea below. The tinted wrap-around windows of her master stateroom sat atop an unusual conning-tower superstructure on the 240-foot science-fiction-like yacht, lending it a submarine-like appearance.

Two massive diesel engines delivered 16,500 horsepower, capable of propelling her at an astonishing maximum speed of 50 knots. Given the nature of their business, the option to move quickly whenever the need arose was critical. At a more modest 25 knots, the yacht had a cruising range of nearly 4,000 nautical miles.

No expense had been spared in building and decorating this beauty. Though it was not her money that built the yacht, even she found the cost obscene. Simply filling its enormous fuel tanks cost hundreds of thousands of U.S. dollars to support the 700 gallons per hour it burned. But the freedom *Syntillate* afforded was one of her few remaining pleasures in life.

Hester's call over the intercom interrupted her thoughts, and she turned her chair to head for the room where he lay. The large Persian cat looked up sleepily from its pillow on the bed before closing its eyes once again.

# CHAPTER 10

"Bus? We're travelling by bus? Why by bus?" Leo asked, incredulous at learning of their travel mode in Uzbekistan. Having spent the previous weeks developing plans, preparing for the mission, and applying for the necessary visas and permits, Quint was now holding the team's final mission briefing over breakfast in the same low-rent hotel conference room where they originally met to discuss the job. While annoying, the sound of hammers and power saws from the musty hotel's much-needed renovations was not loud enough to disrupt the meeting.

"Since our cover is a scientific expedition tasked to map toxins in the Aral Sea, we travel like low-budget college researchers. However, we'll be travelling first class on our eastern European bus ride—we get a seat," Quint said, chuckling at Leo's sour expression.

"We'll arrive at the Tashkent Airport in the capital of Uzbekistan. From Tashkent we fly to Nukus." Quint grinned.

"You're making this shit up." Leo tilted the hotel's battered aluminum urn in hopes of coaxing one last cup of coffee from it.

"Unfortunately, I'm not. Let's hope Nukus means something else in Uzbek. Anyhow, I read some air travel reviews, none of which were favorable. Since one of the reviewers got food poisoning while travelling on Uzbekistan air, I recommend you avoid the in-flight meals. After our three-hour bus ride from Nukus to Moynaq, our guide, Boris, will be there to meet us. Rogers hired him to help as needed and to find us a boat.

"While Kira will accompany us, she'll remain on shore when we begin survey operations, which Mimi will oversee," Quint said, ignoring Kira's cutting stare. Mimi smiled nervously. It was under Kira's tutelage that she became fully qualified to oversee such surveys.

"While we're in Uzbekistan, we need to stick together. No wandering off on your own. It's a dangerous place, and our job will be hard enough without risking a mugging or worse.

"If there are no further questions, we have one more item of business. For those of you who have not already met her, I'd like to introduce our newest team member. After a chance meeting while diving, she later impressed Dawson with her prowess during his latest barroom brawl. So Kira did some background checks, liked what she saw, and hired her. Marcia, please stand up." As she rose, Quint noticed her blushing but was unsure if it was from his mention of the barroom incident or from being in the spotlight.

"She'll be joining us on our Eastern European luxury vacation and will later fill in for—"

"Yeah, by bus, no less," Leo interrupted.

"As I was saying, she's going to be filling in for Kira when she takes off to become a mom," Quint announced, to a chorus of cheers from the team. Kira stood and bowed in mock formality, appearing thankful to have attention diverted from her being replaced on the boat.

"The only kick-ass mom I know," Dakota said as he rose, displaying his latest t-shirt with *Tact: For people who aren't witty enough to be Sarcastic* in bold letters on the front.

"Each of you, please take a minute to introduce yourself to Marcia. This meeting stands adjourned," Quint said.

Kira was the first to approach Marcia. "Glad to have you on the team."

"Why, thank you. I'm really flattered to be joining, but I'm a little stressed out about it."

"You'll do fine. Just remember what my mom always said, 'Stressed spelled backward is desserts.'" Both women laughed.

While most of the group was gathered around Marcia, Dakota headed over to talk with Mimi and Quint. "It seems someone has a new love interest."

"What? W-we've only gone out once," Mimi replied. "Did you know Preston has cancer?" Dakota shook his head. "Only has a few weeks. That's why he's come looking to square things. I guess I feel sorry for him and want to help him make the most of what little time he has."

"Does Dawson know?" Dakota asked as he unsuccessfully attempted to milk another cup of coffee from the urn that Leo had emptied.

"No. Preston was adamant that Dawson not find out," Quint replied.

"I just wish we had met when he had more time, especially with his divorce about to be final," Mimi said, fidgeting with a loose thread on her blouse.

"Divorce? Preston was married?" Quint asked.

"Yeah. That bitch wife of his emptied out all of their accounts. He spent most of what he had left buying this ring for me," she said, flashing a gold ring with an impressive several-carat stone. He didn't even keep enough money to pay his attorney the $4,000 required to finish up the papers. So I loaned it to him until he gets the money from the oil well he sold last week."

Dakota's eyebrows raised. "Preston owned an oil well?"

Mimi nodded. "And he's selling it along with his mansion. He's selling all of his remaining assets to settle his estate before he passes. Plans on giving the money to Dawson."

Quint saw Preston appear, sniffing and nervously wiping his nose. "Is he using drugs?"

Mimi looked down before quietly replying, "Maybe a little. I think it's to deal with his pain from the cancer. Really can't blame the poor thing."

"Good morning," Preston said cheerily as he walked briskly up to the trio. "Enjoying that book I gave you?"

"I am," Dakota smiled. "I found a reference to my grandfather. Chief Luther Standing Bear interviewed him when he was putting together his history of our people. Well, hate to leave, but I've got a bunch to do before we head out."

"Who's she?" Preston pointed at Marcia shortly after Dakota left.

"Our newest team member," Mimi said, her voice betraying a hint of jealousy. "Everyone's been making quite a fuss over her."

"It's good to make her feel at home." Quint looked up at Preston. "By the way, you've got something white on your nose." Preston's hand shot to his face to wipe it clean without offering an explanation.

"Let's welcome her too," Preston said, seeming eager to break things off with Quint. But his escape was thwarted when Marcia came over to join them. Quint noticed Mimi appeared uneasy, shifting her weight nervously.

"Good to see you again, Quint. I appreciated the introduction... except for mentioning the bar fight. Could have done without that."

Quint laughed. "Hey, you're part of the team now. No secrets." Quint thought she seemed weary and guessed it was from holding her own with all of the well-intentioned team members, who appeared quite taken by her.

"Hey, newbie, Preston would like to welcome you aboard," Preston said, approaching with his hand extended. "Certainly an attractive, and no doubt capable addition to the team."

"Thank you," Marcia replied. "And you are... "

"Dawson's brother."

"Oh... I've... heard... Dawson told me about you," she said, her obvious dislike barely concealed.

"What did you do before joining the team?"

"I worked for a private security firm in New York for a couple of years and then one in the Middle East."

"I see. And before that?"

Marcia paused, offended at being interrogated by someone who was not even a legitimate part of the team. "I worked at a diner in New York as a waitress."

"Wow, quite a change. Think you'll like working with the team better than being a hash-house slave?"

"Anything's better than working in that shitty two-bit diner serving shit, taking shit, and cleaning up shit," Marcia snapped.

Mimi broke the awkward silence that followed. "Before you arrived I was the team newbie, so I'll be happy to help you any way I can. My name's Mimi; here's my number," she said, handing Marcia a plain business card.

"Thanks. I'm sure I'll be taking you up on that offer." Marcia appeared to regret her outburst and seemed relieved to be rescued from the awkward exchange when Mimi steered Preston away. She then turned to Quint. "Sorry about losing my temper. It's just that I—"

"No apology necessary," he interrupted, and then continued as a towering black man approached. "There's one other person I don't think you've met. Let me introduce you to Willy. He was tops in his class in the merchant marine academy. Worked two jobs, attended class, and then studied sometimes nearly all night long before rising at 4 a.m. to make it to his first job. He works magic to keep whatever boat we scrounge up running."

Willy, standing nearly seven feet tall and weighing well in excess of 300 pounds, looked embarrassed by Quint's bragging praise and muttered something inaudible before speaking up.

"He exaggerates. I *was* the engineer on our ship *Searcher* before we lost her in a hurricane. Now, I'm trying to figure out what I'm supposed to be doing for the team."

Marcia laughed. "Well, maybe we can do that together."

She shook the big man's hand, "Happy to meet you. Quint mentioned you had a relative, a niece, I believe, with lupus. How's she doing?"

Willy beamed, clearly taken with her show of concern. "She's doing much better; thanks for asking. The uh... experimental medicine seems to be working." As Willy finished, Marcia noticed Mimi and Preston head out the door.

"Is it just me?" she asked, and then continued in response to Willy's puzzled look. "I mean, everyone on the team seems to be really sharp, so I don't get the whole Preston thing. While I admit that I just met him, he sure seems like a snake to me. And yet they all treat him like he's something special," she said, keeping what Dawson had told her in confidence.

Willy laughed, "No, it's not just you. I too think he's manipulative and fake. Some of the others agree but are keeping silent for Dawson's sake. I suppose most prefer to risk looking foolish by giving Preston the opportunity to bury the hatchet with Dawson in whatever time he has left."

Quint nodded. "I'm beginning to have my doubts too. He's always borrowing money, yet I'm constantly hearing about the mansions and oil wells he's selling. And of course, there's the mysterious white powder on his nose on occasion. But Preston does have a way.

He's done a great job of painting himself as someone seeking redemption after seeing the error of his ways. I suppose the issue will resolve itself one way or another since he won't be around for long." Marcia nodded.

The next morning, Quint was at the Miami airport working on his second cup of coffee when the rest of the team began to arrive. "Nice outfit, Leo. Where'd you get it, Pimps R Us?" Dawson asked with a grin as Leo walked up rolling an enormous suitcase.

"Hey, these are nice clothes." Leo seemed defensive about his bush jacket, vest, embroidered shirt, and pants all festooned with pockets and made from what appeared to be silk.

"Maybe if we were going on a disco safari," Dawson teased, giving Quint a wink while ignoring Leo's glare and Dakota's snicker.

The team had a long layover once they reached New York. Quint saw Colin hard at work on his list of baby names. He had noticed that Mimi seemed preoccupied during most of the day's flight and wondered if it was because of her previous evening with Preston. A minute later, Mimi detached herself from the group and walked to a quiet area of JFK airport before placing a call on her cell phone.

"Preston," she said. "I'm in New York and thought I'd call before we left the country."

"Uh... Mimi," Preston stumbled, "I'm so glad you did. Have a good flight?"

"Yes, aside from feeling sluggish because *somebody* kept me up most of the night."

Preston laughed. "Guilty as charged. Are you complaining?"

"No," she quickly responded. "Not at all."

"I hate that you have to leave. Isn't there some way to contact you? I'll worry."

"Aw," Mimi said, and then lowered her voice as Dawson walked by. "Well... Quint has a satphone, but we really aren't supposed to give out the number." She had already told him far more about their mission than was appropriate, but convinced herself that it was okay since he was Dawson's brother. "Besides, I can call you every couple of days."

"I understand. I just thought it might be nice to have a way to get in touch with you. Come on, what could it possibly hurt? Please, it'll give us the chance to make plans for when you return."

"Preston, I don't know. I mean Quint was pretty adamant," she said noticing that he was looking her way.

"Did I tell you my oncologist set up a meeting with another specialist this morning. Don't want to worry you, but. . . just forget it, you don't need to hear about my problems. Maybe I'll be all right until you get back, I—"

Mimi interrupted, realizing that with the cancer he might not be. "I guess it really wouldn't hurt to give it to you. It's not like you're some big spy. But I'll be in lots of trouble if the team finds out."

"I'll keep it a secret. You have my word."

"Okay, I'll text you the number. Just promise you'll keep it to yourself and use it only if you have to. I'll try to call you whenever I can. Gotta go. Bye."

Mimi hung up, feeling conflicted. While pleased that he seemed so concerned about staying in touch, she wondered why he was so insistent, almost desperate. But she ignored the little warning voice in the back of her head as she texted him the satphone number.

Preston waited patiently and barely a minute later, received Mimi's text. He typed a short message and forwarded the satphone number. He was lost in thought when he heard the chime from his phone and read the incoming response: *Excellent, you have done well. Proceed as planned.*

# CHAPTER 11

"Man, I'm starving," Leo said, as the team disembarked from their flight in Tashkent. "I was so hungry I nearly ate the in-flight meal, food poisoning be damned."

Quint laughed as Kira reached into her bag. "Here's another energy bar."

"Thanks, Kira. But don't you have a stale piece of cardboard I could eat instead?" Leo griped, downing the bar in two bites.

The din inside the airport terminal was deafening. Hordes of people stood shoulder-to-shoulder talking, most of them puffing away on foul smelling tobacco. A few ate carryout food from paper containers, and the smell of old grease permeated the bluish haze.

Quint had sought refuge in a narrow hallway near the ticket counter where it was quieter. He was just finishing his status update to Rogers when Dawson's raised voice attracted his attention. "What the hell do you mean, no seats? Our tickets are already bought and paid for," Dawson screamed at the obstinate ticket agent, who seemed oblivious to the fact that Dawson was poised to rip out his throat.

"Excuse me," Quint interrupted. "Kira needs you. I'll see what I can do," he said, hoping to escalate the situation. As Dawson went in search of Kira on the contrived errand, Quint continued.

"I'm sorry, my friend is unfamiliar with your customs and wasn't aware that the... uh... entry fee isn't included in the ticket purchase price." Well aware that a bribe would be required for the agent to simply do his job, Quint pulled two $100 bills from his wallet and laid them on the counter. The agent's eyes bulged as he scooped up the money.

"Ah, glad you understand. Now, let's see. Ah, here's your group's reservation. Everything appears to be in order. I suggest you be standing at those double doors," he said pointing off to his left, "well in advance of boarding time to make certain your seats are still available when you board. The onboard crew is corrupt and will sometimes resell seats." Quint was amazed at the agent's gall in saying this with a straight face after having just extorted a bribe to issue the prepaid boarding passes. As he left the counter, he heard Dawson and Kira arguing while Marcia stood by silently.

"So what do you want me to do?" Dawson asked, the frustration thick in his voice.

"Just treat him like a brother," Kira replied. Despite her initial reservations, Preston had won her over with his seemingly sincere desire to patch things up with Dawson and by accepting the blame for his mistakes.

"As if I haven't tried," Dawson replied as Quint walked up. "Very funny, Kira didn't need me."

"Hey, I was just trying to help you avoid firsthand knowledge of the Uzbekistan prison system," Quint replied.

"Well, you needn't have bothered." Dawson walked away in a huff followed by Quint in search of the restrooms.

"I know I'm the new kid on the team so please don't take offense," Marcia said once they had gone, "but I have to tell you that Preston puts me off. And I'm not the only one. I know Quint is having doubts."

Kira looked at Marcia for a long moment before replying. "Maybe you're right. It's just that I care a lot for Dawson," she said, pausing for a moment, "and I lost my brother at a very young age. I appreciate your honesty; you and I should get along well." Marcia nodded. "My back is killing me. Let's see if we can score a place to sit in the lobby. We've got a long layover." Kira pointed across the room.

"Lots of luck. There aren't any seats," Leo approached, munching on a bag of some sort of chips.

"Damn and it appears that they haven't discovered no-smoking zones either. Let's at least step outside and get some fresh air."

"Negative on that too. I already tried—it's not allowed," Leo said, and then followed her to a small spot near the double doors where they took turns leaning against the wall while enduring their layover.

"Who do you think Mimi's talking to so secretively?" Dakota pointed at Mimi cradling the satphone to her ear.

"I'd guess Preston," Quint replied.

"After that episode with Everett dying in Venezuela, I hope things work out. Preston's not a bad sort; in fact, he's already paid me back some of the money I loaned him," Leo said.

"Paid you back?" Dakota exclaimed. "I lent him $3,500 just before we left to tide him over until he gets his inheritance money. How could he be paying you back?"

"Beats me, but look, we all have hard times. If he wasn't good for it, why would he have paid me back anything? After all, he didn't have to, I was about to leave. It'll be okay; you'll see. Dawson is solid, and I'm betting his brother is too." Dakota nodded, seeming relieved.

"I don't speak Uzbek, but it looks like we're about to board," Quint said, guessing at the reason for the uniformed woman's unintelligible announcement over the PA system and the crowd's sudden surge. Thanks to the advice from the corrupt ticket agent, the team was already in place.

"Finally, three hours late," Kira said while gathering her things. "Well, at least our flight didn't get cancelled."

A few minutes later, Quint filed onto the plane behind Kira and Mimi and took the seat across the aisle. Then they began another hour and a half wait in the sweltering heat of the un-air-conditioned cabin. When the pilot finally appeared in the doorway, Kira started to cheer until she saw he held a half full vodka bottle in one hand and brandished a pistol in the other.

"Welcome," he said in English with a thick accent. "I see we have lovely American women on board. Care to come up front and play with my control stick?" he chuckled. After his invitation went ignored, he shrugged, seeming nonplussed, and ducked into the cockpit.

A moment later, his voice boomed from the overhead speakers. "Put on seatbelts and grab asses. We go to Nukus with slogan, 'If you don't like our city, then Nukus,'" he said, ending with a loud burst of laughter.

Most of the team sat with closed eyes, praying during the flight until they touched down in Nukus.

From the moment the team boarded the overcrowded, decrepit bus in Nukus until they reached Moynaq, Uzbekistan, Quint listened to Leo complain for the entire bone-jarring ride. The team was weary by the time they finally arrived at the stifling hot concrete bus station, which was more like an abandoned storefront located at the south end of what Quint imagined was Main Street. A powerfully built,

barrel-chested man with a full beard and matching
head of tangled black hair was there to meet them.

"Welcome to hell we call Moynaq. My name is Boris,
and this my daughter, Nigora. You are Quint, no?"
Boris said in a thick accent and then offered his hand.

"Pleased to meet you," Quint introduced the rest of
the team members as they shook hands. Nigora
appeared to be in her late twenties and wore long,
blondish hair. Her fine features and slim figure had
the men fawning over her—except for Quint, who
remained busy talking to Boris and Colin, who fearing
Kira's wrath, made a point of ignoring the attractive
young woman.

"Everyone here?" Quint nodded. "Follow me," Boris
said, and led them from the station. "Your man Rogers
want best so hire me. I got you boat. I am chauffeur,
guide, whatever you need, Boris get, no?"

"Your help with securing the boat is certainly
appreciated," Quint replied. The team loaded into a
van that was probably white at one time but was now
half-brown from rust, most of which was concentrated
in the many dents and scrapes covering all four sides,
and even the roof, Quint noticed as he stepped in.

Boris revved the engine and took off in a cloud of
dust. Quint was amazed to find Leo sleeping within
minutes. Yelling to be heard over the loud exhaust and
Leo's snoring, Boris provided a running travelogue
about his country as he steered the van at an alarming
speed over the pothole-ridden roads. Quint gradually
found it easier to understand his broken English.

Finally they arrived at Boris' modest home where he
invited the team inside after kicking off his boots. As
Leo proceeded in behind him, he was nearly jerked off
his feet when Kira grabbed his arm and pulled him
back outside. "Take off your shoes."

"Why, this isn't Japan?"

"Maybe, but it's also their custom to take off one's
footwear when entering the house."

"Oh, well then, by all means let me take off my footwear," Leo sighed as he slipped his shoes off on the steps with a huff.

"I show you house," Boris said, as the team followed him into the living room where they stood packed together. "This living room." He went on for several minutes pointing out each feature and piece of furnishing. "Come," he said moving to the next room. "Bedroom with very own bathroom." Here he repeated the process, pointing out the bed, the sink, the toilet, the tub, and his array of toiletries while those who could fit inside the tiny room stood shoulder to shoulder. "Hot water faucet. You not find in many Uzbekistan houses."

"I guess he has pride in ownership," Quint whispered to Dawson as Boris continued his lengthy diatribe.

Dawson simply rolled his eyes as he shook his head. "You think? At least we're not crammed in there with the rest."

A moment later they heard Boris finish, and the team poured out of his bedroom. "Before I show you daughter room and other bathroom, I repeat tour for you not fit in." Unwilling to risk offending Boris, Quint sighed as he and Dawson entered the bedroom, ignoring Leo's smirk.

After the tour had mercifully ended, Quint briefed Boris on their plans while the team busied themselves preparing dinner from the food stores Rogers had sent along. Quint explained their mission, giving enough detail to establish credibility while adhering to a need-to-know philosophy.

"We'll need two days to prepare the boat you have acquired for us and receive Rogers' shipment of items that we... thought best not to bring with us," Quint said.

"Weapons?" Boris asked and Quint nodded. "Even with corrupt officials, weapons draw attention, though maybe U.S. green backs fix, no?"

Quint simply nodded. "As I was saying, we'll spend a couple of days out on the water to establish our cover, after which we're planning a night mission to Renaissance Island followed by a quick departure the following day. Now, let's see what the team has cooked up for us." Quint noticed Boris seemed torn between being grateful for the team's thoughtfulness in bringing the food and feeling embarrassed at how desperate he and the people of his town had become.

"I figured you already have plenty of Russian vodka and might enjoy some of France's best," Kira said, offering him a glass but limiting herself to water in deference to the baby she carried.

"Na zda·ró·vye!" Boris said as he and Nigora each accepted a glass of Grey Goose and beheld the lavish spread before him. "That's Russian thanks for what you bring. Za vashee zda·ró·vye, to your health. Za ná·shoo dróo·zhboo, to our friendship. And za lyoo·bóf, to love. Now pa·yé·kha·lee —we eat," Boris finished with a hearty laugh accompanying Mimi's snort.

The team chatted among themselves as they passed dishes. Quint noticed almost everyone including Boris was avoiding Leo's contribution to the feast. But Kira was actually tasting a couple of the items. "You do realize you're eating some of Leo's stuff, right?" Quint whispered.

"Yeah, maybe it's the pregnancy but my taste buds are in weird mode," Kira replied, as Boris launched off on another of his tales of growing up with the Aral Sea in its glory. When the food was nearly gone, the team was sated, and Boris had finished entertaining everyone, they toasted each other with Boris' Russian Vodka. While it helped ward off the jet lag, Quint feared it would leave the team feeling worse in the morning.

The men adjourned outside with their vodka where Boris handed out cigars and then fired up his own. The women remained at the table chatting. "Nigora, you have a beautiful name. What does it mean?" Kira asked.

"Beloved, most popular Uzbekistan name. I lucky to have father who give name meaning, no?"

"Your mother, is she—"

"She die when I am ten. My father, he still hurt, still in love. Filth here killed her. Kill all of us. He try find escape for me but not so easy."

"I like him; he seems like a good man," Marcia said.

"Best. His big dream is me go to Amelica."

"Why don't you both go?" Mimi asked as she rose to stretch.

"When poor, not so easy. And my father, he not leave his home and my babushka, or how you say, his mother. And I not leave him."

Mimi borrowed the satphone and excused herself to step outside. A few minutes later, seeming quite upbeat, she returned the phone to Quint. *Things must be going well at home.*

At last, when Quint figured that if the team continued drinking they might soon be incapable of walking, he persuaded Boris to take them to the hotel. Nigora made a big production of hugging each of the team, but when Leo's turn came, much to his chagrin she simply shook his hand.

The Oyabek Hotel was nothing like Leo had described. It was in obvious need of major maintenance. Outside, an overturned bus, stripped of anything useful, lay rusting on its side. "This is it?" Leo seemed devastated. "This looks nothing like I remember when I was last here. Where's the Aral Sea? When you said it had shrunk, I thought you meant it had dropped a couple of feet like the lakes do in the U.S. during a dry year."

"If you'd managed to stay awake during our earlier tour, Boris already covered all of that," Dawson said.

"No problem," Boris laughed. "Tomorrow I show you big tourist spot. You like.

"Normally, cool now but weather change when Aral dry up. Winter come very soon. Then plenty cold. But now maybe hot inside, yes? Maybe sleep in courtyard or fix generator." He pointed to a huge engine that looked to be older than the hotel. "Need parts Rogers send. I leave fuel," he said, as he unloaded a five gallon can of fuel from the back of the van. "Maybe you fix, run fans if you no sleep outside."

"We'll be fine, don't worry about us," Quint replied, having no intentions of sleeping outside. While the team unloaded their bags from the van, Quint wondered why they would want to work on the generator at midnight.

Boris handed out flashlights and then led them through the unlit lobby. The beam from Quint's light pierced the gloomy recesses of the lobby, revealing a sagging counter piled with junk and mounds of furniture stacked at the far end of the otherwise empty lobby space. "Don't worry, I have taken care of checking you in." Having seen no signs of life at the hotel, Quint wasn't sure whether he was joking.

Lugging their bags, the team followed Boris up two flights of stairs and then into an unlit hallway littered with trash and strips of paint that had peeled off the walls. "You can pick any room you like. They are all equally... luxurious." He finished with a laugh before heading back down the stairs.

"For security, it's probably best if all of the women stay in one room and the men in adjacent ones. We don't know who's likely to be coming around," Quint said.

Kira took one side of the hall while Marcia checked out the rooms on the other, seeming to find them equally repulsive. Finally, halfway down the corridor,

Kira announced, "I guess it really doesn't matter. This one will do." Marcia and Mimi followed her into the room to perform a security check. The rest of the men chose the adjoining rooms closer to the stairwell, each featuring several twin-sized beds.

The women explored their room, which featured a toilet, its bowl stained dark gray and appearing not to have been cleaned since it was installed. It appeared to actually flush on the fourth try—taking forever to re-fill with the low water pressure.

"I guess I'll be opting for sponge baths." Kira pointed at the claw-foot tub, perched on the opposite side of the bathroom. It listed to one side, one of its rusted legs having failed. She struggled to suppress a laugh as the other two women nodded, seeming unable to find words to express their horror at the accommodations.

"This certainly takes first place as the shittiest hotel I've ever stayed in. Make that the worst I've ever seen," Kira remarked. "Damn, it's like an oven in here." She opened the balcony door and laid her bag on the bed, judging it to be only slightly cleaner than the grimy floor.

Colin knocked and then entered the room to say good night to Kira. "Call if you need anything, though I doubt we can offer you much," he said, before leaving to join the other men.

In the darkened room illuminated only by their flashlights, Mimi and Marcia did the same on the other beds. Between the glow of the vodka and the weariness from travel, the women failed to notice the stream of mosquitoes pouring into the room. As they rummaged through their bags to find what they needed to prepare for bed, they batted away the pests that flew in front of their faces, paying little attention.

Colin found the men lying with the sheets pulled over their heads. After encountering clouds of stinging pests that swarmed through the open window, the men had coated themselves with some of the military-grade pest spray Rogers had provided.

Dawson tossed Colin a can, and he hosed himself down before jumping in the remaining empty bed. "Now I see why Rogers gave us all that bug spray."

Seconds later, a high-pitched, blood-curdling eeekkk erupted followed by "Shit!" A moment later, Kira came bursting into the room with Mimi and Marcia close behind. Kira shone the light around the room erratically, blinding the men while she continued yelling.

"Our room is filled with clouds of biting bugs, which was bad enough. But then these 747-sized flying mantises swooped in behind them."

Quint climbed from his bed to hand Kira and the other two women a can of the bug spray. "You may not smell as good nor like the greasy film, but at least you won't have all of your bodily fluids siphoned off." He grinned as the women wrinkled their noses and sprayed on a heavy protective layer of the liquid.

Kira tossed the can back when they finished and turned to Colin. "We can't stand the heat with the windows closed, and we're not sharing our room with all of those bugs. Do something," Kira demanded, with the other women expressing their full support.

"Come on, guys, let's see if we can get the generator running," Quint said and saw Kira's oily face beaming.

Willy, who had just entered the room after calling home on the satphone, heard the discussion. "Look, you guys get some rest. I can handle this," he insisted. As he turned to leave, Mimi asked to borrow the satphone again and slipped down the hall.

Two hours later, the generator roared to life, followed shortly by the women's cheers when the lights came on and the fan began to run. But their joy seemed short lived when Kira complain loudly, "This is nice, hot and cold running roaches." With the room now fully lit, Quint could see legions of pests covering the walls and floors of his room and the full extent of the filth.

He then heard Kira's voice once again. "Leave the lights on and the fan running. We'll sleep with the covers up over our faces." Quint guessed it would be a long night.

# CHAPTER 12

Syndy rolled her wheelchair into Hester's spacious stateroom, puffing away on the freshly lit cigarette stuck in her yellowed tube. Before her lay the morbidly obese man. Confined to bed by his paralysis, the industrial-grade bed groaned beneath his nearly quarter-ton bulk.

With little to do but indulge his considerable appetite, Hester had regained all the weight he had lost while recovering after his near death experience in Venezuela. An assortment of gourmet foods and snacks filled the rows of shelves above him in lieu of decorator items, which his blindness would prevent him from enjoying.

A cadre of well-paid servants doted on him, enduring his vile manner. Upon Syndy's arrival, he abruptly ordered his attendants from the room, leaving a black streak of caviar running from the corner of his mouth.

He looked up with sightless, bloodshot eyes set above a wide, often-broken nose perched atop pock-marked cheeks. His mouth was filled with rotted brown teeth. Though never a handsome man, now he was much less so, his hideous appearance matching his attitude. But his considerable financial resources had helped Syndy to gain a certain appreciation for his ugliness.

"You're smoking again," Hester said. "You shouldn't do that; it's bad for your health. It'll ruin your complexion."

"Yes, love," Syndy replied, the mechanical voice removing any hint of warmth from her voice. Though she enjoyed more mobility than Hester, this small advantage was largely offset by her ravaged appearance.

"It's not fair to be paralyzed *and* blind, unable to appreciate your beauty now that I finally have you." Hester knew that Syndy had endured a lengthy recovery in a prison hospital, after which her brief trial ended when the sympathetic judge placed her on probation, wrongly assuming that she posed no further threat.

But Hester remained blissfully unaware of the full extent of Syndy's disfigurement and was the only person to still see her as the beautiful woman she once was. She threatened the staff with their very lives should they ever divulge the truth. "I was just lying here thinking about—"

"Let me guess," Syndy interrupted. "Quint and Dawson, or should I say their painful demise."

"I suppose it wasn't that hard," he said with a laugh. "I've thought of hundreds of ways to kill them." After ambushing Quint's team at the site of an ancient Incan temple, Hester's brother, Pierre, was killed while Hester was buried in debris from an explosion.

"While I lay there in the jungle, paralyzed and blind, insects feasting on my broken body, I thought of nothing else. Then after those idiot natives stumbled across me and nursed me back to some degree of health, I had several more weeks to focus on the subject while waiting for transport back to the States."

Syndy cackled. "Well I too made quite a list while recovering from my bur... I mean my hospital stay. I add more fantasies each week."

"As do I. When the doctor told me that I had permanently lost my sight and the use of my lower body, only the temporary paralysis to my upper body prevented me from killing myself. It was you, Syndy, who restored my will to live when you came to propose our partnership. You've given me hope. Hope that one day, we can even the score with Quint, Dawson, and the rest of their team."

"And so we shall, perhaps soon." Their mutual hatred was the glue that cemented their relationship. "But I think it best if we do it somewhere other than on U.S. soil."

Hester nodded. "So tell me, sweet, how did your meeting go?"

"Our first project is under way."

"Congratulations, partner." Hester clasped his hands together, grateful for even the limited use of his arms. "I do love making money. The only thing more appealing is vengeance. Your idea about the mole was brilliant. Expensive, but brilliant."

Syndy smiled at the compliment. "Yes, we'll beat Quint's team to the bioweapons. I'm hoping we'll luck out and happen across his people while they're there. If not, it's only a matter of time before we catch them outside of the U.S. A million dollars buys a lot of information and, hopefully, a lot of pain once we find them."

They continued to discuss elaborate schemes for inflicting pain on their mutual adversaries. At least once each week, Syndy would read Hester a list of the top ten most horrific methods of execution. "What would be your favorite way to end Quint's days?" she asked.

"Of late I think more and more about scaphism." Syndy shuddered. Even she found the thought of someone lying in their own excrement while being eaten alive by insects repulsive. "And you?" Hester asked.

"I like Vlad the Impaler's approach." Otherwise known as Dracula, Vlad was depicted in a 15th century woodcut feasting al fresco in the company of his victims, who writhed in agony while impaled on stakes planted in the ground. "But then, fire is also dear to my heart."

"I've got an idea. Why not try out each of the ten? That way we could decide for sure the best way to kill Quint and Dawson when the opportunity presents itself."

"Splendid idea," Syndy replied. "What was the name of the snake who sold us those defective weapons?"

"Jose."

"That's right. Jose. I'll arrange for him to serve as our first experiment and have it videoed. Afterward we... I mean I, can watch it on video," she corrected herself, realizing that Hester would not be watching anything, "and describe it to you."

A knock at the door interrupted them. "Come in." One of her senior crew entered and briefed her on a situation involving their guest, Roberto. "I see. It really comes as no surprise. From his file, I expected such and now we'll get to deal with him. I want it all on video." Syndy issued her instructions and then turned back to Hester when the crewman had left Hester's stateroom.

"How timely," Syndy squealed. "It would appear that we are about to conduct the first of our top ten experiments." They visited until a reminder chime sounding on Syndy's cell phone interrupted her.

"Time to resume my meeting. I'll be back," she said over her shoulder as she motored out of the room.

*I enjoy your company, and we do make a good team, better in some respects than with Pierre. But I will always keep my guard in place,* Hester thought. He then gave the voice command to rotate his bed twenty degrees to prevent the formation of more bedsores.

Given his current condition, Hester was forced to trust Syndy, but he would trust only to a point. That was why, as a defensive measure, he had arranged to have a small explosive charge hidden in her wheelchair, activated by his voice command.

"I feel that a demonstration is the most effective way to convey a message," Syndy said to the group reseated at the conference table. She then angled her wheelchair toward the second of two glass elevators, which had been out of service, but which was now ascending from the living quarters below.

"Roberto was given a different time for this meeting to delay his arrival and allow us a few minutes to assemble." The elevator stopped at the end of the room, but the heavy glass doors remained closed. After pressing the door-open button repeatedly, Roberto tried in vain to part the doors with his hands.

"Roberto, I thought I made myself clear regarding the use of cell phones. Did you fail to understand this point?"

Roberto ceased struggling with the doors as the voice echoed loudly through the speakers in the ceiling. He looked across the room at Syndy, and the group seated at the table on the far side of the elevator's glass rear wall. "Yes, ma'am, I understood."

"Then please share with us your reason for disobeying my very clear instructions."

"What? I didn't—" Syndy interrupted him by pressing a button that caused Roberto's recorded voice to burst forth from the speakers.

"Hey, baby. Sorry I didn't get a chance to cancel our date before leaving. I'll make it up. You know you're my girl." The response at the other end of the line was too weak to be intelligible. "Where am I? I'm not really supposed to say, but I'm on this huge private yacht working for a total nut job. You should see this woman—straight out of the weird zone. A great candidate for Frankenstein's bride. She gives me the creeps, but, hey, the money's good so I'll stomach her. Gotta go. See you in a few days. Kiss, kiss."

Once the recording ended, Roberto's live voice continued but with more fervor. "I'm sorry, I didn't... I mean I..."

"Shut up!" Syndy erupted, the first emotion she had displayed before the group. She angrily jerked the controls and rotated her chair abruptly, causing the pillow to slide from her lap and exposing her deformed hands beneath. Her anger quickly turned to embarrassment as the eight men saw the stub of one arm and the blackened claw of the other with bones exposed on two fingers.

The men quickly averted their eyes, struggling to conceal their obvious revulsion. Just as quickly the embarrassment melted away, and Syndy's anger returned, building to rage as her aide scrambled to place the pillow back into her lap along with the plastic remote control unit that had tumbled to the floor.

Syndy composed herself while her aide placed a fresh cigarette in her holder. "Roberto, you've been a naughty boy, and naughty boys must be taught a lesson. Wouldn't you agree?"

"Ma'am, I'm sorry. It was just a quick call... it was stupid... please forgive me. It won't happen again—"

"Of that I'm certain," she replied quietly as her deformed hand pressed a button on the remote. Instantly panels in the top and bottom of the elevator slid to one side. "Goodbye, Roberto. It would appear that our relationship is about to... burn itself out," she finished with a cackle, and then pressed another button, igniting flames fueled by high pressure propane that jetted from the elevator roof and floor.

Roberto danced around the elevator desperately trying to escape the fiery jets. His screams of agony echoed from the speakers above the conference table over the roar of the flames. Syndy seemed as if she were listening to Beethoven while watching the clock beside the elevator. The flames stopped abruptly when she pressed the button once again.

"Precision is what it's all about, don't you think?" she said, as the room full of men nodded with vacant eyes. "You see, it's important to closely monitor the burn time. A few more seconds, and he would have been dead, and where's the fun in that? But as you can see," she said, gesturing toward the blackened elevator, "he's still alive." One of the men vomited beside his chair at the pathetic site of Roberto's horribly charred body crawling through the now opened elevator door, his facial features burned away. "Well, Roberto, I guess I've made my point, wouldn't you say? Kiss, kiss."

While the whole incident had taken mere seconds, it must have seemed an eternity to the men at the table, forced to view the spectacle. With the flames gone and the elevator cooling, two men appeared wearing breathing masks to drag Roberto back into the elevator and accompany his blackened carcass below. The sound of Roberto's moans ceased, but the smell of charred flesh and burnt hair filled the room.

Syndy's pulse quickened over the excitement from torching Roberto, the audible mechanical sound of her breathing conveying a near orgasmic intensity. Once her breathing returned to normal, she continued.

"Now wasn't that much more effective than my just rambling on about the importance of following instructions and fulfilling your commitments? Being the smart men you are, I'm certain no further such exercise will be required. Roberto was the weak one; in fact, I included him on the team confident that he would prove useful for this very purpose. Any

questions? No? Then Arnold, I'm ready for a briefing
on the plan you've formulated."

As a sign of respect, Syndy referred to her senior
staff by their actual name, though Arnold, like the
rest, had his unique identifier "S-10" tattooed on his
neck. The "S" was in lieu of the entire ship's name
required for junior crew members. The lower the
number, the higher the rank with "S-1" being reserved
for the captain.

Arnold, his face still white from the demonstration,
shakily rose from his seat and cleared his throat.
Visibly struggling to focus on the task instead of the
grisly spectacle he had just witnessed, he launched
into his briefing, gradually gathering confidence as he
went.

"I'm impressed with your plan," Syndy commented
when he finished. "However, I cannot stress enough
how important the success of this mission is to me.
You would all do well to remember that I'm counting
on you to bring me an entire container of bioweapons
material, some to sell and some... for... shall we say,
personal use.

"As you saw in your briefing packets, we have also
designated individuals," she paused as her mind
wandered for a moment, "the capture of whom will net
you a substantial bonus. If you have no further
questions, you are free to leave. Except I'd like Arnold
to please remain. Until we meet again, toodle-loo," she
said in her mechanical voice. The men rose, all opting
to use the stairs located to the far side of the elevator.

Once the rest of the men had left, she turned to
Arnold. "I want to stress that if you do stumble across
Quint, Dawson, and their team, I want them brought
to me alive. Do you understand? Alive." Arnold
nodded. "As I promised, I will make it well worth your
while. Thank you, that is all." Arnold nearly leapt to
his feet and a moment later was gone.

Syndy engaged the wheelchair and moved toward her stateroom. As she neared her aide, she spoke again. "34, do make certain they take 'proper' care so that Roberto doesn't come back to haunt us, so to speak, by creating a messy incident with the authorities. And have them take care of it quickly. I want us under way before dark. Have the captain join me in my stateroom," she said as she exited the room, a cloud of smoke in her wake.

Syndy found life aboard *Syntillate* to be more to her liking than she ever imagined. Hester had agreed to indulge even her slightest whim in the construction of the ship. From the handicapped access she enjoyed throughout to the wheelchair-friendly, glass-enclosed elevator with the special features she had desired, the ship fit her perfectly.

She had found it far easier than she imagined to sell Hester on the advantages of a megayacht as a base of operations. Without moving from his quarters, he could be transported to the far corners of the world. It made it easier to conduct business abroad and offered a convenient means of escape. Of course, Syndy enjoyed the same freedom of movement without the dreaded necessity of facing the public's reaction to her hideous appearance. It was also much easier and considerably cheaper to manipulate things to their liking in places such as the Bahamas.

Hester immediately found the idea intriguing. His blindness denied him the pleasure of the spectacular views from his high-dollar homes. So by liquidating his real-estate holdings, he easily raised the necessary cash to fund the ship project.

After reviewing hundreds of possibilities, Syndy settled on the yacht of a formerly wealthy member of the Russian mafia who had fallen on hard times. During an extensive refit in which no expense was spared, the yacht was adapted perfectly for their purposes.

Appearing more reminiscent of a modern-day stealth warship than a luxury yacht, it was designed to be fast. This came at the expense of spacious decks typically intended to accommodate throngs of nude sunbathers, but for which she and Hester had little use. The design elicited strong emotions from those who saw it. Some viewed it as hideous while others saw it as a cool, futuristic vessel. But to both Syndy and Hester, it was home.

Access to her suite was controlled by a state-of-the-art proximity detector, which sensed her surgically embedded transponder and electronic fingerprint scanners for her personal staff. Her rotating bed enabled her to enjoy the panoramic view from all the windows and featured a lift to assist her in and out of her wheelchair.

She loved living on the ship and the freedom it afforded . Here, with a twenty-two-person staff, she ruled the roost, free to inflict pain and misery on the world beyond.

From the vantage point of her stateroom on the top deck, she enjoyed a nearly 360° view of each port they visited. Though she could disembark and visit any country in which they dropped anchor, because of her disfigurement she generally preferred to remain aboard ship away from the stares of those horrified by her appearance. Her thoughts were interrupted by a knock on the door.

"You wish to see me?" the captain asked as he entered the room.

"Yes, please set course for Scandinavia before dark."

"Uh, exactly where in Scandinavia?"

"That's your job; I don't care. But choose someplace far to the north... and to the east." He nodded and immediately left. Syndy relished her authority to command the ship's itinerary, cruising to wherever her heart desired. Often she chose places simply because they were either far away or exotic. But this time, she wanted to be in position to accept the cargo that she had tasked Arnold to deliver.

Syndy moved toward the port window where, perched in her wheelchair, she gazed out at the seagulls soaring overhead, their freedom seemingly mocking her. The fish and even the lowliest of land creatures able to move about at will unassisted did the same.

But she could still take refuge in her mind, where she could imagine anything. These increasingly more frequent episodes of escape from reality were beginning to have their effect. She became more polarized, fixating on her fantasies, which now consumed a great part of each day. Central to these fantasies were Quint and Dawson or more specifically, their agonizing deaths.

# CHAPTER 13

Quint awoke the next morning to silence—the generator had run out of fuel during the night. Though it had powered the fans long enough for him to get some sleep, he was covered with red welts from a host of insect bites.

He rose to join the rest of the team gathered in the hotel lobby where he grabbed an energy bar from the box beside the kerosene-powered stove. The coffee had just finished brewing, and he poured himself a cup. "You mean to tell me that with all the shit we hauled here, there's no vanilla creamer?"

"Oops, sorry. I'll add it to our provisioning list for next time," Kira replied. A few minutes later, the team was assembled in the courtyard for Boris to take them from the hell-hole hotel in his ragged van.

"What you think of country so far?" Boris asked, his smile suggesting he suspected the real answer. Before Quint could think of a proper response, Dawson jumped in.

"I think most of us always wanted to vacation here. Personally, this is the realization of one of my life-long dreams. Yep, the ol' bucket list will be shorter now," he replied, earning a dirty look from Kira.

Boris roared with laughter and then set out at full speed, avoiding only the larger potholes. "I take you to tourist spot as I promise. Moynaq, once paradise and grow apricot trees, watermelon. Fishermen make big harvest from fourth biggest lake in world. Big as Ireland. Thousands of islands."

He stopped the van at a dilapidated factory building beside which stood the gray statue of a fisherman holding a large fish in his hands. "This we call Last Fisherman Standing. Is sad joke. No more fish so no more fisherman. Soon, no more sea. You see, I show you," Boris said and then rocketed off once again.

"As young boy, I live here. But stupid government planners turn into 45,000-square-kilometer poisoned desert big as Belgium, Luxemburg and Netherlands all combine. See what big government do to Aral Sea, no?"

"Why did they do this?" Kira asked.

"Stupid idiots' grand plan to control world cotton market. Divert most of Amu Darya and Syr Darya so no longer feed Aral Sea. Shrink to fourth of size. Water three times more salty than ocean.

"And here our big tourist spot," he said, finally stopping again. The team stared open-mouthed at the incongruous sight of a row of rusting ship hulls, marooned in the desert sands. "When sea disappear, we dig channel, but sea, she shrink faster than we dig. Fishing fleet beached in desert like science fiction movie. Moynaq now 150 kilometers from shore, no more seaport.

"No local fish for cannery, so can fish come on train from Pacific. Those too stupid to leave work in factory or strip scrap from rusting ships to buy food."

Boris continued his series of anecdotes, and after another short, but hair-raising drive, he stopped before a decrepit, high-rise building. "Mother, she live here. You have aspirin?"

"Sure," Mimi replied. She dug through her bag for a bottle and handed it to Boris.

"Thanks," he said, pocketing the entire bottle. Quint smiled at the look of surprise on Mimi's face.

"Be back soon," Boris promised, and left carrying a bag of leftovers from the previous evening's feast.

When Nigora started to follow, he stopped her. "No, you stay. You see your babushka another time."

"What's a babushka?" Mimi asked.

"Uh... my... granny I think is your word," Nigora smiled.

A minute later, Boris reappeared in the window of the corner apartment on the third floor and waved. While the team waited outside the dilapidated apartment building, Quint noticed an ominous-looking group of men gathering farther down the street.

Unarmed, he felt naked and exposed. The worried look on Dawson's face telegraphed his shared concern. Two more raggedly dressed men joined the group a few minutes later, their stares and gestures making it clear that the team was the object of their focus.

"I'm going to check on Boris and see if we can get moving," Quint finally said, the concern heavy in his voice. The rusted staircase swayed with each step he took, threatening to detach from the building at any time and crash to the ground below. When he finally reached the safety of the concrete landing, he took a deep breath and tapped on the door.

Boris invited Quint inside, where a pale and withered old woman looked up from her ancient recliner. Another mid-40s woman with long dark hair hovered over her. "This mother, made me man I am. And here most favorite sister. Only young brother Vladimir missing. This is Quint. He bring medicine and food."

The old woman said something in a barely audible voice that still carried the kindness and inner strength of a woman unbowed before a lifetime of hardship. As she pushed aside her threadbare blanket and struggled to get up, the daughter softly pushed her back.

"Mother, you cannot make tea that does not exist," the daughter said, first in Uzbek and then in English,

Quint assumed for his benefit adding, "It has been
many years since we have had such a luxury."

Unsure how to respond, Quint chose to address the
older woman out of respect, even though she wouldn't
understand. "Oh, no thank you, I can't stay." He then
turned to Boris.

"I apologize for intruding, but I was concerned by
what appears to be a gang gathering down the street."
Boris scowled as he moved to the window where he
could see the group of men who had now eased to
within a block of the team. Without a word, he
disappeared into a small back room, reappearing a
minute later carrying a bundle wrapped in burlap.

"Mother, we go. Vladimir come later." Quint said
goodbye and assured the sister that she was welcome
to keep the aspirin as she gushed her appreciation for
the "drugs." He then followed Boris back down the
wobbly staircase, making certain to remain at least
one flight behind. When he reached the bottom, Boris
was already kneeling to unwrap the burlap package.
Quint recognized the distinctive click when Boris
inserted a long curved magazine.

The group of men had closed to within 200 feet, and
Quint's unarmed team had sought refuge behind the
van when Boris burst into view. As he marched
directly toward the men, the burlap fell to the ground,
exposing the muzzle of an angry-looking AK-47.

When Boris had closed to within 75 feet, the
apparent leader moved to raise a small machine pistol.
Without breaking stride, Boris pulled the trigger, and
the staccato burst of his weapon sounded. He
continued forward, emptying half of the magazine into
the leader, who did a jerky dance before his bullet-
ridden body fell to the ground, his unfired gun lying
beside him. The rest of the gang fled, melting into the
side streets and buildings.

Boris squatted beside the dead man. With closed
eyes he whispered something Quint couldn't make out,

and when he rose, his eyes appeared watery. "Get in van. We go, now," he barked with no further explanation, pausing only to pick up the man's gun off the ground.

He drove to where the dead man lay and stopped. Without giving the team a chance to offer their help, he dragged the limp body behind the van where he tossed it into the back before slamming the doors. A moment later, they were back under way.

A few blocks later, he pulled over and unceremoniously dumped the body into a ravine before driving away. They rode in silence for ten more minutes before Boris finally spoke.

"Forgive them for what they try to do and me for what I did. I should not leave you. Not bad men. I grow up with one I kill. We play sports and friends. But years here make men desperate. Killing leader makes point, for you and for family when I not there. Here they understand only strength. Use force or die. No time to mourn, no time to bury.

"Later, I take rifle back to sister but maybe now she not need it. It is sad world our leaders give us," he said, the disgust thick in his voice. They rode in silence for a few more minutes before Boris spoke once again. "Miss Mimi, thank you for medicine. How I pay you?"

"Don't be silly; I was glad to give it to you," Mimi replied. "I hope it helps your mother get better."

"That, it cannot do—she dying of TB. Maybe aspirin make feel better up here," he said, pointing to his head.

"Ah, a placebo," Mimi replied.

Quint caught Boris' confused look. "A pill that can't cure but gives hope."

"Here we need much hope." No one responded, unsure what to say as they rode on.

"Do the people here fear Renaissance Island?" Mimi finally asked, breaking the silence.

"Fear Vozrozhdeniye? No, not go there. Living here plenty bad enough. After Aral dry up, create big desert. Dust storms blow 100,000,000 kilos of dust, salt, pesticides, chemicals, and poisons from dried-out seabed each year. Ruin water we drink and air we breathe. Make us, how you say, anemic. Make us sick. Kill everything.

"But unlike America, in my country everyone get same healthcare," Boris said, seemingly boasting before adding, "too little and too late." He ended with a loud laugh, slapping his thigh.

A short while later, the team finally reached the current shore of the Aral Sea where their ship awaited. Boris had managed to charter the most dilapidated vessel Quint had ever seen, at a price that would have purchased a much nicer craft back in the States. Quint was amazed that it actually floated. He had to look hard to find any vestige of paint on the rusted hull. Though the deck groaned, it bore Leo's weight.

Quint saw Kira stop to study the boat's transom. "What are you doing?"

"Trying to make out the boat's name. The first two letters are 'M' and 'a' then either 'j' or 'g' and then 'i.' What the hell does that mean?"

Leo, who had joined her, was quick to answer. "If the third letter is a "j," it could be the name of a fictitious planet in the Armstrong Nebula, or a town in Ethiopia. But if it's a "g" then it could stand for modified adjusted gross income, one of the three wise men, or maybe a Zoroastrian priest of the ancient Medes."

Quint laughed as Kira sighed and rolled her eyes. "And you know this how?"

"I'm smart," Leo replied, with his chest puffed out.

"Yeah, imagine how smart he'd be if his mind wasn't filled with that sort of useless brain sludge," Dawson blurted out.

"Look, we've got work to do," Quint protested. "We'll call her *Magic* since it will take plenty of it for her to remain afloat long enough for us to do our job. Dakota, since we chartered *Magic* sans captain to have the freedom we need to conduct our mission, why don't we get busy puzzling out the controls while the rest of the team unpacks our gear and gets it set up."

It took only a minute for the two men to confirm that the boat's pathetic 1970s-era electronics did not work. "Now, aren't you glad I insisted we bring along the portable GPS and radar?" Dakota asked with a smug grin.

"Am I. We'd be screwed without it," Quint agreed as he helped unpack the gear nestled in the foam-filled plastic shipping container they had lugged along.

Quint glanced down and saw the team attacking their small mountain of ancient oceanographic survey gear. While most of it was not functional, he hoped it would create the illusion that this was truly a scientific expedition, at least long enough to withstand a cursory inspection. The two cases containing an inflatable dinghy and an outboard engine, now stowed on the foredeck, were another story. If they didn't work, it would be a short mission.

By the end of the day, the team was tired, but in no hurry to return to the hotel. They arrived just in time to re-fuel the generator and have it running by nightfall. Boris dropped them off and left quickly, claiming an emergency. Quint suspected it was feigned to avoid the embarrassment of not hosting a dinner he was customarily obliged to provide but unable to afford.

Once Quint had finished his cold shower, somewhat of a challenge given the anemic stream of water that dribbled from the shower head, he joined the rest of the team gathered for dinner. Tonight's fare would be far simpler than that of the previous evening.

"Where's Leo?" Quint asked, as he walked in smoothing his wet hair. Willy and Dakota looked off, seeming otherwise preoccupied while he awaited a reply.

Kira finally broke the silence. "He went out for dinner."

"Went out? We brought dinner. Did I not make it clear that no one was to leave the group? This isn't some little backwoods town in Ohio. As we saw this morning, there are some bad dudes here."

"You know how he is about his weird food—" Kira replied.

"Exotic," Dakota interrupted with a laugh as he offered Leo's standard correction.

"Sorry," Kira continued. "Anyhow, Boris told him about some restaurant that serves *exotic* specialties from several eastern European countries. I guess he couldn't resist."

"I think she's right," Dakota chimed in. "He'd been talking about some strange dishes and kvass, a Russian beer made by fermenting old bread in water. I hope never to be so desperate for a buzz that I'd drink that."

"And you didn't stop him because... ?" Quint asked Kira.

"I ain't his mama, and he's a big boy. I saw him whispering to Boris, who smiled and motioned for him to climb in his truck. Dawson was there. He saw him too."

"You were there too and didn't stop him?" Quint turned to Dawson, noting a fleeting deer-in-the-headlights expression.

"Uh...yeah... he went out to dinner. But as she said, he's a big boy. It'll be okay. I'm betting he's having a memorable evening," Dawson said with a grin that suggested he was hiding something, but Quint chose not to push.

The next morning, there was still no sign of Leo by the time Quint heard the van pull up. Boris stepped out and opened the rear doors. "More gear. Just delivered." He pointed to a sturdy-looking wooden crate surrounded by a mound of cardboard boxes. "This one maybe weapons." Dawson immediately pried off the lid and began digging in the crate.

"Thanks. You know where Leo might be?" Quint's irritation was obvious.

Boris's face spread in a wide grin, and he shot a quick glance at Dawson. "He go to Sevdiya's. Restaurant famous for Eastern Europe cooking. I drop him off but arrange taxi. Make sure he have cab fare. He not back?"

"No, and in the future I would appreciate it if you didn't assist any of my team in leaving without my approval."

"Sorry. I go search."

"No, we don't have time. Please have them contact us as soon as—."

"Wait, maybe this him," Boris interrupted, as he reached into the van to retrieve an ancient cell phone the size of a brick. "Yes... yes... we meet at Last Fisherman," he said as he hung up. "Nigora have your friend."

"He's okay?" Quint asked, concern in his voice.

"Yes, I uh... think maybe."

A few minutes later, they approached an ancient Lada parked beside the statue. As soon as Boris stopped the van, Leo leaped from the sedan and came running toward them, leaving Nigora to hand the driver a handful of coins before following. "Man, am I glad to see you guys. What a freakin' night."

"Did you forget the part about the team sticking tog—" Quint said.

"Hey, give me a break... I was kidnapped and raped!"

"Raped?"

"Yeah. Boris dropped me off at this home restaurant specializing in exotic eastern European food. One of those places with no signs, so unless you know about it, you're out of luck. The woman who runs it, Sevdiya, is in her 50's and weighs about 300 pounds with a beard heavier than mine.

"But her English is passable, and the woman can cook. Things went well at first, and we had fun talking about different foods. The problem started when I finished eating and tried to pay. I asked her how much the meal was, and she wanted to barter. It didn't take me long to figure out what she had in mind." Quint noticed Boris and Dawson turn and walk a few steps away, fighting to keep from laughing.

"I thanked her, but told her I'd prefer to pay. Although I certainly didn't tell her why, I make it a practice not to sleep with any woman who outweighs me or has more facial hair. Well, she got all bent out of shape and started yelling in Uzbek. Then she reached under the counter and whipped out this gun. Looked like a blunderbuss or something. Marched me out back to this dumpy little cottage and told me if I didn't perform, she'd shoot off my equipment. She raped me!"

No longer able to keep a straight face, Dawson, Boris, and most of the rest of the men doubled over laughing. Finally, Dawson managed to stop long enough to speak. "Since you've got a beard too, at least you didn't get any whisker burns." This time even the women joined in the laughter. Leo climbed into the van in a huff and remained silent while Boris drove, and Dawson cracked jokes about Leo's tragic experience.

When the teasing had finally run its course, Willy spoke. "So tell us about the food."

"Though it certainly wasn't worth the price," Leo began and then paused to let another round of laughter pass, "it truly was a wonderful meal." Quint saw Leo's eyes glaze over. "She started with this Hungarian chicken soup. It's made in a giant pot with the whole chicken. I got a foot in my bowl!" Quint took this to be a good thing.

"It's supposed to be good luck, though not so much in my case." Leo rolled his eyes as another wave of laughter erupted. "I probably should have gone for the duck-blood soup," he paused for a moment while appearing to be envisioning the dish.

"Anyhow, they had this incredible baked celery, nearly as thick as my hand. Must raise it near Chernobyl. The entree was pork knuckle, a Czech dish. The monstrous joint is served with foot-long utensils stuck in the joint. It's pretty cool-looking, though there's not a lot of meat. The side of kraut was good. I just wish I had ordered a few more kvass beers before the bill came due." This time he was prepared for the response.

When they arrived at *Magic*, Quint managed to get Dawson aside. "You had something to do with Leo's restaurant experience last night, didn't you?"

"Me?" Dawson's feigned indignation evaporated under Quint's glare. "Okay, maybe I did learn that Sevdiya was one hot number in her heyday. And maybe it did come to my attention that she used to sell her favors before becoming a restaurateur. And maybe I did sort of get Boris to take me there so I could pre-pay Leo's meal with enough left over to arrange his... dessert. But please don't tell him."

"Dammit all, Dawson! I won't tell, but you better hope he doesn't figure it out. After all the other stunts you've pulled on him, he'll kill you."

As Quint stormed off, he heard Mimi on the satphone. From the warm tone of her voice, he knew it wasn't family she was talking to. "I said no personal calls!" he yelled.

She spotted him walking toward her and quickly ended the call. When he was still a few feet away, she tossed him the phone and then scampered off before he could lay into her.

# CHAPTER 14

The team spent the day installing their equipment and making repairs on *Magic*. "We can't do much about the yellowed and cracked windows or the corroded engine controls, but we've repaired everything we could and cleaned out most of the filth and debris," Colin said to Quint, the sound of the boat's engine interrupting him. It coughed and wheezed for a minute before settling into a steady rhythm.

A few minutes later, Willy approached, tossing a greasy rag on a pile of trash. "I went over the engine, replaced the belts, changed the oil, tightened all the hose clamps I could get to, and filled the batteries."

"Yeah, sounds like you got it running okay," Quint grinned.

"No one was more surprised than me when it actually started. From the looks of the engine room, I doubt any maintenance has been performed on the engine in the past decade. I'll try to keep it running, but I can't make any promises."

By evening they were within a couple of hours of being done. Quint sensed a change in the air as they drove back to the hotel but thought little of it as he began making plans for the next day. "We need to get to the ship early tomorrow to finish up a few little things. We should be ready to get under way by late morning."

Boris shook his head, "No, tomorrow we stay inside, drink vodka."

"What?" Quint snapped. "And we would want to do that because...?"

"Big dust storm."

"Dust storm? How do you know?"

"Mother say so. She always right."

"Well, I hardly think that should stop us."

"Trust me, you not want to be in dust storm and breathe filth."

"But we would be out on the Aral Sea. Wouldn't we be safe there?"

Boris laughed. "Storms very big, maybe 150-300 kilometers. Boat engine no work so well. You wait until storm pass, no?"

"And how long will that take?"

"Maybe one hour; maybe several," Boris said, with a shrug of his shoulders. Quint sighed, frustrated by the delay.

The team gathered in the grimy hotel lobby, preferring it over their even drearier rooms. Kira, her nesting instincts appearing to have kicked in, pressed several of the men into service retrieving a collection of mis-matched chairs and tables from a pile of furniture heaped on the far side of the lobby. She then oversaw the creation of a makeshift lounge area where they could relax and eat.

She negotiated for the use of the ancient hot plate from the desk clerk during one of his rare appearances, and tasked Dakota to clean it up enough to be serviceable for heating their dinner.

"Syndy, it appears we must delay our plans," Arnold said over the satphone.

"What? Why?"

"An enormous dust storm will make it impossible for us to fly tomorrow."

"Let a dust storm stop us? I don't think so." She triggered the switch to deliver a lungful of smoke.

"If you can't see, I think it unwise to fly through it. Remember President Carter's ill-fated attempt to rescue the Iranian hostages? They lost several helicopters to mechanical failures in a dust storm, forcing the mission to be aborted. I think we want to take heed of his error. We can, however, be ready to launch once the storm is over."

"Very well, but proceed as soon as possible," Syndy replied, the frustration evident even in her mechanical voice. "With Quint and his team outside the U.S., perhaps we can make use of this delay. In fact, it will be a perfect cover for what I have in mind. Our busy mole has provided us with an update on the location of Quint and his team. While you wait for the storm to pass, take this opportunity to capture Quint or Dawson. And maybe kill a few of the other team members."

"But if we divert my men for this new task we won't be poised to proceed with your primary objective."

"Then I suggest you hire someone else."

Arnold smiled, "I think I have just the man for the job: Cary. He's nearby and always ready—for the right fee, of course."

"Very well. One other thing. We have completed negotiations on some other... contraband. The three trucks carrying it will meet up with yours to form a convoy. Combining the shipments will get more bang for our bribery buck." She exhaled a thick cloud of smoke and finished with a ghastly chuckle.

Boris joined the team for dinner in the hotel lobby that evening. With the delay due to the dust storm and fearing it might be a cultural slight to refuse, most of the team members were vulnerable to Boris' seemingly endless toasts with Russian vodka. But they were ill prepared to keep pace with a man virtually weaned on the stuff. Determined to avoid a horrific hangover, Quint escaped early with Kira following close behind, using the excuse of her pregnancy.

The next morning, Quint awoke to the sound of a raging dust storm, just as Boris' mother predicted. He wondered how long the generator would continue running in the dirty air that penetrated their hotel rooms through every crack and seam.

"Rise and shine, party animals," Quint said, taunting Dawson, Dakota, and the rest of his hung-over team.

"Screw you," Dawson finally managed to reply after Quint's fourth attempt to motivate his crew.

"So, I have to take up the slack because my team can't hold their liquor? What a bunch of wussies," Quint replied with a smile.

"Sorry, Quint; I feel horrible," Dakota groaned in obvious agony. "That Russian vodka is nasty shit. Give me a while, and I'll try to get going."

"That's okay; I just felt obliged to have some fun. You guys get feeling human while I martyr myself by going back to *Magic* alone to finish running equipment checks and tie up loose ends," Quint said, laughing as he headed for the door.

He donned the goggles that Boris had left for them, put a hooded jacket over his long-sleeved shirt, and tied a handkerchief around his nose and mouth. For good measure he added a surgical mask hoping the double layer might filter out the poisonous material Boris had warned him about.

Quint braced himself as he eased the door open but was still nearly jerked off his feet as a gust of wind caught it. He managed to hang on and with a struggle, finally got it closed.

Though the goggles protected his eyes, the visibility was still limited to a few feet. Quint pulled the hood tighter against the course grit, which blasted any exposed patch of skin. Even so, he could feel sand in his ears and creeping down his neck as it worked its way inside the hood.

Shortly after emerging from the safety of the hotel lobby, he heard the sound of a truck engine and thought he saw a shadow moving a short distance away. *It appears someone else is as stupid as me.*

Removing two plastic ties from his pocket, Quint strapped a handheld GPS to the handlebars of the borrowed motorcycle. While Boris had not recommended using it in the dust storm, he hadn't specifically said they couldn't. Quint wrapped the air filter with a double layer of cloth, hoping to keep out most of the dust while still letting the motor breathe, and set out for the boat.

Between the ear-splitting sound of the engine absent a muffler and the howl of the dust-laden wind, Quint was effectively deaf as well as blind when a dark shadow suddenly materialized in front of him. He jerked the front wheel hard to the left while slamming on the brakes.

The bike skidded out from under him and he slid into the wheels of the looming truck. He was still trying to extricate himself from the wrecked bike when he caught a shadow of movement and saw a figure kneel beside him.

"Who are y—"

A hand bearing a syringe plunged a needle into his neck before he could react. His fist shot out impotently at the retreating form. As he struggled to his feet, his vision blurred, and his muscles refused to respond. A moment later, he was unconscious.

# CHAPTER 15

"Man, I feel terrible," Dawson said, when he finally joined the team in the hotel lobby a couple of hours later. "My head is throbbing, and my stomach's threatening to erupt."

"My biggest problem is at the other end," Colin replied.

"You too?" Dawson asked. "During the night I was a seven, but this morning I'm down to a four."

"Good for you. I'm still a seven," Colin replied.

"A seven what?" Mimi asked.

"On the Bristol Stool Scale." Dawson smiled at her confused look.

"Huh?"

"How can I say this?" Dawson stroked his chin acting as if in deep thought. "The Bristol Stool Scale is a feces classification tool for diarrhea victims."

"Gross!" Mimi turned away in disgust.

A minute later the door opened, and Boris appeared, his daughter trailing behind. He spotted Dawson holding his head in obvious pain. "You no feel so good?"

"Thanks to the after-effects of your vodka-drinking challenge."

Boris gave a hearty laugh. "Don't feel bad. Living in hell, plenty time to drink vodka. Make our lives almost bearable. Quint here?"

No one replied for a moment until Dawson finally spoke up. "Being wiser than the rest of us last night, he was feeling much better and went to the boat to finish rigging our gear."

"Bad idea, no? Maybe he no find in storm. When storm quit, we look." Boris shook his head.

Dawson was trying to think of something to say when Mimi approached and handed Boris a plastic bag with several over-the-counter bottles of medicine, less what she had reserved to cope with the team's over-indulgence. "Here's some more medicine for your mother. I know this can't cure her, but perhaps it will relieve her pain better than the aspirin."

"Thanks, Mimi. Nice ring, big cubic zirconia, no?" Boris blurted out. Dawson saw Mimi's face turn crimson as Boris realized his blunder. "Sorry. Our culture demand truth, no offense."

"None taken." Dawson saw Mimi hold the ring as if she were now wearing a large spider and knew she was lying.

"My daughter stay with you and help," Boris said, now seeming eager to leave.

"I think she's got the hots for you," Leo said once Boris was gone.

"Who's got the hots for me?" Dawson replied.

"Nigora."

Dawson looked over to where she was sitting with Kira. "What makes you say that?"

"Because she's constantly looking over at you whenever you aren't looking. I can hardly get her to speak to me at all." Leo seemed irritated at having his advances spurned.

Dawson had noticed that Nigora seemed infatuated with the Americans. It wasn't clear to him whether it was due to her having met so few or wanting to practice her English. Or maybe it was in response to the pressure he imagined her family must be placing on her at being nearly 30, still unmarried, and without child.

"Well, she's waaay too pretty for you, my friend. And a little young for me," Dawson replied.

"We'll see once she focuses her womanly charms on you, which it appears she's headed here to do right now. I'll leave so as not to cramp your style."

"You needn't b—" Dawson's reply was interrupted by Nigora's greeting.

"Enjoy dust storm?" she joked.

"Not really, you?"

"I accept and use time." They talked for only a few minutes before Marcia and Kira joined the conversation.

"So, what you think of our country, lush and verdant, no?" Nigora asked Marcia with a laugh.

"You're a real comedian, just like your father," Marcia replied.

Seizing the opportunity to escape, Dawson rose from his seat on the floor, hoping to discourage any romantic intentions Nigora might have. "Speaking of your father, I need to excuse myself to grab some lunch and then go sleep off the rest of his vodka."

Most of the team returned to their rooms, hoping more sleep would help their hangovers. Marcia and Mimi remained chatting with Nigora. "A shame what they've done to your country."

Nigora nodded. "Now we call area around sea Aral-Kum, or Aral sands. Each year, millions of tons of salt and dust from sea bed ruin farm lands and kill our babies."

"I feel guilty that we're not a *real* research team trying to solve your country's problems," Marcia lamented.

"We joke if everyone who come to study Aral Sea bring bucket of water, we refill sea. But not small problem. They say $300 billion to fix. I think maybe even you rich Americans not have so much money, no?" Nigora then turned to Mimi and noticed that she had removed her ring and now held it in the palm of her hand. "My father embarrass you, yes?" Mimi nodded. "He mean no harm."

"I was just shocked to hear that it wasn't real. How would your father know?"

"When young, work in jewelry store while go to school. He love diamonds, very good at valuing. Once sea shrinks, our neighbors force to sell jewelry, ask him to appraise. But now no one have anything valuable. So where your ring come from?"

"A man named Preston, someone I thought was a friend. I suppose it was foolish to think a plain woman like me would get such an expensive gift."

"Mimi, you attractive. Many men here love you, but not afford even fake diamond," she said. All three women laughed, Mimi with her characteristic snort.

"I wonder how many of Preston's other claims are bogus?"

"Don't be too upset. I mean, he never actually claimed it was real," Kira commented.

"You know, you're right. I just assumed it was," Mimi replied.

"Perhaps all he can afford. Or maybe he tricked," Nigora added.

"Maybe." Mimi slid the ring back on her finger.

"So tell me more of your country," Nigora said to Marcia.

"You've never been to America?"

"No, but want to."

"Why?"

"Buh."

"It's duh," Marcia replied.

"Huh?"

"You said, 'Buh' but the expression is duh."

"I see. I want go Amelica and see Hollywood, meet Texas cowboy, drive on freeway, and get big breasts. Oh, and go Disneyville."

"World."

"Huh?"

"You said you wanted to go to Disneyville."

"Yes. I want go Disneyville."

"Well, I hope you do," Marcia said, ending the exchange.

# CHAPTER 16

Quint regained consciousness to find himself firmly secured in a rolling office chair. As he struggled to clear his head he heard a raspy voice say, "Can we talk?"

Quint looked up to see a weathered figure in dirty coveralls and heavy work boots stooped over two 55-gallon drums, which lay on their side. The smell of diesel fuel hung in the air.

The man wore a menacing smile, and his row of rotted teeth evidenced that personal hygiene was not his strong suit. A pool of yellowish brown wax had collected at the bottom of one ear, and a few whitish chunks resided in the other. An occasional wisp of white hair sprouted from his head amongst patches of brown-blotched skin framing a face covered in heavy gray stubble. A square jaw with deep lines, more like creases, outlined his jowls. The circular lenses in his green welding goggles gave him a bug-like appearance, as if he were costumed to star in the horror movie, *The Fly*.

"You know, I like to watch movies. Must've watched a million of 'em. One thing that drives me crazy is when they get the upper hand on some guy but don't properly restrain him. You know, like they leave the secret agent guy in a pool of sharks or a sealed, flooding room expecting him to die. But he never does. Nope, always gets away." The man shook his head while igniting an acetylene torch. "Well not me, buddy boy. No siree."

Finished speaking, he began humming as he resumed his work. Sparks flew as he welded the two drums end-to-end, forming a long tube, open at one end. Quint struggled to free his hands but found them tightly bound together with half a roll of duct tape.

"Almost done now, just a little air hole at the far end," the kidnapper cackled as he cut a hole the size of a quarter near the sealed end. "Now we'll add a small door so they can feed you and maybe a pooper chute halfway down." A shower of sparks continued to arc onto the grease-stained concrete floor from his cutting torch and a cloud of smoke enveloped his head. The smell of burning metal filled the room.

Though Quint couldn't make out what he was saying, the weird man continued to mutter. *Doesn't sound like an Uzbek, maybe he's American, or could be Canadian.*

The man cut two six-inch square holes and then added a crude sliding door over each. When finished, he laid down the torch and walked toward Quint waving a black device. "Know what this baby is?"

"I'm going to have to go with a Taser," Quint replied sarcastically.

"Ding, ding, ding, we have a winner. You'rrrrre right. Right as rain. Now, you can cooperate, or I'll demonstrate it for you and then you'll cooperate—trust me. I was curious and tried it. Knocked the shit out of me. So what be your choice?"

Quint stared at the maniac. "I believe I'll go with the no-Taser alternative."

"Wise choice."

"Who are you, and what is it you want?"

"Forgive me; my name is Cary. And unless I am badly mistaken, your name is Quint," he said with a broad smile. Quint noticed one of his left teeth was gleaming silver. "What I want is simply for you to get your ass inside this here tube." He grabbed the back of Quint's chair and rolled him over to the 55-gallon drum enclosure. "There's someone who wants to see you, and I've been paid, handsomely I might add, to arrange the meeting."

The extended drum was sealed at the far end, and a round piece of sheet steel lay beside the open end. He hoisted Quint from the chair and laid him onto a narrow board with wheels. With the Taser held firmly in one hand, he cut Quint's duct tape binding and then slid the board into the tube until Quint's head neared the sealed end. Quint then saw something slide through the freshly cut hole above. "I'd suggest you breathe through this plastic tube as it may get a little foul in there."

A minute later the clang of metal accompanied darkness as Cary placed the round metal plate against the tube's open end. Quint could hear a crackling sound as the metal cylinder was welded shut, filling the tube with more acrid smoke. Taking Cary's suggestion, Quint slid the end of the plastic tube into his mouth and began to breathe. Though he could still taste the smell of burned metal, it was not nearly as strong. When the noise finally stopped, the man spoke again.

"See, now there's no need for me to worry about you getting out of your little steel tube prison to cause problems." He sealed the area between the hole and the plastic with duct tape, placing a final wrap around the breathing tube to hold it in place. "You know they use these containers for all sorts of things, even make musical drums out of them," he said beating on the end with a hammer to make his point. The sound inside the sealed drum was deafening, nearly bursting Quint's eardrums.

"You know what I call this?"

"No, please tell me," Quint replied facetiously, his voice echoing in the metal prison.

"Quint-in-a-can. Get it? Quint-in-a-can. That's funny shit," he chuckled. "Well, I'm off. Wish me luck 'cause if I don't make it back, you're in deep doo doo."

Quint heard footsteps fade and the sound of a heavy door closing followed by silence. *You're right about one thing, Mr. Wacko, I don't think I'll be escaping.*

The sound of a metal door slamming shut awoke Quint. Without enough light to read his watch, he had no idea how long he had been trapped inside the metal tube and wondered if it was still daytime.

"Hey, Quint-in-a-can," Cary said, laughing yet again at his pathetic joke. "Wakie, wakie. You know, I was trying to think of some way to get you where you need to go when it hit me. You're gonna love this—not as much as me, I'm sure, but nevertheless."

The rattling of chains and the sound of a rolling metal door were followed by Cary's approaching footsteps. "Folks pay big bucks to experience this sort of thing, and here you are about to get a free ride." Quint dreaded whatever was about to happen next, confident it would be anything but fun.

He heard Cary grunt and felt his barrel prison begin to move. With the inside diameter larger than his shoulders, Quint was bounced around the inside of the metal tube as Cary rolled the welded drums. "Get set, here we go," Cary said.

Quint tensed, fairly certain he knew what was about to take place as he felt the metal tube roll faster travelling down a steep incline. He grunted as he was thrown about and slammed against the side each time it landed after becoming airborne for an instant. Though probably only a few seconds, it seemed he was bashed inside the barrel for hours before his metal prison finally came to rest with a jarring thud.

"Now see, wasn't that easy? At least for me, that is."

Quint felt like some cartoon character with its eyes spinning like wheels in a slot machine. His body ached all over. "Give me just a minute to get this rope tied on to the shackle I welded on the end of your 'boat' and we'll be ready for your bon voyage."

Quint heard a rasping sound as a rope was fastened to the end of his steel prison, evidently soon to be a boat. He scooted down until his eye was against the crack where Cary had cut the feeding chute and could see the deck of a derelict but apparently operational boat a few yards away.

A minute later, he was rolling once again though slower this time until he came to an abrupt stop with a splash. He could feel himself bobbing in the water when the sick realization hit him that water was pouring through the metal cutouts. He rotated the drum by shifting his weight until he reached a position where the water stopped pouring in.

Finding his breathing tube now underwater, he quickly put his finger over the end of the plastic tube and breathed the foul air inside the barrels. It sounded like Cary was still fumbling with the other end of the line when Quint heard the sound of approaching vehicles.

"Shit!" Cary yelled and Quint heard him running away. A moment later, he heard what sounded like the boat's engine roar to life.

The sound of gunfire was followed by the noise of the boat engine's exhaust fading in the distance. A minute later, he felt the metal drum move and then begin to roll across the ground. The sound of metal scraping against the steel drum announced the opening of the small feeding chute door near his head.

"Hey buddy, whatcha doing?" he heard a familiar voice ask.

"Dawson? Get me out of here right now."

"Hey, don't get your panties in a wad. Can it, nyuk, nyuk."

"Real funny."

"The least you could do is humor your liberators. We're going to haul you back to that building and cut you out. Give us a minute."

"Well, it would be much appreciated if you could do it without another simulated carnival ride." A few minutes later, Quint was breathing through the plastic tube while they cut through the end of the drum. He felt an enormous sense of relief as Dawson pulled him from the tube and he saw Boris and the team standing around him.

"You know, I sort of liked the idea of having you put in your place, so to speak, and considered leaving you in there for a while. But I figured I'd eventually have to let you out, and you'd be all pissy." Dawson laughed. "Care to tell us how you got canned?"

"I really don't know," Quint said, ignoring the now familiar pun. He went on to relate what little he could remember. "When I woke up, I was in this building with Mr. Nut job welding on those barrels. I have no idea what this was all about. How'd you find me?"

"Remember that little GPS transponder you insisted we each have inserted in our arm pit? Have to admit, that was one of your better ideas. Once the dust storm settled to the point Boris felt it was safe to travel, it led us most of the way here. That is until the signal was blocked, I guessing when he canned you. That's why it took us a while to figure out exactly where you were."

"Did you catch Cary?"

"Nope. Apparently, he was about to take you somewhere by boat. When we showed up, he fired a couple of shots at us before hauling ass. If we hadn't gotten here when we did, you'd have been long gone too."

As soon as they returned to the hotel, Quint dialed Rogers on the satphone to discuss the kidnapping episode. "And you have no idea who it was?"

"No, but definitely not a local."

"Think it could have been simply a kidnapping for ransom?"

"I don't think so. Though he was working alone, he struck me as a professional. Claimed someone wanted to meet me and that he was paid to arrange it. But he never elaborated."

"Well, this really isn't much to go on, but I'll pass the information on to our folks. Doubt they'll have much luck."

"I know, but please do what you can." As Quint hung up, he saw Mimi approaching.

"Mind if I borrow the satphone?"

"I'm afraid I do. We're about to get into the thick of it, and I don't want anyone making personal calls. We need to remain focused, and we can't have any inadvertent leaks."

"Quint, be real."

"Mimi, I am. Need I remind you that I was just taken hostage? This is serious business," he replied, mildly surprised at her unusually aggressive attitude.

"Yeah, that's right. I seem to recall someone... oh yeah, it was you saying, 'While we're in Uzbekistan, stick together and no wandering off on our own.' I guess that doesn't apply to you."

Quint sputtered for a moment before replying. "You're right. It was stupid of me, and as you can see, I got my butt in a serious sling. I put the rest of the team at risk as well. But you're still not using the satphone for a personal call."

"Never mind," she said, and walked off in a huff, mumbling something Quint was certain he was lucky not to have heard.

Later that evening, Quint assembled the team. "Look, we have no idea who Cary was or for whom he was working. Suffice to say, it was no random act. We all need to exercise caution, so I don't want anyone going anywhere alone.

"Have a buddy with you at all times, and if you need to go very far, take a weapon. We might not be so lucky a second time, and I can tell you for a fact, you don't want to get 'canned.' Even if you're not claustrophobic, it was no fun."

# CHAPTER 17

By the following morning, the dust storm had passed. Quint was making a cup of coffee when he noticed Kira staring off into space. When he dropped his spoon on the counter she jumped. "Oh...uh... hey, Quint."

"Deep in thought, huh?"

"Baby names," Kira said. "I figured the right one would come to me at some point, but I just keep going round and round."

Quint smiled. "It'll come to you." Colin had come walking up in time to hear their conversation and reached into his pocket to withdraw a folded paper. "I've been making a list. Maybe one of them will at least help you think of something." He handed her the tattered sheet of paper, one side nearly filled with rows of names, some in pen and others in pencil.

Kira studied it for a moment before looking up at him. "Is this a joke?"

"Yeah. A joke. I guess that's what it is." Colin looked down at his shoes as he walked off with slumped shoulders.

Quint could see the regret in her face as Kira called, "Colin," and then went after him. "I'm sorry. I guess I'm crabby over being excluded from the survey operation. I really think—"

Colin interrupted. "We've been through all of that; you're staying here."

"I know; I just hate not being involved. Actually, I'm sort of glad not to be taking another of Boris' painful van rides. Maybe it's the pregnancy, but I'm not sure I could take more pounding on the rough road. As for your names, some are quite good. Others... not so much," she laughed.

Colin put his arm around her. "Just relax and enjoy a brief vacation in your luxury accommodations." Kira wrinkled her nose. "Boris brought us more fuel, and Willy checked the generator so hopefully it will keep running until we return." He hugged her one last time before joining Quint and the rest of the team boarding Boris' dilapidated van before it quickly pulled away.

"I can't quit thinking about that nut job Cary," Leo said, clinging to the headrest of the seat in front of him to fight the violent swaying motion of the van. "I'm not sure he could get my fat ass inside one of those barrels, but I broke out in a cold sweat last night just thinking about it. Unlike you, I *am* claustrophobic."

Quint laughed. "Well, at least out here, he'll have a little harder time of it. But on the island..."

"You need me with you, no?" Boris asked as he manhandled the van over the heavily rutted road.

"No," Quint replied firmly.

"You caught on island, cover story maybe not work so well. But, with illegal tour guide, would be better, no?"

"But then wouldn't you be in trouble?"

"Yes, but they set you free. Money you pay me ease suffering until my release. And you have trouble, I good with gun, no?"

Quint laughed. "Very well, you can come along, but we'll have to discuss the fee."

The van came to a stop with the worn brake pads squealing in protest. "You leave Kira gun?" Boris asked. Quint shook his head. "Maybe good idea, no?"

Dawson stepped onto *Magic* and returned a moment later with a 9mm pistol and an M4A1 carbine. Quint laughed. "You expecting her to fight a war?"

Dawson shook his head. "No, but if she needs to defend herself, we want her to have plenty of firepower."

After Dawson finished showing Nigora how to use the weapons, Boris hugged her goodbye. "You take guns to Kira. Stay with her. Later I call, you bring back van." She clung to him for a bit, but finally let go as he stepped away.

"Be careful," she said, her voice breaking and eyes watery.

"Always, my princess." Boris followed Quint down the rickety dock to their derelict-looking vessel. Deep ruts along the shore marked where sections of the floating dock had been repeatedly dragged back into position as the sea continued its retreat.

"She's sure no *Searcher*, is she?" Dakota mused, referring to their old ship lost during Hurricane Katrina. Quint shook his head and chuckled as he read Dakota's t-shirt of the day: *When all else fails, try doing what the captain suggested.* A bead of sweat slid down Quint's face, and he wiped his cheek with his shirtsleeve before signaling for Willy to start the engine.

While the rest of the team readied the survey gear, Marcia and Quint entered *Magic's* small combination salon and galley, where they shared the rotating fan. She breathed a long sigh as the moving air dried the sweat from her body. "Man, it's hot," she said.

Quint nodded, the sweat pouring down his forehead into his eyes forcing him to wipe his face again with the bottom of his T-shirt. "How you doing, scared?"

"Not really, more apprehensive. I don't want to let the team down."

"Considering you're a newbie, you could pass on going with us." Quint offered her a final chance to avoid their island trek, but his suggestion was met with a withering look.

"I'm willing and able to go. And since I'm the only one who's studied Rogers' drawings on the lab layout, you need me there."

"Just wanted you to know you could opt out now, and no one would think much about it. But once we're on the island—"

"I appreciate that, Quint, but I won't let you down. I hired on for this, and I'm up for it," Marcia replied firmly. Fairly certain of her response but needing to confirm, Quint patted her on the shoulder reassuringly.

Dakota skillfully idled away from the makeshift dock. No one was surprised when a trawler appeared and shadowed them at a distance. When Uzbekistan granted them a permit, it was understood that they would be observed as they conducted their Aral Sea survey.

Quint hoped that their skill in performing basic survey work would enable them to fake the more technical aspects of their oceanographic operations cover. His plan was to establish a routine in hopes of lulling their shadow into a lax state.

They began working a grid, stopping periodically for hydrocasts to sample the water and sea bottom. Drawing on her experience months spent aboard *Searcher,* Mimi oversaw this phase of the operation. She directed the deployment of the side scan sonar "fish" and the water sampling, enjoying the chance to be in charge.

Surprisingly, the engine ran most of the time, albeit with Willy's considerable attention. But twice, they were forced to stop when the boat's single engine ground to a halt, sending Willy scurrying below to find and fix the problem.

"I've conducted a straw poll and rather than endure another punishing round trip ride to our lovely, bug-infested hotel, we'll remain on *Magic* at night and make the best of its Spartan quarters. The men will take the open topsides and leave below decks for the women to share," Quint announced to the team.

By the following day, the team found the work boring and the heat relentless. Despite Boris' attempt to entertain the crew with stories of his various adventures, midway through the second day, most of the crew was ready to commit hara-kiri. Only their nervousness about the activities planned for that night kept them vigilant. As evening approached, Dakota maneuvered *Magic* within dinghy range of the southern tip of Renaissance Island.

Quint waited an hour after sunset to begin their operation. "Okay, Dawson, Marcia, Colin, and Boris will go with me in the inflatable. Mimi, you and the rest of the crew will continue survey operations to maintain our cover. I know it's boring, but we're screwed if our shadow notices any change in our routine and decides to investigate."

Under cover of darkness, Colin and Willy inflated the dinghy and attached the engine before sliding the small vessel over the transom. "Let's load up," Quint said and they began climbing into the dingy. With Boris joining the crew, the dinghy sat even lower in the water than Quint had feared. He prayed that the wind would not pick up, as even small waves would be a problem with so little freeboard.

"Here are the explosives. Remember, the timers are tamper-proof, so once you set them, you can't stop them. All you can do is remove them," Leo said. Quint nodded and pushed the dinghy away.

Quint assumed that their radio transmissions would be monitored and had arranged to communicate in code. Anything requiring more direct discussion was to be handled over the satellite phone. Once they were under way, he raised Dakota on the handheld VHF to confirm that they were clear. "Ready to change survey lanes."

In response, Dakota swung the decrepit fishing boat about. Immediately, Dawson increased throttle and headed their overloaded craft directly toward the island, taking care to keep *Magic* between them and the trawler. By the time they could no longer hide in its shadow, they were far enough away that their tiny radar image was not likely to be noticed.

The warm waters of the Aral Sea were flat as they scooted over its surface toward the distant island shore. With no moon and the stars concealed behind a heavy layer of clouds, the sea surface was a sheet of onyx broken only by their wake. Ripples from the occasional fish broke the placid surface; otherwise, the largely lifeless waters remained still.

"Okay, Leo, drop the hydrocast array," Mimi said once the inflatable was well under way.

"Yeah, right," he replied.

"What do you mean?" Mimi asked curtly.

"Look, Quint and Dawson are gone so you can quit with the whole 'look who's in charge thing.' I'm not wasting my time and energy taking more phony samples for no reason."

"The hell you say." She reached for the plastic pipe filled with rolled up charts and swung it like a baseball bat hitting him firmly on his left shoulder.

"Ow."

"You don't know whether or not they have night vision on our shadow boat. If they do and spot us breaking routine, we'll have trouble. That's not happening on my watch. Now, get up and help me or I'll wear your ass out with this pipe," she said, as she swung it once again, barely missing Leo as he ducked.

"Bitch," he muttered and then darted outside before she could wind up again. A minute later, he was deploying the hydrocast array. Willy, who had just emerged from the engine room in time to witness the exchange, joined Dakota laughing at Leo's being cowed by a woman half his size.

Using his night vision goggles, Quint was able to see the gentle rise of the island as they approached. He noticed Marcia pull her light jacket tight when the outline of the buildings became visible in the distance. No one spoke, their expressionless faces revealing the shared tension.

Dawson slowed the inflatable, and Quint eased over the side as soon as they reached shallow water. Bow line in hand, he towed the boat through the shin-deep water onto the beach, where he paused to get his bearings while the others stepped from the dinghy onto the sand beach.

The dry air sucked the moisture from Quint's jeans as the group formed and headed from the beach toward the distant buildings. They wore normal clothing in the event they ran into the Soviets. They were also prepared to ditch the explosives, weapons, and small amount of equipment they had brought to maintain their cover story as an oceanographic group out on an unauthorized evening lark.

Marcia slipped the small radio from her pack to signal Dakota they had reached the island. "The fish is in the box," she transmitted with a slight tremble in her voice.

With their earbuds and throat mics in place, each of them performed a quick comms check to make sure the small radios mounted on their belts were working.

Dawson then took the lead and after walking only a few steps, stopped and held up his hand for silence.

"You hear that?" he whispered. Quint gave him a puzzled look. "I thought I heard an engine. You didn't?"

"Afraid not. I think your paranoia is causing you to hear things."

"Maybe," Dawson replied, obviously unconvinced.

"Or maybe it's a ghost, yes?" Boris said with a nervous chuckle.

Having studied the briefing reports and photos of Renaissance Island these past few weeks, the team thought they were ready for what they would see. They were not. No amount of preparation could temper the reality of being in the single most revolting place on the planet. Even the hardened Boris seemed subdued.

The creak of a swing's rusted chains moving gently in the hot night air added to the creepy feeling. Quint saw Marcia hesitate as they passed a stuffed toy lying beside the abandoned playground near the living quarters.

Quint glanced at his GPS for the hundredth time since setting foot on the island, confirming they were still headed toward the target building's coordinates. Like the others, he was anxious to finish and leave behind the chemical and biological death that lay in this godforsaken place.

He glanced back to confirm that Marcia was closely monitoring the handheld "sniffer" that would alert them of any serious bio-agent concentrations. He wondered how many showers it would take to feel clean again.

Quint spotted a corroded monkey cage. "Hawker claimed that at night, the scientists would place these cages on the downwind side of the labs and then explode bomblets of the germ du jour to study dispersal patterns." His own breathing shallowed as he envisioned a cloud of biological filth drifting down upon the unsuspecting monkeys.

As they worked their way toward the lab hugging the shadows, Colin and Boris searched for signs of recent visitors while Dawson scanned the empty buildings with his night vision goggles for any threats. Several times, they nudged one another, pointing to a footprint or scuff mark in the dirt. Though uncertain whether they were from Rogers' man, Dean, or some other group, the marks were recent, and the group grew more cautious. After minutes that seemed like hours, they reached the lab building where the bioweapons cache was allegedly located.

"Okay, Marcia, it's your show now," Quint whispered.

Marcia nodded, reaching into her bag for a gas mask, with the others following suit. Marcia handed the bio-agent monitor off to Colin and took the lead as they entered the building.

Quint hoped Marcia's hours spent studying the directions provided by Dean before his death and memorizing the laminated diagram she now carried in her hand were about to pay off. Backtracking only once, she smoothly guided the group down two flights of stairs to the cavernous warehouse basement, where an expanse of grey concrete stretched endlessly in front of them.

Halfway down the main corridor, they turned the corner toward the secure room and froze at the sight of a body lying just ahead. With the team following cautiously, Dawson took the lead and crept forward, his M4A1 carbine at the ready.

Marcia turned away, obviously struggling to steady her queasy stomach as they approached the bloated form lying face up on the floor. A crusty layer of blood covered the lower portion of the discolored face. A trail of black marks from the man's boots led to the room beyond, where Quint assumed the bio-agent cache was stored.

"I believe we've found Dean's guide," Dawson's whispered. "Based on the fresh footprints and the fact he's recently been moved, it would appear we're not the first ones here since his death."

"And it looks like whoever moved the guide's body is planning to return." Quint pointed at the full pallets alongside a couple of empty ones. *This can't be good.* Proceeding cautiously onward, he motioned for Colin and Marcia to watch their back as they approached the cache door, closed but for a slight crack.

As Dawson eased it open, they heard a slight scrape followed by a thump from something hitting on the far side of the room. This was followed by the sound of breaking glass and then a barely audible grunt, which made it clear someone was in the room. Dawson motioned for Quint to break left as he slung the door open and holding his flashlight in front, broke to the right. Colin and Marcia followed closely behind, guns raised.

"Uh... Marcia, I don't think you need to see this," Dawson said—too late.

"Oh no! Oh no!" Marcia repeated, stepping back outside before lifting her mask and vomiting.

In the middle of the room, the twitching body of a man was tied to the end of a shelving unit, his head taped firmly in position. A slender rope was looped around a pipe on the ceiling with a bag of sand tied to the end.

"It appears that while we were focused on opening the door, we failed to notice the end of that rope, which must have been wedged between the door and the door frame to hold the bag in position. When we opened the door, the bag of sand was free to swing and strike him in the face. Whoever left him here must have taped one of those glass vials in his mouth and the impact shattered it."

The man was writhing in pain, blood pouring from his nose and oozing from his mouth through a hole in the tape. Quint realized the man's few remaining minutes in this world would be spent in agony, but before he could react, Dawson raised his silenced carbine, flicked off the safety, and squeezed off a single round. The team remained still for a minute struggling to regain their composure after witnessing the grisly scene.

"Someone not like him, no?" Boris said.

Marcia re-entered the room, carefully avoiding both the dead man taped to the shelving unit and the pile of boxes into which Dean's guide had fallen. "I don't know how much of this stuff is missing, but it's appears that it may be a lot," she commented. The empty shelves before them were marked with square patches where it appeared that boxes had, up until recently, kept the dust from accumulating.

Quint nodded. "Marcia, get a sample of each different type of vial stored here. Dean's notes indicated he was somewhat hurried when he made his attempt. The recent visitors make it doubly important we know what's here and what they might have taken."

He then turned to Colin and Boris. "According to Dean, those barrels outside the door are filled with diesel fuel. Stack a pile just inside the room while Dawson arms the demolition explosives."

After donning a second set of rubber gloves, Quint searched the dead man still taped to the shelving but, as expected, found nothing. He was helping Dawson rig the remaining charges on the shelving units when he noticed Marcia hurriedly leave the room as soon as her task was completed.

By the time the charges were armed and in place, Boris and Colin had amassed a sizeable pile of barrels in the cache room. Though confident the primary timers would do their job, Quint double-checked the remote detonator to make certain it was operating.

He then rigged a second set of charges on the pile of fuel barrels as Dawson tipped two over, and using his Kabar knife, jabbed a hole in the side of each to allow diesel fuel to flood the cache room.

"We done here?" Seeing nods from everyone, Quint continued. "I'm setting the timers for one hour. We can detonate them early with the remote if we need to." After starting the timers, he motioned for the team to leave.

Once they cleared the building, each of them tore off their masks and gulped in the hot night air. Quint found it surprisingly refreshing to be freed of the mask after wearing it for the past hour in the cesspool beneath the building. With the adrenalin rush fading and their legs shaky, several of the team took a seat on the building's steps while struggling to catch their breath. "Marcia, raise Dakota on the radio to report that we're finished and will be heading back shortly."

"Who do you think beat us here?" Colin asked.

"Don't know, but they obviously didn't care much about keeping it a secret. I wonder how long that poor sonofabitch had been down there?" Quint asked.

"Not long. The tape on his mouth was fresh, and from the way he was struggling, his muscles hadn't had time to cramp up yet," Dawson replied.

"I couldn't have done it, but putting that guy out of his misery was the right thing to do. I wonder how long before he'd have died if we hadn't come along?" Marcia asked.

Quint saw Dawson shrug and then change the subject. "You think it was the Russians or some other group?"

"I'm guessing some other group, maybe even connected to my buddy Cary. Why would the Russians leave that poor guy tied up like that?" Quint asked.

"A better question, is, are they still around and if so, when are they coming back?" Colin said.

Before anyone could answer, the distant sound of engines approaching broke the nighttime quiet. "Uh-oh, I think they just answered your question. I'm guessing they're returning for another load. Spread out," Quint yelled. With the broad expanse of the lab building stretching out too far to make it to the end before the vehicles arrived, they all donned their gas masks and ducked back inside.

# CHAPTER 18

"Dawson, take the stairs and assume an overwatch position on the second floor. Colin, you watch our backs. Everyone else, take up positions in rooms on either side of the front entrance." Quint hunkered down with the others beneath the windows with only his head exposed watching the approaching vehicles.

Two 4-wheelers, each pulling a sizeable trailer, had closed to within 100 yards when they abruptly stopped, and Quint could hear men's voices. As if on cue, the two vehicles separated in a flanking move, stopping behind cover in front of the lab building. After the passenger had dismounted from each vehicle, the drivers went roaring off. Immediately, the men in front began firing at the building.

"Dammit, they must have thermal imaging, and they've spotted us," Dawson yelled, as he came back down the stairs to help develop a plan.

"What are they doing?" Marcia asked.

"My guess is those guys will try to keep us pinned while the others go for reinforcements." Colin joined the team gathered in the hallway, ignoring the incoming fire harmlessly striking the building.

"What about ducking out the back?" Marcia asked.

"With their night vision, they'll see us as soon as we clear the end of the building," Quint replied

"Well, we best come up with a solution quickly; the timers are running," Colin said.

"Good point. Well, we're not removing the detonators, and things aren't going to get any easier when they get back with reinforcements. So I say we fight our way out now and use the remotes to blow the building once we're clear. Hopefully, that will take away their reason to continue fighting."

The team remained silent until Dawson spoke up, "I agree." In unison, they headed for the back, except for Boris. "I stay, return fire. I follow when clear."

"No way, you're coming with—"

"No!" Boris interrupted Quint. "I stay. They get no more filth to ruin other people life. Go!" Boris made it clear his position was non-negotiable.

"Thanks," Quint said, as the team headed for the rear exit. While Boris held of the attackers, the team made it out one at a time, leap frogging while providing cover for each other.

The exchange of fire continued fiercely. Boris changed positions, firing from a different window each time while noting the positions of the gun flashes. Popping up in the next room, he took careful aim, and as soon as the man to his left fired, he pulled the trigger. By the time he heard the scream of his bullets hitting their mark, he was in the next room, where he repeated the process. Once again he took careful aim and squeezed off another shot directly at the flash and heard the second man scream in pain.

"I get both," Boris radioed.

"Okay, now come on," Quint replied.

Boris leapt to his feet and burst through the front door, bounding down the stairs headed toward the end of the building. He was nearly halfway there, completely exposed, when the sound of more 4-wheeler engines signaled that reinforcements were on the way. He hesitated as he considered reversing direction and then glanced up at the windows. Seeing that they were too high, he continued on toward the team.

It looked like he was going to make it when gunfire erupted, and 20 feet from the end of the building he went down. Immediately, automatic weapons fire raked the building corner where the team had gathered, while one of the 4-wheelers headed for the back of the building.

"They're going to try to flank us again. We've got to run for it," Quint screamed.

"And leave Boris? No way," Marcia yelled back, a sick look on her face.

"We can't help him now; if we stay we all die," Quint replied. "We'll take up a position over there," Quint pointed at the next building, "and blow the charges with the remote. Then we'll take a defensive position. After we kick their ass or they leave, we'll go back for Boris."

Dawson nodded and grabbed Marcia's arm, pulling her with him as he ran to the next building and hunkered down behind a low wall. Quint reached into his pack, removed the remote, and triggered it without hesitation. A muffled thud resounded from inside the building.

"That was unimpressive," Marcia said.

"The charges we set on the bioweapons were just large enough to shatter most of the vials, not vaporize the liquids. The thermite charges we placed on the fuel drums are not designed to create a massive explosion but rather a ferocious fire to destroy the bioweapons without releasing them into the atmosphere." Thick black smoke began rolling out of the windows and the gunfire quickly tapered off.

"Look, he's still alive!" Marcia yelled,.

Quint could see Boris crawling back toward the front entrance and out of view.

"Boris, this way. We're over here," she yelled, but he was either unable to hear her or too badly hurt to think clearly.

A moment later, they heard the 4-wheelers circle back to the front of the building out of sight. "We have to do something," Marcia pleaded.

"There's nothing we can do," Dawson said in a low voice. "If we try to go back, they'll mow us down out in the open. I'm guessing they're about to confirm what we did with the explosives, after which they'll leave, hopefully without killing Boris."

A few minutes later, they heard the sound of the 4-wheelers fading in the distance. The four jumped to their feet and headed back to the lab building at a run. As they rounded the corner they saw—no Boris. Quint yelled his name, but they could see the 4-wheeler tracks beside a bloody spot on the ground. It was clear the men on the 4-wheelers had taken him.

"Well, at least they didn't kill him," Marcia said, but no one replied.

"Okay, we'll do a quick check to make sure he's not still inside, and then we've got to leave," Quint said. The team donned their gas masks before entering the building, now filling with smoke from the raging fire below. They searched for Boris, calling out repeatedly. But with no response and no sign of blood, it was clear he was not there.

"Okay, let's get out of here before this thing explodes and comes crashing down on us," Dawson said, disgust in his voice.

"Since we're on an island, they've either got a boat or a plane waiting. Perhaps we can—" Quint stopped at the sound of engines starting. A minute later, he heard the roar of a plane lifting off from the airbase just to the north. Once it was airborne, it changed course flying directly toward the team still gathered on the building's steps.

"Uh-oh, looks like they're headed back for round two. Time to go, folks," Quint said, springing to his feet. With the other three team members close behind, he sprinted toward the gap between the lab and the next building and then turned at the end, as a string of tracers from a mini-gun firing from the plane's side door walked the path behind them.

The plane swept past them, but Quint knew it would return in seconds. He spotted a heavy truck and changed direction toward it. The team dove beneath it just as the plane reappeared over the building beside them to make a second pass. The gunner unleashed another volley at the numerous vehicles scattered about and any piles of debris large enough to conceal the team.

Hardly daring to breathe, the team remained motionless beneath the truck, where they lay shielded by its heavy chassis while listening to the clank of bullets striking metal. The plane made another pass, and they heard a thud as something hit the ground a few feet away.

"Bomb!" Dawson shouted, but after a minute, nothing had happened. "Must have been a dud," he said, as they crawled out from cover with the plane headed away.

"Oh my God!" Marcia screamed, running toward a form lying on the ground 50 yards away. "They dropped him from the plane." On the ground lay the broken body of Boris.

She stopped short when it was obvious he was dead. "He was probably still alive when they dropped him. Those bastards," Marcia said in a low voice between sobs.

"Dammit! He was a good man," Quint said, sick over the pointless killing.

A few seconds later they heard the roar of the mini-gun again, after which the sound of the plane quickly faded into night.

"Uh-oh," Dawson commented.

"What?" Marcia queried.

"I can think of only one inviting target for them to be firing at," he replied. No one spoke as they ran toward the beach. As they neared the boat, their fears were confirmed. Assuming the inflatable would be safe for the short time they planned to be away, they had left it uncovered. Now its flattened tubes were riddled with holes.

"This is nice," Quint commented.

With the island well behind them, Arnold lifted the handheld satphone and speed-dialed Syndy. "We got it," he said, once she was on the line.

"Excellent! Tell me about it," Syndy said in her Darth Vadar mechanical voice.

"The plane we had to use was smaller than I would have preferred and would accommodate only two 4-wheelers with trailers. That forced us to make several trips. We left the vehicles behind to make room, and got more of the 'good stuff' than you had expected."

"Problems?"

"Nothing serious. I caught Lawrence trying to steal a few vials. I suppose he had grand plans of going into business for himself."

"I trust you took care of him."

"Yes, I arranged a little welcome for whomever might come next. At the same time, I made it clear to the rest of the team how we handle such problems." He described how they had left the man tied to the shelving unit with a vial of bio-agents in his mouth.

"Splendid! Simple yet no doubt effective! That type of initiative is worthy of a bonus! I guess if no one finds him anytime soon, he'll have ample time to rue the error of his ways."

"As it turns out, he didn't have to wait long; that's the other thing I have to tell you. Though we had already recovered more bioweapons than you wanted, I intended to make one more trip when we ran into some opposition. We spotted a five-man team near the building and engaged them in a fire fight. They hit two of my men and then triggered an explosive charge in the bioweapons cache. I decided it was best to retreat with what we had already taken."

"Hmm. Quint's team?"

"Probably. Had we known their schedule, we could have been prepared to capture them. But under the circumstances, I chose to focus on getting the bioweapons."

"Good choice. I wish I could have gotten you another update from our mole. He knew they planned to go soon, but it was frustrating that he wasn't able to establish contact again to confirm a more exact time."

"That it was. I would have set an ambush. We captured a poor Uzbek all shot to hell, but he was too far gone to talk. After we took off, we made a pass over them and dropped him off, hoping to draw them out, but they were too cautious to fall for it. We had the video recorder running so we may get something off of that. In any case, they won't be going anywhere soon. We destroyed their inflatable boat."

"If your video footage proves it's Quint's team, what are the chances of going back to capture them?"

"Not good. Once the smoke from that explosion is noticed, the authorities will be crawling all over the place."

Syndy was furious but elected not to let Arnold know, at least not for the time being. "Where are the vials?"

"We're on our way to the warehouse in Uzbekistan where we'll consolidate them into a single shipping container."

"Excellent. You'll then be heading for Russia where you'll join up with three other container loads of cargo. They'll provide more muscle, should it be needed to get the goods to Murmansk, Russia, where we'll be awaiting the delivery."

"Why Murmansk? It's shorter and easier to go through eastern Europe," Arnold protested.

"True, but the chances of having the shipment intercepted would also be much higher; we're not shipping a container filled with melons. The direct approach would require crossing the borders of several countries with sophisticated bioweapons-detection capabilities. By going through Russia, a few bribes here and there, and we'll be home free. Worst case, if we're caught by the authorities, my Russian contact would probably help us transport the shipment for a sizable additional fee."

"Very well, we'll proceed as you wish."

"You need to hurry. The first Arctic cold front of the season is forecast to arrive shortly, and you need to beat it to Murmansk."

"What the hell do we do now?" Colin asked, as he surveyed their ruined boat.

"Good question," Quint replied. "No way Dakota can get in close enough to pick us up without a lengthy swim in those putrid waters. And even if he tried, our shadow boat would be on us in no time."

"What do you guys think about retiring on beautiful Renaissance Island?" Dawson joked, trying to lighten the mood.

"Not much, especially after the authorities get wind of those charges we set off," Marcia replied.

"Speaking of wind," Quint said, "if it picks up and blows that smoke our way, we'll have even bigger problems."

"Hmm," Dawson muttered, as he walked away from the group toward the pier, which stood some distance up the beach. The team watched in silence as he stopped and kicked something.

Quint smiled when he heard a deep metallic thud.
His eyes shot back to the ruined dinghy, and he jogged
over to inspect the small motor. Miraculously it
appeared unscathed. Even its built-in fuel tank was
intact.

"Give Dawson a hand digging; I think he just found
us a ride," Quint said, as he loosened the motor clamps
from the dinghy transom. By the time Quint had the
engine off, the rest of the team had unburied an
ancient aluminum skiff and dragged it to the water's
edge where Marcia continued to scoop out sand.

"While I get this engine mounted, you guys go get
Boris. We can't leave his body behind," Quint said,
while lifting the motor into position on the skiff's
warped transom. He had just finished tightening the
clamps when he saw the two men returning with the
body.

"Don't mean to be a nag, but could you hurry? I'd
really prefer to be far away from here should that wind
shift direction," Quint said. They carefully laid Boris'
body in the skiff and then pushed it into the water
before hopping in. The engine fired up immediately,
but after running for only a few seconds, coughed and
died. The silence was deafening. They all were
painfully aware of the consequences if they were
unable to keep it running.

"Probably just air in the fuel line," Quint
announced, as his hand found the starter cord and
gave it another hard pull—nothing. He took a deep
breath and pulled four more times. He was close to
giving up when, on the next try, the engine coughed
once but caught and continued to purr.

The bow of the boat swung around as Quint
throttled up the small engine, and they eased slowly
away from shore. The angle of the warped transom
forced the motor to sit at a rakish angle, preventing it
from getting a good bite in the water. Quint managed
to force it down far enough to keep them moving.

The gentle breeze had stiffened, giving birth to a light chop which, under normal circumstances, would not have been noteworthy. But the badly overloaded boat had only a couple of inches of freeboard, and as Quint increased their speed, the larger wavelets began breaking over the sides of the skiff.

Dawson removed the gas mask from his pack and bailed the skiff, with the rest of the team quickly following suit. However, Quint was forced to back off on the throttle when it became obvious that their efforts were not keeping pace with the rising water.

"Marcia, raise Dakota," Quint said. She nodded and withdrew the sat-phone to call the ship quickly relating their situation.

"We're headed back, but we've had problems and are moving slow. We need you to close the distance so we can get back aboard before this piece of crap boat sinks."

"We've been on our current survey line headed away from the island long enough that our change in direction isn't likely to raise the attention of the boys on our shadow trawler. We'll be headed your way in a jiffy." Dakota brought *Magic's* bow around and pushed the throttles forward. With the smoking engine groaning in protest, he set course for the island. A few minutes later, he approached the team in the barely floating skiff.

Dawson swung alongside and caught a rope from Willy as the team scampered aboard the old fishing boat. Quint pushed down on one stern corner of the skiff with his foot and it began to flood as Willy released the line. The sinking skiff quickly faded behind them, its engine still running as it disappeared beneath the surface of the dark waters.

Dakota continued toward the island for long enough that it would not appear suspicious when he turned back away. Meanwhile, the team jettisoned all evidence of their shore excursion while Marcia set about hiding the sample vials they had collected for analysis. After removing the front of a piece of electronics gear, she taped the vials inside and then carefully replaced the face plate.

Dakota finally changed direction to steam away from the island with their shadow boat following suit. Quint was pacing back and forth across the stern of the boat, watching the island fall behind. He prayed the flames would not light the night sky enough to be noticed when the engine died.

Willy sprinted for the engine compartment with Quint close behind. "Make sure we haven't left anything suspicious lying around in case our shadow decides to check us out."

As he ducked below decks, he saw the beam from Willy's flashlight stop on a metal line where a small geyser of liquid was erupting. "We blew a fuel line."

"We have a spare?" Quint fired back.

"Not hardly. But we do have duct tape," Willy replied as he began digging through a cardboard box on the floor of the engine room. With a broad smile, he withdrew a large gray roll. Quint held the flashlight as Willy began to wrap the broken fuel line.

"Uh... Quint, we got company headed our way," Dawson yelled from above.

"How far off are they?"

"Not far, maybe five minutes."

"We ready for them?"

"As ready as we can be." Dawson voice lacked confidence.

"Shit. Okay, start a hydrocast. Make it look like we stopped to get water samples and maybe we can get the engine running before they decide to try and board us," Quint replied.

Willy continued to wrap the leaking fuel line, eventually slowing the flow to a mere drip. "Ready to fire the engine back up?" Quint asked.

"I'll have to bleed the air from the fuel system first."

"How long will that take?"

"As long as it takes, I'm afraid. Shouldn't be more than a couple of minutes... I hope."

"You need me?" Quint asked as he heard an approaching boat and the sound of voices.

"No, I got it. You can go entertain our guests," Willy said, as he cracked the first injector.

When Quint emerged from the engine room, the shadow boat had just pulled alongside, and a man dressed in an official-looking uniform was stepping aboard. "We noticed that you were dead in the water. May we be of assistance?" the man asked, in English with a thick accent.

Quint wiped the diesel fuel from his hands on a greasy rag and then extended his right arm. "Thanks, but it was just a fuel leak. We have it repaired and are bleeding the system."

The man took Quint's hand but as he shook it, his eyes cut back and forth checking out their equipment. Mimi and Leo had just hoisted the hydrocast array aboard and were removing water samples. Neither one looked up, focusing on the task at hand.

The man moved toward the salon and studied the survey gear. "I understand you are here to map the pollutant concentrations. Going well?"

"So far, engine problems aside. Just boring work, I'm afraid." Quint gestured at the hydrocast equipment while eyeing the island to see if there was any visible sign of the fire. "Mostly repetitive work."

The man nodded and then pointed at the paper chart recorder. "I didn't know anyone still used those."

Quint stiffened as he spotted a pistol lying on the opposite side of the salon. He cut his eyes toward Dawson and then back to the gun before turning back to the man. "Not many do, but it's hard to get funding for new equipment these days." When he glanced back, he saw that Dawson had edged over far enough to block the man's view of the weapon.

The uniformed man nodded and was about to speak when the sound of the diesel engine starting erupted from below. "It would appear that your problem is solved. Please continue with your work," he said, and stepped back aboard his own vessel. A few minutes later, the shadow boat had dropped back into position, and *Magic* was once again under way.

Quint heard Mimi sigh. "Nervous?" he asked.

"Oh, yeah. We dropped the hydrocast array so quickly I forgot to arm the water samplers. Luckily, he didn't appear to notice."

"Maybe not, but he sure seemed suspicious. The sooner we're out of here, the better."

By sunrise, they were far enough away that even the smoke was not visible, lost in the heavy overcast sky far behind them. Quint joined Dakota in the tiny wheelhouse. "Run a few more survey lines to maintain our cover. Then radio our shadow to declare our 'survey mission' complete and head for the dock. We want to be long gone should our handiwork at the lab be discovered sooner than we hoped." Quint then made his way down to the salon.

"Marcia, call Kira. Have her schedule Rogers' chartered plane to pick us up in three hours. Then ask her to have Nigora bring the van to meet us in an hour. Don't mention Boris. That's a conversation we need to have face-to-face." Quint dreaded telling Nigora about her father.

"You don't think the Uzbeks will link our sudden departure by plane to the island fire?" Leo asked.

"They might, but provided we're long gone, I don't give a shit," Quint replied, noticing that their shadow boat had changed course and was steaming away.

Having served its purpose, all the unneeded equipment and weapons were jettisoned by the time the team reached shore, where Nigora sat waiting in the van. "You have success, no?" she asked.

"Yes, thanks to your father," Quint replied.

"Where is he?"

Before Quint could answer, Marcia took the woman's hand and led her away from the others. Though he was unable to hear what was said, Nigora's sobbing made it clear Marcia had given her the bad news. The team waited beside the van until Nigora finally relinquished her hold on Marcia's neck and walked back toward them. "Where is body?"

"Nigora, I don't think that's a good—"

"I must see," Nigora interrupted Quint. He shat a glance at Marcia after after seeing her nod, reluctantly led Nigora back to the boat, where a piece of canvas covered Boris' lifeless body. She kneeled and pulled back the cover. A single tear ran down her face falling on her dead father's broken body. Tenderly, she stroked his head, smoothing his hair. She muttered something in Uzbek that Quint couldn't understand.

Quint waited patiently until Nigora finally replaced the canvas and stood without speaking. By the time they returned to the van, Nigora had composed herself. "Thank you for bring back my father to bury," she said to Quint. They stood in silence for a moment while Nigora seemed to be about to speak again.

"I go with you," she said firmly.

"Nigora, you belong here with your family," Quint replied.

"Not true. With father dead, he want me to go. His sister and brother take care of babushka. You owe me. He die helping you."

Quint motioned to Dawson, and the two men walked a few feet away. "What do you think?"

"I don't like it, but she's right. Boris did die helping us, and what's she going to do here with no father? Maybe we can't help everyone in this shit hole, but at least we can help the daughter of the man who died helping us."

"And how the hell do we do that?" Quint asked.

"Call Rogers. Make it his problem," Dawson replied.

Quint nodded and walked back over to Nigora. "You win; we'll take you with us. You got a passport?"

"Yes, Father insist we keep papers. I get when I pack. Ready in only ten minutes. You will see. I not be problem. I smart. I work hard. It is good decision you make."

"What about your father?" Dawson asked.

"We take body to house. My family handle."

"But don't you want to stay for his funeral?" Dawson asked.

"Yes, but not possible, no?" They loaded up in the van with Colin taking the driver's seat, and headed to Nigora's house.

"Do we have time for dinner?" Leo asked, seemingly oblivious to the unfolding drama surrounding him.

In an attempt to lighten the mood, Dawson replied without thinking. "Yeah, we could stop at your favorite place. It's right on the way."

"Wait a minute, how the hell do you know where it is?" Leo asked.

"I... uh... Boris told me."

"You're lying. You set me up, didn't you?"

"Would I do that?"

"You're damned right you would. Okay, Dawson, it's on," Leo threatened, and then became silent. Quint imagined he was busy devising a plan for his revenge.

When Colin pulled the van up to Nigora's house, Willy and Dawson carried Boris' body inside where they placed it on the sofa. The team gathered around Nigora in silence for a minute before Quint spoke.

"He was a good man. Boris, you made the most generous sacrifice a man can make helping others. Because of that, your daughter is now left without a father. We can't change that, but I vow to look after her so you may rest in peace."

Tears streamed down Nigora's face as she quietly turned to go pack her things. A few minutes later, they loaded back into the van with Colin behind the wheel once again.

"Okay, let's get going. Drive it like you stole it," Leo joked.

"But we no steal van," Nigora said.

"It's an expression... oh, never mind," Leo said, his attempt at humor having fallen flat.

Nigora looked up as they passed the bus station. "We not take bus back?"

"No. We arrived by bus to maintain our cover. But it's important to leave quickly, so we arranged for a charter flight out," he explained, as Colin drove them to the section of road chosen for their landing strip. Half an hour later, a small plane appeared and after circling once, landed and taxied up to the van. The team quickly loaded up, anxious to make a hasty exit. As they taxied, Nigora called to let her family know where she had left the van and her father's body.

Only when Quint heard the comforting sound of the wheels folding into the plane's fuselage did he finally relax. As they banked after takeoff, he spotted a thin column of smoke in the distance before the low clouds absorbed it. He hoped they were the only ones to make that observation.

# CHAPTER 19

The hum of Syndy's electric wheelchair announced her arrival into Hester's stateroom. The plush furnishings in her master suite stood in stark contrast to Hester's Spartan accommodations. Given the ongoing mess of spills associated with his blindness, and dealing with the bodily fluids of a paraplegic, plush carpeting and surroundings were impractical.

"What a pleasant surprise. How are things going, love?" Hester asked.

"It worked! They have the vials," Syndy replied. "We make a good team." She quickly glanced around the room to confirm they were alone before reaching out with the stub of her left arm to touch his right leg. The sign of affection, normally reserved for her pet cat, was lost on Hester, whose paralysis and blindness prevented him from noticing the gesture.

"So are you saving the best news for last—did they capture Quint? After that debacle with Cary, I was hoping."

"For the last few days, our mole was unable to contact them, so he couldn't feed us updates on their position and schedule. When Quint's team popped up while Arnold's team was busy retrieving the bioweapons, he was unprepared."

"And?" Hester asked.

"And they ended up in a shootout, during which Quint's team blew the remaining bioweapons stash."

"But I thought you said—"

"Arnold had already recovered more than we expected, so he chose not to risk being captured or losing the contraband. Plus at the time, Arnold wasn't positive that it was Quint's team, though he knew they were planning an incursion soon. After examining the video Arnold shot from the plane, we confirmed it was Quint and Dawson."

"Damn!" Hester said. "So close to realizing our dream."

"Yes, I wanted to kill him... to kill him... to kill him... to... " her voice broke as she sobbed.

Hester remained silent until Syndy regained her composure before continuing. "Capturing them alive is as important as the money we'll make off the bioweapon sales."

"I agree," she replied in a much lower voice, "but it just wasn't to be. Arnold acted wisely; we could have lost the bioweapons and still not captured them. At least Quint's little band of do-gooders didn't screw up our operation this time."

She sat thinking of how Quint's team had taken away her beauty, her health, and placed her in a wheelchair. "Perhaps we can lure them into another trap."

"How so?"

"I'm certain they'll try to recover the bioweapons we stole; we have an effective bait. I will instruct Arnold to leak their storage location, in hopes of flushing out Quint and his team. Maybe this time, our mole will have better luck discerning their plans." Tired from the emotional stress, she patted his leg one more time and then retired to her stateroom for a nap.

Syndy enjoyed their floating base of operations, the power that Hester's wealth afforded, and even the closeness that had developed between them. But having learned not to completely trust anyone, she would keep an eye on him. Though the time might come when she would have to deal with Hester, until then, she would enjoy their partnership.

The vibration of his silenced phone caught Quint's attention. A quick glance at the caller ID showed it was Rogers, and he took the call.

"How'd things go?"

"Good news, bad news. We found and destroyed the bioweapons cache."

"Great!" Rogers replied. "I appreciate the risk your folks took to accomplish that. Please pass on my thanks to the rest of your team."

"No problem. That's why you pay us the big bucks," Quint chuckled. "The bad news is we destroyed only part of the cache. Someone beat us to the island," Quint said. He had dreaded this phone call. Not because he felt any sense of guilt; they had done their job. But the thought of that deadly material in the wrong hands sickened him. "It appears they had already stolen a load before we arrived."

"Mmm, not good. Any idea who it might have been?"

"Not really. I doubt it was that nut job, Cary," Quint said. "Let me know what you find out and if we can help chase down the remaining bioweapons. The other bad news is they killed Boris."

"That's a shame; he seemed like a good man."

"He was. We brought his daughter, Nigora, out of the country, and I need your help getting her into the U.S. legally."

"Have you lost your mind?"

"Boris was killed doing your dirty work," Quint replied bluntly. "We owed it to him."

"I appreciate your compassion, but—"

"Don't give me that shit. No buts. Just help us. We owe her... and Boris."

"I'll see what I can do." Rogers abruptly broke the connection.

Quint smelled bacon as soon as he entered the gymnasium-sized cafeteria in time for breakfast. He loaded his plate and joined the rest of the team at a long folding table in the far corner of the dining hall. They had just arrived at the military base in England where Rogers had arranged for them to stay after departing Uzbekistan.

Quint had finished seconds and refilled his coffee cup when his phone rang. It was Rogers again.

"Okay, I pulled some strings and greased the skids to get Nigora into the country." Rogers seemed more calm than he had during their previous conversation.

"Thanks," Quint said. "I know it was tough, but under the circumstances, it was the right thing to do. Any luck on tracking down the stolen bioweapons?"

"Yeah, as a matter of fact, we located them. An anonymous informant gave us the location. It was easier than I expected—almost too easy. Makes me a little suspicious."

"Like maybe they wanted us to know?"

"Exactly."

"Where are the weapons?"

"In a warehouse, still inside Uzbekistan."

"We can be ready in a few hours. I'll mobilize the team."

"Uh... thanks, Quint, but while I appreciate your dedication, we don't need you for this. We were able to get a beacon in place to track the shipment, and we have a team ready to stage an interdiction. Since this involves a simple snatch and grab and not blowing things up, the President is comfortable with using an undercover special ops team for this phase. That is, provided we snatch it before it gets into Russian territory."

"Since we were involved on the front end, I think we should at least provide backup to your team."

"I appreciate the offer, but as I said, we've got this covered. Don't get me wrong, we're very appreciative for what your team accomplished, but this really is a job for a professional commando team."

"Fine, we'll sit this one out and let your *professional commando team* handle it." Quint made it clear he resented not being allowed to finish the job they had started.

"Our team is scheduled to depart shortly. Botz is leading it."

"Botz? The same sonofabitch that set us up twice? I thought you said you had a *professional* team."

"I know you guys don't see eye to eye, but—"

"Don't see eye to eye? That lunatic nearly got us killed."

"Let's not go there again. I know his plan to use you as bait backfired, but he does know his stuff."

"That's open to debate," Quint fired back.

"Look, if not for your team we wouldn't even know about the missing bioweapons, so I called as a courtesy to let you know the plan. But Botz will be leading the clean-up."

"Whatever. Keep in touch." Quint hung up and tossed a crumpled napkin on the remains of his breakfast. Struggling to contain his outrage, he looked over at Dawson. "It appears that with Botz and his team now in the mix, our mission is complete."

Dawson shook his head. "Well, I guess this means we get a break. I know I could use one." The rest of the team voiced their agreement.

# CHAPTER 20

"It appears that Quint's team is being cut out of the mission to reclaim the bioweapons we stole," Syndy said, when she rejoined Hester the next day.

"Excellent!" Hester replied.

"Not really. It appears that they plan to use a professional commando team instead."

"Oh. That sounds like trouble."

"Yes it could be. Parvez, the broker who's acting as a fence to sell our bioweapons haul, has many contacts who could prove useful. I will call him and see what he can arrange." Syndy returned to her suite to make the call.

"You have the... material?" Parvez asked when he heard Syndy's voice.

"Yes, but not in our hands quite yet. I am, however, calling with regard to a new development on that front." She quickly explained the problem.

"Let me check with my sources and see what I can do," Parvez said.

A short time later, Syndy's phone rang. It was Parvez. "As you suspected, your friend Quint is not involved in the bioweapons recovery attempt, but we have identified the military group assigned the task."

"Great, now how do we deal with them?" Syndy asked.

"One of my contacts, a man by the name of Rashid, has a network of fanatical followers, some of whom have been positioned as sleepers for many years. He can arrange to take care of your commando team problem using one of them, but it will not be cheap."

"We will pay whatever it takes."

"He does not want money. He is one of the prospective buyers for your bioweapons, and now wishes to take his share in lieu of payment for dealing with your problem. He also has Russian mafia connections and can arrange to hire as many Russian soldiers as are needed to help defend your shipment afterwards."

"It's better than losing the entire lot, so I suppose we don't have a lot of choice. Tell him it's a deal."

# CHAPTER 21

Quint walked to the front of the conference room at the military base in England, where the team was gathered for a meeting. "Now that we've finished debriefing Rogers' representatives, our job here is done. Ready for some well-deserved time off?" He paused to let the cheer die down. "Where you planning to spend your break time?" Quint asked the group.

"I plan to eat my way through Europe starting in France. Anyone care to join me?"

"I'm afraid I'll have to pass," Quint replied quickly as it became clear that no one else had an interest in participating in Leo's weird food extravaganza.

"I'm riding a Husky," Kira said, a dreamy look in her eye.

"You're going to ride a dog?" Leo asked, sounding stunned.

"No," she laughed, "a Husqvarna Motorcycle."

"Never of heard of them."

"It's a pretty cool company. They started out in their namesake town making weapons for the King of Sweden in the late 1600s, before getting into the motorcycle business in the early 1900s. I've always wanted to ride one."

"Where you planning to ride?" Dawson asked.

"We're joining the Road of Bones motorcycle tour."

"Road of Bones?"

"That's what they call the Kolyma Highway in Russia where the tour ends. Stalin used slaves, and many died building it. Since the land is permanently frozen, the dead were buried beneath or beside the road where they fell. Actually, we can't do the entire 100-day ride from London to Magadan, Siberia. We'll catch up with them in Samarkand for the Silk Road portion of the tour."

"I hear of this!" Nigora squealed. "They go to Shabrisabz too, birthplace of Timur the Lame. You must see ruins of largest mosque in world he build. Much impressive," Nigora said excitedly.

"You're pregnant and planning on riding a motorcycle?" Quint asked.

"Yes," Kira said defensively.

"You think that's really smart? E.R. doctors call those 'donor cycles' for good reason."

"Don't you start; it's not like I'm stupid and forgot that I'm pregnant. I could get hit by a meteor while cowering in my bedroom too. Look, I spoke with the doctor. He says at this stage of the pregnancy there's really no serious risk. Once the baby comes, I sure won't have time, particularly if I'm still single," she said with a sideways glance at Colin. "Nothing will happen; you'll see."

"I just hope you're right," Quint said in resignation.

"What about Nigora?" Kira asked, changing the subject.

"It'll take another day to get all her paperwork straight. Then she's flying back with me to the Keys. Marcia is leaving ahead of us to make arrangements to get her settled in the States," Quint replied.

"And you, what are your plans?" Kira asked Quint.

"I'll be spending my time trying to get things back on track with Evie."

Kira looked at Nigora. "You excited about going to America?"

"Buh."

"Nigora, it's... never mind. I'm not going to waste my breath," Kira said.

"How you waste breath?"

"Good luck," Kira replied, ignoring Nigora's question. "What are you doing, Mimi?"

"Preston is meeting me here, and then we're going to London," Mimi replied. "We'll spend a couple of days in the city, maybe take a day trip to visit Stonehenge or Salisbury Cathedral. After that, he has some sort of business-related Norwegian cruise, and I'm flying back to the States."

"Who's paying?" Dawson chimed in.

"Excuse me, I hardly think that's any of your business," Mimi replied defensively. But seeing Dawson's cocky smile, she continued, "If you must know, Preston ran into an identity theft problem with his credit card. They're sending him a replacement with a new account number, so I agreed to pay and he'll pay me back in full later."

Dawson shook his head in disbelief. "After that business with your ring, anyone want to give me odds on that happening?"

"He should be here any minute. Why don't you ask him yourself?" Mimi replied, her frown turning to a smile as she noticed Preston enter the room.

"Well, I'm gone. Taking the first train to wherever it's going. When I get bored, I'll head back home," Dawson said, beating a hasty retreat.

Preston hugged Mimi and then Nigora as she was introduced. Quint grinned as Marcia skillfully avoided his attempt to kiss her on the cheek.

Mimi excused herself to the ladies room, and as soon as she left, Preston turned to Marcia. "It's good to see you. I was thinking perhaps we could spend a little time together before you head back home."

"I thought you and Mimi were heading to London." Quint winced at the unconcealed disgust in Marcia's voice.

"Oh... yeah, I just thought we could uh... grab lunch... the three of us, I... uh... mean, and catch up."

"Catch up on what? Look, Preston, I'll be blunt. You seem to be doing a good job of bullshitting those on the team who want to believe you for Dawson's sake. But let me make one thing clear; I'm not one of them. I know your type, and the very first time I can prove I'm right, I won't be shy about passing it on. In the meantime, you best not hurt Mimi," Marcia said, and turned to leave.

Quint noticed Preston's face turn dark red, his left hand forming a fist. He took a step forward, stopping when he glanced back at Quint. Preston took a deep breath and unclenched his fist, though his eyes remained glued to Marcia's hips as she walked away.

"What were you guys chatting about?" Mimi asked, as she returned.

"How glad I am to be spending time with you," he lied with a broad smile.

"You waiting for someone on this flight too?" Evie asked the only other woman in the tiny Key West airport lobby two days later.

"Yes, a friend of mine. He's flying in from Europe," Marcia replied.

"Really, what's his name?" Evie asked wide-eyed.

"Quint."

"Your b-boyfriend?"

"Oh no, just a work acquaintance. You know him?"

"You might say so. He's my... I mean we've dated some in the past, and I thought for a minute—"

"That I was competition. You needn't worry about that. I never mix business with my personal life, especially if I know there's an existing relationship. I'm just here to pick up a woman who's travelling with him," Marcia replied. Noting Evie's raised eyebrows, she continued. "The daughter of someone we worked with in Europe is immigrating to the States. Quint was delayed while they got all of the paperwork in place for her to enter the country legally."

"I'm Evie, pleased to meet you," she said with a smile, though her female alarm system still seemed actively engaged.

"And I'm Marcia. Believe me, you have nothing to worry about. During the trip, you're all he talked about. He's got it bad for you. It was Evie this and Evie that."

Evie beamed at hearing this. "So, how did things go?"

"A lot tougher than I had imagined. But what we did was good, I mean... it was a... uh... it was tough," Marcia said awkwardly after realizing she shouldn't be divulging anything.

Evie laughed. "Don't worry, I understand. Plus I'll get it out of him shortly. He's not very good at keeping secrets from me." A few minutes later, the P.A. announced the arriving flight.

Quint was surprised to find the two women waiting. "I see you and Marcia have already met, so let me introduce you to Nigora."

"I happy to meet with you," Nigora said, taking Evie's hand. "Quint tell me much about you. I think he much in love." She winked as she whispered her last comment. "And Marcia, he say you take me shopping. I love shopping. I love Amelica. I love flying. I love—"

"Nigora, why don't you and Marcia head to Miami for your shopping spree before it gets too late," Quint said, interrupting her tirade before she could get started.

"Then we go. Hi, Hi," Nigora said, hugging Evie.

Quint saw the puzzled look on her face. "That's 'Bye, Bye' not 'Hi, Hi,' Nigora," he said, while hugging Marcia goodbye under Evie's watchful eye.

"Wherever," Nigora replied.

Quint heard Marcia correct her as they headed out of the terminal. "It's whatever."

"Huh?" Nigora replied.

"You said, 'Wherever.'"

"Yes, we go wherever you want, you know shopping better than me." Marcia looked back at Quint with a shrug as he followed Evie to her car.

Quint slung his suitcase into the trunk and then ducked into Evie's car. "My flight got changed. How did you find out I'd be—"

"Dawson," Evie interrupted. "He called to check on me, and I decided to surprise you. Got time for dinner?"

"You have to ask?" They chatted as she drove to Louie's Backyard, Quint's hopes renewed that things between them might finally be healing.

While Quint dove into his seared tuna marbles with ponzu, Evie picked at her mozzarella-wrapped eggplant appetizer. During the meal, they worked on reconnecting after the bumpy period of the past several weeks. Evie made no mention of their last conversation, and Quint was certainly didn't bring up the unpleasant episode.

The waitress brought Quint's entree, and he took his first bite of fresh grilled grouper. "Mmm, perfect. Crisp on the outside and flaky warm on the inside." As he eagerly moved the fork to his mouth again, the second bite landed directly on the front of his shirt. "Damn it all!" he swore, setting the fork down.

"Oink, oink," Evie teased. She dipped a napkin in her water glass and made a futile attempt to remove the offensive stain, while Quint struggled against the urge to take her into his arms. With the stain somewhat less noticeable, Evie sat back and looked at Quint. "So tell me about Marcia."

"There's really not a lot to tell. Kira will be having her baby soon, so we hired Marcia to fill in. Plus, we needed to grow the team."

"Oh," Evie replied, causing Quint to sense there might be a problem.

"You don't like her?"

"I like her fine; that's not my concern. It's more that I think she likes you."

"Don't be silly; we just work together. There's nothing between us," Quint protested.

"Perhaps not from your perspective. Not so sure about hers."

"Well, you're wrong, but in any case, it doesn't matter," Quint replied, taking her hand in his. They sat drinking their wine in silence.

"Before you left your wife after you learned she was cheating on you, were things already at a dead-end?"

Quint hesitated for a minute, hoping there was not a hidden reason for her question. "I suppose when we got to the point where 'I love you' was a cliché. Maybe if her miscarriage hadn't foiled our plan to have kids, our marriage would have had more meaning."

"You know, there's something I never told you. I was married once."

"Oh really? I can see how you might forget to tell the person who cares for you most in the whole world that sort of tiny detail. Mind telling me what happened?"

"He lost his left arm in an automobile accident as a teen-ager, and didn't handle the handicap well. He developed some sort of complex, and to compensate, he insisted on being called Edward, often the third, and never Ed or Eddie. Of course, he accepted my calling him Eddie after deciding that Poopsie was even worse.

"We were both young and liked to party, so it was only after we were married that I realized the full extent of his drinking problem, which, of course, he denied. He became increasingly more belligerent when he drank. And then one night, when he was well on his way to being drunk, he asked me to take him to buy more liquor. When I refused, he punched me in the stomach and face before leaving to get it himself. While he was gone, I called the cops and had him arrested. By the time he found a friend to bond him out, I was on my way down here."

"Hmm. I'm guessing that played a role in your rebuffing my attempts to take our relationship to a new level a few months back?" Evie nodded. "Thanks for telling me," Quint said, and toyed with his butter knife for a moment before continuing. "Last time we were together, you made it clear that you weren't ready for anything physical between us. So I want you to know, that's okay. I'm just glad to be spending time back together." Evie smiled without replying.

The waiter returned with the check and Quint's credit card. While he was adding the tip to the credit card receipt, he heard Evie say, "Let's go back to my place."

Though flustered to the point he had trouble computing the tip, Quint hoped this might be the break he had been praying for since her kidnapping and rape episode. Maybe she was finally ready to put that horror behind her and move on with her life—and their relationship.

They rode to her place in silence, Quint feeling uncharacteristically awkward and insecure. While he didn't want to pressure Evie for intimacy, he was afraid she might interpret any hesitancy as a lack of interest on his part. He resolved to err in the direction of moving too slowly as he plopped down on her couch just as her house phone began to ring.

Evie ignored the ringing phone and continued her story. "Aren't you going to answer that?" Quint interrupted.

"Nope," she replied.

"Why not?"

"I never do. Most are telemarketers. Anybody who knows me personally can leave a message," she replied, handing him two glasses and a bottle of Courvoisier XO.

"Wow, the good stuff," Quint remarked.

"Yeah, I figure if it was good enough for Napoleon... While it's no Erte Vendanges, it's the best I can afford," Evie replied, as Quint poured her a glass of the cognac.

"I've been hesitant to get back together because I know you intend to continue working with the team. Given what happened to me, I want no part of that."

"Evie, it's not fair to make me choose between you and the team."

"You're right, and I don't intend to."

"What?"

"I finally realized that it's not fair to make you choose. I want what we have... I mean had, bad enough that I've come to terms with it. Just don't expect me to be joining you on one of your missions any time soon."  Quint nodded and reached for her hand as they sat quietly drinking their cognac.

"I saw you sitting in your car," Evie said.

"Huh?" Quint replied.

"All those nights when you parked down the street to watch my house, I sat in the darkened living room watching you watching me."

"Then why didn't you—"

Noticing Quint's glass was empty, she took it and set it, along with her own half full one, on the table beside the bottle of cognac. As she turned back, her face neared his. "I couldn't. I mean, I wanted to be with you, to have you here with me. I've wanted to... maybe I'm..." she paused. "What I'm trying to say is I wasn't ready then," she said, planting her lips squarely on his.

Prepared for only a modest show of affection, Quint was surprised at Evie's passion. With her mouth still pressed against his, Quint managed to mutter, "I thought you said you weren't ready."

"I am now," she replied, her words muffled as she pressed her lips back to his.

The next morning, Quint awoke feeling like a teenager after his first date. He was thrilled to be back with Evie, though he had declined her offer to stay the night. Opting to take things slow, he had borrowed her car and returned to Dawson's place. There he lay in bed trying to think of some way to build on the momentum of the previous evening.

After dismissing several ideas as being too forward, like skimpy lingerie, or too plebian like replacing her aging iron, he finally settled on what he thought was the perfect gift. He headed back to Key West planning one stop before returning her car.

He pulled up in front of Evie's house, got out of the car carrying a large box with an enormous bow, climbed the three steps onto her porch, and rang the doorbell. Evie started to smile at Quint holding the present when she noticed it appeared to be moving.

"What do we have here?" she asked.

"A gift to commemorate having my love back in my life," he replied, handing her the box.

She nearly dropped it as the weight within shifted, but Quint simply shrugged in response to her puzzled look. Evie walked to the kitchen and set the box on her table, jumping backward as the green head of an iguana poked out.

"Lil Fred. Your new iguana," Quint said with a huge grin.

Evie looked off with a tear in her eye. "No, Fred is dead." He knew she still mourned her pet iguana who died during Hurricane Katrina. "Thanks. I love him.

This one looks more like... a Barney. Yes that's his name, Barney," Evie said, and happily spent the next few hours arranging a home for her new pet.

# CHAPTER 22

Kira had been hoping that Colin might propose to her. Contrary to the popular trend, the thought of raising a child as a single mother did not appeal to her. She felt it important that a child grow up with both a mother and a father—an experience denied her.

She held her breath every time the situation presented an opening for him to ask her, but no cigar. Though she did not want him to propose out of guilt, she desperately did want him to propose.

She smiled at Colin as they left their room before dawn the next morning. *Maybe during our motorcycle vacation he'll pop the question.*

While Colin settled their bill, she exited the hotel. The taxi was waiting across the narrow street, ready to drive them to Samarkand. As she stepped off the sidewalk, her bag slid off her shoulder and fell onto the pavement. Before she could pick it up, a white Peugeot van roared past, its front tire crushing the purse.

Rather than stop, the grizzled old man driving grinned, and Kira caught a flash of silver in his smile. "You asshole!" she yelled.

Colin exited the hotel just in time to see the near miss and came running over. "What happened? Are you okay?"

"Yes, no thanks to that idiot. If I hadn't dropped my purse, he would have hit me."

"I didn't get his tag number, did you?" Colin asked through clenched teeth, handing her the ruined purse.

"No, I was too startled. It was some old guy. Had a silver tooth, of all things."

"You want to go back inside and sit down?"

"No, the taxi's waiting. Let's just go. I'll go shopping later to replace my purse," she said, as they handed the driver their bags and climbed into the taxi.

Though pleasant enough, the driver seemed fixated on early American rock bands. While driving, he watched old videos of his favorites on a small video screen clipped to the sun visor on the passenger's side, much to the dismay of his passengers. When Colin made the mistake of complimenting one of the songs, the driver launched into a 30-minute monologue on rock music.

When they finally reached their hotel, Colin paid him the agreed amount, adding a sizeable tip. The driver thanked him profusely and then added. "Madam, watch out for a crazy politician who comes here to get drunk and kiss female tourists." Kira thanked him and followed Colin into the hotel, vowing to avoid the bar.

Excited about the next day's motorcycle trip, Kira hardly slept. She jumped in the shower before dawn the next morning and quickly donned the outfit she had laid out the previous night. She crammed the remains of her purse into her bag and then headed for her bike which had been delivered to the hotel the previous evening.

After lashing her bag onto the back, Kira slid onto the seat and with trembling hands thrust the key into the ignition. Drawing a deep breath, she started the bike and waited. Colin finally stumbled out and climbed onto his own bike, still struggling to wake up.

With Colin following close behind, Kira eased out onto the main street, giddy from the throaty growl of the exhaust. After a short ride, they stopped where they had been instructed to meet the tour leader—but he wasn't there. With a frown, Kira dug into her pocket for her prepaid cell phone and dialed his number, but she got no answer. Before she could call again, a man came roaring around the corner on a flashy motorcycle, a broad grin on his face, "I am Jamshid. Ready to roll?"

"Been ready," she replied, miffed at being kept waiting for nearly a full minute. "Keep the dirty side down." Dressed in tight leathers, her long hair trailing from beneath a bright red bandana, Kira roared off. Jamshid quickly caught up to lead while Colin hung slightly behind.

With the roar of the bike beneath her and the cool morning air in her face, Kira felt her irritation quickly melt away. She loved the way the powerful bike accelerated and how it cornered as if on rails. *My whole life has been building to this very moment.* She smiled at Colin—life was good.

They met the rest of the tour group on the edge of Samarkand and continued on toward Shabrisabz. It was mid-morning when they pulled into the city. Jamshid pulled to the curbing to begin his commentary, as they learned would happen each time they stopped at one of the numerous attractions.

"This city is known as the birth place of Timur the Lame, so called for the limp caused by his partial paralysis. He was a powerful Uzbek warlord, whose army pillaged and plundered throughout Central Asia. Timur was a greater despot than the much better known Genghis Khan, and conquered Central Asia, Turkey, India, and parts of Mongolia. Showing little interest in establishing an empire, he simply invaded countries, killed anyone who opposed him, and then returned home with piles of 'booty.' After conquering the Ottoman Empire, he placed the captured Ottoman Sultan in a cage in his parlor, where Timur forced the Sultan's naked wives to serve him food and drink while the caged Sultan looked on helplessly.

"To instill fear, he created huge pyramids of human skulls outside each conquered town. After slaughtering a few towns, many of his targets surrendered without a fight, hoping for mercy." Jamshid finished, mounted his bike, and roared off with the group following close behind.

His next stop was the Bibi-Khanym Mosque. "These ruins are believed to be the site of the largest mosque in the world, some 167 meters by 109. A herd of 90 elephants was used to carry the precious stones used in its construction. While Timur was a very effective warlord, he was not such a great architect. The mosque collapsed in a mere five years, though it still was an impressive feat for its time."

They spent half the day touring the city before heading to Bukhara. By the time they arrived, the aching in Kira's seat had offset her earlier euphoria. She was relieved when Jamshid pulled up to the Amelia Hotel. As Colin dismounted from his bike, he caught a glimpse of an old man driving a white van. But before he could react, it turned the corner and was lost from sight.

"Welcome. This is your first time in Bukhara?" the bellboy asked, as he guided them to their room. Kira nodded. "There is much to see. Perhaps you noticed the Kalyan minaret on your way in, that circular-pillar brick tower. It was built in 1127 to summon Muslims to prayer. Later, criminals were executed by tossing them from the top, earning it the name, Tower of Death.

"Here is your room," he said, opening the door with a flourish. Kira was impressed with the elaborate latticework that adorned the massive mirrors on each wall. "Tomorrow morning, you must join us for breakfast in our 18th century dining room. It is a favorite with all our guests." He graciously accepted Colin's generous tip and left the room.

They took quick showers before joining the others in the lobby. It felt good to stretch their legs on the walk to the restaurant. Both Kira and Colin noticed a white van duck into a side alley when the group paused to enter the restaurant. "Did you see that?" Colin said.

"Yeah, but I've seen several. I don't think white vans are all that rare here," Kira replied, before entering the restaurant. Colin hung on the sidewalk for another moment but seeing nothing, continued inside.

The couple opted to have Jamshid order for them as did most of the rest of the group. Those who did otherwise soon regretted it.

"This is laghman, which is pulled noodles with mutton. And this is plov, a one-pot rice dish cooked with vegetables. When entertaining, the men here prepare it with the same pride men in your country display when grilling meat." Jamshid described each dish as it arrived.

"The food is wonderful," Kira said to Colin, after sampling several items.

"Yeah, Leo would be in heaven," he added. The thrill of the trip, coupled with the glimpse she had caught of a small velvet jewelry box in Colin's bag had her excited. She rubbed Colin's hand lovingly as he held her in the booth beside him.

The next morning, with her seat still tender from riding, Kira climbed onto her bike with only slightly less enthusiasm than the previous day. After enjoying riding bare-headed the previous day, under Colin's watchful eyes Kira begrudgingly donned her helmet, which she called her "skid lid." He nodded in approval while donning his own.

Between the afterglow of the romantic evening and being back on the bike, Kira was having the time of her life. They were lagging behind the rest of the group when Kira spotted a large bird, maybe an osprey, soaring high above and excitedly turned to point it out to Colin.

Looking back with her left arm pointing at the sky, she saw Colin's own arm pointing ahead with a horrorstruck look in his eyes. In a scene she would relive in slow motion forever, Kira spun around to find that a white van had burst out onto the highway squarely in front of her. Instinctively she jerked the handlebars to the left, attempting to steer around the truck, but it was hopelessly close.

She skidded sideways, striking the front fender of the van broadside, her leg sandwiched between the bike and the vehicle's fender. Kira heard the screech of her tires followed by a heavy thud. She flew off the seat and hit the van before sailing over iys hood. For an instant she soared like the osprey that still lingered in the distance before crashing down onto the pavement and tumbling down the road like a rag doll. By the time she finally came to a stop, she was no longer conscious.

With slightly more time to react, Colin steered right. He looked into the van and saw a glint of silver in the smile of the old man driving it, before laying his bike down amidst a shower of sparks and screeching metal. His leathers partially protected his leg from being shredded and saved some of the skin on his calf. As he slid past the rear of the van, his bike hit a rock at the side of the road and flipped, sending him skidding onto the grass shoulder of the road.

When Colin finally came to rest, he lifted his head looking for Kira, only to see a small sedan headed straight for him, a middle-aged woman frozen behind the wheel. He rolled to the side as the woman finally swerved to the left while standing on the brakes. Missing Colin by inches, she ground to a halt in a blue cloud of smoking rubber.

Lying in the grass amidst a pile of plastic bottles and assorted litter, Colin struggled to rise a second time, still dazed and unsure how badly he was hurt. "I'm sorry, I'm so sorry, are you all right? I nearly hit you, oh my God, look at her—what happened to her leg? Oh my God, oh my God, her leg, her leg!" the woman babbled as Colin forced himself to his hands and knees. With blood pouring from an assortment of cuts and scrapes, he jerked his helmet off and tossed it aside.

He spotted the white van fading away into the distance and Kira lying on the opposite side of the road, motionless. He forced himself to his feet, and staggered across the road. Belatedly, he jerked his head around to check for more traffic, but the traffic was beginning to form a line in each direction.

Colin approached Kira's crumpled form with Jamshid kneeling beside her. "She's got a pulse," he announced. "Somebody call an ambulance. Quick! She needs help—she may not have much time."

"No, oh, God no, please God, please," Colin moaned, collapsing beside Kira's still form. He moved to undo her helmet, but Jamshid grabbed his hand.

"Let's leave it on until the paramedics get here. We don't want to do any further damage."

Colin withdrew his hand from her battered helmet and examined the rest of her body. Her leathers were torn, and blood oozed from a number of places where the material was worn through. Nothing appeared too bad until he noticed her right leg lying at an impossible angle and her pants leg drenched with blood. Raw muscle was exposed through a tear in the fabric below her knee where the white of bone protruded. Colin could not tell if her mangled leg was even still attached.

He was still kneeling next to her, unsure what to do, when the wail of the ambulance's siren mercifully signaled the arrival of medical help. The first responders ignored him as they assessed Kira's condition.

A minute later the second team to arrive gently urged Colin to his feet. As the paramedics guided him to their waiting truck, his gaze remained riveted to the wheeled stretcher where Kira was being placed. He broke their grasp to stop and watch as Kira's gurney was loaded into the ambulance.

"Come on, we'll check you out on the way," the paramedic told him.

"But I need to go with her!" Colin yelled. "She's pregnant." Hearing this, the medic attending Kira looked up.

"How far along?"

"A couple of months or so." The medic nodded before slamming the doors.

"It's okay; you'll be with her shortly," the medic reassured him as Kira's ambulance leapt forward, headed for the hospital.

.

Colin turned to Jamshid with a confused look. "Don't worry, I'll take care of the bikes." Jamshid placed a hand on Colin's shoulder. "You just worry about her. Please call me as soon as you know anything," he said. He retrieved the couple's bags from their bikes and placed them beside Colin, and a minute later the second ambulance was also headed for the hospital.

A few hours later, with his various cuts and abrasions bandaged and two broken ribs taped, a distraught Colin was staring blankly out a window at the parking lot below when a doctor emerged from the restricted area. "You're with the woman from the motorcycle wreck?"

Colin nodded. "How is she? Will she be all right? What about her leg? What about the baby?" The doctor took Colin's arm and guided him to a chair in the waiting room.

"I'm Dr. Karimov. Have a seat and we'll go over her condition. Both she and the baby are going to be all right," the doctor said. Colin sighed in relief. "But she has several broken ribs, a collapsed lung, and then there's her leg. It's badly damaged—I'm afraid we won't be able to save it."

"Amputate her leg? Are you crazy?"

"Look, we're just as concerned as you. We—"

"Just as concerned as me? That's bullshit. To you, she's just another patient who may live or die. To me she's everything. I hope she's about to be my wife. If she dies, so do I. Now you get your ass on that phone right now. I want the best surgeon in the country in there. Pronto."

The doctor rose and left without replying as an older nurse approached. "Hi, I'm Madina. I'm so sorry about what happened. I know you're hurting and angry, but that was Dr. Karimov and believe me, he *is* the best in the country. We're lucky to have him." Colin nodded silently as Madina softly took his hand in hers.

Colin looked up at her, tears flowing down his face. "I'm sorry; I just want her to be okay. I'd still love her with no legs. Please tell Dr. Karimov I'm on board with whatever he feels is best."

# CHAPTER 23

Col. Botz's team boarded two stealth helicopters and lifted off from the secluded base near the border of Uzbekistan, embarking on their operation to seize the stolen bioweapons. Pvt. Hernandez leaned back with his eyes closed, as if resting before the mission. Unbeknownst to the team, Hernandez was not his real name, nor was he resting, nor was he even Hispanic as he claimed.

Rather he was from Iran, an avowed radical Muslim working for a terrorist named Rashid. He had spent years infiltrating first the United States and then the U.S. military using this false identity. No one in the squad had cause to question either his ethnicity or his loyalty. But after years of wondering whether he would ever get the chance to strike out against the infidels, the phone call from Rashid had finally come the day before.

Flying just a few feet above ground level, they had been airborne for less than thirty minutes when Hernandez opened his eyes. Mechanically, he removed a frag grenade from his combat harness and calmly pulled the pin before lobbing it at the pilot in the forward cabin.

The astonished Col. Botz shouted a warning loud enough to be heard over the cabin noise and that of Hernandez yelling, "Praise Allah; Allah is great." The colonel then launched himself forward, pinning

Hernandez to prevent him from arming a second grenade.

The grenade flew past both the pilot and copilot and landed on the floor, where it rolled beneath the seat. The pilot's hand shot down in a futile attempt to grab it as the copilot radioed "Chopper two, we've got a maverick. We're hot," code for a sleeper terrorist who had gone active. Botz repeatedly punched the man in a face frozen in a sick grin, despite the blood spewing from his shattered nose. An instant later an enormous explosion ignited the heavily loaded fuel tank and blew the helicopter apart.

The second chopper, tracking close behind the lead chopper, was attempting to peel off when the blossoming orange flame washed over it. The lead chopper's huge rotor blade pierced its windscreen, instantly killing the flight crew. With no time to react, the team was tossed about the cabin as the second chopper tumbled before impacting the ground, with the dead flight crew still strapped in place.

Two of the five squad members in the second chopper remained conscious. Though badly wounded, they managed to crawl out the open side doors before the wreckage burst into flames. Ignoring their own life-threatening injuries, the two men tried in vain to rescue the others before the intense heat rendered further efforts impossible. They collapsed on the ground a short distance away. Both helicopters and all but two of the superbly trained squad were gone.

An emergency beacon briefly broadcast a distress signal accompanied by their position before succumbing to the flames. A Blackhawk helicopter on emergency standby was immediately scrambled to the crash site, where they placed demolition charges in the burning wreckage of both choppers before whisking away the two survivors. Over the next several days, a cadre of high-ranking officials in Washington would be dealing with the political fallout from the disaster. Already alternate cover stories were being floated.

# CHAPTER 24

Even before Colin entered the hospital room, he heard Kira crying. She had spent the previous day relieved that the baby had survived and she was still alive. He thought at the time that attitude wouldn't last long; it appeared he was right.

The grief counselor had walked him through what to expect during the recovery process. "According to the Kübler-Ross model, Kira will likely experience five basic emotional stages: denial, anger, bargaining, depression, and acceptance."

"In that order?"

"Not necessarily. There really isn't a specific sequence. In fact, she may not experience all of them, but then again, she may go through those as well as a few others."

"Right now, she mostly seems relieved," Colin said.

"That's not unusual," the woman told him.

"How long do you think this phase will last?"

"Hard to say. But when it ends, you'll wish it hadn't, because it's likely she'll enter the anger phase next."

"At what?"

"Losing her leg, God, herself, you, the world, you name it. When that happens, if she tells you to go the hell away, go the hell away and give her space. But you need to keep coming back to help her through it. She's lucky to have your support, and though it may take a while, she'll realize it." Colin was glad to have all of this explained to him and felt slightly more prepared to cope.

Kira looked up as he entered and began sobbing. "You tried to tell me about the risks of riding bikes while I was pregnant. I was stupid not to listen to you. That wreck put our baby at risk. Oh, Colin, I'm so sorry. I'm so sorry."

"Hey, it's okay."

"No it's not. It'll never be okay. Why didn't I listen to you, why?"

He continued trying to console her, holding her hand until she fell asleep. She awoke a couple of hours later to find him waiting beside her and began crying once again. This cycle repeated for most of the day until he finally fell asleep himself, sitting in the guest chair beside her bed. When he awoke, Kira was still sleeping, and he slipped out of the room, careful not to wake her.

Quint glanced at the clock and saw that it was after midnight as he answered his phone. "Aww, shit!" he said, and then, after listening for another minute, he hung up and went to wake Dawson, who had returned after spending only a couple of days in Europe.

"Colin just called. He and Kira have been in a motorcycle accident."

"How bad?" Dawson asked wiping the sleep from his eyes.

"Bad. They had to amputate her leg. They're still in Uzbekistan, and Colin wants to get her back here for her recovery and therapy. As soon as the doctor says she's stable enough to travel, I promised to get Rogers to fly her back."

Exhausted from lack of sleep since the accident, Colin had slept for nearly two hours. He was awakened by Rogers' call advising him that arrangements had been made to fly Kira back to Miami in a few hours. When the plane arrived at the FBO in Miami, an ambulance was there to whisk them away to the hospital, where Kira spent most of the day being poked and prodded.

It was only the head nurse's persistence that got Colin out of Kira's room while she was undergoing more tests. After helping him arrange for a rental car, she insisted that he make a reservation at a nearby hotel.

An hour later, he was checked in and took a much-needed shower, his first since the accident. The hot water felt good. His back muscles, knotted from sleeping in the chair beside Kira's bed, finally began to relax, and he lay down for just a minute to rest.

He awoke with a start a couple of hours later, after reliving the accident in his sleep. He slipped into a clean oxford-cloth shirt and a pair of jeans, and withdrew the small, blue velvet-covered box from his bag. He admired the diamond engagement ring before placing it in the watch pocket of his jeans with a smile.

By the time he arrived back at the hospital, the darkened parking lot was nearly empty. He punched the elevator button and rode to the third floor. As he emerged, he could hear Kira screaming at one of the nurses.

"Take this slop away! Get me some real food! Isn't it enough to make me into a one-legged, expectant mother without starving me, too?"

"It would appear that she's entered the anger stage of her recovery," Colin said to the nurse, as she fled the room.

"Maybe," the nurse replied. "But she's tired from the trip and everything we put her through today. I'm guessing the specter of being a single mother, coupled with the trauma of losing her leg just got the best of her. I gave her a different type of pain medication. Maybe this one won't make her so... anxious."

Colin nodded and with the ring held in the palm of his hand, cautiously entered her room. Kira looked up to see him still heavily bandaged and limping but cleaned up. "Well lookie here, my baby-daddy's all spic and span. If you only came to give sympathy to the cripple and didn't bring me a greasy bacon cheeseburger—leave."

"Kira, I'm so very sorry this all happened... but I'm here because I love you. I want to be with you... and the baby," he said meekly approaching the bed, poised to kneel his aching body before her and propose.

"How nice that you feel sorry for me. We cripples crave all the pity we can get."

"I didn't say anything about pitying you; in fact, I find you—"

"With fewer limbs, right?" she interrupted. "Just leave. I'm tired of hurting; I'm tired of lying in bed; I'm tired of crappy food; and I'm tired of you. Go find yourself a two-legged woman."

"Kira, I—"

"Go!" she screamed, as he reluctantly backed out the door before the tears began streaming down her face. "Who cares if I never get married?" she cried. "If you were considering proposing before the accident, it was probably out of guilt. And that was when I still had both legs. I don't need you. I don't need anybody. I'll be all right, just me and the baby. We'll do fine."

Colin heard her tirade. But the nurse urged him to leave her alone until she settled down. He slid the ring back in his jeans pocket as he walked away, wondering what he could possibly do next.

After receiving Rogers' call to confirm that Kira would arrive in the States within a few hours on the private plane he had arranged, Quint and Dawson had headed for Miami.

"Yes, sir, may I have your name?" the woman at the hospital's third-floor nurse's station asked.

"Quint," he replied.

"Quint who?" she asked.

"Just plain ol' Quint."

Shrugging her shoulders, she walked into an office across the lobby. A minute later, an older lady approached. "Hello, Mr. Quint. I'm Wendy. May I help you?"

"First of all, it's just Quint and secondly, yes, you may. I'd like directions to find a patient who I believe is on your floor. Her name is Kira, and...," he stopped at the sound of a woman's voice yelling down the hall, and then looked up to see Colin beating a hasty retreat. "Never mind, I think we've found her."

Colin smiled when he saw Quint and Dawson approaching. "Hey, guys, thanks for coming, but you shouldn't have—really."

"How's Kira doing?" Dawson asked.

"As you may have heard, not too well. I would highly recommend you wait until later to visit."

"That's okay, I'll make Dawson go in first," Quint replied. The anger having burned itself out, Kira was quietly lying in bed when Quint and Dawson entered the room.

"Isn't this nice?" she asked, pointing at her stump. "I was just imagining myself with a shiny new prosthetic leg."

"Kira, I'm so sorry."

"It'll be a real kick for junior to grow up with his classmates calling me his 'peg-legged mom.' Or pirate-mom. Now there's an idea."

"I know it sucks, but these days they fabricate prostheses from high-tech alloys that work much better than their old wooden counterparts," Quint said.

Ignoring him, Kira continued. "I'll get a parrot and an eye patch. And maybe one of those three-cornered pirate hats, you know, the ones that—" her voice broke, and she began to sob all over again. After making several more attempts at conversation, the two men stood silent.

Finally, unable to think of anything else to say that didn't sound contrived, they quietly left her to grieve in private. The two men re-joined Colin and headed to the cafeteria.

It was after midnight when Colin checked on Kira again. She was sleeping peacefully when he entered her room and took a seat beside her bed. He found her beautiful in the room's half-light, and he stared as if seeing her for the very first time. He sat for over an hour thinking and savoring the quiet before leaving to get a few more hours' sleep as well. He hoped to find Kira in a better frame of mind the next morning.

"You're back to see the cripple, the one-legged parrot-less mom," Kira began singing to the tune of the Wizard of Oz as Colin entered. "You know, it occurred to me that I can now organize my sock drawer twice as fast as I used to."

"Stop it, Kira. You can't let this turn you into an angry, bitter person. I hate what happened as much as you, but we can't change it. But you can control how you allow this to affect you... that is... us. Plenty of people lose limbs and go on to lead normal lives. No one would choose it, but they deal with it all the same. And that's what you have to do. That is... if you want to get married."

Kira struggled not to reveal her surprise. "Who would want a one-legged wife?"

"Me," Colin replied. "Hey, Heather Mills was an amputee when Paul McCartney married her."

"I heard she was a bitch; is that what you're calling me?" she asked, with a sly grin.

"I can't win." Colin rolled his eyes. "I had planned to ask you during our trip, preferably in a somewhat more romantic setting, sorry. But I'm asking you now. Will you marry me?"

"Yeah, right," Kira said.

"Is that a real answer?"

"Was that a real question?"

"Yes," Colin replied. Kira turned away without responding and began to sob. She felt him wrap her in his arms, gently stroking her back.

Finally, after calming down, she looked up at him through tear-filled eyes, "I would love to be your wife. And this setting works just fine." As they talked about their future, Kira realized the wedding she had dreamed of would now feature her wearing a prosthetic leg. But with Colin there it would be all right. She would make it all right.

# CHAPTER 25

Wearing his favorite ragged khaki shorts and faded Marty Wilson billfish t-shirt with a pair of Top-Siders well past their prime, Quint entered the break room at the team's small office. He fixed a breakfast plate before joining Dawson, Marcia, Willy, and Dakota at the table in the team's small office. "Any word from the rest of the team?" he asked, as he set his plate down.

"Not much. I imagine by now Leo's gained five pounds, and Preston and Mimi are half way to Scotland. When they finish there, she's going to head back and he has to stay to take care of some sort of business," Willy replied.

"Some sort of business? I thought he was dying of cancer," Marcia commented.

Willy shrugged and then paused for a moment before continuing. "You know Dawson, it's probably none of my business, but I think you should give Preston another chance." Dawson began to interrupt, but Willy raised his hand and continued. "Please, just hear me out. He might have done some horrible things in the past, he's still your blood. Give him one last chance. If you later regret it, blame me. But please, do me this favor. I'll not ask another."

Dawson took a bite of his biscuit and chewed in silence while considering what Willy had said. Quint knew that he had a great deal of respect for a man who seldom gave his opinion without due consideration and was pleased to hear him say, "Okay, I'll do it for you."

Quint rose to pour a cup of coffee. "So, Marcia, how did your shopping trip go with Nigora?" he asked, while measuring out a heaping teaspoon of vanilla creamer.

"Quite an experience," Marcia said, with a chuckle. "I love her to death, but she's a handful. I'm not sure you realize what you've gotten us into."

"Well, given the debt we owe her father, we'll have to manage," Quint replied.

"How are things with Evie?" Dawson asked, through a mouthful of biscuit. Marcia looked up from her breakfast and Quint noticed she seemed eager to hear his reply.

"Better, much better. I bought her another iguana."

"Smart, I'm guessing she's still pissed about Dakota killing Fred," Dawson said, with a sly grin.

"Hey, that wasn't my fault. I hated that he got killed but he saved my skin. Without the diversion he created, I probably wouldn't be here today. She's not really mad at me, is she?" Dakota asked.

"No, Dawson's just screwing with you." Quint set his biscuit back on his plate just as the satphone rang. He cleared his throat and then left the room to take the call.

"Quint, we've got a situation," Rogers began. "I need your help recovering the bioweapons before they're smuggled out of Russia."

"Huh? Botz's team was supposed to be handling the interdiction. What happened?"

"They're dead!"

"Dead?"

"Yeah, all but two, both of whom are badly injured. It seems we had a sleeper in the squad who finally awoke. After a detailed background search, they figured out it was a guy named Hernandez. They don't activate sleepers without a damned good reason. I guess that's a measure of the importance of this operation. We can't let those bioweapons get away," Rogers said. "We've missed our chance to intercept them in Uzbekistan, but we still have a narrow window in Russia."

"So your commando squad got toasted and *now* you want us involved?"

"But your team—"

"Our team? You said, 'We need to let a professional commando team handle this.' Am I remembering that right? Well, last time I checked we didn't have a team of commandos."

"Well, now we don't have one either. But even if we did, the President would never authorize the use of conventional forces inside Russia."

"Sorry, but that's not my problem. I offered to help back when we had plenty of time to do things right. Now it's going to be a fire drill, and I'm not putting my team at risk."

"I'm not asking you to put your whole team at risk."

"What?"

"We just need you and Dawson. We can't risk using a larger team."

"Why not just have the Prez ring up the Russians and get them to help?"

"The Russian military is so corrupt we're afraid to ask them for help. If they were to get their hands on these bioweapons, they might try to sell them. We don't have time to get anyone else on site and up to speed. You and Dawson are our only chance."

"How do I know your intel is reliable, and this isn't going to be another fiasco like the one you just had?" Quint paused for a moment before continuing. "Let me talk to Dawson. But it sounds like a mess," Quint said.

"Quint, I hate to point this out, but your job was to eliminate *all* of the bioweapons. These did sort of slip through your fingers."

"Listen to me, you sonofabitch. We did our job.
Whoever stole that container was there before we got
there. If your intel people hadn't had their heads up
their asses, we'd have known about their plan to steal
some of the weapons, we'd have avoided nearly getting
shot, and Boris might still be alive. If we do this, it'll
not be out of guilt," Quint yelled.

"Sorry, I was out of line. It's just that we're in a jam,
and I really need your—" Quint hung up the phone
while he was still talking.

"Rogers?" Dawson asked, as Quint walked back into
the break room.

He nodded, and recounted his conversation. "What
do you think?"

"I think it has all the makings of a disaster,"
Dawson replied.

"So, you're out?"

"Didn't say that. We both know we're going to do
this in the end, so let's not waste valuable time. I don't
know how soon we can get the rest of the team back
from break. They're spread all over hell's creation and
then, of course, there's Kira and Colin," Dawson said,
the concern in his voice ill-concealed.

"As it turns out, that's not a problem. He wants only
the two of us," Quint replied.

"Oh," Dawson replied.

"If you two decide to do this, you should at least
have a team on the ground nearby," Dakota said, Willy
nodding in agreement.

"I agree, plus I could use the field experience,"
Marcia added.

"You sure you three are up for it?" Quint asked.

"You really have to ask?" Dakota replied.

Quint and Dawson stared at each other for a long
moment. Neither one wanted any part of the project
but also knew they couldn't refuse. "Call him," Dawson
muttered.

"We're in," Quint said tersely when Rogers answered. "What's the plan?" Quint was certain he was not going to like what he heard next.

"I have a plane already on the way; they'll pick you up within two hours."

"Cocky, aren't you?"

"No, I just knew you'd do the right thing."

"And that would be cleaning up your mess?"

Rogers ignored Quint's dig. "They'll brief you on the mission details during the flight, provide you with your equipment package, and instruct you on operating the pod."

"Pod?"

"Yeah, we can't very well fly you into Russia with a weapons load and land at one of their bases. So the plan is to use two unmanned combat air vehicles, or UCAVs, modified to carry personnel capsules, or pods, developed for covert operations such as this. Though these prototypes are still under development, they work sort of like one-man gliders. You should have no problem."

"Has anyone used one of these... pods... in an honest-to-God operation?"

"Well, no, but we've conducted extensive tests, and my guys are confident they'll work. Quint, I know you two can do this or I wouldn't ask."

"Yeah, but then it won't be *your* ass on the line, now will it?"

"We'll fly you back to Tashkent, Uzbekistan, where you'll take a commercial flight to Moscow. You'll then drive to Pushnoy where you'll rendezvous in a remote area with the UCAVs and board the pods."

"Why can't we just board the UCAVs in Uzbekistan and have them fly us to wherever?"

"Range. With the weight of the pod plus a person, they suck fuel and can't travel that distance. Plus, this way you won't be on board when they cross the

Russian border, so if they were to be detected, you won't get shot down.

"The pods will deliver you well ahead of the truck carrying the container," Rogers continued. "Before the Botz disaster, we flew a UCAV over and fired a transponder into the top of the container to serve as a locater beacon. That's how Botz's team planned to track it.

"After you land, you'll hijack the truck and then take the container to a harbor near Murmansk, where we'll have a boat waiting. After a short run offshore for a boat-to-sub transfer, we'll get the bioweapons along with the two of you out of the country, and we're done. From the time you board the pod, the whole operation should take only a few hours."

"You make it sound simple."

"It will be," Rogers replied.

"Bullshit. It never is. We want some of our own people stationed close by should things go awry. This is a non-negotiable condition," Quint said, and then paused for a moment. "They need to be on the boat we'll be meeting."

"Agreed," Rogers replied. "In case things go south, you're authorized to blow the container, but civilian lives may be at risk."

"How many?"

Rogers paused. "Could be in the thousands. Any more questions?"

"No, we'll clean up your mess. But Rogers, don't pull that blame-game shit on me ever again." Quint slammed the phone down, dreading Dawson's reaction when he explained the plan involving the UCAVs and pods.

"Sounds like a screwed-up deal. How'd you let him talk us into this one?"

Quint glared at Dawson with raised eyebrows. "Weren't you the one waving the flag only minutes ago? You agreed to it just like I did, so don't you start playing games, too."

"Touchy. If you're going to be an asshole, I'm just not sure I want to go with you and risk getting my ass all shot to hell," Dawson said, feigning hurt feelings.

"I'm sorry to have upset your delicate sensibilities, but your ass is going, right alongside mine." Quint hoped Dawson wasn't right about the risk.

"Prototype pods, flying around inside Russia, retrieving a load of nasty bioshit. What could possibly go wrong with this plan?" Dawson asked sarcastically.

Quint, surprised his reaction wasn't worse, rose to leave. Seizing the chance, Marcia got him to one side. "What about Nigora; what should I do with her? I don't think it's a good idea to leave her on her own yet."

Quint thought for a moment. "I'll see if Evie can help." Marcia nodded. Then, as if on cue, Nigora entered the room with colossal, porn-star-sized breasts. "Nigora... you look... uh, different. Can't put my finger on it but—"

"But you like to? I have big Amelican breasts. Marcia bought them for me. You like?"

"They're sure big," Quint replied. With a broad smile, Nigora began talking with Dawson and Dakota as Quint turned to Marcia.

"Hey, don't start on me," Marcia protested. "She claimed that's one of the things you promised her. We're lucky I talked her into an external prosthesis, at least for now."

"Fine, but did you have to buy her the jumbo, family-sized ones?"

"I didn't, though she wanted them. Those are adjustable. I explained that she could vary the size until she found the look she liked best. Obviously, she chose to start with the max. Let's hope she works her way back down."

"You like my new breasts?" Nigora asked the two men.

"Uh... sure. Kinda big, aren't they?"

"Yes! Saleslady say high-tech. Can fill with water or air so not feel like balloons but not too heavy."

Quint was headed home to pack when Dakota caught up with him and pulled him aside. "I know you were a little uneasy about taking Marcia, but she has a lot of potential, and I think she'll do well. And at the risk of letting Indian superstitions drive me, I have a feeling she needs to be there." Quint nodded without replying.

# CHAPTER 26

By the time they landed back in Tashkent, Uzbekistan, Rogers' man had completed his briefing, and both Quint and Dawson were feeling slightly better about the hastily conceived mission. They disembarked from the military aircraft to find the ground covered with a fresh layer of snow and followed their escort back to the commercial terminal. The same gate agent was there but was considerably more accommodating this time. It appeared that Rogers had already greased the skids so there was no attempt to extort money for their boarding passes.

The flight to Moscow was uneventful. As promised, their IDs and papers held up to the officials' scrutiny, and they cleared customs and immigration on their tourist visas with no problems. Once they exited the terminal, they were met by a man holding a cardboard sign with their hand-lettered names.

He escorted them out to a parking lot covered with dirty slush and piles of snow and pointed to the car Rogers had awaiting them, its headlights illuminating them as they approached.

"That baby would qualify for an antique license plate back in the states," Quint said with a laugh, as the two men approached the car. Dawson wasn't smiling. The dull black vehicle looked like it was carved from a single block of steel.

"We've got to drive eleven hundred miles. This piece of shit gonna get us there?" Dawson asked the driver, who remained behind the wheel laughing. Dawson waited for him to recover as his laugh turned into a heavy smoker's cough.

"This Russian Lada. We not make cars pretty but make tough. Built for Siberia weather and bad roads. Sturdy and heavy like Russian women, no? Only 300,000 km on her, she good for another 150,000, maybe more. She run when we no longer, it is my promise. I think maybe you not return her, but she serve you well."

Unconvinced, Quint saw no other option. The man spent a few minutes showing them how to work the elaborate manual transmission. "No stop unless on hill, otherwise maybe not start, battery not so good. In here," he pointed into the back seat, "are things you friend send. Good papers and name of hotel where you spend night in Pushnoy. In night, someone place second case in Lada. Have large time. Bye."

Quint ducked inside and noted the heavy smell of gasoline. He dug in the crevice of the seat and found the grime encrusted seat belt, dotted with what looked like ketchup and grease. It appeared to have seldom been worn.

"It just keeps getting better," Dawson muttered, as he shifted the car into gear.

"Here we are, in lovely downtown Pushnoy," Dawson announced a full day later. Quint's back ached from the grueling trip as he stepped out of the Lada into the howling wind accompanying the weather front that bore down on them. His face burned from the raw cold as he shuffled through the snow toward the shelter of the warm hotel office.

He wiped his runny nose with a wadded-up napkin and then thrust it back into his pocket. Except for grabbing at a stack of papers that fluttered in the breeze of the open door, the old Russian woman behind the desk seemed not to notice his entry.

After awkwardly waiting for a long moment to get her attention, it became clear she had no intention of acknowledging his presence. "If it's not too much of a bother, I'd like a room. Have any?" She raised her head slowly, peering at him over her half-glasses. After appraising him for a moment, a sour look frozen on her face, she offered a barely perceptible nod.

"Good. Now, might I have one... please" he said, trying to control his temper lest he find himself back out on the frigid street seeking shelter elsewhere. Here, north of the Arctic Circle, he doubted there were many alternatives. He was thankful Dawson had not come in. With his short temper they would almost certainly have ended up out in the cold.

Without a word, she placed a ratty form along with a chewed pen on the counter and resumed what she was doing. Struggling to fill out the registration form with a pen that skipped, Quint indicated the nature of their business to be tourism, though he wondered who in their right mind would come here on vacation.

When asked about the rate, the clerk simply pointed to the amount written on the registration card, $20 higher, he noticed, than the two other registration cards that lay on the desk below the counter. Without objecting, he withdrew a stack of bills and slid them back on top of the completed form. The old woman handed him his room key without having spoken a word during the entire transaction.

"Reminds me of my grandmother," he said, to the man who entered as Quint was leaving.

"Oh, really?"

"Yeah, she was a hateful bitch too," Quint said, in a voice loud enough to cast a parting shot at the old clerk. Though he figured she spoke only Russian and his insult was lost on her, it made him feel better as he stepped out into the cold to rejoin Dawson.

"Got us a nice room, preferably with a Jacuzzi and a masseuse to work out the kinks in our backs?" Dawson asked.

"I wouldn't get my hopes up."

"After driving the whole day in that shitty car, I'm ready to sleep on the lobby floor."

"With that witch at the front desk, I thought we might have to."

Having choked down only part of the two MREs they found in their equipment packs, they were both famished. They entered a small restaurant down the block and shook off the cold. The waiter's English was only slightly better than Quint's non-existent Russian, such that it was impossible to communicate. Unable to read the menu, devoid of any photos or English translations, Quint managed to communicate only that they were hungry and wanted the waiter to just bring them something.

He reappeared a few minutes later carrying two bowls of a reddish soup, which they hoped was borscht. While neither of them was particularly fond of it, each managed to force down half a bowl. The waiter then brought a stack of pancakes and a plate with a jellied meat dish. Before the waiter disappeared again, Quint hailed him while pointing to the menu and shrugging. The waiter walked back to the table and pointed at the word Kholodets and then said something which sounded like "Studen."

Dawson  warily eyed the dish. "What exactly is this?"

"Beats the hell out of me."

Each man took a tentative bite before concentrating on the stack of pancakes. By the time they had eaten enough to take the edge off of their hunger, most of the pancakes were gone, but the majority of the jellied meat dish remained. "I feel like I'm travelling with Leo," Quint said.

Dawson nodded. "Except he would actually have enjoyed this fare. As much as it pains me to admit, some of the weird shit he cooks and even the food at his favorite weird-ass Asian restaurant was better than this. We need to take care of business and get the hell out of this country before we starve."

"I'm more worried about getting arrested as spies by the KGB, or whatever they call the secret police these days," Quint said, as they headed back to their room. He unlocked the door and switched on the light to find a room even worse than he imagined. It was barely a foot larger than the bed, which was something between a twin and a double.

"One bed? You got a room with one bed? It's barely even a bed."

"Quit your complaining. If you don't like it, you can sleep in the car."

"Not in this life. I've slept with far worse than you."

# CHAPTER 27

Despite Quint's concern, they made it through the night without getting arrested. Before dawn the next morning, they left the hotel to once again battle the frozen north. Huge drifts had formed where the wind had blown snow against buildings and vehicles. Luck had smiled upon them, and their car had been parked in the lee where it didn't get buried.

"I just want you to know, it meant nothing," Dawson said.

"What?"

"Last night. I slept with you, but it meant nothing. And I don't want you to think I'm easy or go running around telling everybody."

Quint laughed. "Don't worry. I'll spend months, if not years, trying to block the image of you lying next to me, the sound of you snoring, and the smell of your Russian dinner."

As promised, they found another large, aluminum case inside the vehicle. Dawson drove while Quint inventoried their new equipment and supplies. He found a handheld satphone with a note detailing how to call their contact. Quint followed the instructions and heard a tinny voice answer, "Kelly's pool hall, featuring the toughest balls in town."

"Is this Comedy Central or are you actually going to be of some help?"

"Just trying to lighten things up. In our communication dynamics class, they suggested the use of humor as a way of quickly bonding with folks. It helps efficiency. Plus, us techie-types just work here 'cause they've got the coolest toys. We don't take the military rigmarole too seriously. Provided we take care of business, they cut us slack. I'm Roy."

"Okay, Roy, consider us bonded. Now, how about something useful."

"I can see you guys aren't going to be fun. Inside the case, you'll find two flight suits, along with a heavy set of outerwear—put it all on before you get into the pod. That way you don't wake up frozen if your landing proves not to be as smooth as we might hope. The pods have tight payload weight and volume restrictions so we had to split your equipment between the two. Are you Quint?"

"That's me."

"Sorry, you got the older, slower ride. Your pod will be carrying explosives and miscellaneous electronics. Dawson's will carry the weapons. Both pods contain a receiver to locate the transponder we've placed on the contraband container. You'll take off first with Dawson to follow, but he'll still arrive first in his faster UCAV. After we eject you in your pods, we'll fly the UCAVs back home."

"And where is home?"

"I'd have to shoot you if I told you. No, seriously, we're in China Lake. In fact, I plan on taking a desert ride in my Hummer once I get you guys delivered. The pod is basically a glider, and its landing sequence parameters are pre-programmed. Once you're released from the UCAV, all you do is lie back and enjoy the glide. Oh, and I guess I should tell you that while you've got the slow ride, it's the more dependable, so you may be like the tortoise and beat your hare partner there.

"Back to the case contents. Along with your cold-weather gear, you'll also find MREs, survival gear, radios, and lots of cool electronic gadgets, which you should play with before you get there. Especially the Tactical Unit, which has manuals with info for everything you should need, including maps and a GPS. There are a couple of bottles of water you can refill with snow and tuck inside your parka to provide an endless supply of water. Just avoid the yellow snow, yuk, yuk. Get it?"

"Yeah, I get it, hilarious."

"Call me back with any questions and have a pleasant flight doing whatever it is you guys are supposed to do."

"You mean they haven't told you?"

"Yeah, we know, but we're not supposed to let you know we know."

"Boy, that guy is a real freakin' comedian," Quint said after hanging up the phone.

"What'd he say?"

"You got the fast plane, but yours probably won't make it, which will screw me since you'll have all the weapons."

"Great," Dawson replied.

Quint studied the Tactical Unit and examined the rest of the items, filling Dawson in as they drove. It was nearly midnight when they arrived at the pick-up zone, where they stopped to wait. "The UCAVs are supposed to meet us here by 12:30 a.m., so we might as well suit up."

The men grunted and groaned as they slid into the flight suits and the down-filled outerwear. "I feel like the Pillsbury Doughboy," Dawson complained. "We best not fall down 'cause I don't think we can get back up by ourselves."

Quint nodded. "And we won't fit back in the car either. Of course, it'd be too hot anyhow."

The men divided up the rest of the case's contents and broke open a couple of MREs to snack on while they waited. They were still eating when the buzz of the first UCAV caught their attention. After appearing directly overhead, the unmanned craft circled once before landing. As it taxied toward them, Quint's satphone rang.

"Your ride has arrived. Unlash the clips on the entry hatch and load your gear. Then use the bar mounted on the fuselage to pull yourself inside the pod, sort of like climbing into a fiberglass sleeping bag. Close the end of the pod and let me know when you're ready. Any questions?"

"Yeah, what the hell was I thinking when I agreed to this half-assed scheme?"

"Hey, you'll be a hero. Perhaps not a live one, but a hero, nonetheless," Roy replied. A minute later, with a little help from Dawson, Quint was inside the pod. He wondered how Dawson would fare without the same assistance but was confident that he'd manage.

Quint's shoulders touched the sides of the light gray pod, tight, though not too uncomfortable. *Like an MRI, only not quite so roomy.* Even though he was not claustrophobic, he closed his eyes to shift his focus, trying not to think about the metal barrel prison in which he had recently been held. The pitch of the engine increased, and the pod shook as the UCAV bounced across the snow-covered grass runway. In seconds, they were airborne.

The drone of the engine quickly put Quint to sleep. He wasn't sure how long he had been out when the ringing satphone woke him.

"Wake up, sleepyhead, you're just about on target. When I issue the release command, you'll feel the pod drop, and the sound of the UCAV engine will quickly fade. You'll feel a bump as the pod's glider wings deploy, and then, barring any turbulence, you'll glide smoothly to a landing, which may be a little rough.

"After that, you just unclip the hatch and exit to do your James Bond thing. The container appears not to be moving, so we should be able to put you within a few hundred yards of it. Your receiver will locate the transponder on the container, but as a backup I'll still text you the precise GPS waypoint just before you detach. Ready?"

"No, but I don't suppose it matters, does it?"

"Nope. Ten seconds to release. Oh, and before you leave the pod, don't forget to pull the self-destruct cord. It'll start a timer and the pod will be destroyed an hour later. Can't leave our cool technology lying around, now can we?"

Quint counted down and as he reached zero, felt the pod disengage. Everything happened just as Roy had described, and he began silently gliding. While the turbulence was not as bad as he feared, the landing was much worse. Quint was slung around within the small pod as it lurched and bumped for what seemed like forever. By the time the pod finally came to rest, his neck and shoulders were aching.

He popped the compartment door open and felt the frigid night air pour in. The hairs in his nose froze with his first breath, but the prickly feeling melted away as he exhaled. *Damn, it must be 40 degrees colder here*. Though he had planned to remove the bulky outerwear after landing, faced with the vicious cold, he decided otherwise.

In the distance, he could barely hear the UCAV's engine as it faded into the night sky. After unloading his gear, he found and pulled the self-destruct lanyard and then struggled to his feet once he was clear of the pod.

Quint removed the night vision glasses from his parka pocket and did a 360-degree scan without spotting anything—including Dawson's pod. He searched through his equipment and found a miniature drone.

After a few minutes of fumbling in the cold, he had it assembled and ready to deploy. He started the engine and then hand launched it, per the instructions in the case. The drone began to fly, but as it reached 100 feet, it suddenly took a hard right turn, rolled over, and plummeted into the ground.

*Nice. I hope this isn't indicative of how things are going to go from here on out.*

Even before his satphone rang, Dawson knew something was wrong from the change in the engine's pitch an hour into the flight. "Dawson, we've got serious problems," Roy said, no hint of humor in his voice this time. "Your UCAV is losing power. We're going to have to crash land."

"Can't you just release the pod?"

"No, you're too low. We lost altitude while fighting to keep the UCAV flying. By the time it was clear the problem wasn't going away, we were already too low."

"Okay, so just land and I'll figure out some way to catch up with Quint."

"Uh... well... aside from the fact that you're miles away and there are no roads, we've never landed a UCAV with the pod still attached."

"Well, it looks like you're about to. So Roy, try real hard to get it right the first time," Dawson said. Though plenty worried, he realized his fate was now in Roy's hands.

"We've spotted a flat area with a break in the trees, and we're going in while she's still able to fly. Tighten your harness straps and hang on."

With the first impact, Dawson thought his kidneys ruptured. But before the pain could fully register, the UCAV slid sideways, and the pod detached, tumbling end over end. When he awoke a half hour later, his entire body was riddled with pain. Aside from his lungs aching from the frigid air he had breathed while unconscious and an assortment of miscellaneous aches and pains, he seemed to have survived more or less intact. He was thankful for the advice about wearing bulky outerwear; otherwise he was certain he'd still be unconscious—perhaps permanently.

He unstrapped himself from the remains of the pod and rolled to his side. After finding a way to rise that hurt the least, he struggled to his feet. The burning UCAV lay some distance away, the fire nearly out now that most of the fuel had burned off. The pod hatch had sprung open and separated from the lower portion to which Dawson had still been strapped. Debris was spread over an area the size of a football field, with none of it looking much like the weapons payload.

He was trying to clear his head when he heard the ringing of a satphone in the distance. Turning his head from side to side, he finally got a bearing on the source of the sound, but by the time he was halfway to it, the ringing stopped. He withdrew a small flashlight from his parka and began searching the debris before spotting the satphone. Amazingly, it appeared unscathed but for a few scratches. He took off one glove to punch the speed dial button for the UCAV command center.

"You're alive?" asked Roy, clearly unable to mask his surprise.

"I think so. I've got pain in places I didn't know I had from your abusive landing, but yeah, I'm alive."

"You're a lucky man."

Dawson laughed. "I will say that arming the self-destruct gizmo is going to be a little difficult since I have no idea where the pieces of it might be. Of course, your landing eliminated most of the need for it. Damn it! How come nothing ever goes smoothly? James Bond or that guy on Mission Impossible, what his name?"

"Ethan Hunt."

"Yeah, that's him," Dawson said. "They never have these kinds of problems. Their plans always go like clockwork. But not me,"

"Hey, don't' get all bent out of shape."

"What now?"

"That, my friend, is a very good question. Stand by. I'll call you back." A few minutes later the phone rang again. "Okay, we can get another UCAV to you, but it'll take at least a day to get another pod and make the modifications to attach it. Those things aren't in production yet."

"Obviously, that won't work. What's Plan B?"

"They're working on some way to extract you."

"Wait a minute. My buddy is by himself on a two-man mission. I have to join him."

"Well, Dawson, that's not going to happen."

"Bullshit! You're going to find a way to make it happen or I'm going to come find your skinny ass in China Lake and kick it all the way back here. Where's Quint's UCAV?"

"Not far from you, headed back to base."

"Divert it here."

"What?"

"You heard me. Divert that sonofabitch here, land it, and fly me to join Quint."

"But you don't have a pod."

"It's only a few miles. You and the other whiz kids are going to figure a way to keep me strapped to it long enough to get me there. If I have to hang on to the top of the wings by my fingertips, I'll do it."

"Hang on... err, I'll be right back."

Dawson paced back and forth while he waited. He retrieved an MRE from his pocket and popped a piece of chocolate into his mouth. Finally, the satphone rang again. "Okay, we came up with a way to strap you to the UCAV by making a bridle across the wing pylons, but it doesn't have enough fuel."

"What do you mean, doesn't' have enough fuel?" You planned to fly it all the way back to the base you launched it from."

"Marginally."

"That's plenty to get back here and then take me to Quint."

"Yeah, but not enough to get it back to a refueling point. The added weight makes it suck fuel like a pig."

"That's just too damned bad. You get me to Quint. After that, I don't give a shit what happens to the UCAV. If you can't refuel it, crash the sonofabitch. You know, sort of like you just did with me. Now, you get his UCAV here pronto."

"Yes sir, I'm on it." Twenty minutes later, Dawson thought he heard the sound of the drone's engine in the distance just as his satphone rang. "According to the satellite imagery, you'll need to walk about a mile south to get to an area big enough for us to land and take off again. But before you do, we need you to scavenge some parts from your UCAV to make the bridle." He quickly gave Dawson a list of what they would need and the coordinates for the landing site.

"Uh... Roy," Quint said into the satphone, "any idea where I might find Dawson?"

"He's experiencing technical difficulties."

"What the hell does that mean?"

"You remember the part about his drone being faster but less reliable? Well, his UCAV had problems. We finally got him off the ground, but then he crash landed. He's okay," Roy quickly added, "but we're working on Plan B right now. I'll get back to you in a jiffy with an update."

*Great! Alone in the middle of Russia's frozen tundra, where I'm not legally supposed to be, with no weapons, and tasked to somehow stop a container of bioweapons single handedly. What was I thinking?*

Quint examined the explosives and the electronics packs from the pod to kill time while he waited. He finished in a few minutes, and after great difficulty coping with his flight suit and outerwear, relieved himself just as the satphone rang.

"At Dawson's insistence, we're sending your UCAV back to get him. "

"His pod survived the crash?"

"No, that's the problem; he won't have one. But we came up with a way for him to ride below your UCAV. We'll fly low and slow so that he can eject when we reach your location, assuming he isn't frozen."

"Are you serious?"

"Yep. That's some partner you've got there. I damned sure wouldn't do it. It's long odds he'll still be alive when he arrives, and even slimmer ones that he won't be killed when he drops off. Oh, and the other little issue is that with this delay, the storm front coming your way is about to catch up with you."

Quint's stomach knotted thinking about what his buddy was risking to join him. *I'll definitely have to buy the beer when this one is over.*

# CHAPTER 28

"You know I don't have any weapons now," Dawson reminded Roy over the satphone. "Even if I'd found them after the crash, I couldn't carry them and the rest of this stuff for the bridle."

"That's okay. You probably won't live long enough to need them anyhow," Roy joked.

"You're not making me feel better, asshole."

"You're possibly the most determined man I've ever known. If I ever get stuck in the middle of the frozen Russian wasteland, I want you on my team. Now, better save your satphone battery. Call me when you get to the UCAV."

With his arms burning from carrying the equipment, his legs aching from walking, and the rest of his body sore from the crash, an hour later Dawson finally saw the UCAV parked at the end of an expansive clearing. After phoning Roy for instructions on constructing the bridle, Dawson dove in. Working without gloves, he constantly had to stop and blow on his fingers to prevent frostbite. After a half hour of struggling and cussing, he was just finishing when he heard the sound of approaching snowmobiles.

"We've got company, and I'm guessing it's not the Welcome Wagon. Get this thing off the ground," Dawson told Roy. The drone began taxiing with Dawson still fastening himself into the jury-rigged bridle. As the UCAV picked up speed over the rough field, he was thrust hard against the cables, which dug deep into his chest.

Ahead, the lights of two snowmobiles appeared at the edge of the clearing—it was going to be close. If the riders were armed and quick enough, he was likely to be toast. Just before reaching the tree line, the drone lifted, ending the brutal bouncing. Before the startled snowmobilers could react, he blasted past, too fast for them to bring their rifles to bear. Dawson cringed as he heard rifle fire, and held his breath as the drone cleared the trees by less than ten feet. But he was airborne once again.

Meanwhile, Quint lay on a slight rise, studying a truck 100 yards ahead. His tiny receiver detected the transponder beacon, confirming that he had the right container. To be certain, he donned the glasses in his pack and scanned the truck to locate the infrared beacon. By now, he should be in the cab of that truck headed for the coast, but without Dawson, he had no weapons.

Finally, Quint's satphone rang. "Roy, I don't know how long these guys in the target truck are going to continue sitting here with the engine idling."

"We've got Dawson a ride, but go without him if you're short on time."

"And how do you suggest I do that, throw snowballs?"

"Hey, I just fly the UCAVs; you guys have the field smarts," Roy replied.

"Yeah, but Dawson has the weapons."

"Uh... more bad news. No, he doesn't. Lost 'em in the crash. But I know that somehow you'll get aboard that container before they start moving."

"I hope you're right."

"Hey, you're not the only one having a bad day. With all of your problems, I had to cancel my desert ride. But no sacrifice for the cause is too great, I always say."

"I'm going now before I start tearing up." Quint hung up, resigned to playing things by ear. He had just begun to ease forward when he heard the sound of more truck engines approaching. *What now?*

A minute later, the headlights of three more trucks appeared. The continued past the truck already parked below, and stopped just forward forming a small convoy. *Great!*

The drivers exited their trucks to gather on the downwind side of the first truck for a smoke break. Seeing his chance, Quint eased down from the rise and worked his way toward the row of trucks. He hoped that all of the drivers remained in one group; otherwise, they would spot him and the jig would be up.

Quint crept behind the bioweapons truck and slid beneath its container, hugging the tires on the side closest to the men. Up ahead, he could see the men smoking and talking beside the first truck in line. Luckily, they were facing away with their backs to the wind. Quint was still catching his breath when he heard the group breaking up. His prayers that they would keep to the front of the truck where they might be less likely to spot him were answered.

The sound of the revving truck engines announced the convoy's departure and his truck lurched forward. Crouched low beneath the trailer, Quint continued forward, intending to climb aboard behind the cab. He realized that he didn't have long before the truck would be moving too fast for him to keep up. He preferred not to think about what would happen if he ended up stranded in this god-forsaken frozen wasteland.

With both hands, he snatched a chain hanging on the back of the cab and hopped on one foot with his other heavy boot raised high enough to climb up. His foot slipped on the icy metal, and he nearly lost his footing as he swung outside the edge of the trailer. For a horrible instant, Quint thought the driver might spot him in the rear view mirror but then saw that it was covered with ice.

Regaining his footing while maintaining a death grip on the chain, he continued to run. With the truck now moving so fast he could barely keep up, he planted his boot on top of the upper truck chassis and pulled himself up by the chains. He breathed a sigh of relief when he stood between the cab and trailer, relieved to find the back of the cab lacked a rear window from which he might be seen.

*At least riding on the last truck in line, I don't have to worry about being spotted from behind. But now what do I do?* With no better idea, a moment later, he called to check in with Roy.

"I'm on the bioweapons container truck behind a convoy of three other trucks," Quint whispered and then read off his position and current speed from the GPS. "What am I supposed to do now?"

"I'll get back to you, but get comfy; it's going to be a while."

Dawson's relief at escaping from the snowmobiles was short lived as the brutal cold sent icy daggers stabbing through the gaps in his outerwear. He had been airborne for only a few minutes when the expected front arrived, peppering him with freezing sleet. Even with his parka's hood tied tight and his ski mask in place, it felt like needles were being driven into his face and body. Dawson thought he had experienced every type of misery known to man, but this was as bad as anything he had ever endured.

*I hope Roy's right, and it's not too far. I can't take much more of this.* For the first time, he wondered if he would make it alive. He envisioned himself hanging frozen beneath the UCAV when it eventually ran out of fuel. But then he heard the engine rev twice, Roy's signal that they were on location, and the UCAV began its descent.

When it came time to release the bridle, Dawson panicked to find his right hand frozen tight to the harness. With his stomach in a knot, he jerked his left hand loose as the engine slowed further, signaling he needed to eject. With seconds to act, he grabbed the knife strapped to his chest, gasping when it nearly slipped from his numb fingers. With the flat snowy expanse less than ten feet below, he placed the blade on the release point of the bridle and sawed back and forth with all his strength. Finally, the cable parted, releasing him from the drone. He hit hard on the icy ground only to be jerked back up by his gloved right hand, still frozen to the bridle.

Dangling helplessly from the bridle while being bounced across the ground, it seemed like his arm was being ripped from the socket. Dawson knew that the UCAV pilot could not see him, and he was a dead man if the drone began to climb with him still dangling. Before he could decide what to do, the glove ripped free and he plummeted back to the ground and began sliding.

His left foot dug in, quickly changing his slide to a tumble and he rolled across the slick snow at fifty miles an hour. Finally, his speed bled off, and he came to a stop nearly 100 yards later. For several minutes, he lay still trying to convince himself he was still alive before struggling to his feet.

After confirming that nothing was broken, he reached inside his parka for the phone. "The turkey has landed."

"You made it?" Roy asked, incredulous.

"Piece of cake, but you need to work on the quick release aspect of the bridle, and an in-flight heater would be nice."

"We landed you well ahead of Quint's estimated position so that they wouldn't spot your UCAV. It'll take him an hour or so to reach you so you should have plenty of time to meet up at the coordinates I just sent you."

"Okay, gotta go. I'll check back when I'm in position."

Quint considered his limited options and decided to confirm that the bioweapons were in the container. The only trick in his bag was the explosives. *I'm afraid they might hear even a small C-4 charge, but maybe I could just use the detcord to help me cut a hatch.*

Slowly, he eased up the back of the truck cab, taking care to place his foot securely each time before pulling himself up. Once he cleared the top of the truck cab, the wind-driven cold poured in through each gap in his outerwear, and the icy snow pummeled him. Bracing himself against the frozen wind and struggling to keep his balance as the truck lurched over the icy roadway, Quint slid onto the container.

He withdrew a section of detcord from his backpack and formed a u-shape on top of the container about a third of the way back between two rows of rivets. He held it in place using tiny pieces of plastic explosive. *Not sure if this cord will cut through the metal roof, but if I blow up any of the bioweapons it'll put a quick end to the mission and me.* With the explosives in place, he slid back toward the front of the container.

A sudden lurch of the truck sent him sliding toward the side of the container roof, and he frantically flailed and clawed to keep from falling over the side. His gloved finger tips finally found a seam in the metal roof and stopped the slide. Taking a deep breath, he continued toward the front of the container, where he fired the detcord.

He worried that the driver might have heard the loud crack but relaxed when the truck continued. The blackened area of the roof had cuts on three sides. Using the screwdriver tool on his folding knife, he pried the flap free and pushed it down.

Peering inside, he saw a row of wooden crates four feet below. Concerned about the prospect of leaking bioweapons, he held his breath before swinging his legs down to land gently on the crate below. He cautiously inhaled to test the air, though with the frigid cold he knew it was impossible to smell anything. If there were any leaks, he guessed he would soon be dead.

*Well, if the bioweapons get me, at least it'll be quicker than freezing.* Standing on top of a crate, he pushed the metal roof section back into place, grateful for the still air. He explored the container with the beam of his flashlight and found it completely filled with crates, stacked nearly to the roof leaving a two-foot space just below him. The hazardous warning labels matched the ones he had seen back on Renaissance Island. He had indeed found the bioweapons, so he reached for his phone to call Roy.

Dawson was trudging through the blinding snow, when he heard the satphone ring again. *What now?*

"What's your location?" Roy asked.

Barely able to see his GPS screen held inches from his face, Dawson finally manage to read off his position coordinates.

"You've got thirty minutes to make it a quarter mile. Shouldn't be too bad."

"Yeah, well you're not the one slogging through a 30-knot blizzard wearing heavy gear, after having your ass soundly kicked... twice."

"Oh, quit complaining. At least you're alive, much to everyone's surprise, I might add. Contact Quint if you need an update, and good luck."

Dawson was dog tired and fought the nearly overpowering urge to lie down for a few minutes. But he knew it wouldn't be for only a few minutes—it would be permanent. So fueled by sheer willpower, he forced himself onward, concentrating solely on taking the next step. Beaten half to death, nearly frozen, on foot, and with no weapons, he was determined to help his buddy—somehow.

Quint withdrew a chemical hand-warmer from his pocket and worked to get the feeling back in his limbs. He was just starting to feel his fingers when the satphone rang.

"Okay, Dawson is almost in position; be ready to pick him up in about twenty minutes."

"Uh... Roy, that's going to be a little tough. I'm sitting inside the container with no weapons, so how do you propose I do that?"

"Don't know. You'll come up with something—and you best be quick." Quint hung up, wishing he shared Roy's confidence. Maybe he could use some more explosives to create a distraction and get the drivers to stop, preferably without blowing apart the cab and

himself. He worked a small piece of the explosive into
a ball before placing a detonator inside. Then,
dreading the cold, he refastened his jacket and left the
shelter of the container to climb out onto the back of
the truck.

Quint reached as far as he could toward the top
passenger side of the cab to wedge the ball of
explosives into a small seam. He then crouched low to
put distance between himself and the charge. *Here
goes.* The explosion in the confined space deafened
him, but his thick parka absorbed the blast. When he
looked up, the top corner of the truck cab was blown
partially open. *That damned sure ought to get their
attention.*

An instant later, the truck came to a screeching
halt, and the passenger door swung open. Quint stood
poised. As soon as the passenger jumped out, he
launched himself on top of the man, knocking him to
the ground. Quint elbowed him in the face twice and
grabbed the gun from his limp hand. He then heard
the driver, unaware of what had happened, yell to his
partner while stepping down from the far side of the
truck.

Aiming beneath the truck's cab, Quint fired twice,
striking the driver in the left ankle. He then fired
twice more into the man's torso when he fell. By the
time Quint stood back up, the passenger was regaining
his senses and began grabbing at Quint's legs. Quint
shot him square in the chest.

Knowing he had only seconds before the driver in
the next truck would wonder what happened, Quint
leapt back to his feet. He ripped the passenger's
bloodied parka from his body and jammed it into the
hole in the roof before climbing into the cab.

He quickly scanned the truck's controls, noting a
faded diagram depicting the shifting pattern on top of
the gearshift knob. With gears grinding, Quint
engaged the engine, but the truck didn't budge.

Frantically, he glanced around the cab before spotting what looked like an emergency brake release and tripped it. The truck lunged forward, and Quint worked through the gears.

The radio came to life with a Russian voice he assumed was someone up ahead trying to contact him. Quint keyed the mic while making his best imitation of static. Following the truck tracks barely visible in front of him, he pushed hard to close the gap. When he could finally see tail lights of the truck in front, he blinked his headlights, hoping the driver would interpret it as an okay signal. The radio erupted once, but after another of his static imitations, it went silent again, and they continued driving.

Protected from the howling wind and with the truck's heater blasting, Quint unzipped his parka to keep from sweating and breaking down its insulating ability. He withdrew the satphone from his parka and noticed the battery was getting low.

"Hey Roy, I pulled a rabbit out of the hat and got control of the truck. Where's Dawson?"

"Close. Better hang up; he should be calling you." Seconds later, the phone rang.

"Quint, I see headlights," Dawson said over the satphone. "I'm lying flat so they shouldn't notice me."

"I'm driving the fourth truck at the end of our little convoy."

"I'll waddle as fast as I can in this bulky gear, but you'll have to stop for me to get in."

"Okay, but be quick. You've got to be on board before they notice I've stopped."

Dawson lay glued to the snowy ground, sweating but afraid to unzip his parka. Finally he heard the sound of truck engines. "One... two...," he rose to his feet once the third truck passed. Moving as fast as he could in the cumbersome gear, he waved his arms at what he hoped was Quint's truck and saw it slow and then stop a few yards away. Dawson opened the door as he jumped onto the running board. "Go!" he yelled and swung into the seat while closing the truck's door.

With gears grinding and the truck's engine screaming, Quint accelerated to catch up with the truck ahead of him. He raced through the gears, exhaling only when tail lights appeared. "Not even a radio bleep this time," he said with pride. Dawson nodded, still catching his breath after his harrowing episode.

"As part of our Plan B, we've got enough C-4 to blow our container if we can't get it out of the country, but now we've got three more to worry about," Quint said.

"Do we know what's in them?" Dawson asked.

"No, but we can't afford to assume, now can we? We have to either capture the entire convoy or take it out. Any ideas what to do with the other trailers?"

"Let's take control of them and then figure it out once we know what they're carrying."

"And how do you propose we do that?"

"At least now we have the pistol you took from the driver." Dawson pointed at the pistol lying on the dash. "You'll think of something,"

Quint's eyes narrowed, "I've been getting that a lot lately." They drove on through the blizzard for what seemed like hours before the lights on the truck in front signaled it was braking. "Okay, it's show time. Ideas?" Quint asked.

"You run up on the driver's side waving your hands like a wild man pointing back here. When they step out of the cab, start running back. I'll wait behind their truck and clothesline the passenger while you take out the driver. We'll check them for more weapons and then move on to the next truck, hopefully better armed," Dawson said.

"How come I get to be the wild man?"

"Need I answer that?"

Quint laughed. "And what about the other two trucks? How do we take them?"

"Same plan and hope?" Quint shook his head and brought the truck to a stop a few feet behind the one in front. Immediately, he leapt from the truck's cab to run toward the driver's door, while Dawson ducked behind the trailer in front. A moment later, Quint, screaming like a mad man, came running back by him.

Crouched behind the trailer, Dawson heard the driver following Quint and then the passenger heading back on the opposite side. Just as the passenger walked by, Dawson stepped out and swung the pistol into the man's face, knocking him to the ground. Dawson placed the pistol against the side of the man's head and fired, confident the sound would be muted by the blizzard and the sound of the truck engines.

He darted around the truck and saw Quint trading licks with the driver. Dawson fired twice, hitting the man in the torso with both shots. They checked the men for guns and found a pistol for Quint. With both men now armed, they sprinted toward the next truck in line. Once again, Quint saw the driver and yelled pointing back and began to run with the same effect. The passenger, however, was already well ahead, walking toward the first truck in line.

Dawson couldn't see any lights or buildings ahead so he assumed they had stopped for a bathroom and smoke break. He cursed himself for failing to check how many rounds he had left, but realized at this point it didn't matter—he was committed.

He caught up to the second truck's passenger just as he paused to light a cigarette. Without breaking stride, Dawson fired two rounds into the man, but as he fell, the passenger in the first truck had already dismounted and saw what had happened. Dawson raised his gun to fire, missing to the right. He squeezed the trigger again only to hear an empty click.

"Shit!" Dawson turned and ran with the man in hot pursuit struggling to extract his own gun. Dawson rounded the corner of the second truck in time to see Quint shoot the driver.

"Quint, I'm empty. Shoot the guy chasing me," Dawson yelled, dropping to the ground. Quint raised his pistol and fired as soon as the man rounded the corner. "Okay, only the driver from the lead truck left. You see him?"

"No," Quint replied as Dawson grabbed the pistol from the man Quint had just shot. "Let's go find him."

Once again, the two men crept on either side of the first truck toward the cab, where they hoped the driver would be. Quint was halfway to the driver's side of the cab when his sixth sense kicked in. He turned just in time to see the driver emerging from behind the rear wheels of the trailer, gun raised. Without pause, Quint lunged away from the truck and fired twice, tensing for the impact of the bullet he knew must be coming. He hit the ground with a thud and rolled onto his back, raising his gun once again but there was no need—the last man was dead.

Quint rose and walked back toward the body of the last driver just as Dawson came around the front of the truck. He joined Quint staring at the driver and saw a red splotch over the man's heart. "I'm not that good, must be luck," Quint said, explaining to Dawson how he had taken the shot while diving to the side.

"That or God is *really* looking out for you, my friend."

"Okay, let's see what's in the other three trailers," Quint said. The first two were filled with barrels labeled in Russian. "I'll send some photos back to Rogers for translation so his folks can identify what's in them. Check out the remaining trailer."

He was still sending photos to Rogers when Dawson reappeared. "No barrels in the third one. It's filled with heavy weapons. Looks like our friendly terrorists have been shopping at Scumbags-R-Us."

"Maybe," Quint said. "Let's go back to our truck and wait to hear back from Rogers." Quint poured water to activate his MRE's chemical heater and gave it a minute to warm his entree. "I've got chicken fajita, my very least favorite of all. How 'bout you?"

"I've got chili. For your sake, I hope that adding water doesn't recharge the methane in the beans," Dawson said with a chuckle. The two men wolfed down packs of crackers while waiting for their meals to heat. Quint had already given up on choking down the rest of his entree when the phone rang.

"As you suspected, those trailers are loaded with bad-assed stuff. It appears to be an assortment of nasty chemicals. In the hands of terrorists, they could be used to produce some lethal dirty weapons. While they're not nearly as lethal as the bioweapons, they need to be destroyed."

"And how do you suggest we do that? How about you launch a cruise missile?"

"To hit a target inside Russia? Fat chance. We need to come up with a way to destroy the stuff without spreading it over the countryside. I'll brainstorm with my guys here and get back to you."

"We can't leave these trailers out in the middle of nowhere like this," Quint said after he hung up.

"No, and while I've no lost love for Mother Russia, we can't just blow this shit and scatter chemical waste everywhere, even if we had enough explosives to do it. I'd hate to risk hurting any locals unfortunate enough to be living out here," Dawson said, nibbling on a chocolate bar while Quint studied the GPS map.

"Well, we can't just sit here," Quint said. "There's some sort of facility a couple of miles up ahead. You drive the weapons truck, and I'll take our truck. We'll meet there and come up with something." Dawson pulled his truck alongside Quint's as they arrived at the facility a few minutes later, and both men dismounted.

"Looks like an industrial facility. I'll check the place out while you disconnect the cab of your truck," Quint said. He ejected the magazine from his gun to confirm it was fully loaded save the rounds he had fired. Sliding the gun into his pocket, he headed for the guard shack.

Drawn by the headlights and the sound of the trucks' engines, the guard stepped from the small building to investigate. As Quint approached, he gestured back toward the truck and mumbled into the wind. He heard the guard reply with what Quint assumed was a question while continuing to approach.

When the guard was only ten feet away, Quint removed his hand from his pocket with the gun pointed directly at the guard's chest. The guard immediately stopped and following Quint's gestures, placed his hands on top of his head and then turned back around. Quint marched him back to his post where he motioned for the man to lie on the floor.

Quint jerked the phone cord from the wall and used it to hogtie the man. He had just finished and was about to step back outside when the door opened and he saw a second Russian guard.

"Found this one making rounds around the perimeter," Dawson said, as he forced the man inside.

"Thanks. Now what do we do with him? They only have one phone and we don't have any tape or ro—" The roar of Dawson's gun and the second man falling to the floor shocked Quint.

"Problem solved. Now he won't be going anywhere." Dawson turned and headed back to the trucks.

Quint saw that the bullet had pierced the fleshy part of the man's thigh, enough to disable him without doing any major damage. The man gave a bewildered look to which Quint just shrugged and followed Dawson.

"I think this is a propane gas depot." Quint pointed to the row of pressure vessels. "I've got an idea." He walked back to his truck and climbed in. A minute later, he re-emerged with a canvas bag and headed toward the row of long, slender bullet-shaped storage tanks. When he was finished, he turned to Dawson, "Okay, let's go get the other trucks."

The two men climbed into the truck Dawson had disconnected, and headed back down the road. It took Dawson a minute to adjust to driving without a trailer. Halfway back, the satphone rang. "Other than using explosives to disperse the stuff, we've drawn a blank," Rogers said. "But you've got bigger problems. Our satellite picked up trucks moving your way fast. You guys better get out of there."

Dawson pulled up to the remaining two trucks as Quint hung up. "Trouble?"

"Yeah, we need to hustle—company's coming. I'm guessing that somebody's figured out what we're up to. Maybe one of the guards had a cellphone and called for help or triggered an alarm by not reporting in. We'll leave this truck and drive the other two back."

A few minutes later, Quint pulled his truck up alongside the row of tanks, and Dawson parked beside him. "Scrounge us up some weapons from the arms truck. I'll get an update from Rogers," Quint said dialing the phone. Rogers answered on the first ring. "How far away are those two trucks you spotted?"

"No more than ten minutes."

"I'll get back to you," Quint replied, and jumped from the truck. "Dawson, meet me at the bioweapons truck in three minutes—no more." Quint stopped when he reached the row of propane tanks and fiddled with the bundle he had earlier placed on the ground. When he returned to their truck, he saw Dawson with three automatic weapons slung on his back, busy breaking out the tail lights on the bioweapons trailer with the butt of his pistol.

"This'll make it harder for them to spot us."

"We've only got a few minutes until show time," Quint said.

"Grab these rifles and this bag of spare ammo. I'll get us going." They could see trucks approaching as Dawson finished scraping ice off his mirror and climbed into the cab. With a grinding of gears, he set their truck lurching forward. "I'll leave the headlights off. Maybe we can be out of sight by the time those trucks reach the propane depot." They rode on, keeping an eye on the rearview mirror for approaching trucks.

"Blow it! Blow it!" Dawson yelled. "No, wait! Don't blow it yet; wait a minute. They stopped just short of the facility and seem to be trying to decide what to do." A minute later, he saw one of the trucks stop at the depot with the other continuing toward them. "Okay, blow it! Blow it!"

Quint triggered the remote for the explosives. A massive blast sounded behind them, and an orange light filled the sky. A few seconds later, an enormous shock wave blasted their truck, nearly causing Dawson to wreck as he fought to keep the big truck headed down the road.

As the sound faded, Quint stared at the rear view mirror and watched the pursuing truck slide sideways and stop. But a few seconds later, it resumed its pursuit. The ringing of the satphone made him jump. "I'm betting that's Rogers."

"What the hell was that explosion we picked up on the satellite imagery?" Rogers asked.

"You told us to take care of the other three containers, didn't you?"

"Yeah, but not recreate Hiroshima. What in Sam Hill did you two do?"

"Being enterprising sorts, I used our explosives to blow up the propane tank depot, along with all the trailers and one of the trucks you spotted following us," Quint replied.

"You didn't blow the bioweapons too?"

"Nope. Blowing the chemical weapons was one thing but I figured the locals would appreciate it if we didn't disperse the bioweapons. And since I couldn't be sure the blast would incinerate them, we're bringing them with us."

"You guys are incredible."

"Well, before you tear up, the bad news is that the remaining truck is still on our tail. We're headed to meet the boat, but with these guys after us, I'm not sure how this is going to play out. We've got a good 70 miles of bad road between here and the rendezvous." A long silence followed, and Dawson thought the connection had been broken. "Rogers?"

"I'm here. Keep me posted."

# CHAPTER 29

"They're gaining on us," Dawson groaned a few minutes later. "I'm guessing they have the latest and greatest Russian truck technology as opposed to our old piece of shit. I can't see how they can run any faster than us on this iced-up road, so they must be able to accelerate quicker coming out of the hard turns. They'll be on our butt before we can make it to the evac point."

"I'll check the GPS and pick a spot to engage these guys where we'll have some chance to put up a fight. Drive as fast as you can, but try to keep the truck on the road, please." He laughed at Dawson's sour look.

Quint loaded the rifles and then studied the GPS in the lurching truck. "About a mile ahead, there's another industrial complex of some sort. I don't see much else; pull in there."

As the truck approached the guardhouse beside the gated entrance, two men stepped out and began firing from their right. Quint opened his door and leaned out with his AK-47 leveled. With bullets striking the truck's right fender and door, he pulled the trigger and raked the building before adjusting his aim to hit both of the guards.

Dawson crashed through the gate a second later and whipped in between two buildings, before skidding to a halt in the alley. The two men grabbed their weapons and the bag of spare ammo before leaping from the truck. The heavy steel doors to the building were locked, and before they could find a way to break in, they heard their pursuers' truck approaching.

Heavy automatic fire raked the building as the two men dove for cover. Dawson did a shoulder roll, sprang back to his feet, and then bolted for the corner of the building, the sound of automatic weapons fire spurring him on. As Quint peeked around the corner of the building to return fire, he heard a grunt behind him and feared Dawson had been hit.

"Whoever's firing must have night vision glasses to have spotted us in this mess. We're over a hundred yards away," Quint said, but got no response.

"Damn!" Quint said a minute later when he realized he was on his last magazine and Dawson, who had their spare ammunition, was nowhere around. He sensed as much as saw a form crawling along the building from behind him, but relaxed when he recognized Dawson's parka with the two yellow stripes on the left arm.

"You okay?" asked Quint.

"Hell, no, I'm not okay. I'm shot to hell. I took a round in the leg and one in my arm."

Quint knelt to help his buddy, and confirmed that the whole right side of Dawson's parka was matted with blood—this was no scratch.

"Quint, ol' buddy, I'm not thinking my clearest right now, so it's up to you to get us out of this jam. But whatever you come up with, you best be quick. I can still move, but don't know for how much longer."

"If we try to get inside the building, we'll get our asses shot up again. But if we stay out here, we'll be Popsicles before long."

"Not me. I'll bleed to death first," Dawson replied. "Check my leg."

Quint withdrew his knife and carefully slit the pants leg stiff with frozen blood. Inside, a river of bright red blood flowed down Dawson's lower thigh.

Without speaking, he removed the sling from his rifle to fashion a tourniquet.

"You sissy, it's just a scratch," Quint said, attempting to conceal his true concern. "Hold the free end of this strap tight. It'll stop the bleeding. Did you see how many of them there were?"

"I saw four get out of the truck. I nailed two before they shot me," Dawson replied.

Quint searched for his satphone, only to find the battery dead. A quick search of Dawson's pockets yielded his, but with a large hole where a stray bullet had pierced it. Quint removed the battery from Dawson's ruined phone and swapped it with his before dialing Rogers. "We're pinned down. Dawson is seriously injured and needs immediate care. You've got to get us out of here."

"Quint, you're in Russia; there's not much I can do."

"Maybe you didn't hear me. If you don't evac our asses out of here, the Russians are going to have the bioweapons and two prisoners or two corpses. Either way, you'll have some explaining to do. I don't have time to argue. Get us out of here!" Quint yelled, before hanging up.

"We're on our own until Rogers can get us help. We have to get you out of here. I know you're hurting, but I can't carry you and provide covering fire too. You'll have to lean on me."

"Wasn't that a song?" Dawson asked.

"Huh?"

"Lean on... never mind," he said thickly, while struggling to his feet. With Quint's help, he hobbled to the corner of the building, where Quint eased him back into a sitting position.

"Give me five minutes to work my way to the corner opposite this one," Quint said. "Then stick your rifle around this corner and fire three round suppression bursts so that I can spot their return fire. When your magazine is empty, lob this flash-bang grenade as high as you can so it goes off in the air. While they're blinded, I'll do my number."

"Not an entirely bad plan given the circumstances."

Quint noticed his voice was weak and wondered if it was from the pain or loss of blood. "Just hope it works," Quint calmly replied. He reached the far side of the building just as Dawson opened up, right on cue.

Two heavy caliber weapons returned fire with deadly accuracy, raking the corner of the building behind which Dawson was sheltered, enabling Quint to locate the positions of the two shooters. Shortly, the sound of Dawson's weapons ceased, and Quint closed his eyes to avoid being blinded. With the deafening explosion of the grenade still ringing in his ears, he leapt to his feet and charged forward.

Quint squeezed off several rounds as he reached the first man's position and heard a grunt. Without pausing, he continued running toward the second man, still firing. It was a calculated gamble, since if he had not taken out the first target, his back was now exposed. But, if he hesitated, the second gunman might open up on him. As he reached the second position, Quint threw himself to the snow-covered ground, his gun fixed on the form in front of him. Seeing no motion, he grabbed the wrist of an extended arm and could feel no pulse. The body was cold—it was one of the men Dawson had shot earlier.

Quint was surprised to see the body dressed in a Russian military uniform, a rocket propelled grenade lying beside him. *Glad he didn't have a chance to use that RPG.* Pulling himself nearer, he groped around for the night vision glasses he knew had to be nearby, and finally found them beneath the body. Quint donned them and scanned the area to locate the last man. Seeing nothing, he started to crawl away, but paused to sling the RPG over his shoulder. *This might come in handy.*

Quint made it back to the first man he had shot and found him still breathing. He too was dressed as a Russian soldier.

"I'm not going to leave you here. Let's get you on your feet. Maybe we can patch you up." As Quint reached for the man's left arm, the man rolled toward him and a knife appeared, slashing deep into Quint's shoulder. He recoiled backward while raising his gun, and squeezed off two shots. The first missed but the second stuck the man in the throat just as the knife plunged down again. The man collapsed, no longer breathing. Quint did a quick check of the puncture wound in his shoulder. While it was deep, he didn't seem to be losing much blood.

Quint scanned the surrounding area and seeing nothing, crouched low as he worked his way back to Dawson. He edged around the corner and saw Dawson's form, right where he had left him. "It's Quint. Dawson?" Hearing no response, he crept closer. He saw a series of bullet holes that had penetrated the corner of the metal building.

"Those boys are serious, using metal piercing rounds," he said to himself, as he edged closer. "Aww, shit!" Dawson had been hit again, and the entire left side of his head was a bloody mess. A quick inspection confirmed that Dawson needed medical help—and soon.

Grunting from the pain of the knife wound, he lifted Dawson in a fireman's carry, his rifle still in his right hand. With the night vision glasses in place, he scanned in all directions, hugging the wall of the building while working his way back toward the truck.

Quint laid Dawson in the passenger seat and then, having seen no sign of the remaining man, grabbed his gun and an extra magazine from Dawson's stash. *I need to get Dawson out of here. But if this guy is still alive we'll never make it out of here.*

Quint made a sweep around the building some 50 yards away. Despite the urgency to get Dawson help, he worked slowly, taking pains to move silently while missing nothing. Halfway around the building, he saw a faint image and froze. Behind a snow berm, he spotted a shape moving toward the truck.

Quint changed course and angled to intercept the man. When he was still 30 yards away, he slid into a prone position. He held his breath as the man closed from his left. With the gun sighted he took a deep breath. Just as he was about to squeeze the trigger, an explosion of gunfire erupted from his right.

"Damn!" Quint grunted from his shoulder wound. Too late, he realized that while focused on what he thought was the last man, he had missed a fifth one. Quint squeezed off two rounds and took down the man on his left. He then rolled twice before raising his rifle and despite a withering fusillade of lead, opened fire.

He heard a scream, and the gunfire ceased. Unwilling to risk another mistake, he confirmed that both men were dead—noticing that they too were wearing Russian military uniforms before making his way back to the truck. He tossed the RPG inside, and got the truck back on the road.

# CHAPTER 30

Quint drove with one hand while retrieving the satphone and dialing Rogers with the other. "Okay, the next words out of your mouth better be, 'Quint, I've got a chopper on the way.'"

"Quint, I've got a chopper on the way."

"Really? You got it okay'd?"

"Hell, no. It'll be my ass, but it's done. I managed to dig you up a stealth one, so maybe we won't end up pissing off the Russians. It's fast and can hug the ground."

Quint glanced at Dawson and hesitated for a moment before replying. "Just get it here soon."

"Your call sign is Saber and theirs is Tiger. Give me your coordinates." Quint read his position off his Tactical Unit. "There's a small town about 6 miles ahead of you. On the south side, just before you get there, is what appears to be an airstrip with a couple of warehouses. They'll meet you there in 25 minutes."

"I appreciate what you did for Dawson's sake."

"You'll have to blow the bioweapons," Rogers said.

"Can't. We used the explosives to blow up the other containers at that propane depot."

"Well, we can't just leave them there."

Quint was silent for a moment. "After they evac Dawson, I'll continue on. If I can stay awake long enough, I'll make the rendezvous," Quint replied.

"I know it sucks, but the boat will be waiting for you in Murmansk. They'll contact you with directions on where to meet them at the harbor. As soon as you offload the container, the boat will get under way to meet the sub, which is standing by in international waters."

Quint hung up and struggling to keep the truck on the road while maintaining his speed, checked on Dawson again. He cinched the strap on his wounded leg tighter and confirmed that the bleeding from his other wounds wasn't life threatening. The head wound worried him the most. From the looks of it, the left eye was history, and Quint wondered how Dawson would cope with that—assuming he lived.

"Hang in there, buddy," he said, when he saw Dawson's good eye open nearly an hour later. "We're nearly to the extraction point."

"Screwed the pooch on this one. May not make it."

"Shut the hell up. Only the good die young. You'll break 100."

"How bad is it? Don't shit me."

"It's bad, buddy, I'm afraid real bad. But we're going to get you out of here," Quint said, as he pulled the big rig off the road and stopped behind a derelict factory building, where he was to meet the chopper.

"What about my eye? Is it—" Dawson stopped as he heard the muffled sound of a helicopter approaching.

Quint keyed their handheld VHF radio. "Tiger, Tiger, this is Saber." His second attempt was rewarded with a response.

"Saber, this is Tiger."

"Tiger, we're standing by for immediate evac. You can land at the edge of the parking lot to the north of the building. There's a transponder and a blinking infra-red light on top of our 18 wheeler." Ahead, he could barely make out the chopper emerging through the wind-blown snow as he slammed the truck into gear. Without slowing, he pulled away from the concrete building, kicking up snow as he came to an abrupt stop alongside the helicopter.

Quint leapt out of the driver's door and ran around to drag Dawson out. By the time they reached the chopper, the door had swung open, and the paramedic was ready to pull the unconscious Dawson into the cabin.

"Holy shit! You guys are a wreck," the paramedic exclaimed, seeing the full extent of Dawson's injuries and Quint's bloody shoulder.

"Things didn't go quite as smoothly as planned," Quint replied.

"No shit. Let me see your wound."

"Just worry about Dawson. How bad is he?"

"His pulse is weak, and his left eye is ruined. He's in bad shape. You've done all you could for him. Now it's up to us. If we don't get him to a medical facility quickly, we may lose him. I'll have a surgical team ready as soon as we land, but it's still two hours away. You don't look so hot either. I'll get you fixed up after we lift off."

"I'm not going with you."

"That's crazy. If we somehow manage to make it out of here, we can't come back for you."

"I understand. But I've got to get that load of bioweapons out of here."

"At least let me look at that shoulder." The paramedic pointed at Quint's blood-soaked parka sleeve while wiping his hands. Quint begrudgingly agreed now that they had an IV started on Dawson.

"You're one lucky SOB. The knife wound is deep but it missed your arteries so it doesn't look like it did any serious damage. I'll give you a shot for the pain and stitch you up, but it won't be pretty." A few minutes later, he was finished. "Try not to put too much stress on the stitches, and you'll be good as new in a couple of weeks."

In the distance, Quint saw the headlights of an approaching truck. "Another truck? Give me a break. Move it," Quint yelled. The paramedic signaled the pilot over the intercom, and the chopper's engine spooled up.

As the truck closed, Quint saw the flicker of automatic weapons fire. Though they were out of range, in seconds that would no longer be the case. "Incoming fire," he yelled, as he bolted toward the bioweapons truck. The pilot responded by jamming the throttle forward, lifting the chopper off the ground.

The truck was nearly within firing range when the sound of gunfire ceased. Quint's puzzlement over the abrupt change quickly evaporated when he saw the reason—a man stood in the back of the truck with an RPG resting on top of the cab. Quint realized that as soon as the truck stopped, they would steady the RPG and fire. Then Dawson would die.

Quint jumped back into their truck and drove it like a sports car, darting behind the building to gain distance and cover. *Okay, I'm an army of one against a truck full of pissed-off Russian soldiers, or terrorists, or whoever the hell they are. If I don't get this truck out of here, they'll get the bioweapons. But if I do, they'll see me as soon as I clear the building. Plus they're going to try to take out the chopper. What happens next is bound to be ugly. Wait a minute...* He stopped the truck behind the building and jumped out.

With the RPG he'd found slung over his good shoulder and carrying the AK47, he sprinted through the driving snow toward the corner of the building. Skidding to a halt, he saw a man standing atop the enemy truck with an empty launcher in his hands; an RPG was already in the air.

He glanced back over his shoulder and saw the chopper drop, trying to duck behind the farthest building to escape the missile headed straight for them. An instant later, Quint saw the chopper disappear, followed by a bright orange cloud of flame. His stomach cramped at the sound of the explosion— he knew what it meant.

Quint raised his own RPG and fired in one smooth motion. He could see the driver's face frozen in horror, and an instant later, the truck exploded, throwing men in all directions. Holding the AK47 in his good arm, Quint continued toward the truck, firing at anything that moved. Wounded and alone, he had no doubts about what would happen if any of them survived.

"Damn it all!" Quint yelled at the burning pyre where Dawson's chopper had been only seconds before. He sunk to his knees, unable to accept that his best friend was gone, and unwilling to consider continuing on without him. For a long time he remained kneeling, ignoring the cold and the ache in his shoulder.

Dawson was one of those rare friends who was like a brother. They had endured so much together that even after long periods apart, their friendship was unaffected.

Quint considered trying to recover Dawson's body, but knew it would be hours before the wreckage would cool enough to approach. And the reality was, there would likely not be much left to recover.

Realizing it would serve no purpose to remain longer and risk losing the bioweapons, he forced himself up and back into the truck. He had left it idling during the entire episode to prevent the oil from becoming so cold the engine wouldn't restart. The relative warmth of the truck's cab was a relief from the brutal cold outside, but with the heater going full tilt, the coppery smell of Dawson's blood filled the truck cab.

Quint sat with his head on the steering wheel, trying to muster his last ounce of will to continue. He was tired, so very tired. He took a deep breath and pulled back out onto the road.

A hundred feet from the smoldering truck, Arnold was regaining consciousness. The rest of his men had been killed by the RPG Quint had launched. Only his distance from the explosion had saved him.

Syndy would be furious over the loss of the explosives and weapons. But if he could bring Quint back alive, and maybe even the bioweapons, perhaps he could still avoid a fate like Roberto's. The image of the man being roasted alive in the elevator still haunted him. He removed his satphone to dial his Russian army contact.

# CHAPTER 31

The road was covered with icy chunks broken loose from the pavement by the pressure of passing trucks. The truck's tire caught a particularly deep rut shaking the entire vehicle and knocking the parka out of the hole in the back of the truck cab. A sudden gust of cold air accompanied the parka's exit.

Each bump and jolt telegraphed waves of pain through Quint's upper body from his stab wound. Now that the shot had worn off, his left arm was throbbing. He flexed it periodically hoping to keep it from becoming as stiff as his bloodied jacket.

For the first hour, Quint replayed the scene with the RPG and the chopper over and over in his head, unable to accept Dawson's loss. *He's gone; he's really gone. I should never have called in that chopper. I should have driven him to meet the boat. If I had, he'd still be alive.*

Quint knew he had to stop obsessing over his buddy; there would be plenty of time for mourning later. With or without Dawson, and whether or not he wanted to, he had a job to do. And he would do it; he had to do it.

Beaten, battered, and fighting exhaustion, Quint desperately wanted to pull over for a few hours of sleep. But if he was going to prevent the bioweapons from falling into the hands of terrorists, he had to continue. The ringing of the satphone startled him.

"Enjoying your tour of northern Russia?" Dakota asked.

"Oh yeah. The bullets are beautiful this time of year," Quint replied.

"Glad you're not bored." Dakota laughed and then explained where to meet the boat.

"Just you, Willy, and Marcia, or did any of the rest of the team join you?" he asked, and then winced as the image of Dawson's face flashed through his mind.

"Nope, we're the only ones who remain vigilant. The rest are in pursuit of wenches and grog."

"Oh," Quint replied, without a sarcastic retort. When he spoke again, his voice was somber. "Dawson's dead."

"What? How'd that happen?"

"He got shot up bad and the bastards that shot him nailed the evac chopper with an RPG before I could return the favor."

"I can't believe it."

After they hung up, Quint was lost in thought about Dawson when the ringing satphone interrupted him again. But when he answered, no one was there. The same thing happened twice more a few minutes apart. *That's odd.*

The truck's heater was unable to overcome the cold pouring in from the open hole in the truck's cab. Moisture from his breath began frosting over the inside of the windshield, and he used his good arm to wipe the foggy window. He eyed the fuel gauge and realized that he was getting low, with no place to refuel. *Great! Like I need something else to worry about.* At least the snow had eased off.

His eyelids seemed to weigh a pound. Visions of a thick steak, a glass of red wine, and a warm fire filled his mind. Quint rolled the window down until he could no longer stand the icy needles stabbing him in the face and then sang silly songs at the top of his lungs in a desperate effort to stay awake. Just as the satphone rang, he saw a sign indicating only another 30 kilometers to Murmansk.

"I figured after finishing with the UCAVs, that'd be the last I'd hear from you. What, missing my voice?" Quint asked as soon as the call connected.

"That, and we're a full-service drone unit. You have the dubious distinction of being our first victim... err passenger, and I care," Roy replied with a chuckle, before his voice turned serious. "Since few people are cleared to know what you guys are up to, Rogers asked that I continue to provide whatever support I could. We've been having a tough time with our satellite recon due to the heavy overcast, but a clear spot temporarily opened over your region. It appears there's a roadblock ahead."

"Who set it up?"

"Does it matter?"

"Good point. Damn! I can't catch a break. Any ideas? I'm too tired to think."

"Yeah, you've still got that tactical unit we gave you, right?"

"Of course, I'll treasure it always."

"Good," Roy replied, without any further attempt at humor. "I'll send you a map with a route marked on it that will bypass them. But it won't take them long to figure out you're on to them, so you need to haul ass."

"But even if I get around them, they'll just meet me at the harbor, won't they?"

"I had the same concern, but with all of the witnesses there—to say nothing of the security guards with itchy trigger fingers—I'm told we shouldn't worry too much about that."

"Of course, it's not their butts on the line. But I suppose that does make sense. How in the hell do they keep tracking me?"

"Do you have any idea who they are?"

"The last ones were wearing Russian army uniforms."

"Hmm. Well aside from the fact that there aren't too many roads, there also aren't too many satphones in that neck of the woods. They might have the capability of tracking the signal, so that's one way. Try not to use it unless you have no choice."

Quint felt a small burst of adrenalin. Maybe it would give him the boost he needed to get through the next twenty minutes.

He carefully followed the route marked on the tactical unit's screen, knowing he couldn't afford to make a wrong turn. The route meandered through several back roads before finally putting him back onto the main highway. He saw several vehicles in the distance behind him but noticed they no longer seemed to be shrinking into the distance.

"Damn!" Quint yelled, as he pushed the accelerator to the floor, increasing his speed to the point he could barely stay on the road. He blew past the city limits sign and took the right turn marked on his tactical unit. The lights behind him grew steadily larger, so obviously the vehicles were continuing to gain on him.

Ten minutes later, he saw the port in front of him, and took his first deep breath as he saw the vehicles chasing him stop a scant quarter mile behind. *Don't know who those boys are, but it would appear they're not authorized to enter the port—at least for now.*

Quint slowed down as he approached the port and saw the first check point, replete with heavy locked gates and armed guards. He retrieved the clipboard that had fallen from the dash onto the seat beside him. It appeared to have a shipping manifest, which he hoped would be all he needed to get him through. Quint had no idea what the manifest indicated he was hauling, though he was certain it wasn't bioweapons.

With a pistol tucked beneath his left leg, and the AK-47 leaned against the door, he stopped as a guard exited a small building and approached. The several guards who remained inside appeared eager to use their weapons. Quint had little doubt how a gun fight would end.

The surly guard snatched the clipboard and gave it a cursory look. A cloud of moisture from the man's breath enveloped his head. Quint prayed he wouldn't ask any questions, as his inability to speak Russian would bring an instant end to the charade. After a few seconds that seemed to last forever, the guard grunted and scribbled a signature with a pencil near the bottom. He motioned Quint forward and quickly headed back to the warmth of the small post.

"Nice ride. I was expecting some old piece of shit," Quint quipped, as he climbed down from the cab and approached Dakota. In front of him sat a boat that looked even worse than the rusted hulk they had used in Uzbekistan. It appeared to be an ancient wooden fishing trawler with the fishing gear stripped off, leaving an open deck big enough to accommodate the container.

On its stern, the name *Sostenuto* was crudely written. "I'm guessing that *Sostenuto* is Russian for, ugly turd?"

Dakota stepped out from the bridge while donning a heavy coat. Quint got a quick glimpse of his t-shirt which said: *There is no "I" in team but there is a "U" in suck!*

"Despite what you might think, Murmansk doesn't offer a wide selection," Dakota replied, appearing slightly offended as Marcia and Willy both grinned. "And doing anything without arousing the already suspicious Russian authorities is a bit of a challenge."

"Well that big-assed yacht over there would have made a better choice." Quint pointed at the ship

docked at the far end of the harbor. It bore the name
*Syntillate* in huge gold leaf across its stern.

"I voted for that, too." Willy stepped down onto the
dock and shook hands, "but was overruled."

"Glad you were able to join them," Quint said.

"Couldn't keep me away. I figured somebody had to
keep them straight with both you and Dawson gone. I
mean..." Willy halted. "Sorry, I heard about what
happened. I didn't mean any—"

"I know." The memory of the chopper fiasco came
flooding back, even after Quint had worked hard all
day to suppress it. "I've spent most of the last few
hours alternating between grieving and blaming
myself for somehow not preventing it from happening."

"Quint, there's nothing you could have done—"
Dakota started to say.

"I know that... in my head. But in my heart, well,
that's another matter."

"Damn, it's hard to believe." Willy looked down, and
the group stood in total silence for a moment.

"Look, I managed to bypass a roadblock meant for
me. Once I got back on the main road, someone
followed but evidently didn't have port credentials. But
I'm guessing that could quickly change with a couple of
bribes in the right places. So we need to get the show
on the road."

Dakota nodded. "Willy and I will arrange for a crane
to offload the container, but it'll take us a few minutes.
You're beat, and with your injured shoulder, you
wouldn't be of much help anyhow. So why don't you let
Marcia find you some clean clothes and check out that
bloody shoulder."

Marcia led Quint into the boat's small wheelhouse
and pirated a fresh shirt from Dakota's bag, and a
spare parka from the galley. "I'll redress your wound
after you're done cleaning up." A few minutes later,
Quint was feeling slightly better and looked vastly
improved. He stepped out of the bridge in time to see

the massive crane set the bioweapons container onto the stern of the small boat

"You hungry?" Dakota asked, and saw Quint's nod. "Why don't you go with Willy? While he clears us out at customs, you can get something to eat at that little place up the hill. Meanwhile, I'll see if I can round up our captain and get the ship ready to get underway."

"Dakota, we need to get out of here now," Quint protested.

"I'm as eager as you to get the hell out of here. But if we try to leave without clearing out, they'll arrest us. This is Russia. Nobody is in a big hurry here, so it'll probably take at least a half hour to clear customs. Might as well get something in your stomach. If you're not back when we're cleared to go, we'll come get you." Resigned, Quint nodded and headed off with Willy.

Willy entered the small customs office and took his place in a long line of people already waiting there. Quint continued on to the café and collapsed into a booth, exhausted. He ached all over, but his shoulder was really killing him. Still sick over Dawson, he had little appetite but knew he had to eat something. Maybe it would make him feel better. The waitress appeared with a menu. Unable to read a word, he pointed at a block at the top, hoping it was the daily lunch special.

*I hope it's just something hot and bland, not weird.* She nodded and Quint pointed at the bottle of beer on the adjoining table. He wearily watched the perky waitress disappear into the kitchen. She reappeared moments later with an open bottle of beer and a steaming plate of food—bland and hot.

In the process of hoisting the container onto the boat, they had attracted the notice of several Russians. Though Dakota had paid the dock master a sizeable bribe, it was only a matter of time before somebody alerted the authorities, who would certainly inquire what they were up to. "Sir, it is time to go," the captain yelled to Dakota, who stood beside the container overseeing the dockworkers lashing it down.

"Did Willy and Quint make it back?" Dakota asked Marcia.

"No. I'll try calling them."

Dakota nodded and climbed the ladder to the bridge to speak with the captain. "My two guys should be back any minute."

"We've got to get the hell out of here now or we will not be leaving at all. A man who I pay to be my ears in the harbor tells me that we have attracted the wrong type of attention from the wrong type of people. We must leave."

"But my man is not back yet from clearing us through customs."

"We can't wait."

"I thought you said we might be arrested if we don't have our paperwork approved."

"True. I'm not sure what you have in that container of yours, but given the amount you were willing to pay me to carry it without knowing, if they find us with it on board, we may be shot. I'd rather take our chances. If we make it out and your guy hasn't cleared customs, I'll pay some bribes when I return to deal with it."

"Give me one minute." Dakota ran out the door to find Marcia.

"It looks like they're about to drop the hammer on us, so we need to get this bioshit out of here before we end up in serious deep doo doo. I'm not sure what they'd do if they caught us with this stuff, but I definitely don't want to find out." Though normally calm, Dakota was panicked. "Can you go deal with finding Quint and Willy while we get under way?"

"I hate to leave you hanging. You don't need the rest of us?" Marcia asked.

"At this point, it doesn't make sense to risk having more than one of us aboard if the Russians seize the boat."

"No problem," Marcia said. "Go ahead and leave without us. As long as you're on board to coordinate the meeting with the sub, I'll find Quint and Willy and we'll catch a flight back to the States."

"Give me a minute," he said, and then ducked below as the engine on the trawler fired up. He returned a moment later carrying two bags. "Here's your bag and Willy's. They won't do you any good on here."

"Thanks." Marcia set the bags on the dock and helped cast off lines.

Quint wolfed down a belly full of meat and potatoes and had just finished guzzling the second of two beers when he saw Willy enter the restaurant, a sheaf of papers in his hand.

"We're cleared out." Willy slid into the seat across from Quint while waving off the waitress.

"That was quick."

"I slipped a few of the folks in front of me a couple of bucks and got moved up in line. You done?" Quint nodded. He paid his tab and the two men left the restaurant, headed back toward the harbor. They crossed a small alleyway without noticing a mound of cardboard boxes and debris piled at the end. They never saw the two men who stepped out behind them holding Tasers, which they fired in unison.

The captain of the *Sostenuto* eased the ancient ship away from the dock. They were halfway to the mouth of the harbor when Dakota's handheld satphone rang.

"The sub is standing by to meet you once you clear Russian territorial waters," Rogers said. "They've rigged chocks on their deck, so that they can surface beneath your boat and lift it out of the water. That way, you can offload the material even in heavy seas. They'll have only a short window so be ready. Do you have a davit to hoist off the barrels?"

"Not a functioning one. We used a crane back at the harbor to hoist the entire container onto our deck, but I'll come up with something." Dakota felt the heavy swells as they cleared the harbor and set course for the rendezvous with the sub. He glanced back one last time and saw the large yacht, *Syntillate* moving sideways away from the dock using its thrusters. Just before he lost sight, he saw it headed for the harbor mouth.

# CHAPTER 32

An ambulance was standing by with a wheeled gurney ready when the chopper landed. Once the doors swung open, the waiting paramedics placed the unconscious body on the gurney before loading it into the ambulance. The pilot watched the ambulance roar off with lights flashing and siren screaming headed for the nearest hospital's emergency room.

He turned back to join the ground crew swarming around the helicopter examining the fuselage and badly damaged tail rotor. "What in the hell happened? How'd you manage to keep this thing in the air?" One of the ground crew asked, clearly amazed at the extent of damage the chopper had sustained.

"Just as we were taking off, the buddy of the guy we rescued warned us of an incoming RPG," the pilot replied. "I had nearly dropped behind the cover of a building when the missile struck the roof, peppering us with shrapnel. I thought we were going down but that tough bird kept flying. I'm surprised the vibration didn't shake her apart."

The co-pilot shook his head. "He's being modest. If not for his fancy flying, that RPG would have had us. Not many could've pulled off that stunt," he said, slapping the pilot on the back.

"You guys must be living right," the head of the ground crew replied. "Beer's on me."

"What does the ship's name, *Sostenuto,* mean?" Dakota asked, as the former fishing boat pounded through the heavy seas in the dark.

'The previous owner was Italian and named it for his mother's musical passion. It means sustained, as in the pedal on a piano," the captain explained, with a shrug. "We don't get to choose, so I'm stuck running a boat with a stupid name. At least I've got a job, even if it is running this stripped-down fishing boat as a freighter."

Dakota felt somewhat out of place not serving as crew, but the owner was adamant that his captain and engineer run the tiny ship. "You don't need me here wringing my hands. I'm going to go get some coffee. Want some?" Dakota asked. The captain shook his head and openly took another hit from the flask he carried in his pocket, not offering to share.

Dakota exited the bridge, leaving the captain to his vodka. He made his way down the ladder to the tiny mess hall and poured the remaining coffee from the urn. *They call this coffee? It must have been strong when they made it, but now I need a fork and knife. Maybe the sub will have better... that is if we make it that far.*

Above on the bridge, the captain studied the radar display. "Problems?" his mate asked.

"Maybe," the captain said, as he looked up. "A ship left the harbor after us and is closing, on our same bearing. I'm guessing it's *Syntillate.* Not too many other possibilities."

"And that's a problem?"

"The only reason to be headed our way is to meet another boat. There's nothing else in this direction except ice."

"You don't think it's just a coincidence?" The captain shook his head. "What do we do?"

"Nothing. We're running as fast as this hulk will go. There's no harbor nearby, and if we try to return, we'll run right back into them. If they're looking for trouble, we won't be giving them much with our one pistol."

An hour later, the mate studied the radar. "Looks like we've got another 20 minutes before they catch up. It's probably too early, but you think we should try contacting the sub?"

"Couldn't hurt. Go below and have the American make the call," the captain replied. After the mate had left the bridge, he picked up the ship's VHF radio mic to hail the pursuing ship.

"*Syntillate, Syntillate*, this the *Sostenuto*."

"*Sostenuto* this is *Syntillate*."

"You are on our same heading and closing. Please state your intentions."

"Intentions? Just taking an evening cruise to watch the northern lights. Why?"

"Just being cautious. Not much ship traffic here," the captain replied, and altered course on the autopilot to the west by 15 degrees. He was still glued to the radar display when the mate reappeared on the bridge.

"What's happening?" he asked the captain, who held up his finger and then replied a moment later. "I knew it. I altered course and they did too. I don't know what they're up to, but I don't like it." Ten minutes later, he no longer needed to look at the radar; the ship was close behind.

"*Sostenuto, Sostenuto*, this is *Syntillate*."

"Go ahead," the captain replied.

"Step out on the port wing of your bridge. We want to show you something."

The captain rubbed the back of his neck before shaking his head at the mate and stepping out the port side of the bridge. With its name illuminated in large neon letters along the side and the soft illumination from the staterooms and salon within, the yacht was striking against the darkened sky as it pulled alongside some 50 yards away.

A blonde-haired man stepped from the yacht's bridge and gave a friendly wave. As the captain raised his hand to respond, he saw the man lift a tubular device onto his shoulder. A moment later, a tongue of flame erupted, and a missile leapt toward them. It struck the captain in the chest before he could duck, slamming him against the wheelhouse and killing him instantly.

On the deck below, Dakota was dressed and about to head topside with his satphone when he heard the sound of the wheelhouse being destroyed. He ran up the ladder to find the remains of the captain and mate. With the roof blown halfway off and all the glass shattered, the frigid wind stabbed him with its icy fingers. Outside, he could see the yacht and guessed what had happened.

*Damn! What the hell do we do now?* He quickly realized that there was no *we* any longer; he was it. He dropped back to the deck below, his mind racing as he scrambled to find his parka. He had one arm in the jacket when he felt the ship shift upwards.

With a smile, he raced below to the engine room where he hit the emergency stop and then returned topside while still fastening his parka. By the time he stepped outside, the conning tower of a gigantic sub loomed ahead of the ship. A moment later, he heard a stream of automatic weapons fire as the yacht crew unleashed a volley at him.

Dakota ducked back inside and then peeked out from within the smoking remains of the wheelhouse. Heavy weapons fire was now coming from the conning tower of the sub, and he watched bullets shred the side of *Syntillate.* He then heard the radio come alive.

"This is the U.S. Navy. Cease fire and change your course 90 degrees to port or we will sink your vessel. Do it now!" Immediately, the gunfire ceased, and the yacht altered course to steam away.

Dakota stood on the stern of the ship and stared at the submarine that had surfaced beneath the wooden fishing boat, lifting it from the water. Chocks steadied the ship as intended but were too wide, allowing it to list to one side. A seaman approached on the sub's deck and caught his eye.

"We're inside Russian waters and can't stay long. We need to unload your cargo quickly. Do you have a davit to hoist it down to our deck?"

"Sure don't," he replied. "But give me a minute." Dakota disappeared and a minute later was firing up a chain saw he had spotted earlier in the tool shack by the engine room. The saw ripped through the transom, the rotting boards falling away as he made his second cut. The crewmen below helped to put two boards in place, and they began sliding crates out of the container down the improvised ramp onto the sub. The crew began storing them in the sub's outside "garage," a small enclosure mounted on the deck. The sudden sound of heavy machine gun fire once again drew Dakota's attention.

One of the sub's crew was examining the writing on the crates and had already kicked several over the side. A man on the rear deck was firing at the floating crates and had already shredded several. "What the hell are you doing?" Dakota yelled down.

"As you might have noticed, we can't fit all of these crates inside our small outside storage garage. And for some reason, the captain wasn't too excited about storing biological weapons inside the sub," the man replied, without looking up. "So we're jettisoning the more benign stuff like anthrax."

He was interrupted when the XO shouted down from the conning tower, "Boys, you need to hurry. The Russians have a patrol boat headed our way, and we're submerging in five minutes whether you're done or not. Rig a demolition charge on the hull of that fishing ship and set it to detonate in ten minutes."

Several more of the sub's crew joined Dakota and the others as the mound of crates inside the container steadily shrank. The last crate had been offloaded and the men were now all below deck. With the patrol boat less than five miles away, the sub sank beneath the frigid waters. The thump of the demolition charge sounded a moment later, leaving the abandoned boat to founder in the building seas amidst the remains of the jettisoned crates, and a boatload of Russians to puzzle over what had happened.

# CHAPTER 33

Having grown up poor in New York City, Marcia had never been too far from home. Her trips to the Florida Keys with her father took her the farthest she ever travelled as a child. And up until her job as a security professional, she had made few trips outside of the country. So she still enjoyed the adventure of travel to new places.

But in the hours since she had last seen Quint, worry had replaced the thrill of her adventure. After dropping the bags off at the hotel where they had spent the previous night, she headed for the café. Failing to find Quint and Willy there, she searched the area between it and the harbor, even checking the bars in the unlikely event that the two men had become distracted. Finally, she returned to the café to show each of the patrons a photo of Quint on her phone. A man at the counter paying his bill glanced at the picture and then spoke to the cashier.

"He does not speak English," the clerk said to Marcia, "but wanted me to tell you that on the way here, he saw two men, one of whom looked much like your friend, being helped into a taxi."

"Oh, thank you. Does he remember anything about the taxi?" Marcia asked, and waited for the clerk to translate.

"He say it was an old Volga. There are many, but this was an old black one with a dented right front fender painted red. Check with the other taxi drivers."

"Please thank him for me," she said, and smiled back at the man, who nodded after the clerk had finished translating. "Could you please write a description of the taxi and the men I am looking for in Russian, so that I can just show it to the cab drivers?" The clerk nodded and scribbled a note on the back of a receipt. It then occurred to Marcia that even if she found a driver who seemed to know something after reading her note, she would be unable to understand him.

"Better yet, can you help me find a taxi driver who speaks English?"

"Certainly. I'll call one for you," the clerk replied. Marcia slipped a wad of bills into the woman's hand and stepped outside to wait for the taxi. *Maybe they made it back after the ship left and are waiting for me.* But she feared the phrase, "being helped into a taxi" spelled trouble.

"Ah, you must be the beautiful woman who asked for an English-speaking taxi driver," a middle-aged man said, as he pulled up alongside Marcia. "I am Oleg, the best driver in all of Murmansk, at your service."

"I'm Marcia," she replied. "Oleg, I need to find a taxi."

"But you have one," he said, gesturing at his own cab with open palm.

"No, a particular one," she said and explained. Oleg immediately accepted the challenge, stopping at each taxi they saw, inquiring about one with a dented red fender. The fifth driver admitted knowing the cab they were looking for, and after the proper amount of currency had changed hands, told them how to find it.

Oleg followed his instructions, and ten minutes later they spotted the taxi with the red fender parked

near the docks. Oleg approached the driver and
showed him Quint's photo on Marcia's phone.

"We must pay him."

"I'll pay him, but only after I find out what he
knows." After a brief exchange, Oleg turned back to
her.

"He says he took your friends and two other men to
a yacht at the harbor."

"Yacht? You mean that old, beat-up supply boat?"

"No, he says a fancy yacht."

*Hmmm, that's odd.* "Which one?" she asked and
waited nervously as Oleg translated. She saw the man
point at a luxurious yacht pulling away from the dock.

"He says the one leaving now."

"Damn! Oh, excuse my language," Marcia said.

"He says your friends didn't look so good, like maybe
they had been in a fight." Marcia grimaced as she paid
the man for his help, and then asked Oleg to take her
back to her hotel.

Marcia approached the front desk to rent a room so
she would have a place to sort things out. She
retrieved the bags she had dropped off earlier from the
bellman and headed for her room. In her exhaustion,
doubts began edging into her mind.

*What am I going to do? I'm in over my head. I never
should have—no, I can do this. I will do this. Just need
to settle down. Okay, first step, let's get some
resources and support.* She picked up the phone and
called Kira. When she didn't get an answer, she
continued trying the team members whose cell
numbers she had added to her address book. Finally,
she got Mimi.

"Mimi, we've got big problems."

"What's going on?"

"I haven't been able to reach Quint. I'm afraid he
and Willy are in trouble." She quickly explained whet
she had learned so far.

"I don't know whether or not Rogers can or will help us inside Russia, but let me give you his number. Give it a shot."

"Thanks," Marcia said, as she reluctantly broke the connection. Never before had she felt so alone. She took a deep breath to calm herself and then dialed Rogers.

"Ah, Marcia, you're the new recruit Quint told me about. Enjoying your trip to the Motherland?"

"Not particularly," she replied, somewhat irked by his dismissive attitude. "Look, we've got a problem," and repeated the story she had just told Mimi.

"So, you can't find Quint but suspect that he and Willy might have been kidnapped and taken aboard some yacht. But you have no proof that they're on the ship or, for that matter, even missing. Hmm. Where's the rest of the team?"

"It was just Dakota, Willy, and me; everyone else is still on break. When Quint and Willy didn't show back up, Dakota had to leave with the bioweapons or risk being discovered by the Russians, so I'm working by myself."

"And what is it you want me to do?"

"Help me find them."

"How about the tracking transponder implanted in him?" Rogers asked.

"The implant requires a handheld unit and works only in relatively close proximity. Can't you get his position off his phone?"

"Give me a minute. I'll call you right back." A minute later, her phone rang. "His last position before he went off grid was on the west side of the harbor there in Murmansk."

"That's precisely where the yacht was."

"Was?"

"Yes, it left a while ago. Can you use a satellite to find it?"

"I can try, though it may take a while."

"We don't have a while. We've got to go after that ship and rescue him."

"Marcia, I can't authorize an attack on a civilian ship, especially with no hard intel confirming Quint is even aboard. And it would take a lot longer than we have to get formal authorization."

"I'm not asking for that, just give me whatever help you can—that's all."

"Marcia, don't take this the wrong way, but I don't think this a good idea."

"And I would have to agree with you. But I don't see that we have much choice." She took a deep breath and thought of Quint and Willy, probably being held hostage—or worse. *I won't let you guys down.* "I'm all we've... I mean, they've got, and I'm going after them with or without you. So are you going to help me? Please do it for Quint; you owe him."

"That I do," Rogers sighed. "I'll see what I can do."

"My people are working on a plan, but I have some information for you now," Rogers began a few minutes later. "The yacht's name is *Syntillate.* We have reason to believe it was purchased by a man named Hester, who may be working with an accomplice whose name is Syndy. These are not nice people.

"As for a plan, I'll email you what my folks are putting together as soon as they're finished," Rogers said. "Marcia, I feel obliged to tell you it's unwise for you to attempt this. It would be tough even for an experienced squad of special forces. You really should reconsider."

"Okay, you've officially covered your ass. And though I appreciate your words of caution, I'm going to try."

"I expected as much but felt obliged to be the voice of reason. That being the case, I wish you the best of luck," Rogers said, his attitude seeming to have softened. "We've arranged a charter flight to Oslo. They're ready to go as soon as you can get to the airport.

"I can also help you acquire the necessary weapons, equipment, and resources. I just wired a rather large sum of money to a Norwegian bank. Let me know what else I can do to help. I want the team back as much as you do."

# CHAPTER 34

Marcia spent the flight to Oslo in Rogers' chartered plane reading the briefing he had provided. The informal report had been prepared by one of his staffers with a sense of humor.

*"Syntillate was built by the same German company that constructed the Nazi Battleship Bismarck. While the design is unusual, many find it to be quite spectacular.*

*Hester's associate, Syndy, oversaw its refit, and it would appear she was mad at his money, as she purportedly seemed determined to get rid of as much of it as possible. The interior features bath faucets costing tens of thousands and a stair banister reputed to cost nearly $100,000. The interior incorporates exotic animal hides of almost every description, ranging from African lions to stingray hides, for the furniture and wall coverings.*

*"The aft of the ship supports a three-story watch tower structure. Due to her knife-like hull design, she can achieve a speed of up to 50 knots. She has two swimming pools, the aft one featuring a glass bottom, which serves as a see-thru ceiling for the salon situated directly below. There's a helipad on the bow with a helicopter hangar located directly below, though our sources tell us there's no copter aboard at the present time. At the yacht's aft end, a large garage*

*houses two Jet Skis, a tender, and a speedboat, which
are deployed through a large door in the stern.*

*"While her outside design is well-known, the
interior deck plan is somewhat a mystery. With
considerable difficulty, we were able to obtain a few
drawings, included herein. Our best guess is that
Hester and Syndy will be in the owner's suite on the
top deck or the VIP guest suite on the deck below. The
six guest suites can apparently be reconfigured via
movable walls satisfy changing needs, so the current
layout is indeterminate.*

*"Boarding the vessel at sea will have to take place
at night when the ship operates at vastly reduced
speed. Otherwise it will be difficult, if not impossible,
to catch much less board it. This will be especially true
in heavy seas."*

Marcia studied the drawings but was frustrated by
the lack of detail. She then reviewed the suggestions
Rogers' team had made to help develop her plan.

After the plane landed in Oslo, she checked into a
hotel to have a base of operations for the next few
hours. Exhausted from the long day, she looked at the
bed longingly but chose not to lie down, fearing she
might not wake up for hours.

After confirming that the cash Rogers was supposed
to have wired was indeed available, she freshened up
and changed into a comfortable pair of jeans, a dark
grey pullover sweater, and boots. She phoned the
contact Rogers had given her in her package and
arranged to be picked up across the street in ten
minutes. Grabbing her thick coat and small backpack,
she headed for the lobby.

Ignoring a chorus of angry yells, Marcia walked past
a long row of taxis to the one waiting across the street,
and after confirming it was her contact, hopped into
the warm backseat. She chatted with the driver while
they drove to the bank, where she withdrew the funds

Rogers had wired. With little alternative, she took the driver into her confidence, hoping he could help secure the weapons and other equipment she needed. If this proved to be a mistake, she was confident Rogers could get her bailed out of jail, though by that time, Quint and Willy might be dead.

She started with the easy items: heavy gloves, a knife, suitable clothing, and coils of rope. Once she had a duffel bag half-filled with gear, she sucked in her breath and broached the sensitive subjects, hoping Rogers' contact was as solid as he claimed.

"I need guns and ammunition. Can you help me buy them?" Marcia held her breath as she awaited the driver's reply.

"You are not Norwegian. You have a license?" he asked appearing surprised.

"Uh, not exactly. That's the problem."

"Our country has strict gun control laws with very severe penalties. You are prepared to take such a risk?"

"Yes, I am. Look, I was told you could help me. The life of two good men may depend on it," she said, not sure if it was true and hoping she was wrong.

"We have a mutual friend to whom I owe a favor. Plus, I think the laws are foolish. So I will help you but if you are caught, I was not involved."

"Understood."

Thirty minutes later, the driver stopped in front of a seedy bar. "Ask for Edvin. Tell him Peter sent you. It is too dangerous for me to wait here. I will return in an hour." Marcia stepped from the taxi hugging her wool coat tight against the frigid wind while also keeping a death grip on the cash-filled backpack, now serving as her purse.

The handle on the bar's massive wooden door was bent, and the ancient wood was split and gouged. The squeaking of rusty hinges announced her entrance, and the half dozen men bent over their beers looked up to see who had entered.

Marcia ignored the unshaven leering faces in the smoky haze and focused on the far side, where the bartender was filling a mug with beer. She walked brazenly across the room, stepped up to the bar, and asked, "Are you Edvin?"

Without a reply, the man finished pouring the beer and set it on the bar, extracting a bill and some change from the pile of cash in front of the customer. He then turned back to her. "Might be. Might not be."

"Who are you?" asked the customer at the bar beside her, obviously enjoying the other men's snickers.

"Someone who needs to find Edvin," she said, put off by this nosy customer, with his acne-filled face and greasy hair.

"Why?"

"That's between me and Edvin." The man laughed again and leaned toward her.

"Oh really? Not if you can't find him. We don't get many high and mighty women in here, at least none that stay that way for long."

The customer's hand darted out and hooked the back of her head, pulling her toward his face. She was close enough to see his grungy teeth and catch a whiff of his sour-beer breath before her instincts kicked in. She grabbed his arm and rotated, jerking the man off his stool. She rolled him over her hip, dropping him onto the floor flat on his back, where she placed a foot on his throat.

"I don't know you, and don't believe I care to. But if you can find some manners, I'll let you up." The red-faced man nodded as he struggled to his feet amidst a chorus of taunts from the other patrons. Then, mustering as much dignity as possible, he snatched his money off the bar and headed toward the door, leaving his beer behind.

Once he was safely outside, he turned back to her and yelled, "Bitch," before swiftly closing the door behind him.

Marcia stood silent, unsure what to do next. She saw the bartender's eyes cut toward a man in the far corner, and she turned to see who it was. With his back to the wall, the man had watched the mini-drama play out without joining in. His face remained impassive and he said nothing for a moment before he smiled and beckoned her toward him.

"I'm Edvin. Have a seat," he said quietly, and then raised his voice. "Lennart, bring the lady a beer and another for meself." Edvin appeared to be fiftyish, perhaps Irish, with shaggy gray hair and a pot belly.

They sat in silence as Lennart drew two more beers and brought them over. By the time he returned to the bar, the men seated at the other tables had resumed their conversations.

"You handle yourself well. I like the way you clipped that ass's wings," he said, taking a heavy pull off his beer as Marcia took a small sip of her own. It was warm and bitter but to avoid appearing ungracious, she showed no reaction.

"Thanks. I've been taught it's not so much the force you use as how you apply it."

"Whoever did your teaching did it well," he said, before changing the subject. "You know who I am. Now who are you, and why are you here looking for me?"

"I need to buy guns. I hear you're the man to see."

Edvin eyed her in silence as he drank down half of his beer. "And who, might I ask, told you to find me?"

"Peter said you might help."

"And you have a permit?"

"No."

"Owning a gun without a permit is illegal, as is selling one to you," Edvin said, staring her in the eye. Marcia remained silent while sipping her beer. "Buying such... risky weapons is expensive. You have the cash?" Marcia nodded. "Ha, you have stones, I'll say that. Don't find many women carrying that kind of cash who would storm into a place filled with horny men, knock a man off his barstool, then look to buy illegal guns."

"I'm flattered. Now, you selling or am I wasting my time?"

"Ha, I like you. You're spunky," he said, and then his eyes narrowed to slits. "I'll sell you what you need, but if you're a cop or working with them, I'll slit that pretty throat of yours."

"I'm not a cop. There are two men, friends of mine, whose lives are in danger and need my help. You sell me the guns; I'll pay your price, and that's the last you'll hear of it. We never met, and I found them if anyone were to ask. I'll need a silencer too."

Edvin raised his eyebrows before shaking his head and draining his mug. "You're not much older than my daughter. What you got yourself into?"

Marcia took a long pull on her beer and set it back on the table. "I'd like to tell you, I really would, but I can't. All I can say is my friends are prisoners on a very big yacht full of very bad people and are about to be very dead. I'm their only chance. I know I'm playing into a crappy hand, but it's something I've got to do."

"Scared, aren't you?" he asked with a soft smile.

"Never more."

"You got $5,000?" Marcia nodded. "Stay here. I'll be back in a few minutes," he said, and rose to walk out the door. No one seemed to notice and the rest of the men in the bar continued drinking beer and smoking their cigarettes.

Marcia exhaled deeply and continued nervously taking small sips of her own beer. She had finished the beer and was considering leaving when the door opened, and Edvin entered. "Lennart, two more beers." Marcia winced at the thought of another beer. Already, she was feeling light headed from the strong brew and did not need or want another.

Edvin reclaimed his seat and placed a paper sack on the table. When Marcia started to reach for it, he shook his head. A minute later, Lennart placed two fresh mugs on the table, picked up the empties, and returned to the bar. Edvin nodded at the bag and Marcia slid the heavy sack toward her. Cautiously, she opened it and examined the gun inside.

"It's a 9mm Walther PPQ pistol with a 15-round magazine. Anybody needs to know why you have it, you like to compete in shooting tournaments. There's one this Friday and that's why you bought this from a skinny, young German guy with frizzy black hair and a pockmarked face you've never seen before. Got it?"

"Got it. What's the metal can-looking thing?"

Edvin laughed. "That's a homemade silencer. It's heavy and doesn't look pretty, but it works."

"Five thousand's a lot of money for a pistol and homemade silencer."

"And selling a gun to a cocky woman with no permit is against the law," Edvin replied, and then continued in a near whisper. "There's a beat-up black sedan in the alley around the corner. It's unlocked. In the trunk there's a duffel bag for you. Don't get caught with it."

Marcia smiled and furtively dug in her backpack to withdraw the cash. She deftly passed it across the table, making certain no one could see. In a smooth motion, Edvin swept it off the table and deposited it in his jacket pocket.

"You're not going to count it?" she asked, as she placed the paper sack with the gun and box of rounds into her backpack.

"Nope. I'm betting you're not stupid enough to short me."

Marcia smiled and looked at her watch, noting that it had been an hour. She took a final draw on her beer and rose to leave, pausing to touch his unshaven cheek. "Thanks," she whispered.

She saw Peter waiting in his taxi as she closed the bar door behind her. She held up a finger indicating that she needed another minute and ducked into the alley, where she found the ancient sedan waiting just as Edvin had promised. With a quick glance behind her, she lifted the trunk lid and retrieved the tattered duffel bag. She then crossed the narrow street and slid into the backseat of Peter's taxi.

A few minutes later, they pulled up in front of her hotel. She passed a wad of cash to Peter and said, "Give me a minute to check out and I'll be back for a ride to the airport." Grabbing the two duffel bags and her backpack, she opened the door and stepped out.

"If you're coming back, you can leave that here."

She hesitated for an instant, but replied, "No, thanks," deciding not to further press her luck. She entered her room and opened the bag Edvin had sold her.

"Wow!" she said out loud, as she found a disassembled rifle, boxes of ammo with spare magazines, a large folding knife, and even a hand grenade. *I could wage my own war!* At the bottom of the duffel, she noticed a small oilcloth bag. She opened it to find a second pistol with an ankle holster and a note from Edvin that said, "Just in case."

*Thanks, but I hope not to need that.* She closed the bag and then stuffed everything she needed inside her own duffel bag, leaving her suitcase and most of her personal items. *I won't be needing this stuff where I'm headed and no sense in carrying along dead weight. I can replace it all later, provided I survive the next 48 hours..*

As she passed by the counter, she slid the key across to the same clerk who had checked her in only a few hours earlier. "My plans changed. Guess I won't be staying after all. Just close me out," she said, and without waiting for a reply, headed out to her waiting taxi.

The chartered flight Rogers' team had scheduled to Hammerfest, Norway, was uneventful, and she arrived without incident. Refusing the ground personnel's offer to carry her bags, she headed into the FBO, where she arranged for a taxi to take her to the port. A few minutes later, she paid the driver and started up the gangplank of a well-maintained ship, inexplicably named the *Pigoriak*.

A crewman noticed her approach and blocked the gangway. "May I help you?"

"Yes, I'd like to see the captain."

"Oh really. And you are... " he asked, the arrogant superiority thick in his voice.

Her earlier doubts now erased after her incident with the jerk in the bar, Marcia's patience was strained. "I'm the one who agreed to pay a small fortune to charter an anchor-handling icebreaker tug named after swine, who is tired, and not in the mood for a bunch of bureaucratic bullshit. So why don't you just take me to him. Now!" Taken aback by her verbal barrage, the man stared at her for a long moment before motioning her to follow him to the ship's bridge.

"Captain, this *lady* claims to have chartered the ship," the crewman said, his disbelief evident as he stepped inside the bridge.

"Ahh, you must be Ms. Marcia—"

"Just plain Marcia."

"Well, just plain Marcia, please have a seat in my quarters. Care for something to drink? Perhaps some tea and biscuits?" he asked.

"No, I'm fine," she replied, still full from the heavy beer. The captain dismissed the crewman as he guided her into his quarters, his hand on the small of her back. Marcia bristled at his touch, but chose to let it go for Quint and Willy's sake.

"Do you have the inflatable tender and the other items I discussed with the broker?" she asked, as she took the farthest seat at the small table and quickly surveyed the room. She slid a list of items she had requested across the table.

"Uh, yes... well, that is... I believe we do," he replied while scanning the paper, flustered at her directness.

"You believe so? Well, do you or don't you?" she asked abruptly, quickly establishing that she was not some empty-headed bimbo to be taken lightly.

Raising his head, he eyed her over his glasses. "We do," he replied firmly.

"Very good," she replied, while retrieving an envelope filled with cash. "The charter fee was wired to your broker. Here's payment for the other items."

In contrast to Edvin, the captain meticulously counted the cash. "This seems to be a little short."

Marcia stared directly at the man until he finally broke the stare. "No, that is precisely what was agreed."

"The inflatable cost more than expected, and we had to buy a larger motor than you requested because that was all they had in stock."

"That's your problem..."

"And now it's yours."

Marcia was certain he was jerking her around. "If you wish for us to get along, please do not take me for a dithering fool. Do we need to call the broker to straighten out this matter?'"

"Call anyone you like. I will need an additional $10,000 if you wish to proceed."

"And what if I decide to get my money back and go elsewhere?"

"You're welcome to go wherever you like. I can provide you with the number of other local ship brokers if you wish. But you have chartered my ship, and you can use it or not as you please. We don't do refunds."

"That will not be necessary," she replied, knowing she lacked walk-away power. This was the only available ship capable of doing what she needed. Realizing it was more important to help Quint than to win this negotiation, she changed her attitude. She withdrew another $10,000 from her backpack and tossed it on the table, resolving to square things later.

"By the way, you would not have found another ship at this point, particularly one willing to become involved with you." Marcia nodded. "Okay, now let's discuss your departure schedule and plans." She took a deep breath and related the details of her plan. When they were finished, the captain called one of his crew.

"This is Sven. Show this lady to her quarters, and then take her to the cargo hold where her equipment is stored. Help her with whatever she needs." The strapping blonde-haired young crewman greeted her with a friendly smile and led her to a small cabin beneath the bridge. She dropped off her duffel bag and backpack, deciding that it now held so little cash, theft was not a concern. Nonetheless, she locked the door and pocketed the key he had given her.

They made their way to the hold where a new inflatable sat, rigged with the largest engine she had ever seen on such a boat. "That's a big engine," she commented.

"These are not popular items here since few locals can afford them, so the captain spent a great deal of time finding it for you. We tried to get a smaller one, but none were to be found. It will take you wherever you need to go in a hurry."

Marcia felt a twinge of guilt, as it did appear that the inflatable was much more  boat than she had expected or really needed. She went through the stack of items piled inside the boat, satisfied that everything

was there. The ship was already under way by the
time she returned to her cabin and dialed Rogers on
her satphone. "We just got a new update," he said, and
gave her the current coordinates and heading of
*Syntillate.* "Were you able to get everything you need?"

"Yes. The inflatable is a bit of overkill, but I'm on
the ship and we're headed to meet *Syntillate.*"

"Call if I can help you with anything else. And good
luck," Rogers said as he hung up the phone.

*For Quint's and Willy's sake, I just hope I'm up to
the job.* She headed for the bridge where she handed
the captain the latest set of coordinates and watched
as he entered them into the chartplotter.

"In these seas, it will take us eight hours to reach
them. That will put our arrival at 3 a.m. when it's still
dark as you had requested. I suggest that you get some
dinner in the galley and then try to sleep. I will have
someone wake you in a few hours." Marcia nodded,
thanked him, and headed below to take his advice,
certain that she would need to be well rested for what
would come next.

The roll of the ship put her quickly to sleep. It felt
like she had been in bed for only a few minutes when a
knock on the door awoke her. She looked at the clock
on her phone and saw that it was 1:31. *Boy, that was a
quick night.* She forced herself from the warm cocoon
of her bunk to pull on a set of nylon thermals, a pair of
heavy black jeans, a dark wool sweater, and boots. She
loaded everything she thought she would need into her
duffel bag and headed to the galley for a cup of coffee.

Sipping the nearly solid, dark liquid, she entered
the bridge where the captain greeted her. "Get some
rest?"

"Not nearly enough," she replied with a laugh.
"Where are we?"

"Still on track to meet the ship on schedule,
assuming they have maintained course and speed.
We'll be there in a little over an hour. Still up for this?"

Marcia nodded, her hands clenched into fists to keep her trembling fingers from betraying her. "I'll go get things ready. I could use some help; any chance you can spare Sven again?"

"I'll have him join you. We'll notify you when we have their ship on radar. Good luck." Marcia nodded and headed below, a huge knot forming in her stomach.

*What am I doing?* Trying to collect her courage, her thoughts went back to that safe warm restaurant where she once worked, what seemed like a lifetime ago. Being there with the smell of soup cooking and a winter storm raging just outside suddenly seemed appealing. *I'm a waitress, not a special forces type. No, that's not true. I was a waitress, but that's behind me now. I'm much more than that, and I better start thinking like it, unless I really do want to be back working in a restaurant again—or worse.*

When she stepped into the cargo hold, she saw Sven busy at work on the inflatable. "She's filled with gas; I double checked the oil and made sure she would crank. The lifting harness is rigged, so she's ready when you are. You sure you're up for this?" he asked, the concern obvious on his face.

*Nooo,* the voice inside her head screamed but she heard herself reply, "Absolutely. It'll be a piece of cake, and I'll be back on board with my freed hostages before you know it." He nodded, the sadness in his eyes suggesting he doubted he would see her again.

She secured her equipment in the boat and was in the process of triple-checking things when she heard the intercom. "We have contact. Prepare to deploy. Will advise when we have closed to within two miles." A moment later, the hatch above her swung away, and a cable descended from the crane above. The cold air poured in, dropping the temperature of the compartment well below freezing.

She clipped the ring of the lifting harness to the hook and motioned that she was ready to lift. Marcia closed her eyes and prayed that she would be granted the courage to go through with her crazy plan and the good fortune to survive it. Her prayers were interrupted by the captain announcing the contact coordinates and heading over the radio. She had just finished keying them into her GPS when she heard his voice again.

"Deploy inflatable." The wind caught the inflatable and thrust it sideways as soon as she cleared the ship's hold. Only Sven's steady hand on the control line kept her from being battered against the ship. She hung on, grateful for the heavy wool watch cap and parka hood as she bowed her head against the wind-blown spray.

She felt the boat come to rest on the water and fired up the engine before releasing the lifting hook. As she advanced the throttle, her heart leapt when the motor sputtered then died. For a horrible instant, she thought the seas were going to bash her against the hull before realizing that she was on the lee side and protected from the wind. Frantically, she turned the ignition switch and heard the muted sound of the outboard coming back to life.

She slowly eased the throttle forward, and this time the boat moved away from the ship. She glanced at the GPS strapped to her wrist and swung the wheel to head the boat on a course to intercept the yacht, the doubts flooding back into her mind.

*Who am I trying to kid? I'm no James Bond type. I'm not Quint or Dawson, but if not me, then who? It's not like we could just call the Russians. And by the time the rest of the team arrived to help, Quint and Willy would be long gone. I'm all they have.* That realization gave her the courage she needed, and she repeated to herself, *I won't let them down. Ever.*

# CHAPTER 35

For several hours, Syndy struggled to get to sleep, but her excitement over the capture of Quint and Willy was keeping her wide awake. Finally, she gave up and interrupted the peaceful slumber of her assistant for help getting into her wheelchair. The young girl placed one of the porcelain masks on Syndy's face and put a lit cigarette in her yellowed tube. Syndy dismissed her and took the elevator to the lower deck, headed to Hester's room to begin the "festivities."

Willy awoke from the intense pain in his arms to find himself naked and facing the foot of an enormous bed, with his arms tied above his head to the industrial-looking bedframe. The muscles beneath his glistening black skin rippled as he tested his bonds. An odd collar was around his neck, and his head was pounding from whatever drugs they had given him.

A blonde-haired man noticed him awakening and stepped from behind, placing a handful of unused plastic ties on the table beside the bed. "Hello, Willy, I'm Arnold. I believe you've already met Hester and Syndy."

Willy looked around the room. *Okay, the blob lying on the bed is Hester, which means the freak in the wheelchair behind me must be Syndy.* He felt a mixture of revulsion at seeing the pair, and fear at the prospect of their unbridled sadistic nature. "Yes, I've had the misfortune." Willy struggled to clear the cobwebs from his head.

"Enough chit chat; time to get things started. Let me introduce you to our master of ceremonies, who's travelled quite a ways to be here tonight. Without further ado, ta-ta." On cue the door opened and a man entered the room.

If Willy was surprised to see Syndy and to find Hester still alive, he was stunned to see who had just walked in. Dressed as if for a dinner party, the man walked shamelessly over to the far side of the bed where he stood squarely in front of Willy. "Preston! What're you doing here?"

"Why, Preston is working for us." Syndy smiled. "Funny how things have a way of coming back to bite you on the ass, huh? What, no clever comeback? How disappointing. Well, no matter. We're about to have fun. That is, at least I am." Syndy toggled the control on her chair and rolled closer to the big black man.

"Settling the score with Quint's team has become an integral part of our daily conversations. I hope your niece is coping with her lupus." She laughed at the surprise on Willy's face.

"I dare say that we know almost everything about your team including, obviously, that Dawson has a long-forgotten brother. It's not cheap to be Preston, what with his appetites for gambling, drugs, you name it. Though he was somewhat hesitant when he found out what we had in mind, he got over it in about, oh, I'd say in about two bags of cash. Come to think of it, this Judas cost a hell of a lot more than 30 pieces of silver."

"You're working for these scumbags?" Willy asked while continuing to tug at his bonds in hopes that he might free himself. It quickly became clear—he was in serious trouble. "*This* is the Norwegian cruise Mimi helped fund?"

"Afraid so." A smug grin crossed Preston's face as he looked Willy directly in the eye. He smoothed his silk shirt and picked at a tiny piece of lint.

"You must have wondered why Dawson's long-lost brother suddenly appeared," Hester said. "Well, you can thank your buddy's bro' Preston here for your being with us tonight. Though I hate that we were unable to get our container of bioweapons back, capturing you certainly takes away the sting. Your team cost me my brother's life, my sight, left me paralyzed not to mention what you did to—"

"Not to mention the pain and suffering you caused me," Syndy interrupted.

"How did you give us up, Preston? You couldn't have known where we were."

"It really wasn't all that difficult. One of the fruits of my romance with Mimi was getting the team's satphone number, which I passed on to Syndy. As soon as they dialed the phone a few times, Hester's folks were able to track Quint's position."

"How could you? The team loaned you money and tried to help you."

"Just goes to show that you *can* fool some of the people all of the time." Preston smiled and smoothed the wrinkles from his shirt. "But Mimi told me that you, my friend, had some ugly things to say about me. I don't appreciate that, and paybacks are hell."

"Well, it would appear that I was right."

"Okay, boys, that's enough," Syndy broke in. "We didn't bring you here naked just to humiliate you, though I must admit that's an added benefit. It was to prepare you for our little party. But I'm afraid that may not be as popular with the ladies by the time we've finished with you.

"Hester and I have waited so long for this opportunity, though it won't be so much fun for you,

I'm afraid. I've been thinking about this all day, and I'm fired up. And guess what? You're about to be also, though more literally."

She motioned, and Preston, after hesitating for an instant, walked toward a cardboard box on the table at the far side of the room. He withdrew a propane torch and ignited it. Willy could hardly believe that he could be so callous.

"You know, Willy, when I was a small child, I had goldfish," Syndy said. "I suppose lots of girls did. But I doubt many had my... sense of... curiosity. Yes, let's go with curiosity. One day, my mother left me alone while she went to the store. I took my goldfish into the kitchen where I set their bowl on the stove. I wondered what would happen if I turned on the burner—how they would react, how long they'd last, you know. So I did it.

"For a while nothing happened. But pretty soon they started swimming around like crazy, faster and faster—until they died, that is. You know what I discovered that day? I liked it—a lot. The feeling of power. Not just having it, but using it. Now that we have you all to ourselves, let's fire things up," she said with a giggle. "Preston, Willy looks dirty; wash him with those cleansing flames."

Preston carefully adjusted the flame before approaching Willy. "Preston, you don't have to do this."

"Ah, but I'm afraid I do," he replied, and without pausing, ran the flame rapidly over Willy's left shoulder blade, causing him to scream in pain.

"I wish I could see it, but I must admit, just hearing you brings tears of joy to my eyes. Syndy, I admit you were right; this is well worth our wait," Hester said.

"Willy, I'm just following orders. It's nothing personal," Preston said softly.

"Roasting my ass with a propane torch is pretty damned personal to me."

"Once more a little lower, but not for as long, we don't want to overdo this too quickly," Syndy ordered, as Preston swung the flame over Willy's lower back. After allowing time for his screams to die, Syndy spoke again. "Okay, let's spread the pain around. Do a little one on the back of each leg." Syndy cackled as Preston followed her order.

"Perfect. See, the whole secret is finesse. Just a little at a time, and we could have fun for weeks, maybe months. But since we're saving Quint for later, we have the luxury to indulge ourselves with you," she said, nodding to Preston, who resumed working the flame over Willy's back, scorching his flesh.

"Damn, that stinks," Hester finally complained. "Open the balcony doors to air it out in here."

"Okay, enough for now," Syndy said in response, while entering a code on her remote to unlock the balcony doors and a second code to open them.

They listened to Willy's low moans without speaking until he finally broke the silence. "Water, please. I'm so thirsty." Desperate to end the suffering, Willy hoped for a chance, even a slight one, to end the torture.

"Preston, get him a glass of water."

Willy drank greedily and drained the glass of water that Preston held to his lips. "I have to go to the bathroom."

"I'm afraid you'll have to hold it."

"Look, unless you want my pee all over this bed, I need to use the bathroom."

Syndy summoned two guards, who entered the room brandishing serious-looking machine pistols. "You," she said pointing to the guard on the left, "go down to the cell where we're holding his partner, Quint. If you don't hear from me in four minutes, kill him." The man nodded and left the room.

"Okay, Preston, take Willy to the bathroom so he doesn't soil the bed and carpet, but bring him right back. You," she said, pointing to the remaining guard, "make sure he doesn't get any ideas about escaping." She then turned back to Willy.

"If you aren't concerned about getting yourself killed, then for the sake of your partner, I suggest you behave. Even if you somehow managed to overpower this guard, Quint would be dead before you could find and save him."

Preston freed Willy's hands from the bedframe but bound them together with a plastic tie before helping him toward the bathroom. Willy flinched as daggers of pain shot through his body from the burns on his back and legs.

Once they were alone, Preston whispered. "They're just trying to scare you."

"Well, it's damned sure working. I can't believe you're a traitor."

"What choice did I have? I'm broke with no prospects and living off the kindness, or at least the naivety of others. After this, I'll be set for the rest of my life."

"I'll pray it's a short one, you bastard. What about Mimi? She cared for you."

"Who cares about that pig? She's just a tool."

"You've been leaking information to them the whole time?"

"Guilty as charged. But look, those burns will heal, and I'm sure they'll release you once they've had their fun."

"You can't be that stupid."

"Willy, I had no idea what they had planned and being forced to be a part of it makes me sick."

"Then don't do it," Willy said

"While I don't care for the torch; I prefer to be on my end of it," Preston replied, as he glanced back at Syndy. Willy took the opportunity to pick up a nail file from the counter with his bound hands. Though he had no idea how he could use it, he figured that desperate times called for desperate measures.

Once Preston had retied Willy's arms to the frame at the food of the bed, Syndy called the guard to cancel her earlier instructions regarding shooting Quint. Before she could resume torturing Willy, Hester spoke. "Let's take a break. Are you hungry, Sweet?"

"Not really."

"Very well, Preston, send in my stewardess with a snack, and then let's all be back in thirty minutes. And please close the balcony door. The smell is gone, and it's getting chilly in here."

Once Preston left the room and the balcony door was closed, Willy looked at Syndy. "You plan on killing Preston too?"

"Not necessarily, but boys like him nearly always overplay their hand and end up crossways with folks like us. Take you, for instance. Were it not for the fact that you'll soon be feeding the sharks, I imagine you'd be looking to square things with him. While I'm glad he's a traitorous scumbag, he's still a scumbag. And as such, one must be careful dealing with him 'cause he'd sell us out just as quickly as any other mark."

The stewardess brought in a large plate filled with an assortment of fried finger foods, which she fed to Hester, who greedily devoured them. By the time Preston returned, they were finished, and she left with the empty plate.

"You're familiar with the old adage 'An eye for an eye' I take it," Hester said, while waving a remote control of some sort. Willy nodded. "Well, your team took both of mine so..." Hester motioned to Preston. "Proceed."

Frantically, Willy worked the file against the plastic tie that bound his hands while pulling hard against the bedframe, trying frantically to free his arms. He was not quick enough to avoid the excruciating pain as the flame licked his left eye. He let out a gut‑wrenching bellow and pulled with all of his strength against the partially severed plastic tie. He winced as it cut through his flesh all the way to the bone, but with a mighty pull, it finally gave way. With his arms free, he lunged forward, knocking over Syndy's wheelchair.

"Press the collar remote, Hester. Press it," she screamed.

Willy turned to tackle Preston, sending him stumbling backward and dropping his flaming torch at the side of the room. Hester fumbled with the remote, nearly dropping it in the process before his finger finally found and pressed the top button. Willy stopped in mid stride as a loud bang accompanied a geyser of blood erupting from his neck and his severed head fell to the floor. His headless body then toppled onto Preston, drenching him in a river of blood.

"Shit!" Preston exclaimed as he wormed his way out from under Willy's body, wiping the blood off his face with his silk shirt sleeve.

"Quick, call Arnold on the intercom," Syndy ordered. "Now! Take that blanket off Hester's bed and fight the flames." Preston took the blanket and standing as far away as possible, flailed it at the flames.

Moments later, Arnold arrived with a fire extinguisher. He quickly put out the fire and then helped Syndy back into her chair. Once again, she opened the balcony door to air out the room. "Preston, go get cleaned up while Arnold brings Quint up," she ordered.

"Sweet, don't you want to take a break after all that?" Hester asked.

"Hell, no. I'm not about to let this ruin my fun; we're just getting started," she said, with a maniacal laugh.

# CHAPTER 36

As she topped a large swell, Marcia saw the running lights of the mammoth yacht in the distance. Suddenly, her plan to board the looming hull from a dinky boat bobbing on the ebony roller-coaster seas seemed like the insane idea it was.

The full weight of what she was doing pressed heavily upon her, and doubts flooded her mind. But if she were to save Quint and Willy, there was little choice but to continue on course to intercept the yacht. With *Syntillate* headed toward her, the distance shrank quickly; she would intercept in a few minutes.

Ice formed on the tiny boat's bow railing, and frigid knives of spray cut into her face. Silently, she rode over the enormous swells, unable to take advantage of the powerful engine lest she become airborne.

She fumbled through her pack to find the obsolete night vision monocular, purchased off a dusty shelf at the marine supply store back in Oslo. Though costing more than she would have paid for the latest technology version back in the States, she was grateful to have it. She scanned the foredeck of the yacht for any sign of movement—a shadowy torso or the glow of a cigarette—but saw nothing.

She glanced at the docking device. It consisted of a long line with a bracket outfitted with a suction cup attached at the end. On the floor at her feet lay the grapnel atop its neatly coiled line—the backup plan she hoped not to need. With the docking fixture held in one hand and the steering wheel clutched in the other, she swung her inflatable alongside the massive hull, the knife edge of the yacht's bow now only a few feet away.

In a move she had rehearsed a thousand times in her mind, she carefully adjusted the throttle to match the yacht's speed and leapt to the front of her boat. She braced her feet against the tubes of the inflatable and wedged the toes of her booties into the crevice where the fiberglass deck met the tube's fabric.

She took off her gloves and felt the bitter cold bite into her skin. Tightly clutching the suction cup fixture in her left hand, she leaned forward and slammed it in place against the yacht's bow. Her fingers searched frantically for the locking lever with only seconds before the heavy seas would force the two vessels apart.

She found it but her fingers slid off as the yacht pounded the side of her boat. Straining her entire body, she found the lever a second time, flipped it, and the docking device locked onto the hull. Thrilled that her plan seemed to be working, she drifted away from the yacht paying out line to her suction cup "anchor."

A large wave slammed into her boat, jerking the line taut. Marcia could see the force being placed on the line but before she could react, the suction cup popped off of the hull. In seconds she would begin to fall behind the yacht and in these seas, she would never catch back up. There would be no second chance.

She jettisoned the line overboard and snatched the multi-hooked-grapnel off the floor. An instant later, she sent it sailing through the air to land on the yacht's foredeck. As the line tightened to take the weight of her boat, the grapnel slipped free and came flying back, a fluke grazing her forehead.

With blood flowing into one eye, she retrieved the grapnel for a second shot and spun the steering wheel to take her in closer to the yacht. She advanced the throttle to keep her boat from sliding farther astern before launching the grapnel again. This time it caught on the bow rail where it remained.

Gradually, she pulled back the throttles while paying out line. When she neared the yacht's stern, she cleated off the line, and the inflatable swung toward the yacht until it rested against its fiberglass side. Forcing away the image of sitting snugly before a fireplace with a glass of wine, she took a deep breath and ran through the next phase of the plan in her mind.

She wiped the blood off her face with her sleeve and confirmed that the wound on her forehead was superficial. She donned her backpack, slipped her gloves back on, and screwed the homemade silencer onto to her pistol, strapping the second pistol to her ankle. With her pack and the rifle slung over the same shoulder, she peeked across the expansive swim platform into the cockpit of the larger boat.

On the far side she watched a man armed with a wicked-looking machine gun flip a cigarette over the side and then step into the boat's main salon. Seeing no one else, Marcia grabbed a handrail and pivoted around the back onto the cockpit floor where she froze while checking for more guards.

Seeing none, she headed for the shadows along the side of the ship with her gun and clunky silencer raised. Her wetsuit booties left damp footprints but made no sound.

She was halfway across the cockpit and nearly out of view when a guard on the deck above saw her. Thumbing off the safety, he fumbled to bring his gun into position, and accidentally hit the trigger, firing wide into the frigid darkness. Marcia looked up, startled at the noise, and saw the man leaning over to get a better angle.

Fighting the weight of the clunky silencer, Marcia swung her pistol up and had a clean shot at point-blank range. But having never actually killed anyone, her finger remained frozen on the trigger, despite the angry, hate-filled look on the bearded man's face above. The continued movement of his weapon broke the spell and she fired instinctively, striking the man squarely in the chest and toppling him over the side into the inflatable.

With only seconds to react, Marcia eased beneath the stairs into a tiny storage locker where she hid breathlessly, listening to the sound of running men drawn by the noise. A second guard ran from the far side of the deck above, took one look at the figure in the blacked-out tender, and opened up.

Bullets raked the small boat, deflating the hull and allowing water to pour in. The force of the water drove the bow farther down, ripping away the cleat that held the bow line, and the boat quickly sank.

"What happened?" she heard another man yell excitedly.

"I ran over when I heard gunfire and spotted a small boat tied alongside. Somebody was trying to board us so I blew the hell out of him and sank his boat."

"Any more with him?"

"Didn't see any but we should make a sweep." For the next thirty minutes, Marcia sat in the cramped locker, her gun ready, but praying not to be discovered. Finally she heard voices again.

"Anything?"

"Nothing, must have been a loner. Go get some coffee. I'll report and then join you," he replied.

*Okay, I made it this far. Now what?*

Marcia emerged from the compartment and crept back to the cockpit where she had spotted controls for raising the door to the water toy garage. Taking a chance, she pressed the lever switch to open. She jumped at the sound of the motor. *Damn, that thing is loud.*

She held her breath, listening for an alarm or voices but heard nothing. When the door was barely open, she leapt inside. But just as she found a matching set of controls and pressed the button to shut the door, a man flung himself in behind her, landing on his stomach beside her with a thud.

His gun skidded across the floor, and he looked up to see her staring back frozen, the silenced pistol dangling from her hand. In a lightning fast move, he kicked her hand, sending her gun tumbling toward the back of the garage. She turned to retrieve her gun as the man jumped back to his feet.

Realizing that he would be on her before she could get to her gun, she turned toward him and saw his patronizing grin. It vanished when she landed several karate kicks in quick succession.

It quickly became clear that he too was skilled in martial arts as his quick responses blunted the force of her blows. A chop at the base of her neck followed by a punch to her face sent her reeling. In an instant, he was on top of her with his hands around her throat, a wide grin on his face.

She fought to break his grip, but he was too powerful. She beat on his back with her fists and kicked, trying in vain to squirm free. Already, her vision was narrowing. In seconds she would be unconscious—permanently.

A thought crossed her dimming mind, and she brought her right foot up as far as she could. Then reaching with her right hand, she fumbled with the snap on the ankle holster. Mustering all her strength she withdrew the small pistol, pressed the barrel against the man's left buttock, and pulled the trigger.

He arched backward, a blood-curdling scream escaping his lips. Marcia rolled away, the blood returning to her head. Knowing she could not give him a second chance, she pulled the trigger at point blank range again and again and again.

The sight of the bloody mess before her sent her stomach into convulsions, and she vomited. Afterwards, she lay on the floor to catch her breath, waiting for her stomach to settle and her head to stop throbbing. She listened for the sound of anyone entering the garage, but it appeared that no one had heard the sound of the struggle nor the gun firing over the roar of the massive diesel engines.

*Okay, the boat's under way, so no one should come looking here.* Beside the pair of Jet Skis she saw the yacht's inflatable tender with the keys in it. *Assuming I can find Quint and Willy and live through it, at least we might have a way out of here.*

She took a minute to check out the tender. After switching on the battery, she confirmed that it had fuel and turned the key. As soon as the engine caught, she shut it off, satisfied that it would run when she needed it.

From inside her jacket, she withdrew the diagram of the yacht and continued past the Jet Skis to ease open a hatch on the port side. Seeing that the companionway was clear, she emerged. She ignored the single hatch on her left marked Engine Room and slid down the hall toward the exit hatch at the far end. Peering through a porthole she saw that it opened into another empty companionway.

She felt it was unlikely that Quint and Willy were being held in a regular stateroom. This meant they were either imprisoned in a compartment in the bowels of the ship or in the upper staterooms where

Syndy and Hester could savor their captivity. Marcia chose the latter.

# CHAPTER 37

Quint woke up with a dry mouth and a hammer pounding inside his head. What felt like dried blood covered the left side of his face, and the bandage on his shoulder was soaked a deep red. *Where am I?*

He raised his aching head to look around the tiny room. He lay naked with his arms and legs strapped to the corners of an icy-cold metal bedframe in a windowless room illuminated only by light oozing from beneath the door. The motion told him he was on a boat. *Where the hell am I?*

He had no idea how long he lay there shivering before he heard the sound of approaching footsteps, and the door opened. "Rise and shine," a tall blonde-haired man boomed. Behind him stood another man armed with an automatic pistol. "I'm Arnold. Come with me," the man said, untying Quint from the bed.

Quint blinked, blinded by the light. He struggled to get the feeling back in his limbs while the man prodded him to his feet and marched him, still naked, into the starkly lit hallway. "How about some clothes or at least a blanket?"

"You'll be warm enough soon. You've got a... hot date, so to speak." A passing crew member gave a nervous smile at the sight of a naked man being led through the hallway in the Spartan area below decks. At the end of the corridor, they entered an elevator, stepping out a moment later into more plush surroundings.

Through a nearby porthole, Quint saw that it was night. "What time is it?"

"Time for you to die, or at least wish you could," Arnold replied. "By the way, thanks a lot for avoiding my roadblock and getting the bioweapons to the port before we could intercept them. You damned near got me killed," Arnold said, and slammed the barrel of his pistol into the back of Quint's head for emphasis. "The only reason I'm still breathing is I managed to catch your sorry ass."

As they entered the stateroom at the far end of the hall, Quint got a glimpse of Arnold's watch—it was 3:45 a.m.

"Here's your boy as requested," Arnold announced as they entered Hester's stateroom.

"Quint, so nice to... well, thanks to you, I can't really see you, but happy to have you with us, nonetheless," Hester said. He lay sprawled in a massive bed adorned with motors and cables and a frame that extended some six feet over the bed.

"I thought you were dead!" Quint exclaimed.

"The fact that I'm living is certainly no thanks to you after you left me for dead and in this condition. Nice bed I've got here, huh? Had it designed so they could rotate me. Helps keep down bed sores, as I don't move around much these days, again thanks to you. Please forgive the mess."

As Quint was prodded forward toward the bed, he spotted Willy's headless body, on the floor in a huge pool of blood. A series of ugly burn marks covering his back explained the foul smell of burnt flesh that filled the room. Willy's mutilated head sat on a sideboard like a trophy.

"Damn it all! Hester, what've you done?" Quint yelled.

"We were just partying down. I guess we got a little carried away, and your old buddy sort of... lost his head." Hester let out a loud bellow of a laugh.

"Unless you want to have the shit beat out of you, cooperate while I secure you," Arnold said as he tied Quint's hands to the bedframe above. "And here's your very own collar as well." Once the device was in place around Quint's neck, he saw Arnold retrieve a small remote control unit from his pocket and press the middle of three buttons. Quint heard the collar click.

"The middle button locks and arms the collar. The lower one, which I doubt we'll need any time soon, unlocks and disarms it, and the upper one triggers the detonator inside the collar. So behave and don't lose your head like your buddy," Arnold said with a laugh, as he placed the remote in Hester's hand.

"Want me to throw his buddy's body overboard now? Arnold asked.

"Please." Hester was silent while Arnold dragged Willy's body onto the balcony and unceremoniously dumped it over the side.

"Call if you need me," Arnold said as he headed for the door.

"Arnold has not, how shall I say, had the opportunity to develop the same... strong feelings for you that I have, so he prefers not to stay for the party," Hester said.

"Nice outfit, Quint. What's that birthday suit, pink?" a Darth Vader-like voice added.

Quint was shocked to see a small figure adorned in a flowing red wig seated in a wheelchair enter as Arnold left the suite. But it was the garishly painted porcelain mask that made him gasp. "I'm afraid you have me at something of a disadvantage."

A sinister laugh broke from behind the mask, "You have no idea how true that is. Surely, you remember our wonderful dinner followed by the little episode in my hotel room that your buddy Dawson interrupted.

And then there was the one where you ambushed us at Hester's place. I *know* you must remember that."

"Syndy? You're still alive... and free?" A chill ran up Quint's spine, and he felt sick to see her for the first time since the phosphorus grenade mishap. He remembered her charred body lying on the ground, and her voice begging him to end her life. *As strange as she appears wearing that mask, I can only imagine what lies beneath.* It took him a moment to regain his composure.

"Syndy, the Torch. It's been so long I hardly recognized you. I always did like your 'fiery' personality, and I particularly enjoyed your Buddhist Monk imitation last time we met. You are aware of how they used to set themselves on fire in protest back in the '70s." Quint noticed her tense as she struggled to control her rage. "And did I miss Halloween? What's with the—"

"Uh... so you... uh, do recognize me," Syndy interrupted, as she shot a glance at Hester. "Can't fool you, can I?"

Syndy gave another mechanical laugh. "Quint, I see your sense of humor hasn't suffered. We'll see how long that lasts. You look cold, but don't worry. We'll warm you up shortly, just like I did your old friend Bart and more recently your buddy Willy.

"We had things well under way when Willy sort of broke up the show. It then occurred to me that you really should get to see him one last time. So we took a short break to bring you up from below. Our master of ceremonies will be joining us shortly; he's getting cleaned up after the mess your buddy made.

"You know, you can find so many wonderful things on the Internet," Syndy said. "Recently I found the 10 most painful ways to die. Hester and I thought, 'Wouldn't it be fun to try out all ten just to see for ourselves?' Though I wish we could try out all of them on you, it's impossible. So perhaps you can understand my quandary trying to pick just the right one for you.

"One that made the top ten was called the bull. It was a steel figure made in the shape of a bull. On the side was a door through which they would load the... err participant. A fire would then be lit beneath the belly, and one could hear the screams coming from the bull's mouth as the person inside was slowly roasted.

"Then there was John Sage. Ever heard of him, the head torturer at Chillingham? No? Well, his favorite was to put people in a cage hung above a fire and slowly roast them. He's always been one of my heroes. But then, I'm getting ahead of myself. I'm not sure what method we'll choose for you."

"If you kill me – then what'll you have to live for?"

"Oh, I could live for years on the memories," Syndy replied. "But relax, we don't intend to kill you any time soon. Hester and I plan to whittle you away. Why, we want you to share the joys of living as we do."

"Yes, we're determined to make your life as *interesting* as you've made ours," Hester added.

"Syndy, I didn't do anything to you. If you remember it was your defective phosphorous grenade that—"

"Enough! My version of events works just fine for me. I like it," she interrupted, and then looked toward the door as it opened.

Quint immediately recognized the grizzled man who had just entered. "Cary!"

"That's right, you two have already met. Cary, you now have a chance to redeem yourself after letting our victim, I mean our guest, slip away. Light the torch over there, and let's get the party rolling again."

Cary eagerly walked to the table and snatched up the torch and igniter. "Come on, time's a wasting." Syndy encouraged him, and under her direction, he swept the lighted torch quickly across Quint's back. As he touched the flame to different spots, he showed little emotion at Quint's blood-curdling screams. Finally Syndy ordered him to stop.

"Okay, that's enough for now. We definitely want to drag this out. Tell me, Quint, have you ever thought about becoming a eunuch? I figure once we're finished you won't be needing that equipment anyhow. So as a favor to you, I thought we'd go ahead and eliminate those unneeded parts. Plus, I'll admit, I just thought it would be fun. Let's take a short recess while I prepare to do away with your manhood," Syndy said, as she left the room.

# CHAPTER 38

"Perhaps it's a stupid question, but what's your problem, Hester?" Quint asked, trying to keep his mind off the pain of his burns and the aching in his limbs, tied spread eagled to the frame at the foot of Hester's bed.

"My problem?" Hester asked. "Actually, I have several. For starters you foiled my plans to acquire that treasure in Venezuela."

"Acquire? You mean steal from us."

"One man's booty is another's loss. But to finish answering your question, there was that explosion Dawson engineered that left me in my current state. Then there was leaving me for dead in the jungle where I spent several days helplessly paralyzed with bugs eating my flesh. And killing my brother, Pierre; right up there near the top of my list. There are so many reasons I hate you, but those are the biggies.

"Okay, I answered your question; now afford me the same courtesy and answer my question. What's your favorite painful way to die?" Hester wore a sadistic smirk as he described some of the methods he and Syndy had spent hours discussing. He paused when he heard the sound of his door opening and the whirr of Syndy's approaching wheelchair. Cary followed behind, carrying a leather case. He continued past her, set the case on the table, and retrieved the propane torch and igniter.

"Welcome back, my love," Hester greeted her. "Quint and I were just having a splendid conversation about his preferred way to die."

"And which did you pick, Quint?" she asked, though Quint ignored her. "Not answering? Perhaps you need another session with the torch. I do so love the smell of burning flesh," she said, nodding to Cary. He immediately ignited the torch and with a wide grin, brushed the flame against Quint's neck, eliciting a scream.

"Care to answer now?"

Quint heard her breath quicken, and he wearily raised his head. "The most painful way I can imagine dying is being bored to death by you and Hester. But I promise you one thing. When I get free, I'll make certain to end your twisted lives quickly."

Behind the porcelain mask, Quint imagined Syndy's face contorted in her version of a smile. "I see that being bound and burned hasn't affected your cocky attitude. Excellent. We have big plans for you, and it wouldn't be fun if you were docile. But enough for now."

"I'm tired of toying with him. I'm tired of waiting for him to feel real pain. If we're going to do the eunuch thing, let's do it now. Right now, this very second," Hester yelled, throwing a childish tantrum.

"Very well," she said, and turned to Cary. "Summon our... master of ceremonies, who I know is just dying to see Quint. Hand me the surgical kit. And go prepare a fresh torch; we'll be needing it to cauterize things when we're finished."

Cary placed the open leather case in Syndy's lap and stood beside her, holding the new flaming torch. Syndy scanned the array of instruments before selecting a long scalpel. "I'm guessing our master of ceremonies has never done this procedure before. So when he joins us, I'll explain how to make certain our patient survives. No need to end our party just yet."

"You bitch! I should have killed you when you begged me to end your pathetic life," Quint yelled. Syndy nodded and Cary swung the torch across Quint's upper arm.

"I can't take that smell. Could you open the balcony door again, Sweet?" Hester asked.

"Certainly." Syndy pressed a button on her remote, to open the sliding glass balcony door, and then resumed her inspection of the surgical tools. "I think this longer, narrow scalpel will do the trick."

Marcia worked her way down the companionway, easing open the door of each stateroom to look for Quint. But after a quick scan with her night vision monocular, she found only empty rooms or sleeping crew.

She closed the last door and continued through the forward hatch to an elevator lobby. On either side of the small lobby, a hatch led outside. After hesitating for a moment, she decided to risk using the elevator to ride to the top deck and work her way back down.

She stood poised with her gun ready when the elevator door opened into another empty lobby. A single door on the aft side had a keypad and what appeared to be a handprint scanner. She listened at the door but heard nothing. *Getting in there is going to make a lot of noise. If I can't find him, I'll try here last.*

Seeing no other staterooms, she pressed the button for the next level down. Leaving the elevator, she eased open the first door on her right, which read "Captain" and scanned the darkened room. A snoring man lay on his stomach beside a second form, whose long hair covered the pillow. An empty whiskey bottle was overturned on the bedside table beside several pill bottles. She eased the door shut and continued down the hallway to the next room, where she heard muffled voices. She froze when she heard a man yell in agony and recognized the voice. *Quint?*

With her silenced pistol raised, Marcia threw open the door and stepped inside. To her left, a bizarre looking woman sat in a wheelchair facing a morbidly obese man, who was lying in an enormous bed, staring blankly at the ceiling.

The bed was surrounded by a heavy framework, at the end of which Quint was standing bound and naked. The smell of scorched flesh filled the air, and her stomach knotted as she saw the ugly burn marks on Quint's back. A man held a flaming propane torch, and on the lap of the wheelchair-bound woman lay a gleaming set of scalpels.

Hester, unaware an intruder had entered, yelled, "Come on, let's get on with the show. I want to hear Quint suffer."

Instinctively, Marcia fired at Cary's arm with her silenced pistol. But as she pulled the trigger, his arm moved, causing the bullet to rupture the propane torch. The force of the exploding torch created a wall of flames, igniting the man's clothing and turning him into a human torch. He raced across the room toward the open balcony door, struck the railing at full force, and toppled over the side. The icy ocean waters extinguished the flames when he landed two stories below, and he disappeared in the ship's wake.

"What just happened? Is Quint dead? I don't want him dead; he hasn't suffered nearly enough. What just happened? What was that explosion?" Hester asked, his sightless eyes shifting frantically about.

"Shut up, you fat bastard," Marcia yelled, and pushed the stateroom door closed behind her. She quickly moved toward the bed as smoke began to bellow from the burning draperies and flaming carpet at the far end. "I'll shoot the first one of you two who says one more word."

She then turned toward Quint, withdrawing a six-inch folding knife from her pack. Before Quint could react, Hester began yelling at the top of his lungs, attempting to draw attention from the crew while he fumbled for the remote.

"Help! Help! Terrorists! Somebody save us!"

"Stop yelling and trigger Quint's collar, you fool," Syndy screamed, while moving toward the balcony. Quint saw the remote by Hester's left hand atop his stomach. As soon as Marcia freed him, Quint snatched the gun from her hand and fired. The bullet grazed Hester's hand, causing him to drop the remote, and continued on to enter his chin and blow out the top of his head. Quint's second shot destroyed the smoke detector.

"Quint, she's getting away," Marcia yelled, as Syndy made it through the open door and then spun her wheelchair back around.

"That's the balcony. There's no place for her to go," Quint replied and retrieved Hester's remote to deactivate and unlock his collar.

"Is that..." Marcia's voice faded away as she stared at the severed head on the table.

"Yeah, they got Willy before you got here. They threatened to do the same to me." Jerking the open collar off of his neck, he tossed it and the remote onto the bed. "And that bitch had plans to make a eunuch out of me if you hadn't arrived when you did," he said, as he turned and leveled his gun at Syndy's head. But he stood frozen at the sight before him.

The wind had blown her wig off, exposing her scarred and blackened skull. She raised the blackened claw of her right hand and ripped away the mask, letting it shatter on the deck beside her red wig. Quint looked at the horrific face no longer concealed by the porcelain mask. For a long moment he stood, his gaze locked with hers. He desperately wanted to shoot her but was unable to force himself to kill this pathetic being.

"You can't shoot me, can you? I knew it." Syndy laughed in her mechanical voice. "Is it because you're weak or because you know it would be doing me a favor? Every day I consider ending things but can't quite bring myself to do it. So please, you've already done me one favor by causing Hester's demise; I'll inherit everything. But do me a bigger one and shoot me. Free me from this wretched body. Come on, I was about to eliminate your manhood. Be a man. Get mad. Shoot."

"I've got a better idea," Quint replied, as he retrieved the collar and remote and turned back toward her. She saw the device in his hand and before he could take two steps, she entered a code on the remote control unit in her lap. Instantly, the balcony door slid shut. She quickly entered a second code, and he heard the click of a lock. She entered a third code, triggering the high-pitched shriek of an alarm.

Quint raised the pistol and fired three times at the door, but the slugs only crazed the bulletproof glass. "Damn it!" Too late, he realized what she had done. "I'm not letting that bitch get away."

"Quint, we don't have time. We've got to get out of here—now!"

Quint nodded and turned back toward Syndy. "Crawl back into your hole. But rest assured, the next time I see your ugly evil face will be the last. I promise to kill you on sight," Quint spat, tossing the collar onto the bed with a flourish. Outside, he saw Syndy move as if laughing, though he couldn't hear her through the closed door. She stopped laughing when Quint fired twice more, destroying the control mechanism for opening the door.

Quint scanned the room for something with which to cover himself, and snatched a blanket off the end of the bed. "You got a plan to get us out of here?" Marcia nodded and motioned him toward the door, the rifle now in her hands. After a quick check to make certain the corridor was empty, Marcia led Quint to the elevator, the shriek of the alarm echoing throughout the yacht.

"They sank my inflatable but there's a tender in their water toy garage, located at the stern," she whispered, as they slipped along the corridor. "If we can make it there before they find us, we can use it to get away." Quint paused to trigger another fire alarm which he hoped would create further chaos.

"While I appreciate your saving my ass back there, this outfit isn't working for me. It's more of a 'let's-drink-wine-by-the-fireplace' ensemble than a 'let's-shoot-a-bunch-of-folks-and-escape' one." Marcia smiled, trying not to recall her vivid memories of his recent nakedness.

It was still over an hour before dawn as they worked their way toward the garage. Halfway down the corridor, they saw a hatch opening. Marcia grabbed Quint's arm and pulled him into an empty stateroom. While they waited, Quint checked the closet and found a too-large pair of pants, a shirt too small in the shoulders, a warm jacket, and a set of boots that were too small but that he managed to squeeze his feet into. "Your burns need to be treated, but I guess that'll have to wait for now," Marcia said, while helping him don the shirt and jacket.

Quint nodded as he cracked open the door, noting that the alarms had finally been silenced. They made it to the water toy storage area without further problems.

"The odds of us deploying the tender without being noticed are slim. We need a diversion." Quint searched the garage and located two full gas cans, and found a flare pistol with extra cartridges in the tender.

Marcia reached into her backpack, withdrew the hand grenade, and handed it to Quint. "Damn! Where'd you get this?"

"A woman never tells those sorts of secrets. Even with your diversion, anyone in the salon can see the water toy garage door opening. Since there's a glass-bottomed pool over the salon, I thought this might prove useful in your diversion plans."

Quint smiled. "Ready the tender to deploy and start opening the door in ten minutes. Start the tender's engine so you can run as soon as you're in the water. I'll join you as fast as I can, but don't wait for me. You can, however, keep an eye out for me in the water, in case I'm forced to take a plunge to link up with you."

Marcia nodded and handed him her silenced pistol and a fresh magazine, keeping the rifle for herself. "Good luck." As Quint turned to leave, she reached down to her ankle and removed her backup pistol. "Take this too."

Quint tucked the pistols in the pockets of the baggy pants, along with the grenade. He then worked his way back toward the front of the ship carrying the plastic fuel cans and flare pistol. He stopped at an empty stateroom and picked up an armload of bedding.

He found his way outside, where he dumped everything on the yacht's foredeck below the bridge. After dousing the bedding with gasoline from the first can, he fired a flare into the pile, and quickly stepped back inside the ship.

Gathering a second pile of bedding from another stateroom, he piled it inside the elevator, doused it with fuel from the remaining can, and ignited it with a second flare. He then jabbed the button for the top deck. As the doors closed on the blazing inferno, Quint ran toward the back of the yacht, through a door, and out onto an open upper deck.

On the deck below, he spotted the glass-bottomed pool. He pulled the pin on the grenade and lobbed it squarely into the middle. A moment later, he heard a deep thump and then saw thousands of gallons of water go crashing into the salon, scattering the men inside. He was headed back to join Marcia, and had just entered the corridor near the elevator, when his luck ran out.

The door at the opposite end of the corridor opened, and before Quint could hide, the three armed men entering saw him. Immediately they opened fire, and he fired the unsilenced pistol around the corner, no longer concerned about stealth. A loud grunt was followed by fire from two more automatic weapons. With the most direct way back to the garage blocked, Quint headed outside.

As Marcia began to open the garage door, she knew it was time to go. She cranked up the tender engine, ignoring its roar, and activated the winch to deploy the inflatable. By the time the door was halfway up, there was enough clearance, and she climbed in.

It appeared that most of the crew had been drawn to the fire on the bow. But two men emerging from inside the ship saw the tender deploying and opened fire. Bullets carved a row of holes in the garage door, sending a shower of fiberglass raining across the stern of the yacht and into the tender.

Marcia knew that if they disabled the inflatable, she and Quint were as good as dead. She leapt from the tender clutching her rifle, as she heard one of the guns go silent. Judging it to be empty, she stepped out of the garage and squeezed off shots at the two men above, hitting the first one. She ducked back as the second man slammed a fresh magazine into his rifle and resumed firing.

Near the door she spotted a large plastic boat fender. Grabbing one end, she heaved it with all her strength and sent it flying through the air off the side of the ship. With the second man's attention drawn by the fender, she put two bullets into his chest.

By this time, the inflatable was in the water, so she dove into it, unclipped the winch line, and slammed the throttle in reverse. She hung on tightly as the tender roared backwards away from the garage.

Once clear of the ship, Marcia whirled back around and fired at a man positioned above. He plunged head first down the steps, landing in a pool of blood on the cockpit deck. She then fired at the glass doors on the upper deck where a man was emerging, drawn by the gunshots. The shower of tempered glass sent him into retreat after which she fired at anything that moved until her rifle was empty.

She eased far enough away to no longer be visible from the yacht. On the ship's foredeck, Marcia could see three men fighting a blazing fire while smoke poured out of an open door midway on the upper deck. *But where is Quint?*

Two decks above, Quint emerged from inside the ship just as Arnold was returning from fighting the fire on the bow. Before Quint could react, Arnold jumped him. While they fought over the pistol, Quint realized in seconds the others would come swarming out after him. Feinting to one side, he shoved himself backward with Arnold's jacket held tightly in his free hand, and they both toppled overboard. Taking advantage of the unexpected move, Quint jerked his pistol free and smashed the butt of it into Arnold's face just before hitting the water.

The force of impact knocked the breath out of Quint. As he struggled to get his head back above the freezing water, he saw Marcia in the tender and waved. After emptying his pistol at the ship, he tossed it aside.

"Grab on!" she yelled and threw him a line. He held up the end to show that he had it and she steered the boat away from the yacht, bullets ripping the water around them. Quint saw Arnold burst through the surface behind him and catch a bullet in the back of his head from one of his own men.

More bullets tore through the inflatable's steering console and starboard tube. Marcia retrieved another magazine from her backpack and jammed it into the rifle. Steering with one hand, she returned fire until the yacht had pulled out of range, at which time she helped Quint aboard.

"D-damn, that w-water's c-cold!"

"A 'Thanks for saving my butt' would be nice," Marcia said, with a smile.

"T-thanks for s-saving my b-butt," Quint replied through his shivers.

"The tender's had it," she said, as she scanned the inflatable with her flashlight. The starboard tube was halfway deflated, and the boat was taking on water as they continued to move forward.

"B-better th-throttle b-back."

Marcia nodded and pulled the throttle back to neutral. Both of them held their breath waiting to see what the ship would do.

"Thank God," she said, when it appeared to be continuing on course. "With all the confusion, by the time they figure out what happened, they'll never find us in the dark." Marcia thrust her hand into her backpack and withdrew a small VHF radio. "Plan B. Plan B," she shouted over the radio, and waited for the echoed response. She gave their position from her handheld GPS, using a previously arranged code.

"Hopefully, the captain of the *Pigoriak* and not the *Syntillate* will find us now."

"P-p*igoriak?* How emb-barrassing," Quint stuttered.

On the top deck of *Syntillate,* Preston had observed the fight with Arnold and had seen Quint's and Marcia's escape. He made no attempt to rescue Arnold or recapture Quint and Marcia, choosing to simply watch as they all vanished into the thick veil of night. He then headed below, where he found Syndy reigning over the chaos.

"Make sure the fires are out. Then clean up Hester's stateroom. I don't want his blood ruining everything that survived the fire," she yelled at two crewmen.

"What about Hester? You want us to bury him at sea?" one asked.

"Hell, no! We're taking him back to have a death certificate completed, after which we'll see about a proper burial." Syndy's feigned largesse was fueled by her interest in inheriting his estate. Having had the foresight a few months earlier to trick Hester into signing a new will designating her as sole beneficiary, she was determined to have his demise properly recorded.

"Get as many crew members as needed and haul his body down to the ship's freezer. But make sure to bag him properly. Use a tarp or shower curtain or something. I don't want him leaking all over the food. Preston, come with me." Her wheelchair whirred as she left the room, a soft hum filling the air around her.

The two rode the elevator in silence, save for Syndy's humming. She noticed a dramatic change in his mood; he seemed far more upbeat than he had only a short while before. As they entered her suite, she noticed a hint of white on his left nostril and realized the reason for his mood change. She chose not to comment. "While I hate that Quint killed Hester and then escaped, I suppose there is a silver lining in that I'm now free to proceed as I wish."

"Arnold is gone too."

"That so?"

"I saw him get shot and fall overboard," Preston replied. "I imagine with both of them gone, you'll be needing a consigliore, and I would be most happy to—"

"I'm so glad you stand ready to help," Syndy interrupted. "But since your cover was not blown, your greatest value is in your ability to remain close to Quint and his team. What with your recent excellent performance, I believe a substantial bonus is appropriate to secure your continued services."

"Why, thank you, but I just thought I might serve you—"

"I am well aware of your, uh... abilities. But with Quint having now caused Hester's demise, nothing is more important than evening the score. When we reach port, I want you on a plane headed back to rejoin the team. We will decide later how to proceed. We must take our time to make certain that nothing goes awry with our next attempt. That would greatly displease me; I'm certain you understand."

"Why y-yes, absolutely. N-nothing will, you have my w-word," Preston replied and quickly headed for the door.

"Oh, and Preston, if you really are serious about becoming a more... integral part of my staff, I'll expect to see 'S-203' tattooed on your neck next time we meet." Syndy's laugh echoed from within as Preston closed the door behind him.

# CHAPTER 39

Once aboard the *Pigoriak*, Quint and Marcia collapsed into their assigned bunks, exhausted from the ordeal. When they awoke early the next morning, the ship was docked back in Hammerfest. Marcia had been up long enough to make their return travel arrangements when she found Quint in the galley working on his third cup of coffee.

"Our flight leaves in three hours. I'll tie up loose ends with the captain while you finish breakfast." He nodded and then borrowed her satphone to call Rogers.

"So Wonder Woman rescued you, huh?"

"That she did. You know, there are some decisions I've made in life that I later questioned. Hiring her isn't one of them."

"I must admit, I was skeptical when I first spoke with her, but you've got a gem there. Need any help with your travel arrangements?"

"No, Marcia's got us booked on a flight that leaves in three hours," Quint replied and read him the flight details Marcia had handed him on her way out. "They got Willy," Quint said.

"Damn, I really liked him."

"Me too," Quint replied and breathed a long sigh before continuing. "I guess you heard about Dawson."

"Yeah, losing an eye really sucks."

"I'm guessing that leaving a good-looking corpse wasn't high on his list of priorities," Quint replied, clearly confused.

"Oh, that's right, you don't know. Dawson's not dead."

"What are you talking about? I saw an RPG take out his chopper."

"No, it didn't." Rogers explained the close miss.

"What?"

"The RPG round struck the building, and though it showered the chopper with shrapnel, the pilot kept it in the air and they made it out."

"Where is he?"

"In a hospital in Germany being treated by their best specialists. But they're about to fly him back to Miami on a military transport. He should arrive shortly after you get back. I'll make sure you're on the list of those cleared to see him."

Quint hung up the phone, thrilled his buddy had cheated death once again.

Evie picked up Quint at the Key West airport, and they went back to her place so he could freshen up before dinner. Quint eased down onto the couch, favoring his badly burned back.

"You've had a long day. Relax while I get ready," she said, handing him a beer before leaving the room.

"By the way, where's Barn—ooofff," Quint had started to ask about her iguana when a streak of green launched itself off the floor onto his stomach.

"What's that? I didn't hear you," Evie asked from the bedroom.

"Never mind," Quint replied, and reached out to stroke Barney. "Hey, fella', what're you doing?" Without hesitation, the lizard clamped its jaws around the side of Quint's hand and bit down hard. "Ouch, you little—"

"What? I still can't hear you."

"Nothing, Barney and I are just... playing." Quint replied through clenched teeth, struggling to work his hand free from the lizard's mouth without losing too much flesh. He then joined Evie in the bathroom in search of a Band-Aid.

"What happened now?" Evie yelled with surprise.

"Your lizard bit me; that's what happened."

"What did you do to him?"

Quint looked at her with disbelief. "After he attacked me on the sofa, I tried to pet him, and he bit me."

"You didn't hurt him, did you?" She ran into the living room to check on Barney.

*No, but I considered carving the lizard into chunks.* Quint thought, but instead said, "He hates me."

"That's ridiculous, you big dummy. He doesn't hate you. Why, you're the one who gave him to me."

"How I regret that," Quint muttered.

"What?"

"Nothing." After Evie finished bandaging his wounded hand, Quint realized his pride would have to heal without her soothing attention.

During dinner, Quint felt as close to her as ever. They had finished their dinner at Commodore's and were enjoying a tawny port for dessert when she broke the silence. "I missed you... a lot."

"Ditto. It seems like I was gone a lot longer than I actually was. You been okay?" he asked, hoping her recent trauma was not still haunting her.

"You mean dealing with the rape thing?" Quint nodded. "Though I know it'll always be there, I think I've finally come to grips with it. At least, to the point it's somewhat manageable." He reached for her hand and held it gently. After a few seconds of silence, he thought it best to change the subject.

"Dawson was supposed to arrive last night."

"Wonderful. Where are they taking him?"

"Rogers said to the same hospital as Kira. I'm heading up to Miami to check on them tomorrow. Want to go with me?"

Evie nodded with a broad smile. "Try leaving without me." After they finished their wine and Quint had settled the tab, they returned to Evie's place where they spent an evening that matched even their best times together.

Exhausted, Quint slept till mid-morning the next day. He noticed Evie was not in bed and with a start, remembered Barney. After a quick check to make certain he was not being stalked again, he saw, to his relief, that the bedroom door was closed. He took a quick shower and slipped on a clean pair of cargo shorts and a fresh t-shirt before joining Evie in the kitchen cooking breakfast.

"Hey, sleepy head," she said, thrusting a coffee-filled mug into his hand. "Notice I made sure to have your beloved vanilla creamer?" Quint smiled and nodded. "I was just about to wake you. We can eat the muffins I made on the way to Miami. Let's get going."

He fired up his bright orange '69 Road Runner and backed it carefully out of the Evie's garage where it had been stored while he was gone. Thirty minutes later they were crossing the bridge near Big Pine Key, holding hands while listening to the deep purr of the big block engine with Zac Brown cranked up on the stereo.

They both enjoyed the palette of ocean blues until crossing over Blackwater Sound to the mainland. Only a few miles from the hospital, they stopped for brunch in Coconut Grove. Evie couldn't resist the Macadamia-crusted mahi-mahi, while Quint opted for the Gazpacho Grouper.

Dawson was asleep when they arrived, so Quint went in search of the head nurse. "You're on the approved list, so I can brief you on his condition while you wait for him to wake. As you might be aware, he was shot several times." Quint nodded noticing Evie's grimace. "The bullet wounds in his body missed crucial organs, and one barely missed an artery. His right eye is gone, but there doesn't appear to be any brain damage. He's stable but won't be released for a while.

"His injuries will require physical adjustment, but the mental effect of losing an eye can be much worse than the physical. He's likely to be irritable while he works through this. Try not to hold that against him. That's about all I can tell you. There's a lounge down the hall, second door on the left. Go relax. I'll have someone come get you as soon as he wakes."

"I appreciate it, but we have another friend to visit. Here's my cell number; please have someone call if he wakes up before we return," Quint said, before ambling down the hall, Evie close by his side.

"So, how we doing?" Quint asked as they walked into Kira's room.

"Hey, guys. Thanks for coming. I'm doing great— lost over 20 pounds. Can't honestly recommend this particular weight-loss regimen." She forced a laugh while motioning toward her missing leg.

"Seriously, how are you?" Quint placed his hand on her shoulder, struggling to conceal how upset he really was.

"How do you think? I have bad days, and I have really, really sucky days. Right now it's about a draw as to how many of each. But at least I have Colin; he's been great. You know, he asked me."

Quint looked puzzled while Evie shrieked, "Oh, Kira, that's wonderful. Have you set a date?"

"No, but I'll let you know when we do, and the two of you had better be there."

"Where is Colin?" Quint asked.

"I made him go get some sleep. I've been having to force him to leave."

They made small talk for the next twenty minutes until Quint's cell phone rang and interrupted them. He turned to Kira as he slid it back into his pocket. "Dawson's awake. We need to go check on him, but we'll swing back by to see you before we leave."

"Dawson? He's here?" Kira asked.

"You didn't know?"

"I, uh… guess Colin forgot to mention it."

"He might not know. Dawson just got here sometime last night. He's on the floor below." Kira just nodded. They said their goodbyes, leaving her with a distant look in her eyes.

Dawson was awake when they got back to his room. "Hey, buddy, how you doing?" Quint could never seem to find the right words in these awkward situations.

"You're a smart guy; I bet you can figure that out," Dawson snapped, and then backtracked. "I'm doing about as well as can be expected after being shot full of so many holes the doctor said I now qualify as pegboard."

Quint laughed. "Well, I see it hasn't affected your warped sense of humor."

"I have a feeling I'm going to need it to deal with this." He pointed to the bandaged side of his face. "At least I have one eye left, though I guess 3-D movies are a thing of the past," he said, with a weak laugh.

"Syndy and Hester killed Willy," Quint said.

"I trust you returned the favor," Dawson replied, through clenched teeth.

"With Hester. But Syndy got away."

"You planning a service for Willy? I'd like to go if they'll let me out of here."

"With no body to bury, the team will just wait and plan a service for him after you get out of here," Quint said.

Dawson nodded and remained silent for a minute, seemingly reflecting on the loss of a good friend and team member. Finally, he spoke up. "So, I heard you thought I was dead."

"When that RPG exploded, I saw this giant fireball and no chopper, so yeah, I figured you'd bought the farm."

"From what I understand, that pilot saved my sorry ass with his fancy flying. I also heard that you were terribly upset," Dawson added with a smile.

"Me, upset about being shed of you and your bullshit? Not a chance," Quint teased.

"Speaking of bullshit," Evie piped up as both men laughed.

"Has he told you?" Dawson asked Evie.

"Told me what?"

"Oh, I was hoping he had confessed," Dawson replied with a grin. "While we were in Russia we slept together... but I swear it meant nothing. It was just a one-night thing for me, nothing more, though I'm not so sure with him."

Quint shook his head and quickly explained how they had been forced to share a bed in the Russian hotel.

"You two are sick," Evie replied with a laugh.

"By the way, what happened to your hand?" Dawson asked Quint.

"Attacked by a man-eating lizard." Quint ducked Evie's punch.

Kira had resisted the nurses' persistent attempts to get her out of bed, partly due to the pain but mostly due to her depression. So when she pressed the buzzer, she knew the young nurse who responded would be surprised to hear her request. With great effort and the help of the hospital staff, a few minutes later Kira was sitting in a wheelchair.

"Would you mind pushing me down the hall, please? I need to get out of this room." The nurse nodded and eased her out into the main hallway. "I'd like to go to the next floor down," Kira said, when they neared the elevator. The nurse looked surprised but pushed the down button.

"By myself," she added, when the elevator doors opened. "Don't worry, I'm just going to visit a friend on the floor below. I promise not to run away and get you in trouble." The young nurse hesitated, so Kira wheeled herself into the elevator and pressed the button before she could object.

Enjoying her new-found mobility after being cooped up for so long, she opted not to stop at the nurse's station to ask for Dawson's room number. Instead she worked her way down the hall until she found his name scrawled on a piece of tape outside a room near the end. She paused for a moment, took a deep breath, and pushed open the door.

Inside she saw Dawson lying in bed, a massive bandage covering half of his face. For a moment, she hesitated and had almost decided to leave when he turned his head and saw her. "Kira, what are you doing here?"

"Vacationing," she replied. Dawson laughed, and she caught him stealing a glance at her missing leg. "You know, I've considered becoming a pirate. Now with my missing leg and your eye, we would make a hell of a pirate team."

"Yeah, all we need is a parrot and some grog," Dawson said with a sigh.

"I'm working on both of those."

"Quint told me about the wreck. You're lucky to be here."

"As are you," she said.

Neither spoke until Kira broke the silence. "Colin proposed to me."

Dawson looked away for a moment before replying. "So, I guess this is the part where I'm supposed to be happy for you?" Neither spoke for some time until Dawson finally gazed directly into her face with his good eye and said, "Come closer." Kira wheeled her chair forward until the right wheel touched the bed. He reached for her hand and held it as he continued.

"You're a good woman. Too good for me, I—"

"Don't say that—"

"Let me finish. This may be the last time the two of us can talk openly. I've always cared for you. But what with Colin, my problems getting over Cathy's death, and our working together, we never had... I mean... you and I, we never would have worked. I think we both know that. Colin's a good man. He'll make a good husband and a hell of a father.

"Kira, I know losing a leg has got to be tough for you. It would be for any woman. But you're better than most. And I'm not talking about your looks, though you're more gorgeous to me today than when we first met. I'm talking about what's inside. You've got brains, a big heart, and real guts. But it's your spirit, your zest for life that defines you.

"Some women couldn't face life with such a disability and would give up. I hope you're not one of those. You deserve better, but so do Colin and the baby you're about to bring into this world. If only for them, you've got to get past this. I know you can. I know you must want to. I hope you do."

By the time he finished speaking, Kira's face was streaked with tears. She gazed back at him for a long moment, then lifted his hand to her lips and kissed it before wheeling herself to the door. She stopped and glanced back one last time before she left the room.

The next day, Colin entered Kira's room armed with a bouquet of flowers. "How sweet," she said. "Stargazer lilies, my favorite. Thanks so much." Colin stood silent as she held his hand. "You know, I've been thinking."

"Uh oh," Colin joked.

"Ha ha. No seriously, I've been a real bitch and –"

"Kira, losing a leg while you're pregnant gives you plenty of reason, you –"

"No, it doesn't. Colin, you've been a prince, more than I deserved, more than I could ask for. So now it's payback time. I've decided that starting today, I'm going to become the wife-to-be that you deserve," she said, and then became quiet as tears coursed down her face.

Colin pulled her close with his free hand and stroked her hair.

# CHAPTER 40

A few weeks later, Kira, still struggling to cope with the loss of her leg, eagerly accepted Nigora's offer to help plan the wedding. "I so excited. Have many questions. Ready to talk about wedding, no?" Nigora asked.

"Sure, what questions?"

"Have much to do. Location you like only good for few guests. Need bigger. Must call men in Colin's family to have meeting. They set wedding date, talk about divorce, tell Colin when to step on your foot. Must make list of gifts you want, get artist for to draw henna designs on your hands, maybe arms too, and—"

"Hold on, hold on. What are you talking about? We're only having a few dozen people, and I will pick the date. What the hell are henna designs?"

Nigora sighed, appearing to explain as if to a child. "In Uzbekistan, from birth of first child, family save money for big wedding, maybe 1,000 people. Henna is plant used for dying bride's hands, buh. Is tradition."

"Okay, let me make this easy... on both of us. I appreciate your help, and I respect your customs. But I will tell you what I want and what I need you to do, okay?"

"Humph. Just want that you have proper wedding, like I have one day."

"I appreciate that, but this is my wedding, and you must respect *our* customs." Nigora nodded. "And why would Colin need to step on my foot? And why would we talk about divorce?"

"Is tradition for groom to lightly press on foot of bride, sign of a respect. And is tradition to talk about divorce before marriage in my country."

"Well, I'll accept that he respects me without stepping on my one remaining foot, and there will be no discussion of divorce—I don't care whose tradition we break." Nigora nodded reluctantly, and Kira began to explain what she wanted. After accepting that this would be an American, not an Uzbek wedding, Nigora proved to be an enthusiastic and invaluable resource to Kira.

*"Jimmy Buffett says that Margaritaville*
*is wherever you want it to be.*
*But this Saturday at 7 p.m., it will be at the*
*Ernest Hemingway home on Whitehead Street.*
*Please join us there for our wedding reception.*
*Dress is tropical casual."*

Preston placed the invitation back in his pocket and continued to walk down Duval Street. Most of the team was already gathered on the grounds, seeking the comfort of the cool shadows when he arrived.

He removed a stack of checks, making a big production of distributing them to everyone who had loaned him money, trying his best to make this event about him. He spotted Marcia talking to Quint and Evie and quickly made his way over. "Hey, Quint. Sorry it took me longer than planned, but here's the rest of what I owed you," Preston said. He shook Quint's hand as he handed him his check, making certain that Marcia noticed.

"Why, thank you," Quint replied, appearing somewhat surprised.

"What happened to your hand?" Preston asked.

Before Quint could reply, Evie interrupted, "Just a paper cut."

Preston nodded and turned to Marcia. "Sorry, no check for you, though I'm sure we could come up with a consolation prize," he said, giving Quint a look that suggested he was joking.

Marcia rolled her eyes. "Oh, really? Well, maybe Mimi could help you with that."

"Help with what?" Mimi asked, as she walkied up behind Preston.

"Uh, h-handing out checks. Here's yours. Payment in full," he said, giving her a quick peck on the cheek while eying Marcia, who ignored him. "Come on, I need to give Leo his." Preston quickly dragged Mimi away from the others.

They caught up with Leo and Preston handed him a check. "Why, thanks."

"Preston is happy to see that you made it back from Europe for the wedding. How was it over there?"

"Splendid. I ate my way through most of France and the better part of Germany. Le Rubis' Tete de Veau, or calf's head, was divine. It's easy to see why that was one of Chirac's favorite dishes. And then there was the partridge, the bulots, and oh, the Ris de Veau, calf's pancreas, served in this sauce, which—"

"It sounds like you had a wonderful time," Preston interrupted. "I think we'll get a drink before they get started." Leo nodded, and looked off wistfully with glazed eyes.

Once they were out of earshot, Mimi gave a snort. "That was rude but thanks for saving us. He was just getting started and already my stomach was complaining." She then lowered her voice. "It's good to have you back."

"Preston is happy to be back." She accompanied him as he worked the crowd until this stack of checks was finally gone. Mimi glanced at Dawson each time Preston handed over a check to make certain he was witnessing this process. Then, armed with fresh drinks, Mimi steered Preston in his direction.

"Hey, Dawson." He responded with a quick nod. Before he had time to offer any cutting comments, the crowd quieted. On the balcony above, the small wedding party had just appeared.

Given the heat, the guests appeared grateful the wedding invitation specified tropical casual rather than more formal wear. However, at Kira's insistence, the bride and groom were dressed formally, though in mild protest Colin's bowtie and cummerbund were festooned with gaudy parrots and tropical flowers.

"Kira looks great, doesn't she?" Mimi said, and Preston quickly agreed.

"Oh, splendid," Dawson agreed without enthusiasm.

The vows were read, and a few photos taken, after which Colin quickly disappeared. He resurfaced a few minutes later in shorts, sandals, and a tropical shirt reminiscent of his former tie and cummerbund. Kira remained in her wedding gown, which offered the advantage of concealing her prosthesis.

Trays of finger foods, boiled shrimp, and sushi abounded. For those not satisfied by one of the dozen types of beers iced down in a large skiff at the back of the bar area, an array of mixed drinks including pitchers of mojitos, and margaritas were available.

Preston proved to be the hit of the wedding reception. His was by far the most eloquent toast. He showered praise on each of the newlyweds, after which he asked to make one last toast.

"Not to place a damper on such a wondrous event, I just wanted to recognize someone who is not with us today nor, unfortunately, will he ever be again. Here's to Willy, an all-around good person. I hope that those responsible for his death will be found and punished appropriately." The team responded with a chorus of amens, and then everyone drank, except for Dawson.

When Preston had finished, Dawson spoke up. "As long as we're making toasts for those other than the guests of honor," he paused and glanced at Preston with his good eye, "I'd like to toast Marcia for saving my best friend and the team's fearful... I mean fearless, leader." The group joined his toast with enthusiasm. While Preston proceeded to regale the crowd formed around him with tales of his past, he noticed that Dawson was the first to leave.

"So you plan on eating the placenta?" Quint heard Leo ask Kira. "It's quite fashionable these days."

"Leo, sometimes you are more disgusting than I can even fathom," Quint replied.

"I understand that those with weak stomachs who find the thought distasteful can have it powdered and encapsulated. Believers claim it's a miracle pill that helps to ward off postpartum depression, improve breast milk supply, increase energy levels, and even prevent aging. One study claims it helps relieve pain in rats; don't ask me how they figured that one out. I hear one place even makes placenta prints that you can hang on your wall."

"Thanks, but I think I'll pass. You want it?" Kira asked.

"Yuck!" Mimi exclaimed, and left to find Preston.

"Quint, I'd like you to meet my sister, Jenny. She came all the way from England to be my maid of honor." She had Kira's good looks, and appeared maybe a couple of years younger. Her tan made it clear she was an outdoors-type. That or maybe she spent a great deal of time in a tanning bed.

"My pleasure. Was your husband able to join us too?" Quint noticed the wedding ring as he took her slender hand.

A flash of red crossed her face, and Jenny shifted uncomfortably. "Uh... no, Brad had to stay to get the sailboat ready. We're about to leave on the first leg of our journey."

"Where too?" Quint asked.

"Around the world, we hope, eventually." Jenny laughed. "We've spent the past few years sailing rental boats and planning our adventure. We got a great deal on a boat from a couple who had actually been sailing it around the world, but gave up when they reached the Seychelles. Brad's down there now getting it ready, and I'm joining him after the wedding."

"Where will you be heading?"

"We'll sail back to England for the first leg of our adventure. Depending on how things go, we'll save up for a next leg, maybe to America."

Quint frowned. "Seychelles to England. That means you'll be sailing near Somalia, land of pirates and all types of scum."

"Yeah, but Brad has it all planned out. He plans to stay well offshore and slip through at night."

"Hmm," Quint said, electing not to comment further. Jenny excused herself to meet some of the other guests, and Quint caught Kira's eye.

"I share your concern," she said softly. "Tried to talk her out of it, but she's bull headed."

"I wonder where she gets that from?"

Kira laughed. "Brad doesn't know it, but this trip is her last stab at fixing their marriage."

Quint nodded. "I just hope marital problems remain the extent of her troubles."

Noting that the party seemed to be winding down, Quint loudly addressed the remaining group. "Why don't we adjourn to the Bull and continue the festivities on my nickel." He didn't have to offer twice, and the remaining crowd followed him down Duval Street. They had been there for over an hour when a loud commotion drew everyone's attention. The bartender caught Quint's eye.

"Your friend is back there beating the crap out of some guy." Quint bolted for the back of the bar.

"Nigora! What in the hell are you doing?" he yelled, pulling her off of a man who lay bleeding on the floor. With Nigora back on her feet, he noticed the front of her blouse was soaking wet, and one of her massive fake breasts was deflated.

"Look what he do? Drunk idiot grab me, ruin my big Amelican breasts. So I kick his ass."

# EPILOGUE

The following week, Preston arrived early to the team's breakfast meeting in their regular hotel conference room and placed a sack of doughnuts by the coffee service. After scanning the room to see that no one was there yet, he quickly slid a small black box, slightly larger than a pack of gum, out of his pocket.

He peeled a strip of paper off the plastic housing and reached under the table to press the box into position. He held a set of headphones up to one ear to confirm that the transmitter was working and had just finished when the sound of Dawson's voice made him jump.

"Preston! What the hell are you doing here? You're not part of the team."

"I know," he said, as he looked up and saw Dawson and Quint entering the room. "I only wanted to make a gesture."

"You brought us doughnuts again," Kira said, while opening the bag to help herself.

"Yes, and I understand that you're having a closed meeting. Please just let Mimi know I'll be in the bar down the street having Bloody Marys when she's finished," he said, before leaving the room.

Quint's bandages were gone, and the knife wound in his shoulder was aching less. He looked at Dawson, who now wore an eye patch, and felt lucky they had both survived the mission, more or less intact.

Dawson's broken ribs and arm would heal, and the bullet holes would largely disappear. But Quint knew the loss of his left eye would, of course, be permanent, and he was under no illusions about how tough that would be for his buddy.

When Quint saw Leo, among the last to arrive as usual, he called the meeting to order. "We have a few housekeeping items to discuss before we get to the main reason I called this meeting," he said and proceeded to tick down the items on the agenda, including a debriefing on their recent Aral mission. Finally, he reached the last item.

"Rogers says that the fortress deal is about to be approved! The Cuban island called 'Tears of Coral' will soon be ours to use as a base of operations. As we've discussed in the past, life will be a lot simpler with a permanent operations center. Given the types of things we get into, being non-U.S. based will be a major plus.

"Most everything we've done of late is sanctioned by the feds, but being based elsewhere will make it more comfortable for everyone concerned. And there are some tax benefits as well. Actually, it was Dawson's idea, so perhaps I should let him tell you about our new base." Quint turned the meeting over to Dawson.

"This neat but little-known island lies a few miles off the coast of Cuba. According to my research, the Germans developed it during WW II. When their senior folks saw the handwriting on the wall, some used it as a stopping-off point as they fled to South America. It lay dormant until the '60s, when it was used by the Ruskies until they abandoned it after the Cold War ended.

"Its remoteness offers little commercial appeal and since it also offers no particular strategic advantage to the Cubans, they, too, had abandoned it. But it's perfect for our needs," Dawson explained. "It has high elevation, deep water, an old airstrip, and some existing facilities that we hope will be suitable for use as an opcenter."

"But what about the little problem of U.S.-Cuban relations?" Leo asked.

"Well, since ol' Fidel is out of the picture, things are not as cold as you might think based solely on what you hear in the news. Behind the scenes things have been warming a great deal, largely due to how cash-strapped the Cubans are. Rogers' folks handled the negotiations to lease it, in lieu of the bonus Rogers promised on the job we did in the Pass, and we'll soon have title to use it."

"Sounds too good to be true," Kira said. "But how will that work being in a location controlled by Cuba, especially given our previous run-in with the Cuban navy?" she asked, referring to their earlier unpleasant encounter while working a wreck in Cay Sal.

"Part of the deal will grant us complete autonomy to operate as we please, with regard to both the Cubans and the U.S. Government. As far as their navy, with that nasty Admiral out of the picture, only his crew and captain would recognize us, and none of them know our names.

"The agreement will allow anything we import to go through a duty-free zone in Cuba to avoid tariffs. We will have permission to fly or travel by boat both to and from the island without clearing customs. We'll need only file transit papers in advance." Dawson nodded to Quint that he was finished.

"When Rogers gives us the final go ahead, we'll go down to sign the papers. We'll then do a site visit to see firsthand what we have to work with. Upon our return, we'll develop a plan for setting up the base. Be thinking of a clever name in the meantime."

As the team filed out, Mimi went in search of Preston. She found him sitting in the far corner of the bar just putting away a small set of headphones. "Ready to grab lunch?"

"Sure." He paid his bar tab, and the couple walked toward Dante's at Conch Harbor. After they had chosen their table and placed their orders, Preston turned to Mimi. "Good meeting?"

"Yeah, we're getting this cool operations base," she blurted out without thinking. "But I... uh, can't talk about it."

"Mimi, the team has its right to privacy. I don't want to hear another word," Preston replied. They finished their meal, and he gave the waitress his credit card. "I need to go to the restroom. I'll be right back, and then let's go do something fun," he said.

Preston left the table and headed for the bathroom. After glancing over his shoulder to confirm that he was out of Mimi's field of view, he ducked outside to make a phone call. A metallic voice answered.

"You have information for me?" Syndy asked, inhaling through the yellowed plastic tube.

"Oh, yeah. And you're going to love this."

**The End**

# NOTE FROM FRANK

"Thanks so much for reading my third novel, *The Aral*. I know you have many choices of what to read and appreciate your investment of time. If you enjoyed it, please take a minute to place a review on **www.GoodReads.com**, the retailer's website, or on my own **www.FrankWilem.com.**

"Oh, and please tell your friends. And look for my fourth book, Tears of Coral, soon to be released."

## COMING SOON, FRANK'S FOURTH NOVEL:

# Tears of Coral

In the 4th book in Wilem's Quint and Dawson series, the team is getting settled in their new base on an island just off the coast of Cuba when they learn one of their own has been kidnapped by pirates in Somalia. Appalled by the violent lawlessness of these murderous savages, the team sets off, bent on rescuing their friend and putting an end to the Somali pirates' reign of terror. But one of the team's old enemies is hot on their trail, seeking vengeance to settle an old score. Things heat up quickly as the team struggles for their very lives, caught between bloodthirsty pirates and a crazed nemesis.

# AUTHOR NOTES

The Aral Sea area is the world's worst man-made ecological disaster. Through their colossal blundering, the Russians succeeded in turning the 4th largest lake into a toxic wasteland. So everything in my book, *The Aral*, related to this area is true.

The world's largest bioweapons lab discussed in my book is also real. Acting as a front company, Biopreparat ran the lab. This pharmaceutical firm was privatized and is still in business today, run by Russian ex-military officers. Open-air testing on Renaissance Island using live animals was conducted just as I described.

The mention of a genetically altered super-virus weapon is true, as is the burial of live anthrax mentioned in the book. In fact, live anthrax spores have been found in over half of the burial sites. Below, I have included some links you might find of interest related to the Renaissance Island story.

http://www.phaster.com/news_articles/germ_factory/
http://www.siumed.edu/medicine/id/bioterrorism.htm
http://fire.biol.wwu.edu/trent/alles/AralSea.pdf

Background on bioweapons such as anthrax
1

http://www.backwoodshome.com/articles2/duffy73.htm
l

The Road of Bones motorcycle tour that Kira and Colin joined is real. The end of the trip takes the route of this infamous road, built by Stalin with slave labor. It was named for the bones of the workers who died while building it and could not be buried in the permafrost.

http://www.telegraph.co.uk/news/worldnews/europe/russia/1404085/Road-of-Bones-where-slaves-perished.html
http://www.environmentalgraffiti.com/featured/stalin-road-of-bones/19454?image=0
http://www.motorcyclistonline.com/features/122_1102_the_road_of_bones_vladivostok_to_magadan/viewall.html

Timur the Lame was an interesting tyrant I stumbled across while researching this story. His ruthless exploits were all true. More can be found about him at these links:

http://www.badassoftheweek.com/tamerlane.html
http://en.wikipedia.org/wiki/Timur
http://www.bbc.co.uk/news/magazine-20538810

# ABOUT THE AUTHOR

Frank J. Wilem, Jr., is an entrepreneur living in Gulfport, Mississippi with his wife, Dee Dee, and daughter, Brittany. Frank's love for the sea blossomed during his high school years at West High in Torrance, California when a friend convinced him to snorkel off Lunada Bay in Palos Verde. When it was his turn to use the mask, one look beneath the chilly Pacific waters and he was hooked.

After graduating from Texas A&M with a Bachelor of Science in Electrical Engineering, the call of the ocean led him to the University of Miami where he earned a Masters degree in Ocean Engineering. Frank worked in the R&D departments for two Fortune 500 companies before his love of the ocean led him to join Computer Sciences Corporation at NASA's Stennis Space Center.

He left there to become a founder of Triton Systems, Inc., which he and his partners grew into a $100 million company and the nation's largest manufacturer of automatic teller machines. With the sale of Triton, Frank purchased his sportfish boat Vixen and pursued his passion for bluewater fishing. Most days he and Captain Eric Gill can be found in the northern waters of the Gulf of Mexico or the Bahamas, chasing billfish, tuna, wahoo and dolphin.

*The Aral* is Frank's third book.